PRAISE FOR NOEL SCANLON

"Fast moving. The background is colourful and very convincing. *"Irish Independent*

"Full marks to Mr Scanlon for background on this one. He has lived and worked for years in the Middle East and obviously knows what he is writing about at first hand. Furthermore he knows the Arabs, their hopes and fears, their ambitions to Arabise the West and their present frightening power. He is also aware of the flaws in that power – the jealousies, the lust for pointless violence, and the clash of policy between the various paramilitary groups. It's an exciting read with a guaranteed thrill on each page." *The Irish Times*

"Tension and adventure in Southern Arabia. The background and detail of the events are splendidly authentic." *The London Times*

"Many years in the Middle East and India plus a degree in Arabic studies have qualified Noel Scanlon to write a book about Arabia. He tells of a web of international intrigue and an incredible journey across the sands of Arabia's Empty Quarter. No book could be better timed from the topical angle." *Sunday Independent*

"A whopping good read." *Sunday World*

"The setting is the queasy world of Southern Arabian politics. The author obviously has an inside knowledge of the Middle East." *Belfast Telegraph*

"Apart from containing a lively action story, Noel Scanlon's novel is of considerable interest for what it conveys and tells about life in the Arab world. It lends itself for reference to the introductory chapter of 'the Seven Pillars of Wisdom' by T E Lawrence. The Peninsula of Arabia is one of the huge fulcrums of international affairs and Noel Scanlon could not command such a historical perspective through dialogue unless he himself had much first-hand experience of the territory and its people of which he writes." *Australian Press*

"Irish writer Scanlon's colloquial style is charmingly deadpan." *Kirkus Review. USA*

"A rattling good and topical yarn about guerrilla action in an oil producing state in Arabia." *Derby Evening Telegraph*

"An up-to-the minute thriller. Mr Scanlon brings to his story keen insight and colourful detail." *Western Daily Press*

"The author writes of Arabia with skill and obvious knowledge and understanding. His novel makes very interesting reading and a grim picture of guerrilla war in the intense heat, the appalling cruelties practised, the poverty and misery in the midst of legendary wealth and luxury." *Irish Press*

"A resourceful hero, a taut situation with much high-level nail biting and an author who never slackens his grip." *Methodist Recorder*

"It's a good tale, with a very topical angle." *National Newsagents and Books*

"A fast-moving thriller with an interesting and highly authentic Arab background." *The Birmingham Post*

"Highly readable. Full of freshness and originality. Grabs you from the opening and holds you all the way to the last full stop." *Gordon Thomas*

Also by Noel Scanlon

NOVELS

Quinn
Quinn and the Desert Oil
Apparitions
Black Ashes

Radio Plays
Radio Documentaries
Short Stories

THE GULF

NOEL SCANLON

THRILLER PUBLICATIONS

Published by
THRILLER PUBLICATIONS
email: thrillerpublications@eircom.net

Copyright © Noel Scanlon
ISBN 978-0-9556002-0-3

Cover by Anu Design
Typeset by Typeform
Printed by ColourBooks

For Joan
My companion, soul mate, friend, wife, editor and that's just for starters.

PROLOGUE

Ayatullah Abd al Wahhab studied the faces of the small group of men gathered in the bare reception room of a crumbling house in a back street of the remote town of Mehriz in Iran.

The men were seated on cushions set close to a cement wall once white in colour but now stained by the perspiration of the many heads and backs that had rested against it. The house was ringed by bodyguards armed with machine pistols but the bodyguards took care not to be conspicuous. Their function was to provide protection, not to advertise their presence.

If anyone in the town knew of what was going on, they gave no sign. They either hurried past, eyes downcast, or avoided the house and took another route. It was well understood that to know too much was dangerous. It could lead not only to your own throat being slit but that of all your family in a raid on your house that night.

In the bare room with the shutters drawn the sounds of the *suq* were muted, a distant sound like waves breaking on the shore. The heat and humidity was suffocating but the men gathered there seemed not to notice. They were accustomed to intense heat. And they were concentrated on, gripped by, the words, the charisma, the aura of their leader.

After the initial lengthy greetings and embraces, there had been little or no small talk. The importance of the occasion made the participants solemn. Important decisions were about to be taken, decisions that would change the face of the Middle East.

Ayatullah Abd al Wahhab was dressed in a long black robe and head cloth. He seemed to be frail. Until he spoke. And then something extraordinary happened. He grew in stature. He expanded until his presence filled the room.

"The time has come to strike," Ayatullah Abd al Wahhab said. *"Let*

1

blood be spilled. Let the blood of our oppressors be spilled. Let the blood of the traitors be spilled. Let the blood of the infidels be spilled..."

There was the noise of raised voices outside. A scuffle. Then a quick burst of machine gun fire. Someone had strayed too close to the house where the meeting was being held. Someone had asked questions. They wouldn't ask any more.

"The time has come to strike down those Rulers who oppress their people and who are friends of our enemies, inviting them, their oil companies, and now their soldiers on to sacred Moslem land, defiling it."

There was a murmur of agreement as the men listened not only to the words the Ayatullah spoke but to the resonance of the Arabic rhetoric of which Abd al Wahhab was a noted and powerful exponent. He spoke in classical Arabic. He knew well the subconscious link with the holy Koran his words forged in the minds of his listeners, its deep emotional effect. He knew how to appeal to wounded Arab pride. He knew how to work on the deep sense of humiliation, the deep longing for revenge felt by every man in the room.

They all wanted a strong leader to follow and believed that in Ayatullah Abd al Wahhab they had found one. Most of them were already active in the cause, had at some time carried out assaults against the enemy, raids from the desert and the hills into the heart of enemy territory. All present were men hardened to suffering and cruelty, to both the death they meted out, and the death and torture that would eventually befall themselves.

Their fervent support gave the Ayatullah the elation of power. It came to him as an excitement, a sharpening of the senses. An awareness of the deaths and disruption and chaos that would arise from decisions taken at this meeting was present as a warm glow inside him. It raised him above ordinary limitations so that he was levitating across the room.

Euphoria was coursing through his veins. He was no longer a thin frail man but an all powerful force. A darkness hung around him, a dazzling darkness charged with some extraordinary power.

"When our plan is executed we will control all the Gulf oil the West so desperately need for their cars, their industries, for their debauched way of life.

"They will live to regret the day they declared a crusade against us and our brother Moslems......"

When Ayatullah Abd al Wahhab finally sat down, he shrank back to the thin frail man he had been.

After the Ayatullah, Sheikh Ramani took the floor. The Ayatullah had expounded his visionary concept. Sheikh Ramani, the strategist among them, went into the practical details of the proposed plan. They would foment uprisings in all the Gulf states. The offensive would begin with Ayatullah Abd al Wahhab returning to his home state of Khor Fahal where he and the men chosen to go with him would begin the Jihad. After that in quick succession leaders would be sent to Dubai, Sharjah, Doha, Bahrain and Muscat.

Much detailed planning had still to be done and secrecy had to be maintained. Spies and informers had to be sought out and summarily executed. Much preparation had still to be done.

But at that meeting in the town of Mehriz in Iran the die was cast and the future of the Middle East with all its oil resources would depend on the outcome of the Ayatullah's plan.

NOEL SCANLON

CHAPTER 1

In the pre-dawn hours, a single unmarked police vehicle drove quickly through the empty streets of the Old City in the Gulf state of Khor Fahal and on to the road that led to the beach jetty. The out of uniform lieutenant told the driver to douse his lights. In the back two men steadied the body in the body bag that was being jolted about by the rough road.

A pie dog barked, then yelped as someone struck it to silence it. The houses in this area were built in the old Arab style with ornate carved wooden doors. The windows had no glass; their shutters were open to allow in any breath of night air. But most people slept out of doors. Hearing a vehicle pass, men stirred in their sleep on string beds on the mud roofs of their houses and wondered who could be out and about at this time.

It was still dark when the boy moved down the dirt track towards the beach. He had walked from the shanty town where he lived in a crowded shack. The shack, like hundreds of others, was built from pieces of tin, plywood, old boxes, and plastic sheets suspended on poles.

The boy heard the sound of an approaching vehicle which, as it passed close to him, he identified as a police vehicle. The very sight of it started his pulse racing, filled him with dread and apprehension.

He dodged off the track and into some low dunes. Lying there, he watched as the police vehicle pulled into the grounds of the Fishermen's Mosque.

The boy wondered why it was there and if it was connected with the rumour going around that the police had arrested the mullah in the mosque the previous evening.

After some time, he heard the noise of a boat approaching from the sea. At the same time the police vehicle drove out of the mosque grounds and down on to the beach to where the boat was landing. There was a flurry of activity as a body bag was removed from the back of the police vehicle and loaded on to the boat.

In the slowly dawning light, the boy watched as the boat shoved off and headed out to sea, growing smaller and smaller, the figures on board gradually becoming stick figures.

A little later, the boat dropped anchor at a small rocky island called Al Kabir. From that distance and in that light the boy found it difficult to see exactly what they were doing. He wished he possessed a pair of binoculars but, living on the breadline as he did, it was highly unlikely that he ever would. In the event, he didn't need binoculars. The sun rose out of the sea, the boat swung around and he could clearly see the sack the police had loaded being dropped into the sea.

The boy realised that he had by chance come upon an important piece of information. But how could he best use it? He might try to barter or sell it. But he must handle it carefully.

It could be useful.

It could also be highly dangerous.

CHAPTER 2

D avid disentangled himself from Deborah's naked body and slipped from bed. Memories of the night before lingered in his mind. Their love making during the night had had a more than ordinary intensity about it. Was this passion brought about by the intense heat? Or was there something darker and deeper involved here, a need for reassurance from one another, a reaffirmation of life brought on by the tensions that had been building up in and around them over the past weeks? He lingered by the bedside and, leaning over, implanted a kiss on his wife's forehead. She murmured and turned over, without waking up.

He quickly pulled on a t-shirt and shorts and moved quietly down the stairs of the apartment block and into the heavy heat of Khor Fahal in the Arabian Gulf. There was a short period now for an hour or so of slightly less intense heat than what was to come later. As often as possible, he got up early like this. He liked to enjoy what little cool and what little breeze there was before going to work in the Trucial Bank where he was the senior executive.

The rented apartment they lived in was one of six in an old Arab house, the property of the merchant Darwish. Darwish was a multi-millionaire like all the old established merchants but didn't believe in spending money on upkeep and, as a result, the whole block was more or less crumbling away.

In the garage, David checked the coupling, then drove the Land Rover with the Dory speedboat on the trailer from the garage and headed towards the nearby beach. It was really because of the easy accessibility of this beach that they lived here on this side of the creek as opposed to the other side where almost all the expats tended to live together in luxury accommodation but cut off from the general populace in compounds. This was definitely the wrong side of the creek to live on. But they preferred it. If you were in Arabia, it seemed logical to live in Arabia rather than among

Europeans. Anyway, that is what they had mutually opted for. It was an environment David was comfortable with having lived in numerous similar locations as a child when moving all over the Middle East as a consequence of his father's various postings in the bank.

He weaved his way now through streets and alleyways so narrow that in places the Land Rover was just about scraping the sides of houses that were set in an irregular jagged line, their wooden shutters still mostly closed. Little laneways ran down to the creek that lapped against the houses on the front. The raucous voice of an Arab woman shrieking against the background of Arabic music suddenly stopped, as if throttled. On the flat mud roofs where the populace slept, bodies were beginning to rise up now as if from the dead, rolling back assorted bedclothes.

The whole area here was so ancient that it looked as if it had just been unearthed by archaeologists, dug out from under centuries of sand. The coastline he was driving along was known in the 19th century as the Pirate Coast, a long coastline between the desert and the sea, a land dotted with forts and watchtowers.

In the early morning now, the houses were light brown. Later, exposed to the harsh glare of the sun, they would whiten out. The dirt would disappear. They would become bright and clean, transformed by the bright Arabian sun.

This was the side of the creek where the Shi'ites and the stateless lived. Mostly in poverty. The area had never been properly developed and probably never would be. The Ruling Family who controlled the state's wealth had no intention of improving the lot of those who lived here. They left the whole area decrepit and neglected as it had always been.

It looked almost exactly the same as it had when David's father had opened the first bank here in the suq and, as a young boy, David had watched Baluchi coolies sweating in the sun as they heaved a Chubb safe up the steps and into the converted merchant's shop that was to be the first bank in the state and issue the first currency supplanting the Maria Theresa dollar which the tribal Arabs considered much superior. You could test it with your teeth, which was something you couldn't do with the new paper currency.

He was approaching the Shi'ite mosque known locally as the Fishermen's Mosque. It stood out from all the other buildings. With its minaret, slender and shapely, there was something about it, some aesthetic appeal that drew your eye to it.

But it wasn't the minaret that caught David's attention that fatal morning. It was the police vehicles drawn up in the mosque compound. For some time now, relationships between the Sunnis and Shi'ites in the state had been deteriorating. But David had never seen police vehicles in the grounds of a mosque before. This was a first and it was a sight that made him feel apprehensive. It was a bad omen.

He crossed the creek by the old bridge and drove on to the wide-open beach. The sight of those police vehicles had put a dampener on the lift he normally got heading out at this time of the morning.

The boy, whose name he didn't know and if asked would be given a false name anyway, was waiting for him on the shoreline in his tattered t-shirt, tense with nervous excitement, eager to be allowed out in the boat. Sometimes when he got here the boy was waiting like this. Sometimes he would disappear for weeks. All David knew about him was that he lived a precarious knife-edged existence in the shanty town where the illegals and the dispossessed lived. Most of them had never had any proper employment. They were displaced persons without rights. They waited to be deported, dumped over the border, undocumented and destitute.

David allowed the boy to help out with the boat. He didn't know the boy's history and didn't want to. There was always the possibility that he might be a spy for the regular police or the religious police. On the other hand, he was much more likely to be what he seemed to be, a youth desperate to survive as best he could. And, even if he was a spy, and the place was riddled with spies, why would anyone want to spy on him? He was only going for a spin in his boat.

David backed the trailer into the waves until the water had risen over its wheels and waves slapped against the hull. The boy shoved the speedboat clear while David parked the Land Rover and trailer above the high-water mark. Paddling the boat out into deeper water now, he lowered the outboard engine. The movement of the sea under him felt good.

He looked back towards the Fishermen's Mosque where he had seen the police vehicles. A crowd was gathering. They seemed to be agitated.

"What's going on at the mosque?" David asked the boy in Arabic. He had learnt his Arabic as a child. "Have you not heard," the boy said, pleased to have information to pass on. "The police arrested Mullah Hussein last night. Inside the mosque. All the Shi'ites very very angry. They say their holy place has been desecrated. Arresting the mullah will cause too much trouble." He spoke with nervous intensity, looking around him in case someone was listening which hardly seemed likely out in the open sea. But then his life depended on his wits.

Up until now, the police had been careful to respect the sanctity of the mosques, even when the Shi'ite mullahs preached seditious sermons. David's commercial assistant, Mohammed, kept him up to speed on everything that happened locally. The latest word was that the mullahs were getting more and more in your face provocative.

In Islam, unlike the Christian tradition, there has never been a formal separation of church and state making it quite usual for religious leaders to preach highly political sermons. Whatever the mullahs preached, up until now the mosques had been strictly out of bounds to the police. Given this tradition, it was all the more remarkable that the police had all of a sudden arrested a mullah in a mosque. It wasn't something you'd ever expect to happen. It looked like a new departure, an ominous change in government policy. The more David thought about it, the less he liked its possible consequences.

Through his various contacts, he had been getting the feeling for sometime now that someone was stirring it up. The Shi'ites were in the majority but had little or no power. The power of the Sunni Sheikh Suleiman Bin Himyar Al Yas, his extended family and supporters was more or less absolute. The state was called a sheikhdom. In plain fact it was a dictatorship.

"Look look," the boy said now pointing towards the mosque. David looked and he didn't like what he was seeing. Police were milling around and a crowd had begun to gather. Suddenly the police began firing off rounds of tear gas at the gathering crowd.

At the same time, the outboard engine started with an explosion of noise and they shot out to sea.

CHAPTER 3

Light ricocheted off surfaces. Everything was hard edged, clearly defined. Deborah paused, blinking her eyes in an intensity of light that temporarily blinded her. There was too much light, too clear a definition of things, too much exposure.

She crossed to the clothes line on the roof and took down the clothes Abdul had hung out the night before. They were dried stiff and felt gritty and sandy.

When they had first come to live in this apartment block, before she had landed her present position as editor of the *Al Jameela* magazine, she'd had a period as a stay-at-home wife. Before coming out she had thought that she might rather enjoy being a lady of leisure lounging up here in her deck chair sunbathing or perhaps flicking through magazines or the odd novel by way of diversion. A life of luxury and ease in the sun. But it hadn't worked out quite like that. The dust blew into her eyes, the sun made her face red and sore; the light was too bright to read in. And the landlord formally objected to even the partial exposure of a Christian female body on the roof of this Moslem building. It was her first brush with a strict patriarchal society with all its staggering hypocrisy.

She thought she was alone on the roof now but, turning at a sound behind her, saw her Arab neighbour, Yasmin from Apartment 3, begin to leave, pulling her veil across her face, looking embarrassed and guilty.

Yasmin had been the only woman in the block to respond to her invitation to morning coffee - the others just hadn't turned up leaving her with piles of Arab sweetmeats. Yasmin seemed a nice person but her almost non-existent English and Deborah's halting Arabic made communication difficult.

Yasmin's husband and the lord of her life worked in one of the ministries. After he swept off in regal manner in his chauffeur driven car to his office every morning, Yasmin seemed to spend the rest of the day alone with her Filipino maid, locked away much like a nun who had joined an enclosed order.

Deborah said now, in a breezy, friendly manner, "Good morning. *Sabah al Kheir.*" She hoped she'd got that last bit right. She had begun learning Arabic as soon as she had arrived and had a little colloquial, that is all she really needed. To read and write in a strange script was too much for the moment.

Yasmin seemed to be confused at being addressed at all. She barely muttered a reply before scurrying away. Something must be wrong. Had that arrogant husband of hers told her not to speak to foreigners? It was difficult to grasp the degree of power men out here exercised over their wives. And what about Maria, the Filipino maid? The word was that all the Arab men screwed their Filipino maids as well as keeping them as slaves. Filipino maids and nannies were regularly beaten and raped and, if they got pregnant, they got eighty lashes and a few years imprisonment. Naturally nothing happened to the man.

Penetrating behind the veil of purdah wasn't turning out to be that easy, even for someone as curious and persistent as Deborah. God knows what went on in that apartment across the hall, sexually or otherwise.

In the matter of sex, being out here in a strange culture in all this endless sunshine hadn't done her own sex life any harm. Relations between herself and David had never been better. Maybe it was the heat.

She glanced down at the creek where dhows were anchored. A fishing *sambuk* lay on its side; a group of Arab men were working on it. A boy, quick and lithe, was paddling a dugout, swerving between the moored boats, narrowly missing obstructions. A naked child swam nearby, clinging to an old tyre in the sticky salty water. A small boy was throwing stones at a scrawny pie dog. What a cruel little brat.

Looking out to sea, she picked out their boat farther out than David usually went.

As she was leaving the roof, a shrill voice she was sure she hadn't heard before, blasted out from the mosque, making her start. This didn't sound like the usual call to prayer. It had a different tone with a definite edge to it. Did any religious group pray as much or as often as the Moslems? The Irish used to pray a lot until the advent of the Celtic tiger when all the dosh flooded into the country and as a result everybody had to work so hard to get rich and to stay rich that there wasn't much time left for praying.

Back down in her apartment, old fashioned and a bit shabby but spacious with big wide balconies protected from the sun and with a fabulous view overlooking the creek, she caught the smell of mocha coffee coming strong and pungent from the kitchen. Making coffee was one of the very few culinary tasks Abdul was up to.

"Abdul," she called out but there was no reply from the kitchen. Abdul was supposed to be getting the breakfast but he hadn't done anything other than put the coffee pot on. Hearing voices, she went out on to the balcony and, looking down, there was Abdul gossiping over the compound wall with an Arab man she had never seen before. Typical. Her dogs, Honey and Poochie, warily kept their distance. They looked up at her now on hearing her voice.

She called down, "Abdul, come up here and get the breakfast."

Deborah had never had a servant before and had looked forward to it as an exciting new experience. But it had turned out near enough the opposite of what she'd expected. Her relationship with Abdul wasn't exactly the mistress servant relationship she had envisioned. Not by a long chalk. Abdul was over-familiar, obstreperous, argumentative, opinionated and irresponsible, not exactly the qualities apparent in the butler in 'The Remains of the Day', which she had vaguely expected or at least the Arab equivalent thereof.

This, Margaret, the wife of Andy Wilson of the Standard Chartered Bank, had told her, and Margaret knew everything about everything, was her own fault for hiring an Arab. No Arab makes a good servant. A camel driver. A slave driver. A sheikh, whether dirt poor or filthy rich. A merchant, ditto. An idle retainer. Any of the above. But not a servant. She should, Margaret told her, have hired an Indian. Indians are naturally servile. Arabs are naturally assertive and superior. Like their camels. That's the fault of their religion. Arabs are like that because they're Moslem. Now Hindus are another story. A Hindu will accept anything because if he gets a bad deal in this life he can always look forward to his next reincarnation, which is a lot better than his being bolshie to you now in this one like all Arabs are. Religions have a lot to answer for.

So Margaret philosophised in the Phoenix Bar, where they sometimes met for a drink. Deborah pretended to be in full agreement with all Margaret's colonial style views of the natives. Margaret was so formidable that it would have been suicidal to contradict her. So Deborah didn't dare tell Margaret that her views were out of the last century, from the days of

Empire in India or even the American south, at any rate unenlightened and completely out of date. She was too craven to tell Margaret that she didn't want servility in a servant, that her social conscience wouldn't allow it.

She went into the kitchen now and began preparing the breakfast herself.

As she was eating a slice of papaya at the dining room table, Abdul came rushing in. He was in a state of high excitement.

"I have news," he said importantly. He paused for effect. "Police they shoot too many people at Fisherman's Mosque this morning."

Abdul's words gave her a cold sudden stab of fear.

"I'm sure you're exaggerating."

Abdul was always exaggerating. He seemed incapable of properly distinguishing reality from fantasy. He had an almost total inability to tell the plain truth about anything without embellishment. Something might have happened down at the mosque but she didn't believe Abdul when he said a whole lot of people had been shot. No way.

As she was finishing breakfast, her mother came in wearing her dressing gown. Maybe it was the bright light out here but she looked older and more drawn as if she'd aged years since coming out.

At the time they'd planned it, it had seemed a good idea for her mother to have a good long restful holiday in the sun. But it hadn't quite worked out that way. She didn't like the climate. And she particularly didn't like the people.

Her mother said querulously now, "Carolyn is feverish. I don't think you should take her to school today. She got too much sun yesterday." She said this disapprovingly. "If you're not careful, exposure to the sun out here will give the child skin cancer."

"Yes mother." That was Deborah's normal response to anything and everything her mother said. Her mother saw all sorts of disasters waiting around the corner. For all that, her mother made Deborah feel inadequate. Just her being here, her presence, even if she never said anything critical, had this effect. So naturally in the matter of Carolyn's alleged fever, Deborah gave in. In this situation, as in most situations, acquiescence and retreat seemed the best tack to take. "All right. She can stay away from school. Just for today."

"I think you're making a wise decision, dear," her mother said as she sat at the table and Abdul elaborately served her a slice of papaya.

Deborah looked in on Carolyn. Her room was filled with toys, Harry Potter and Spiderman and Bart Simpson posters among numerous others on the wall. She hid her face now. Deborah felt her forehead which seemed normal. "Would you like to stay home from school today?"

"Yes. I like to stay with gran."

"That's all right then. Gran will look after you while I'm at work. Come here and give me a hug." She held her daughter tight and stroked her sun bleached curls.

Deborah was late for work as she ran downstairs and went to her car. Her dogs, Honey and Poochie, came bounding after her and jumped up at the car trying to get in to go for a ride. Poochie was a pure black and white west of Ireland collie, thin and so highly geared that she was hyperactive. Honey was golden-coloured, part saluki and part god knows what.

"Keep the dogs in the compound," Deborah called up to Abdul, who was out on the balcony, a wet dishcloth thrown over his left shoulder.

Honey and Poochie, both females and devoted to one another, wagged their tails excitedly.

Driving away, Deborah wondered why David still wasn't back from his boat trip. She had always been against these early morning trips to go diving in shark infested water. But she couldn't stop him any more than she could stop herself now fantasising disaster, a mood that had been brought on by Abdul talking about people being shot. She had flashes of David being drowned; she could see the boat upturned in the sea, he was trying to cling on to it but the sharks, even bigger than the sharks in Jaws were ripping his legs off.

What did all these sinister, graphic images mean?

That she was uncertain and fearful? That she hadn't settled properly into Khor Fahal, that she didn't trust her surroundings?

There was a blasting of horns as two police vehicles drove past at unnecessarily high speed and cut in on her, the armed police officers inscrutable behind their dark glasses.

A frisson of fear ran through her. It was the first time she'd had such a feeling. But it wasn't to be the last.

NOEL SCANLON

CHAPTER 4

David was cruising along parallel to the coastline that slid past, a narrow strip of sandy beach which stretched for hundreds and hundreds of miles. A thin line on the edge of Arabia.

The feeling of unease he had had on seeing the crowd gather outside the mosque was blown away as he sped over the unchanging sea fringed by a white unspoiled shoreline. Well, not quite unspoiled. Various oil spillages had brought oil pollution, changing the quality of this deserted coastline. Even after some big clean-ups there were still pockets of pollution in lonely hidden coves. A worm had entered this land that had remained untouched for so long.

They were far enough out now to get a view of the gravel plain. Beyond the plain, the interior was shrouded in a heat haze. Away in there was a treacherous sand desert of dunes and quicksands known as the Empty Quarter.

The boy was gesticulating. "Out there," he said. "Out there at Al Kabir rock. Very good diving. Very good fish."

They headed out in that direction passing a lone fisherman in a small dugout riding the swells, throwing out a line. A bonito bird sat prim and pretty in the water. The wind rushing past emptied David's mind of all but the sensation of movement and he would have liked to have gone on like that, caught in a time warp, the world reduced, simplified.

Approaching the Al Kabir rock he cut the engine and threw out the anchor.

As he zipped up his wet suit with its weight belt, fixed the compressed air tank on his back and pulled on his fins, the sun was still low. The coastline had a light orange-coloured glow.

"Look after the boat," he said to the boy. "Don't let it drift."

"Yes yes," the boy said. "No problem."

Pulling his face-mask over his head and adjusting the air tube, David threw himself backwards over the side of the boat, his loaded spear gun in his hand.

Alone in the quiet world of the underwater, he propelled himself forward with a slight movement of his fins, sinking into a vast fairytale world, a seascape of valleys and hills of colourful corals, of dainty angel fish with yellow and blue stripes that swam close to his face.

Sinking into deeper water, there were fewer colours, less light penetrated. It was eerie down here in this mysterious valley where so many sea creatures lurked.

Sinking lower and lower, he was retreating from the world above, descending into another dimension. It was tranquil down here, hypnotic, inducing a feeling of peacefulness, of time slowing.

But not for long.

When almost on the ocean floor, he spotted, just ahead, a black sack around which curious fish were hovering and nibbling. As he got closer, he saw an outstretched human hand. The sack seemed to move, to breathe. Then suddenly it was splitting open. A body, white and wan in those murky depths, began to float free, then stopped, anchored to the sea-bed by a stone which whoever had dumped the body had tied to the sack.

Floating and waving behind the body and loosely attached to it there appeared a piece of cloth, a brown turban unwinding. And a cloak. A mullah's cloak. The boy had told him that Mullah Hussein had been arrested in his mosque the night before. Well he hadn't lasted for long. After a summary execution he had been dumped here.

Who had murdered him? Who had dumped him here and why?

Was he really dead? Of course he was dead, what else could he be. And yet the eyes, bulbous and fish-like, seemed to be staring up at him from their watery grave as if animated by some residual life-force. The lips of the corpse writhed away from the teeth, the dead Mullah Hussein undulating as if in some sort of grotesque underwater ballet.

Quickly David kicked away. Jerked out of his previous state of tranquillity, he felt an overwhelming rush of apprehension. Whatever was going on here he wanted nothing to do with it.

Suddenly, the sea all around David became darker. A shoal of tiny fish was heading away, disturbed and frightened. He began to back off, sorry that he had seen what he had seen. He had no wish to become involved in any way in the death of the mullah or the Moslem fundamentalism the mullah represented.

He had only moved a short distance away when he sensed a movement in the water. Forms, dark on the periphery of vision, became lighter coloured, with a hint of silver-grey, as they came gliding down towards him. Sharks!

What should he do? Make a mad dash for it? But any sudden movement would only attract the sharks. Grasping a spur of rock, he pulled himself behind it. He tensed and remained immobile.

These sharks were smooth and streamlined, their dorsal fins cutting through the water. They circled slowly and carefully, sizing up the situation.

Suddenly and swiftly, as if they had heard something, a signal, a communication of some sort, they all closed in on the body bag. Its jaws open, the lead shark ripped off an arm. The second shark took a leg.

The Shi'ite mullah had become a meal.

David kicked for a surface that was made of glinting glass. Crashing through it, shattering it, he was overwhelmed with relief at this transition from the underworld into the upper world, with its bright light and blue sky.

Swimming not far from him was the boy who must have dived in after him, and must also have seen the body.

Reaching the boat and pulling himself aboard panting and gasping, the boy already there hauling up the anchor with quick lithe actions, well attuned to fear and danger, always on the look out for it coming at him in the day as in the middle of the night, as sharply attuned to danger as the sharks were to the smell of blood.

David sweated starting the engine and headed for the shore at full throttle. As they struck the beach, he saw that there were even more police vehicles over by the mosque.

He said to the boy, "Get to hell out of here. Make yourself scarce. And keep your mouth shut. Don't mention a word about this to anyone..." He had barely finished the sentence when the boy had already disappeared as if into thin air.

Driving off the beach with the boat loaded on the trailer, David caught the acrid smell of tear gas drifting over from the mosque area which was swarming with armed police now.

The protesters had retreated to the little narrow laneways between houses that were closed and barred, blind, surrounded by high walls built within a few feet of the house itself. Some were shouting but most looked sullen and angry. Many were holding wet cloths to their faces, coughing and choking and others were trying to stem the flow of blood from an injury.

As he drove on, he passed a group of old men sitting on the sand in their robes, staring at him hostilely while telling their amber beads.

Suddenly, a hail of stones clattered against the side of his Land Rover.

He felt a blast of hatred directed at him. In all the times he had passed along here, he had never encountered any trouble before. It had always been peaceful and pleasant. Somnolent even. Well not any more. The stones clattering against the vehicle reverberated back and back down the tunnels of his mind.

With that blast of hatred directed at him for the first time, he knew that something vital in the equation, in the balance of their lives here had altered. He could feel it slipping away from him. Their life here had suddenly become fragile and threatened.

David had seen it all before in the long ago when living with his parents in various parts of Arabia where they had settled down into a pleasant lifestyle with set routines and the Arabs were friendly and everything seemed fine and solid like it would never change and indeed in the case of his parents, they went on like that for years and years and years. Until the first stone was thrown. It never seemed to be significant at the time. Or its significance was not appreciated. What significance should be attached to a youth, a mere child, throwing a stone at a passing vehicle, at the windows of the bank? There was no need to exaggerate such minor trivial incidents. Everything would go on as it had always gone on.

But everything did not go on as it had always gone on. The throwing of that first stone proved to be the beginning of a great unravelling, of a long colonial rule, of an empire, of white supremacy, of a way of life for all the expats who had inhabited it.

Suddenly everything began to crumble and fade. Years, decades, folded in on themselves and collapsed. Who even remembers the East Aden Protectorate, or the West Aden Protectorate, though they were solid enough for long enough. Who remembers Mukulla or the Hadhramut or Seiyun with its tall mud skyscrapers polished with melted sugar where his parents had lived and laboured? Pretty well nobody remembers them. And the exodus of the expats who lived in all these places began with something as seemingly harmless as a stone striking the bonnet of a car.

So David was well aware that the missiles clattering against his Land Rover now were aimed at him with intent, with deep hostility and nothing would ever be the same again.

The stone throwers began to melt away as a police vehicle drove up and followed him. Checking in his rear-view mirror, he saw the police still behind, slowing when he slowed, picking up speed when he picked up speed. In the front sat two officers in dark glasses staring impassively in front of them.

NOEL SCANLON

CHAPTER 5

The boy bought a glass of tea from a *chaikhana* with rough tables constructed of boxes on which tea was served in little glasses by an old man who boiled the water in a battered kettle salvaged from a dump.

Then the boy went to lie on his rope bed in the shack he shared with six others. Just now, he had the space to himself. He was lying on his bed drinking his glass of tea and smoking a *beadie* when he thought he heard raised voices in the distance.

With the money he had been given, he would later buy a plate of rice and dhal but first he wanted to enjoy his smoke. The rest of the money he had buried. He had put it about the *suq* that he had information and eventually he was brought to a man in a small room at the back of a cafe. And there he had recounted his sighting of the dead mullah in the sea. The man whose name he didn't know and whose face he didn't see, had spoken kindly to him and told him that his contribution would be remembered. What he didn't tell him was that the boy had just supplied the information which would ignite the uprising.

The shack he was in was built on desert land without sanitation or running water. The open sewers stank. Between the shacks ran winding narrow paths littered with debris where pie dogs roamed. Rats and vermin bred in the refuse.

The boy had entered Khor Fahal as one of an imported army of labourers. They were not citizens and they had no rights. They were exploited by recruiters in their country of origin who charged them exorbitantly to transport them here. And, when here, they were exploited by the contractors who employed them on a daily basis. When they could get work they worked and sweated all day labouring in searing temperatures that reached 140 centigrade, labouring in that hellish heat for a pittance. When they could, they sent money back to their families. They dreamed of returning to their village with money in their pockets.

Most of the men however were, like the boy, unemployed. Occasionally he got work as a day labourer on a building site but after he hadn't been paid for weeks he had given that up.

Everyday he walked or hitched a lift to the Old City to see if he could pick up anything. There were better pickings in the New City but that was out of bounds for him. The Sunnis ruled supreme there. It wasn't safe for the likes of him. He stood a fair chance of being arrested by the police. And, even if he managed to avoid the police, the mansions and apartment blocks over there were bristling with security.

So he hung around the *suqs* of the Old City watching for a stall-holder to look the other way. Which didn't happen very often. The stall-holders were sharp and smart and if you did manage to snatch something they would pursue you down the winding *suqs* and alleyways and if you were caught you could expect a good lashing.

The boy heard the sounds again, close-by now.

Always alert to danger, he leapt up and looked out.

Police!

The police were demolishing a shack nearby, tearing it to pieces. They handcuffed its occupants and then began to flog them. Two police held each man down while another flogged him with a whip, raising it high above his head and holding it poised for a moment then, with a swift movement, bringing it swishing through the air and on to the man's bare back.

The shanty town was regularly raided by police looking for criminals or fugitives or just collecting bribes.

The boy crawled on his hands and knees out of the back of the shack. He crawled towards a *chaikhana* where a group of men were drinking the jungly whisky they extracted from palm trees.

The men waved at him to go away.

The illegals the police were beating screamed the boy's name and pointed. The police dropped them in the dirt and rushed towards the shack.

They seized the boy before he even got as far as the *chaikhana*.

As the police dragged him away, the men in the *chaikhana* went on playing *tric trac* with an indifference bred of heat and desperation.

CHAPTER 6

A bout a mile from their apartment block Deborah bypassed the Old City which was down a road to the left. With its leaning buildings crumbling away, its dirty laneways, its open fronted shops crammed with merchants' wares, its open-air markets spilling into the gutter, the whole area was a web of alleyways, a maze of tiny shops, a jumble of tradesmen, a bustle of people. It was the original City by the creek, once walled but long since spreading and sprawling outwards, a lively teeming over populated largely Shi'ite area with the great arid empty desert lapping at its edges.

Seen from the distance, it looked ancient and romantic. But Deborah didn't buy into the romance. The Old City was plain filthy and unsanitary. It was still as primitive as the whole country had been only a few decades ago, when almost no one had even heard of these small insignificant Gulf states like Khor Fahal.

Then came the discovery of oil. The incredible bonanza of oil gushing up out of the barren desert. Not just a little oil. But vast oil deposits.

All the numbers, all the apples, all the fruit, clicked into line. The one armed bandits were spewing coins out into the arcade until it was pouring out into the street in an avalanche of cash. It was like winning the Lotto. Every day. For ever.

One day the old Sheikh of Khor Fahal, Sheikh Jilyani Bin Himyar Al Yas, was dirt poor, the next day he had millions. Which quickly became billions.

Of course there were problems. The first one was that the man who had won the Lotto didn't want the Lotto money. Of Bedouin origin the then Sheikh was happiest when hunting with his falcons in the desert. He didn't like his routine being interfered with. He didn't like foreigners; in particular he didn't like the oil companies. He thought they were trying to

NOEL SCANLON

take his country from him. Which of course they were. They, for their part, couldn't understand why this ignorant and impecunious tribesman who had spent most of his life scrabbling about in the desert, wouldn't take his Lotto money and be glad to get it. He should have been down on his knees to them thanking them. After all they were offering him wealth beyond his dreams. But this uneducated and illiterate man didn't seem to understand. He just wasn't capable of appreciating the glittering prize they were holding out to him. And he was stubborn. He couldn't be made to realise that his country was going to change big time and that he wasn't going to stop it.

There was nothing else for it. He had to go.

So he went.

The old Sheikh was replaced by his younger brother and the deposed Sheikh was sent off to live obscurely in his desert palace with his retainers to amuse himself whatever way he liked but without being allowed any participation whatever in government.

His brother, the new Ruler, Sheikh Suleiman Bin Himyar Al Yas, agreed to co-operate with the west and play the game by their rules. He was handed oil contracts to sign and he dutifully signed them. He was advised to build a whole new city in the sand and so he did. A deep-water harbour was built to berth the ships bringing in the material to build the city. Also an international airport. There followed roads, hospitals and schools. The great transformation had begun. An awful lot of lolly was handed out, a lot of companies, a lot of people became very quickly very very wealthy.

These thoughts ran through Deborah's mind as, crossing the bridge over the creek now, she fast forwarded a few centuries from the medieval past into the modern present. It was like moving into another time dimension.

High-rise buildings shimmered and shone as if they were not quite real, as if they and the rest of the New City were only a mirage.

It wasn't Disneyland but it was Fantasyland for sure. Super luxury hotels, some of the tallest buildings in the world, and, on the far side of the city, walled off villas surrounded by exotic gardens. Wide streets were flanked by towering new department stores crammed with everything western countries could offer in return for oil to fuel their homes, their oil fired central heating, their gas guzzling cars, their industries.

Everything shimmered in the hot sun. The gold domed Great Mosque. The miles of marble. The tower of the Al Yas international airport. The highway lined with drip-fed palm trees. Super tankers moving in and out of the deep water harbour.

26

Chauffeured limousines sped past Deborah as she drove on to the wide six-lane highway headed for the New City, another world, another century. As always, she was struck by the incongruity of such a close juxtaposing of the ultra modern and the medieval, the high tech. and the primitive.

She saw all this every morning. But, familiar as it was, there was still something unbelievable and unreal and fairytale about it.

Not quite fairytale though. There was a police road block up ahead.

Deborah hated road blocks. Sometimes you wouldn't see one for days and sometimes they were all over the place. At home being pulled by the police never bothered her. Here it made her nervous. There had been unpleasant incidents. Moslem women weren't allowed to drive at all and foreign women were discouraged. If you did drive they made you feel that you were doing something really terrible and highly immoral. You couldn't believe their attitude. And if you were unlucky enough to have an accident, you would most likely be thrown in gaol.

So she pulled up and waited in line.

When it came to her turn and a young constable was examining her papers, a squad of *Muttawa* or Religious Police drove up. These Religious Police belonged to the Department of Virtue and Extermination of Sin. Which sounds risible. Except when you are the person in the car in their country being pulled up by them. These *Muttawa* were no joke. They were highly intimidating. They were ultra orthodox with the mission of policing the morals of the state. This included women dressing strictly according to the law, their law that is. They were religious fanatics.

A thin, cloaked man, bearded and carrying prayer beads, approached her. He stared at her with that glitter, that glaze in the eyes of all religious fanatics. Addressing her in Arabic, he ordered her out of her car with the harsh uncompromising air of the ultra self-righteous.

She felt flustered and didn't obey at first, pretending not to understand though it was perfectly clear what he meant. Losing his temper at her slow response, the man yanked the car door open, shouted at her to get out. She wondered what sort of a family man this long bearded crazy was. What sort of a life did his wife, or two wives, or three wives, have? Did he whip them every night?

Hastily grabbing the *abbaya* that she always carried for such eventualities and trying to cover her hair with a chiffon scarf, Deborah slowly got out of the car. The *Muttawa* gathered around her like so many birds of prey around a kill, chattering and screaming and arguing. There was the smell of heat and sweat all around her and the feeling of being in close proximity to fanatics who were more than capable of doing extreme things if you pressed the wrong buttons. She knew that she had to keep her cool. Awful things happened to women who didn't.

They gestured to her to turn around and, before she realised what they were doing, they were measuring the distance from her hastily pulled on *abbaya* to the ground. It was all so ridiculous, laughable really. But at the same time frightening. The power these men had over you was awesome. They could whisk you away on a whim. They actually believed that an inch here or there in dress was a flagrant incitement to men's lust, totally wanton, distracting men from spiritual thoughts. Did these men have spiritual thoughts? Or lustful ones? It didn't really matter. What did matter was that they could give you up to forty lashes for breaking the dress code rules.

Chilled by the thought of what might happen to her at the whim of one of these zealots, she kept her head down. Finally, after a shrieking consultation among themselves, the *Muttawa* let her go. Reluctantly.

As she drove on, she felt shaken. And furious. The claim of these Religious Police that they were imposing morality was total and absolute hypocrisy. They weren't imposing morality; they were suppressing women and denying them their rights.

Things weren't what they seemed in this glittering New City. The appearance wasn't the reality. There was this flaw, this contradiction. The dazzling image was only a surface image. The fairytale didn't exist; it was only a back projection. The city appeared on the surface as ultra modern with more five star hotels than most European cities. But, in its philosophical underpinning, it was still back in the Middle Ages.

The trouble was, you could visit here or even live here and be seduced by all the surface signs of civilisation into thinking that the state was really modern in every way. But it hadn't emerged from the Middle Ages in its most fundamental aspects. For all its modernity, beneath the surface this was still a medieval feudal state.

And quite a nasty, dictatorial state at that.

CHAPTER 7

David hurried up the steps of the Trucial Bank head office building, a large modern block in the banking sector in the New City with a forecourt, a fountain and a soaring piece of abstract steel sculpture.

Immediately on entering the building, he was struck by cool air coming from the huge central air-conditioning plant; the air had been chilled so that it felt cold even chilly on the skin. He walked through the banking hall towards his private office.

His office was spacious and well appointed though not opulent. Opulence was reserved for the chief executive officer, CJ, and the suites for the use of the chairman and other directors.

Still suffering from the shock of discovering the mullah's body on the sea-bed, David sat at his desk for a moment absorbing and being reassured by the order and normality that lay all around him: his computer terminal, his fax machine, his micro cassette digital recorder, the orderly pile of financial magazines and documents neatly arranged on his desk. Whatever about what was happening outside, the world in here hadn't changed. Everything was as it should be. Everything was in its place. He was surrounded by comforting facts and figures, by reasoned economic analyses. It might be a disordered and dangerous world out there. But in here everything was strictly in order, precisely quantified, a finite, clearly defined world of facts and figures.

He checked his mail, played back his answering machine, glanced at the financial papers, switched on his computer and checked the markets. The Khor dinar was steady against all currencies.

He looked at the previous day's foreign currency transactions, then at the stock market. The Nasdaq had recovered thirty points from the two hundred point drop of the day before. A real recovery or a technical adjustment? The Dow and FTSE had eased slightly. Asian stocks seemed to have bottomed out.

He checked his diary and rang through that he was ready for the first of his appointments.

During the morning, he saw the representatives of a hotel chain who wanted to establish themselves in Khor Fahal, and a tyre manufacturing company who wanted the name of a local merchant who would be suitable to represent them. Both were typical of firms exploring the possibilities of establishing in the Middle East: they wanted names, they wanted information, they wanted to know the lie of the land to enable them to evaluate the prospects of their success in what was a highly lucrative market. They wanted to know the snags, who in the ministries had to be bribed, there was no point in bribing the wrong person, but, above all, they wanted to know the reliability of the local Arab merchant who would become their partner as required by law.

After he had given the visiting reps what help he could, he saw several large customers about their planned imports and a merchant who placed an order for a consignment of gold he wanted flown out from the UK by a chartered flight.

In between dealing with these people, David signed correspondence, sanctioned the issuing of letters of credit, passed the overdrafts that needed his decision. The banking hall was divided into various departments: Letters of Credit, Inward Bills which dealt with bills of lading and the documentation of imports, a Foreign Exchange Department, a Securities Department, a Drafts Department, and a Cash Department though in a bank of this nature cash transactions with the public were a small part of its overall activities.

Here on the ground floor they dealt with everything except for the special accounts which were exclusively dealt with in the chief executive's office upstairs.

As David worked away at his desk, an image he had been suppressing all morning jumped into his mind as if it had been lurking in the shadows all the time waiting to pounce.

The body bag was splitting open. Something was creeping out. A cloak. Then the body of the dead mullah, white and wan but clearer and more vivid than ever. David put his hand to his forehead. He had to stop this flow of images or his mind would go skidding off into all sorts of undefined and frightening areas.

He got up, went to the window and looked out. A police car was parked a little way down the street. One of the policemen was speaking on his mobile. Who was he ringing, what was the significance of his call? Maybe he was becoming paranoid. But it seemed to him that the presence of the police outside was ominous, that it must mean something.

It had been so quiet when he had lived here as a boy. The six lane highway he was now looking out on had been a dirt track negotiable only by a four wheel drive vehicle.

Most weekends the family would go on an expedition up the *wadi*. The bank driver had been a desert driver, skilled at negotiating the sides of dunes. In winter David remembered him in the early morning regularly using a rag burning with petrol to encourage the engine to start. Apart from his driving duties, everyday he used to fetch large ghee cans of water drawn from the local well and deliver them to Bank House. That's how primitive things had been. How rapidly and completely everything had changed!

Banking had changed along with everything else. It was no longer the leisurely and gentlemanly pursuit David's father had followed. In those days Sheikh Jilyani Bin Himyar Al Yas, long since deposed, used invite him to the palace on a regular basis and take his advice on the disposition of the millions that had just begun to roll in, money that was, at that time, kept in the Sheikh's very own private account, the state bureaucracy not having yet evolved. Sheikh Jilyani knew nothing about banking and it was natural that he should take advice from the only resident bank manager. At that time, there had been only one bank. Now there were scores. As a result, banking had become vastly more competitive. Khor Fahal was fast becoming one of the financial centres of the Middle East. This had accelerated greatly after the invasion of Iraq when Arabs began to withdraw massive amounts of money from America and the U K on the basis that they felt it was no longer safe, might even be seized under the new anti terrorism laws. Most of this money was re-deposited in the Middle East and the Trucial Bank experienced a huge inflow of funds.

David looked up to see Mohammed standing in front of his desk. He hadn't heard him come in.

Mohammed, in his Arab dress, a long *thobe* over his thin body, shoulders rounded, *kheffiya* held neatly in place by black rope, was his right hand man. He looked after commercial intelligence and brought in new business. He had connections with all of the major trading families and various members of the bureaucracy, including members of the Ruling Family. He gathered and relayed information, a task he was excellent at since by nature he was a gossip. He was David's eyes and ears in the *suqs* and the merchants' offices and the bureaucracy. Very little happened in Khor Fahal that Mohammed, with his widespread contacts, didn't get to know about.

Mohammed said now, "Have you heard about the rioting at the Shi'ite Fishermen's Mosque this morning?"

"I was there. Shortly after, that is."

"Then you were out in your boat early?"

David nodded and sat back in his swivel chair. "What have you heard?"

"The word is that it all began with the mullah being arrested in the Shi'ite mosque last night."

"What do we know about this mullah?"

"Mullah Hussein is known to be anti-government. But no one expected him to be arrested. No mullah has ever been arrested before. And, even worse than arresting him, is that no one has seen him since his arrest. The police just whisked him away."

"So where is he?"

"The rumour is that when the police got him into their custody they murdered him."

"What do you think?

"I don't know. Perhaps they did murder him. Or perhaps he had a heart attack. Or perhaps he died after being beaten up. Or perhaps he is safe and well in police custody."

"What do the police say?"

"They've issued an absolute denial. Though they admit arresting him."

"On what charge?"

"What they have leaked is that they have proof that he was plotting against the government. They claim that he has been making secret visits to Iran and that they have seized tapes incriminating him. They say they are holding him pending a trial but the people do not believe them. Rumours are running rife. Unless the police actually produce the mullah, the people will believe the worst."

David pondered this. "So, taking a worst case scenario, what could happen? What would be the most extreme reaction from the Shi'ites as you see it?"

Mohammed took a drag on his cigarette. The bank was meant to be a smoke free zone but Mohammed was an inveterate smoker who just couldn't give it up. "It could be disastrous. Arresting ordinary Shi'ites or even disappearing them is one thing. Profaning a mosque and arresting a mullah is something else. It's really inflammatory. Murdering a mullah could be the match that sets the state ablaze. I think the police made a mistake. If things aren't very cleverly handled, the whole state could explode."

"You think so?"

"It could happen if they don't produce the mullah."

David restrained himself from saying that this would be rather difficult. "And if they don't produce him what can we expect?"

"Demonstrations. Civil unrest. Rioting. That sort of thing. As you know the people throughout the Arab world are incensed just now. The Shi'ites are just looking for an excuse. Nothing they'd like better than to overthrow the present government which is a lot too western orientated for their liking."

"So, if all this were to happen, how would the government react?"

"Strongly. They'd try to quell it, take out the leaders, that sort of thing."

David changed the subject and went on to discuss various matters of bank business. He liked Mohammed but he could never be one hundred percent sure of him. He never knew for sure whether Mohammed was telling him the truth or what he thought he wanted to hear. He suspected that Mohammed played several sides at the same time. He doubted if Mohammed relayed information exclusively to him as he was supposed to do. Information, after all, fetched a high price in Khor Fahal.

Still, by and large, he trusted him. Mohammed did very well out of his position with the bank. He drove around in a Mercedes sports and without a doubt he had money salted away. He also, to David's certain knowledge, owned property, a taxi firm and dabbled in the gold smuggling that was endemic in the state; everyone was into gold smuggling including leading merchants and various members of the Ruling Family. High powered *dhows* regularly slipped out of Khor creek to meet and off-load gold into boats outside Indian territorial waters. Payment for the smuggled gold came in through the bank sometimes in the form of silver bars, sometimes in the form of bags of cheques and drafts.

"The Chairman is leaving the building," Mohammed commented, looking out the window.

"Really? At this time of day?"

"He seems to be in a hurry to go."

David and Mohammed watched Sayyid Sultan ibn Khalifa, the

chairman of the bank, having come down in his personal elevator, descend the marble steps to the bank car park where he strode towards his Rolls Royce, his long regulation white starched *thobe* flapping about his body, surrounded by his armed guards and retainers who roughly brushed aside anyone who tried to approach him, his chauffeur holding the car door open and ushering him into its air-conditioned luxury. On the rare occasion David got to see him, the chairman made a point of keeping him hanging around while he spoke on one of his numerous onyx telephones, keeping David waiting at his whim in order to show who was who and what was what.

"He told his flight crew to be ready for a flight later today," Mohammed said.

"To where?"

"He didn't say. He'll tell them when he's airborne."

"Indeed," David said.

The Chairman was something of a mystery man. No one knew how or why he had achieved his present high position which he could only hold with the acquiescence or backing of the Ruler. That was how things worked in the state, a nod from the Ruler decided who got what contract, who got a slice of the cake and what size slice they got. Bin Khalifa had the Ruler's ear and this was enormously valuable. Many a fortune had been established just on that basis. But what was odd here was that he was not a local, not of the tribe but an outsider. By and large all high positions were held by the family, by the tribe. No one knew Bin Khalifa's past or how he had gained such influence.

Mohammed furtively stubbed out his cigarette and left the office.

David's mind was made up. Mohammed had confirmed his own reading of the situation.

The germ of an idea had been forming in his mind right from the moment he had got safely back on shore, in fact from the moment he had found the mullah's body he had immediately spotted a financial opportunity. He had had a strong hunch. Of course he had had hunches before and not all his hunches turned out to be right in the past as he had disastrously found out. But this situation was different.

He checked the currency markets again. The Khor dinar was still steady. He was ahead of the game. He had seen the dead mullah. He had the evidence of his own eyes that the mullah lay dead at the bottom of the sea, murdered. And eaten by sharks. Also he had seen the police in the mosque compound and the disturbance that had ensued with the police firing on the small crowd. It might all fizzle out. But his instinct was that it wouldn't.

If there was trouble, real political trouble with the Shi'ites in the state, he was convinced that the value of the currency would fall in world markets, how much depended on how bad the trouble was. He had to get in before that fall began.

He briefly thought of contacting CJ but decided against. Currency dealing was his responsibility. And CJ wouldn't want to be involved. That way he could blame David if it all went wrong.

The first thing was to cover the bank's position. He cyphered and encoded an order to sell short, then e-mailed the encoded order to the bank's brokers, placing a forward contract to sell dinars in the amount of fifty million which he contracted to buy back on a given date at the then prevailing rate.

If the rate went up, he, or rather the bank lost. If it went down, they won.

But what about himself? What about a modest little gamble on the side. Nothing too way out. Just a million or two. This was a once off chance, one not likely to come his way again.

His mind was made up. He'd go with his instincts. As he took this decision he realised that dealing was still in his blood, more than he had thought. He felt again the rush of adrenaline that came with it. He was taken aback at the strength of the rush and how much he missed it, missed the hectic hysteria of the trading floor. It's so easy to make large sums of money when the markets are going with you, that it's hard to accept you're liable to lose equally large sums when the tide turns against you. As it so easily can. A word from a finance minister, or a central bank announcement of an interest rate change, up or down or even a strong hint or rumour can wipe hundreds of millions off the markets in minutes, can start a wave of panic in the trading rooms around the world with computers being worked maniacally, phone boards flashing, traders screaming. Nowhere does hysteria set in faster than on a trading floor. Nothing in the world behaves as irrationally as stock, commodity and currency markets. Caught in the wrong position, long when you should be sort, short when you should be long, your tendency when you start losing is to double up and hope the markets will change in your favour rather than accept the loss staring you in the face.

That's what happened to David on the trading floor of the Schroder Bank in the offshore financial centre in Dublin where things went so disastrously wrong that David among others lost his job in the company leaving him and Deborah figuring out how to pay the mortgage on an extremely expensive house in Killiney not to speak of their accumulated debts.

But this time was going to be different. This was pay back time. He e-mailed another order to sell short, this time on his own account. If everything went all right nobody need ever know. And the profit from a decent percentage fall would just about pay off his present debts, his overdraft, the mortgage and so on. If the currency collapsed he could look on being well set up for retirement and good bye to money worries. But if the Khor dinar rose in the market? Better not think about that.

He had just finished e-mailing his order when his telephone rang. Mohammed was on the other end. Colonel Rachman of the police department was in the bank and wanted to see him straight away.

CHAPTER 8

Mohammed ushered Colonel Rachman into David's office with a great show of solicitude. A visit from Colonel Rachman was not something anyone welcomed and it made David feel decidedly apprehensive. Rachman was an aide to Chief of Police Qassim.

Chief of Police Qassim was the most feared man in the state. He and his police were legendary for organising raids at night, the dreaded knock on the door. Anyone suspected of disloyalty or subversion was immediately arrested and imprisoned. Many had disappeared over the years and were never seen again.

Mohammed, who had a keen appreciation of the power of the police and what they could do to you, fussed and fawned, muttering solicitously, "*Ahlan wasahlin. Tefuddel, tefuddel.* Welcome, welcome," while he pulled out a chair for Rachman and then backed obsequiously out the door.

Colonel Rachman, in his heavily braided uniform, his skin the colour of teak, was strikingly handsome with a strong suggestion of cruelty and arrogance. His aquiline face in profile emphasised his hawk nose, his tribal descent. Like all those in a position of power in the state, he was a Sunni.

He began by being fastidiously if ironically polite.

"*Salaam aleikum.* Peace be on you."

"*Aleikum asalaam.* And on you peace," David replied

"*Keif Halak.*"

"*Tayyib, al humdilallah,*" David said as required by custom.

The formal greetings the Arabs use in ordinary social intercourse sounded like a mockery coming from the mouth of someone who had committed the atrocities and supervised the torture Colonel Rachman was known to have been involved in.

David rang for coffee and immediately a Pakistani boy brought it in with alacrity on the silver tray kept for special customers, pouring from the type of coffee pot with the curved beak to be found all over Arabia though this one was made of silver with Persian designs while the run of the mill pot was of beaten copper. The boy poured expertly beginning from a height and descending swiftly to the small cups without spilling a drop.

Sipping his coffee, Colonel Rachman dispensed with any further formalities and cut to the chase.

"I believe you were out in your boat this morning?"

It was what David had expected. The call had to be about the mullah; there wasn't anything else the colonel would bother to call on him about.

He wasn't sure how to answer. It would be foolish to lie since the colonel obviously knew he had been out in his boat. After all he had been followed from the mosque by two police officers in dark glasses.

"Yes, I went for a short run before breakfast."

"To your usual spot on the promontory?"

How did Rachman have all this information? How much did he know?

"I went for my usual run," David said evasively.

"But not to the promontory?"

"No."

"Where then?

"To the Al Kabir rock."

"And why did you change your destination?

"No particular reason. I dive all over the place." He paused. "And before we go any further, would you mind telling me what this is all about?"

"Just clearing up a few matters."

"I haven't done anything against the law."

"That's for me to determine."

How right he was. David was well aware that the colonel could do what he liked. This was not a democracy. There was no judiciary, at least not as understood in the west, to restrain the police. There was a code of justice of sorts but the Sharia law administered by a religious court was far removed from the western concept of justice.

Colonel Rachman took out his prayer beads and began telling them. His apparent politeness had been replaced by hardness, an implacability. "Were you alone?"

David hesitated. There was the fate of the boy to be considered. He remembered the boy's eagerness and delight as they sped across the sea. If arrested, he would to be tortured and quickly broken. He decided to try to protect the boy.

"Yes, I was alone."

"Are you quite sure you were alone?"

"Yes."

As soon as he had uttered the lie, he knew by Rachman's reaction that he had made a mistake. Possibly a big mistake. They knew about the boy. Realising this, he wanted to take the lie back, haul it back into his brain. But of course he couldn't.

Rachman's demeanour became more hostile. His face altered. A thin smile and a cruel twist of the lips appeared on his face. David felt like he was getting a quick glimpse into a dark pit, a glimpse of the cruelty for which the police were famous.

David wanted to point out that the bank was not an interrogation centre. He wanted to ask the colonel what right he had to cross-examine him. But, of course, he didn't.

Rachman twirled his beads. He was like a cat with a mouse.

"What you said just now about being alone in the boat gives me a problem. You see my men picked up a youth this morning. This youth claims to have been out in the boat with you. And since he was also seen by my men coming ashore in your boat, perhaps you should start your story again. And it would be better for you to tell the truth this time."

"All right," David said. "I didn't want to implicate the boy because he's vulnerable and I know precisely what your men do to youths like him."

Rachman bristled. "Stop maligning the police and tell me everything that happened while you were out in your boat."

David told him more or less what had happened that morning only because he had to and because they already knew, having beaten it out of the boy. Otherwise he would have said nothing.

As he told his story, he was back in the underwater depths as they turned dark and menacing. The body bag was splitting open again, the mullah's body in the murky half light hung there indecisively, suspended. His mouth was open. The corpse began to speak, or at least to communicate. What was he saying?

When David had finished his revised version of what had happened, Colonel Rachman sat there saying nothing, staring out of unblinking eyes. David was on trial and Rachman was the judge weighing up the evidence.

Eventually he broke the silence. "You claim to have found a body. Why did you not report it to the police?"

"I was about to. I've had a busy morning."

"Not to report finding a body is a criminal offence. Now according to your story you saw the body of the dead mullah on the sea bed. Did you know the mullah well?"

"I wouldn't say that. I've seen him once or twice in passing."

"In that case how did you identify the body as that of the mullah?"

"Because I knew him by sight. I know it was the mullah. I recognised him. And the body was wrapped in a mullah's cloak."

The colonel smiled his twisted smile again. Or was it a grimace. "The cloak proves nothing. The cloak could have been anybody's."

David didn't reply.

"Let's go over this again. You were underwater which means the light was poor. You claim you saw a black body bag tethered to the sea-bed by a rock. But you never got close-up because you were frightened off by sharks. Is that correct?"

"Correct."

"So, given that you didn't really know the mullah, had in fact only ever seen him at a distance, your impression that it was him is only a supposition. At best, it's a long way from a positive identification."

David was beginning to catch the drift.

"Given the circumstances, I am going to suggest you cannot be certain of what you saw."

"I'm sure I saw a human body," David said. "And if it wasn't the mullah it was someone who looked like him."

Rachman said, "I'm sure you made a genuine mistake. And I am trying to help you. I am trying to see a way for you to get out of this mess. I don't think you appreciate the danger you are in.

"The position from the point of view of the police is that I now have a report from you that you found a dead body. Following on this, and while further enquiries are made, it is up to me whether or not I arrest you for being implicated in murder."

At the threat of arrest, David felt his blood run cold. He knew only too well what happened to those arrested by Rachman on murder charges.

He was back in an old nightmare. He was being led down corridors in a secret prison. He could hear the screams coming from the cells all around and combined with this and the damp oppressive heat was the smell of urine and human sweat and vomit. A dim yellowish light shone through barred squares on either side. At one of these, a face, ravaged and disfigured, suddenly appeared. It was a familiar face, a face he knew.

Coming out of this nightmarish back flash, he said, "So what do you want of me?"

"I do not want anything. I am only trying to help you, not for yourself, but because of your CEO's friendship with Chief of Police Qassim. Despite that, however, if you were to continue to claim that you saw the dead mullah in the sea or even that you saw a body in the sea, I would have to detain you for questioning."

Colonel Rachman let him ponder the implications of this for a moment, then said, "Fortunately this little matter can, I think, be resolved." He smiled a thin twisted smile. "You see, you could not possibly have seen the dead body of the mullah because we released him shortly after we arrested him. Released him and expelled him from the country because of his proven subversive activities. I myself escorted him out of the state. So whoever or whatever you saw, it was not the mullah." His voice was harsh and threatening. "Do I make myself clear?"

"Absolutely," David said. "You make yourself crystal clear."

It could hardly be plainer. If he didn't keep his mouth shut, something very nasty was going to happen to him.

"Good, good," Colonel Rachman said. "I think we understand one another. You didn't see anything unusual when you went diving this morning and there will be no malicious rumours spread that might in any way involve the police in this matter.

"The mullah is safely in Iran. Should you be foolish enough to say anything to the contrary, to start some rumour that would give ammunition to the enemies of the state, I must warn you that it would have the most serious consequences for you and your family."

He rose to go and, right on queue, Mohammed was in the office bent over in his *thobe* like an obsequious Arab Uriah Heep, ushering Colonel Rachman out.

NOEL SCANLON

CHAPTER 9

Putting what had happened with the *Muttawa* at the police checkpoint out of her mind, Deborah worked her way through the morning's mail.

The magazine office was shabby as offices went in this oil rich state. *Al Jameela*, being a woman's magazine, was naturally accorded minimum status. Deborah's office was partitioned off in an open plan area that accommodated the dozen staff, all female and wearing long sleeved ankle length dresses that covered their bodies more or less completely.

Separated from the area where the women worked, was a room with its own entrance occupied by Fawzi, their male reporter, and a photographer. The men never entered the women's office space and if Deborah wanted anything from them she had to go to see them.

She had been offered the editorship of the magazine when her predecessor, a Lebanese woman, had been suddenly deported for reasons unknown. The girls either didn't know or wouldn't tell her how this woman had transgressed, though they hinted strongly that she had been caught having an illicit affair and had been lucky only to be deported.

Deborah's official designation was that of editor. The editor in chief was Sheikha Sharifa who was connected to the Ruling Family, but apart from an initial interview at the Sheikha's luxury villa, Deborah had never seen sign or light of her. She never came to the office but nonetheless maintained a suite that was kept permanently locked. So far, Deborah had been left to her own devices in running the magazine.

When she looked up from her work now, Aisha was in her office, quietly standing there. Aisha's hair was covered with a silk headscarf. She wore glasses and had a serious, studious demeanour. She was the daughter of a government official who sent a driver with her every morning and collected her after work. She was of an age when she should have been married off and she confided in Deborah her difficulties at home trying to fend off suitors presented by the females of her extended family who came to her house making offers on behalf of various males seeking wives. Aisha had so far managed to avoid marriage to someone she strongly objected to marrying. But for how long could she resist?

Despite the apparent outward sophistication of the city, young women like Aisha were still regarded as objects to be bartered and marriage as a contract between families for their own mutual advantage.

Deborah said to Aisha now, "Thanks for doing the translations. You must have come in early."

"What do you think of the contributions?" Aisha asked, anxious for her opinion.

Deborah had made a request in the last issue for contributions written by women and the response was turning out to be phenomenal.

"Great. Fantastic. A real eye-opener."

The fact was that Deborah was gob smacked by what was pouring in from women all over the city. There was an intensity, a nakedness about some of the personal intimacies which she hadn't expected coming from such cloistered and subjugated women. In here among them were some real cries from the heart. She had unexpectedly and quite by chance been given a glimpse into a room usually closed and locked, a glimpse into the hearts of young Arab women expressing their frustrations and passions.

It was nothing short of amazing what these women were prepared to commit to paper such revelations about their private lives and thoughts and dreams in a society where women could be whipped for breaking the dress code not to speak of having an assignation with a man.

Deborah was trying slowly to widen the scope of the magazine. When she had taken over, most of it consisted of photographs with accompanying text of the Ruler or some dignitary arriving at the airport or members of the Ruling family at endless functions. She had introduced new elements. She had a Jordanian female doctor contributing a weekly article on women's health. She had started a series of interviews and articles on social issues. In her wilder imaginings, Deborah had this idea that she was going to make *Al Jameela* the leading woman's magazine in the Gulf and one that seriously tackled issues from a feminist viewpoint.

After Aisha had left, Deborah noticed through the glass panel in her office Fatima, the youngest member of staff, pretty and feminine, heavily made up and perfumed, arrive late as usual. Fatima was a rebel. She threw off her black *abbaya* and *yashmak* with a flourish. Underneath the *abbaya,* her hair was teased up to about twice its size and dyed red. Last week it had blonde streaks. She was wearing a tight fitting light yellow v-neck t-shirt which made her look provocative. Fatima liked to live dangerously. She took off her sandals now and put on a pair of stilettos. In the office, the only gesture she made towards the Moslem dress code was to cover her hair with a gossamer-like diaphanous silk headscarf.

Some time later the phone rang again and Deborah picked it up.

"Is that you Deborah?" her mother asked. "Your voice sounds very faint. Are you all right?"

"Yes, Mum."

"What's wrong with David? He was in a very bad mood this morning. Snapped at me when I asked him a simple question."

"He was just in a rush to get to work."

"Well, there was no need to take it out on me. I think he was annoyed about the men sitting outside."

"What men?"

"Two policemen in a police car. They followed him when he left. I don't know if he saw them. But I did."

Deborah wondered what that was all about.

"Anyway," her mother went on, "what I'm ringing to tell you is that Carolyn's temperature is down and I've let her out of bed."

"Good," Deborah said.

When her mother spoke again her voice sounded formal and stilted. "I'm dressed and ready," she said. "I hope you haven't forgotten that today is Sunday and you're taking me to Mass."

Deborah had forgotten all about Mass. She had to get out of this somehow. She had too much on her plate to leave the office and go and fetch her mother right now. "I've been trying to get away but something important has just come up." Well, that was at least partly true. "Otherwise I had intended to take you. Is Abdul there?"

"Yes. Why?"

"Tell him to run down to the taxi rank and get you a taxi."

"I don't like going in a taxi on my own in this country."

"You'll be perfectly all right, Mum. I'll tell you what, get Abdul to go with you and wait outside to take you home."

"But are you not coming? I thought you'd be coming?"

Of course her mother expected her to drop everything and leave the office in order to take her to Mass. Naturally. In fact Deborah had completely forgotten that today was Sunday. With Friday the Moslem holiday, and with Thursday and Friday the weekend, you were inclined to forget about Sunday. David didn't go to church services, hardly anyone in the state did, and she herself rarely went to Mass. She had gone the first couple of Sundays with her mother who had been shocked to find that the Mass was conducted, not in a church, but in a room in a private house with only a handful of people and a visiting Italian priest. It didn't seem to her mother to be like Mass at all when compared to the Catholic churches back home in Ireland which were packed with people.

"Aren't you coming?" her mother asked querulously.

"I'd love to," Deborah lied, "but I just have to be here."

Deborah could tell that her mother was making a great effort not to complain. All the same, she managed to make her feel guilty. Before her mother's visit, she had become used to the expats lack of interest in religion, but her mother's visit had resurrected childhood feelings and memories she thought she had completely forgotten about but which her mother reminded her of in no uncertain manner.

"Just because you're living among Moslems, you are still a Catholic and you have obligations. You should set an example. Even the Moslems go to their mosques and, if they can fulfil their obligations, why can't you?"

"I'll go next Sunday," Deborah promised and put the phone down.

A little later there was a light knock on the door and the tea boy came in, his tray laden with small glasses and two pots.

"*Finjan chai?*" the young tea boy asked.

"Yes, please," Deborah said without looking up. She went on with her reading, flicking over a page. She was aware of the boy going through the ritual of pouring tea from his battered copper pot ornamented with brass.

She reached out for the glass of tea on her desk. The boy was still standing there. He was glaring at her.

"That's all thanks," Deborah said.

But the boy didn't move.

Why was he looking at her like that? He was looking at her with a mixture of insolence and fanaticism.

Deborah said sharply, "You can go now. You are not to stay here."

The tea boy, very thin in his dirty gown and skullcap, was often about the office but she had never particularly observed him before; he was one of those urchins who had free passage everywhere even into the women's quarters.

When she told him to go for the second time, the boy still didn't move. He just stood there staring at her.

"Please go now," Deborah repeated sharply.

The tea boy leaned across the desk. His hand snaked out and struck her sharply across the face. He stood there glaring at her with hatred in his eyes. Then disappeared running through the doorway, the little glasses of tea and coffee rattling on his tray.

NOEL SCANLON

CHAPTER 10

_____

"So what's going on?" demanded CJ, the chief executive officer of the bank.

For all that he affected the air of a frank laid-back man of the people who peppered his conversation with expletives and profanities, CJ had done very nicely for himself. His reported worth was over eighty million but no one really knew its full extent. Years ago he had been in the same bank as David's father at a time when new Arab banks were springing up and were on the lookout for executives already experienced in international Middle Eastern banking and capable of running a newly formed bank. CJ had seized the opportunity, jumped ship and built the fledgling Trucial Bank into one of the most successful and highly profitable banking organisation in the whole Gulf area.

'It was easy at the time,' CJ had told David many times as he kept him up late drinking in the Phoenix bar. 'Your father could have done the same or better. He was senior to me at the time and knew more about banking than I did. But nothing could move him. He wanted to stay where he was in a good steady job for a British company. I told him there was more scope for using your initiative in an emerging Arab bank but he just wouldn't buy it. Maybe he'd still be alive today if he had.'

At this point, depending on the amount of drink he had taken, CJ would become maudlin to the point of tears over the sad and tragic end that had overtaken his good friend David's father.

That was CJ late night in the Phoenix bar. This was daylight, and CJ in his official capacity as CEO was stone cold sober in his opulent suite looking out over the city.

"So what's going on?" he asked.

"What do you mean?"

CJ pointed out the window. "For a start, would you mind telling why there are two policemen sitting out there in a police car watching the bank?"

David checked. They were still there. "I have no idea."

"Well you ought to, considering they arrived here right on your tail this morning."

CJ had been in before him, something that almost never happened. He had noted his Mercedes in the car park.

CJ went on, "And while you're at it, would you mind telling me why Colonel Rachman paid you a visit just now?"

David wasn't surprised that CJ knew about Rachman's visit. He'd either had a phone call from the police or someone in the office had told him. It didn't matter which. CJ was where he was because he made it his business to know what was going on.

He raised his hand now. "And don't try to tell me it was bank business. I know it wasn't. If you're in some sort of trouble, I need to know about it. If you're in trouble with the police, the bank is in trouble with the police."

David considered what he would have to tell CJ and what he could leave out. A certain amount but not too much. Behind the amiable front, CJ was devious and ruthless. Shrewd too. He hadn't made his millions without being shrewd. So David had to be careful about how he told his story.

When he had finished his version of what had happened out in the boat, CJ exploded, "I can't believe what I'm hearing. You should never have got involved in something like this."

"I didn't get involved in anything. All I did was go for my usual boat trip."

"Why did you go diving? There was no need to go diving. I can never understand why anyone in their right mind would want to dive in seas everyone knows are infested with killer sharks"'

David opened his mouth to speak but CJ stopped him.

"Don't say another word. I don't want to hear any more details. I've heard too much already. Whether you meant to or not, you've gone and got this bank into a difficult and tricky situation. I have always taken great care that none of my staff gets into trouble with any state officials. Especially the police."

"I'm not in trouble with the police. I haven't broken any laws."

"Colonel Racham doesn't make calls just to pass the time of day and, in case you haven't worked it out, he was acting under instructions from Chief of Police Qassim. And when that fucker or one of his leg men calls on you, you're in trouble, whether you think it or not. I hope you co-operated with him?"

"I told him the truth which is that I saw the body of the dead mullah."

"God Almighty! And what did Rachman say to that?"

"He refused to accept my story. I didn't like his attitude. I didn't like being told what I saw or didn't see."

"Have you no common sense whatever," CJ exclaimed. "Couldn't you see that the man was doing you a favour? He was just giving you a little steering so that you got things straight in your mind and you didn't get yourself into trouble unnecessarily."

So it had been a phone call. Could it have been from Qassim himself?

A little more placatory, a little more man to man, CJ went on, "You don't want getting mixed up in any of that dead body sort of thing. Very dangerous. There's nothing in it for you only trouble. Rachman was offering you a way out."

"What about the truth?"

CJ was getting exasperated.

"Who gives a fuck about the truth? And what is the truth anyway? There are a lot of different interpretations of the truth. And how can you be sure what you saw? All those fucking mullahs look the same, dead or alive, in or out of the water."

David said nothing. This man had given him a job with an almost embarrassingly high salary at a time when he was unemployed, after being let off by the Schroder Bank, given him a job for which there was no doubt dozens of well qualified applicants. Why had he done it? Because of his father? Because he was a fellow countryman? Because he was someone he felt he could easily control? Because he had Arabic? Because he was someone he had a hold over? Because it made him feel good? Who knows? Despite his bluff open manner, CJ was a complex character. He was by no means an easy man to read. One thing David knew was that, in return for giving him his present job, CJ wanted and expected complete and absolute loyalty.

CJ went on, "Don't give me any grief here. And don't tell me about your moral scruples. I don't want to hear about them."

He sat back and looked thoughtful. "This is how we're going to play this. The official line is that this mullah fellow was escorted out of the country. What we do is accept the official line. Unequivocally. Do you have a problem with that?"

"Not at all. Except that it isn't true. The mullah is dead. I saw his body on the sea-bed."

"That's not the point."

"So what is the point?"

"God give me strength! The point is that we go along with the official line. The point is that that is what I have decided we do. We go along with what they want. In case you've forgotten, they're the people who pay us our outrageous salaries. They're the people who keep us in the luxury to which we have become accustomed. They're the people who put the bread on the table.

"This state has been good to me," CJ went on. "And it'll be good to you if you play your cards right. And that means keeping in with the authorities, not spitting in their face.

"Without the protection and co-operation of the people in authority in this state, none of us would have got anywhere. I wouldn't have my present position. And you certainly wouldn't. How the fuck do you think you got the job? Did you think you got it by fair and due process?"

When David didn't reply, CJ went on, "You got the job because I gave it to you. Otherwise you wouldn't have had a hope in hell. With your record, no one would be offering you the sort of position and remuneration you have here. You'd be fecking (occasionally overcome by some distant moral Catholic ethical memory, CJ introduced an e into the f word, an Irish way of making it somehow respectable) you'd be fecking about back home in Dublin applying for jobs, sending out CV's, and your CV isn't all that great. It has some negative points in it that I overlooked because I'm soft hearted. In return I expect your co-operation."

"I always co-operate."

CJ sounded mollified. "I must say, by and large, you do. And it wasn't your fault that you happened on that dead body, whoever it was. I don't give a feck who was murdered, if they were murdered. I don't give a feck if a hundred Shi'ite mullahs were murdered. What I do care about is that you've put yourself into an unfortunate position. That's a pity. But I'm sure we can deal with it provided no rumours are put about. At least no rumours concerning or touching this bank in any way."

"I'm not going to say anything," David said. "But you can't stop rumours. It's already common gossip in the *suqs* that the mullah was arrested and there's bound to be a lot of speculation about what happened to him."

"I don't give a shit what's common gossip in the *suqs*. So long as we're not in any way involved," CJ said.

"If the mullah isn't produced they're going to put two and two together anyway."

"That's their problem. Which brings me to another point. What with this present commotion and all, I want you to move out of your apartment on the far side of the creek as soon as possible. I'll get you accommodation on this side. A desirable property with swimming pool, grounds, the lot. Prices are going up like crazy, but I'm sure we can find one of our more indebted customers to give us the right deal."

"Deborah likes it where she is," David said.

"For godsake. Deborah is a nice girl but she's got to understand her position. She's a bank wife and she has to behave like one. She's living in accommodation provided by the bank, she has responsibilities and she has to act accordingly. By the way, I'd prefer if she didn't work. The salary we pay you is more than adequate to maintain a household. A girl like her shouldn't be mixed up with that rag she works for. It doesn't reflect well on the bank."

"Deborah will be delighted to hear that," David said with heavy irony.

"It's up to you to make your wife understand her position."

David didn't respond. It came into his mind that he hadn't told CJ about the fifty million forward sale of the currency. Would he tell him? Or just leave it? Maybe better leave it just for them moment. See which way the market went. Pick his time to tell him

"That's fine then," CJ went on. "Don't rock the boat. Keep your mouth shut, and this ridiculous incident of the dead mullah will blow over. The police will let it drop. Do the right thing, keep your nose clean and I'll look after you. But remember this. Get yourself into trouble or let your wife get you into trouble and you'll find yourself back home. On the dole."

NOEL SCANLON

CHAPTER 11

Davidid looked about the Phoenix Hotel bar which was crowded as usual with a largely male crowd. Faces were flushed with liquor after the deals that reps and delegations had made or thought they had made. The crowded tables looked like a miniature meeting of the United Nations - English, American, German, Nigerian, Pakistani, and a Japanese delegation who had come to Khor Fahal in the hope of obtaining the multi million dinar contract for the new airport runway.

There were very few Arabs among them and those there were were young and talking loudly and defiantly, defiant but guilty as if they were being watched by the serried ranks of their strict living alcohol-abhorring forebears. Though quite a few of the wealthier Arabs drank, some of them to excess, going from total abstinence to total drunkenness, they did so largely in private. If they drank in public at functions, the alcohol was disguised as a soft drink passed to them by a pliant waiter.

David had just dropped in for a beer after work. He was glad to get in out of the heat. Outside temperatures had really begun to soar. Heat was moving into a new dimension, the sky leaden and the wind searingly hot. Work finished early in the Gulf; at least it did in the banking world which usually knocked off around two o'clock. The suqs and merchants' offices closed for a siesta then re-opened in the evening. The banks didn't re-open though sometimes David would take Mohammed with him and visit merchants in the evenings, despite the clammy heat.

The expats were as usual gathered in a corner of the Phoenix bar. Most of them were hard drinkers but none more so that the young and unaccompanied men who on occasion stayed here drinking all afternoon, evening and into the small hours. They needed a few, and maybe more than a few, beers to maintain their liquid levels and prevent dehydration. Throughout the Gulf, alcohol consumption was high. It was not a stay-at-

NOEL SCANLON

home environment. For the great majority of expats, it was not a place you settled into. Here you were forever an outsider, especially, if, as was often the case, you spoke little or no Arabic.

In Khor Fahal, east appeared to meet west and west appeared to meet east and certainly the signs of the west were everywhere: in the Coca Cola signs, the MacDonald's, the supermarkets, the automobiles, the plethora of consumer items. These sign bearers of western culture were cheek by jowl with the mosques, the calls to prayer, the *thobes,* the *abbayas*, the veils, the committee for the Promulgation of Virtue and the Elimination of Vice.

The two cultures appeared to meet. Indeed the western consumer culture seemed to be washing over the state in a great tidal wave. But the two cultures didn't really either meet or understand one another despite their close proximity. There was no meeting of minds. Both shamelessly used and exploited the other. The Arabs met only the greedy consumer side of western capitalism, the people who wanted their oil, the reps who wanted the big contracts. They met only the consumer side and mistook the dross for the real thing. They never got beneath the surface, never came to know what really made the west tick.

The westerns, for their part, never got beneath the surface of Arab culture either. Defeated by the language, the customs, the religion and the heat, they retreated into one another's company and stayed there.

His own father had managed to spend his entire working life in the Arabia without learning the language, totally incurious about Arab culture, living the transplanted life of a colonial in a hot inhospitable land, attending and giving innumerable cocktail parties at various Bank Houses in various states where the format was always exactly the same, the men dressed in black evening dress or, in extreme heat, black trousers, cummerbund and open necked white shirt, barely noticing the Arab bearers in white tunics proffering the obligatory small eats western style and the inevitable drinks. His father was socially active in the British Club, the Bridge Club and the Golf Club where, in those days, they played their golf on sand instead of grass. But his social activities were confined to the expats. During his decades of living out here he seemed scarcely to have noticed the Arabs.

David didn't know if it was his imagination but, in the Phoenix bar now, he sensed an air of tension, glances over the shoulder, a momentary pause as there was a loud bang outside that turned out to be only a car back firing but could have been something more sinister than that.

56

He felt a hand on his shoulder.

"How's it going?" Andy Wilson of the Standard Chartered Bank asked, as he took the bar stool beside him and ordered a beer.

"I hear rumours that there was some shooting early this morning over on your side, down in the grounds of a mosque. Is that true?"

"Absolutely. I was in the area at the time bringing my boat in. There was a crowd around the mosque and the police were there but all I saw them fire was tear gas."

"Given how touchy they are about the sacredness of mosques and all that, the police mixing it with the Shi'ites in the mosques doesn't seem like a great idea."

"No it doesn't, does it."

"And no one seems to know what's happened to the mullah fellow over there. I hope he hasn't been martyred. Nothing seems to get them going like having a few martyrs they can carry around roaring and bawling and calling on Allah."

"Too true."

There were raised voices and gesticulations at the Japanese delegation table.

"Head Office got into a bit of a flap when they heard about it, wanted a full up-date on our security precautions. They suggested that if things escalate we should start making plans as to how best to protect the staff, perhaps even consider flying the women home. They always tend to fuss a lot in these situations though I must say they do leave it up to the staff on the ground to make the final decision after they have consulted with the embassy. Of course you don't have the problem of consulting with Head Office what with your Head Office being right here."

"That's right," David said. Where had the Chairman been off to this morning in his private jet? A meeting of some sort? But where and about what? Did he know something none of the rest of them knew? "I don't imagine anyone on the board of the Trucial Bank is losing any sleep over what may or may not happen to their staff. In fact our esteemed chairman flew off in his private plane this morning."

"So?"

"Nothing, he's just off on one of his jaunts."

"Lucky man. So what's your assessment of the situation? Is there something going to happen, something more than a few rounds fired off by the police? You're closer to the Arab mind than most of us."

"I don't really know. You can't make too much of one incident with the police and a bit of rioting."

"My commercial assistant seems to think there's some incitement going on," Andy said. "And there's always some tension what with Shi'ites making up two thirds of the population and the Sunnis having all the money and power."

"That's always been the situation, there have always been tensions but it's never blown its top yet."

"There's always a first. And we could be the unlucky buggers to be in the wrong place at the wrong time.

David remembered the look in Colonel Rachman's eyes as he leaned forward to threaten him.

"That's a possibility we can never rule out"

They chatted on desultorily about business, about this and that as waves of expats gossip and speculation washed over them. There weren't as many European expats in the state as during the very peak of intense construction and expansion, but Khor Fahal still attracted them like bees to a honey pot.

You might ask what sane person, especially from a temperate northern country, would want to live in a climate that took years off your life, made you old before your time. The answer was: plenty. They mightn't like the climate. They mightn't like the Arabs. But they liked their money. There were plenty of takers for the jobs on offer so long as people went on being paid double or treble what they could make in their home country, with company-paid accommodation, a company car, children's school fees paid, and a generous pension scheme thrown in for good measure. And, above all, the glorious fact that in Khor Fahal there was no income tax. Can you imagine: no revenue taking half your earnings off you or hounding you for capital gains not to speak of the plethora of indirect taxes, can you imagine no tax whatever?

It might be hot as hell out here. It might even get dangerous. But, stick it out for a few years, save ninety percent of your salary minimum, and, even after one contract, you were going home with a tidy little sum, enough to set you up back home in some line you fancied. If you survived that is.

Andy had left and David was thinking of leaving when Rosemary Forbes came up to him.

"Long time no see. What are you drinking?"

Rosemary accepted a glass of red wine. David had known her on and off since she was a child, a colonial child like himself hawked around with their parents to wherever they were posted. After university, Rosemary had joined the British Foreign Office and was back out in the British Embassy on a tour of duty.

She looked smart in her lightweight linen suit and her tan. Her facial expression was always a little too severe but compensated for by pleasant blue eyes that sometimes twinkled. She looked competent and reliable. David vaguely recalled some gossip he had heard about her. Hadn't there been an affair that ended disastrously? For such a sensible seeming girl, it seemed that she chose her men badly.

They chatted for a while about what had happened to mutual acquaintances and places in the Gulf where they had both lived as children: Doha, Abu Dhabi, Bahrain, Kuwait. The Gulf in this context meant the expats who lived there mainly in either the banking or diplomatic service. Given that context it came down to a pretty small number.

"How's your father keeping?" David asked.

"He's retired now and living in Scotland in a little cottage on his own. He's secretary of the Trucial States Association. They have a dinner every year in London and talk about the old days. Even sometimes arrange trips out to the Gulf." She paused. "Have you managed to pick up anything new about your father's disappearance?"

"No," David said. "Too many years have passed. I think that trail has been dead for a long time now." He changed the subject. "Anyway tell me how your career is going."

"It's going along."

"I don't suppose the posting out here will do your prospects any harm."

Rosemary like himself was fluent in Arabic.

"I don't suppose it will. It was made clear to me back home that to advance further I needed to take a posting in the Middle East. A position in Khor Fahal came up and here I am. To tell you the truth, I was disappointed when I first got here. It's changed so much. It was like a totally different country from the one I remember."

"That's exactly my impression too. The place has changed beyond recognition. I had a call from the police today," David said. "A certain Colonel Rachman."

"Oh him. Anything serious?"

"I don't know yet. But then I'm sure you and your spooks know more about it than I do." David had always known that Rosemary had something to do with Intelligence. She had let something slip once about interrogating prisoners which pointed in that direction. He kept referring to it as a joke and to see how she'd react.

But she wasn't going to let him take a rise out of her. "That's right," Rosemary said. "We have spies crawling all over the place."

CHAPTER 12

Ayatullah Abd al Wahhab, closely protected by a band of bodyguards and followers, wound their way through the crowded warren of narrow streets and alleyways of the Old City.

The first step to implement the decisions taken at the meeting in Mehriz was being about to be carried out. But he wanted to keep his entry as quiet and unnoticed as possible. It was better that way, secrecy and stealth worked better than any display of force. That would come later.

The Ayatullah was as ever dressed in a long black robe and black head cloth. He seemed to be frail. He was supported on either side by strong men who, like the rest of the entourage, were heavily armed. As they skirted the old harbour area, from a short distance away came the sound of water lapping against the sides of the *dhows* anchored in the old harbour where the *nakoodas* and their crews were resting.

On a promontory jutting into the sea was an old Portuguese fort where political prisoners were once chained, manacled and incarcerated. High up on the mass of base rock, a stranded goat bleated; it looked down the precipitous side, stained with the refuse of generations, trying to make up its mind to jump on to the next crag.

Ayatullah Abd Al Wahhab and his entourage had crossed quietly at a remote desert border post a couple of days earlier. The border guards were sympathetic to him, or most of them were. Those who weren't had been eliminated.

The Ayatullah had been expelled from Khor Fahal for sedition many years before. Sitting in his flat in exile, he had watched as the old Sheikh was deposed and the new Sheikh quickly grew oppressive and intolerant and dictatorial. He watched and waited with satisfaction while discontent grew and festered. With each repressive act his hatred of the Ruler grew. It was in his nature to hate and he did so with a bitter and deep hatred. He lusted for revenge. But he also lusted for power. And not only physical power, but power over people's minds.

He had been planning his return for over a decade, making contacts, seeking out like-minded people, carefully building his reputation. He planned and intrigued and plotted. He kept in close contact with his supporters in Khor Fahal, building his base, his *Mujahadeen*.

And it had all paid off in that crucial meeting in Mehriz. There he had won over the support he needed to put his plan into action.

Once the fateful decision was taken, his supporters inside Khor Fahal kept him up to date on a daily basis with everything that happened within the state. After hearing of the arrest of Mullah Hussein and the wave of resentment it was causing, he knew it was time to act.

The cortege wound its way through by-roads and alleyways.

They entered a very narrow lane with high walls on either side. It was in the heart of that part of the Old City that was still medieval in appearance, an area full of ancient houses with courtyards each with a well and ancient pulley from which dark blurs of figures drew water.

The cortege stopped in front of two huge double doors brought in from India by *dhow* a century ago. These wooden doors were fortified with metal spikes. Rarely used, they swung open now and, as soon as Ayatullah Abd Al Wahhab and his followers were inside, were quickly closed and barred.

CHAPTER 13

Headed home across the bridge after work, Deborah drove faster than usual.

She was so upset and angry that when a transport truck flying little flags with ornate Arabic lettering plastered all over it blasted its horn at her, she blasted her horn back. The *kheffiahed* driver, with all the superiority of the Arab male macho man drove past contemptuously.

She wasn't doing too good. Apart from her brush with the *Muttawa,* she had just had her first direct contact with Arab violence. She had known all the time that there was a certain amount of latent violence about. But to be actually struck by a tea boy made it up close and real.

It was fine to watch violence on TV. But to feel the hot breath of it in your face was something else. The fact was she hadn't been prepared for it and it had left her shaken. Also it brought home to her that she knew even less about this part of the world than she thought she did.

Was she ever going to understand anything about this country or its people? The women's contributions that had come pouring in to the magazine had led her to think she might actually be getting somewhere, getting some valuable insights into the mind of the veiled down trodden and maltreated Arab woman. The outpourings in the scribbled notes and letters had had an effect on her, they were so intense. But, in the end, so pathetic. There was nothing the women who had written to her could do about their situation. They simply had no power nor any means of expression in the patriarchal society in which they lived. And there wasn't much she could do for them. She had no illusions that anything she might publish in *Al Jameela* would have any significant effect on anything.

And there was something else that was getting to her, something that didn't make her future in journalism in the state look any too bright.

Before leaving her office she had checked her answering machine. When she pressed the playback button she was taken aback at the sound of a deep hoarse female voice saying, "Why is there not someone there to answer my call? Is that you Deborah? Are you listening? I hope so because I am most upset."

The voice speaking in heavily accented English was that of the Editor in Chief, Sheikha Sharifa.

Deborah was startled by the sound of the voice because the Sheikha had never left a message on the answering machine before. She never attended the office. She had never worked in journalism and knew nothing about it. All Deborah knew about the woman from her brief meeting in her villa and from general gossip was that she was connected to the Ruling Family and had taken on the editorship as a sinecure.

The disembodied voice went on, "I have recently reviewed the last issue of *Al Jameela*. Frankly I was shocked. I expected better of you. It is obvious that you are trying to use it as a vehicle for propagating a liberal and libertine philosophy that is totally unacceptable in this state. It must stop immediately. I will be watching what you do and I will be in contact soon."

That was all. But it was enough. That bitch who knew sweet damn all about journalism was telling her, an independent and independent minded journalist, what she should and should not do. Well she wasn't going to take that out of anyone.

And what was the Sheikha trying to say anyway? What did she mean by philosophy? The magazine didn't have a philosophy. The only mildly informative pieces ever to appear in the magazine were those Deborah had introduced.

Why, having remained silent and incommunicado for so long, was that bitch beginning to interfere? And what did she object to? The interviews? Or the articles on health? She hadn't been specific. Not that it mattered. The message in her call came over loud and clear. She wanted the magazine to revert to the sycophantic pictorial affair it had been when Deborah had taken over.

Well it wasn't going to happen, not on her watch. It went against all journalistic principles. She was damned if she was going to be prevented from publishing whatever she decided to publish. She wouldn't get away with it of course. What had she to put up against the Sheikha's influence and power? Not a lot.

If the Sheikha really went ahead and blocked her, stopped her publishing the material she had lined up for the next issue, she would resign and write reportage for the newspapers back home with which she had maintained a connection. And the Sheikha could bugger off.

As Deborah drove up to their apartment block, her mother, looking distracted, was waiting for her inside the carport with the dogs.

Deborah knew immediately something was wrong.

Her mother's new straw hat was perched on her head to shade her from the sun. Her face was pale, her legs white and veined with varicose veins.

"Carolyn has disappeared. I can't find her anywhere."

Deborah felt an immediate blast of panic.

"I thought you were looking after her."

"I was but I must have nodded off for a few minutes," her mother said stiffly.

Deborah was about to unleash her feelings, her invective, on her mother but her mother looked so frail, so beaten, that she bit her tongue and smothered the reprimands.

Having established that her mother had no idea where Carolyn might be or even what direction she had gone in, she ran to her car and jumped in. She didn't know where to look or which way to turn.

Distracted, she drove back the way she had come. It was all her fault. She expected too much of her mother. After all she was old, in a strange country, in a hot climate. In fact, she shouldn't have her out here at all now that the situation in Khor Fahal was turning nasty. It certainly was no place for an elderly woman who had never been abroad let alone in the Arab world.

Where could Carolyn have got to?

She looked to left and right, studied the sun-scoured dusty scene ahead. It looked like a tableau congealed in hot heavy air that had solidified, encasing everything and everybody in its glutinous mass.

Old men squatted in the shade. Statue-like in their robes, they stared out on the creek.

She pulled up beside a group of them and jumped out of her car.

She shouted, "Have you seen a small girl pass this way? Dressed in t-shirt and shorts?" She tried her inadequate broken Arabic. "You see, girl? White girl? *Nazarani?*"

The old men stared back at her as if they didn't see her, hadn't heard a word she said, as if she was an apparition from another world.

She drove on until she came to the turn off to the *suq* when she pulled in to the side of the road. Should she search down there?

The heat was so intense that you would think it would stop all activity but it didn't seem to have. From the *suq* came the sound of men shouting and women ululating. Some emotional tide was running down there among the Shi'ites and the heat wasn't slowing it down. Perhaps it was even accentuating it. Heat tires the body but it doesn't quieten the mind.

Looking down the road to the *suq*, Deborah saw a crowd of people carrying banners and shouting. Though she could neither read the banners nor tell what they were shouting, she felt uneasy. In the blinding sun the figures were ethereal, unreal. Like a mirage, they wavered insubstantially in the overheated air. The crowd was moving towards her like a wave. And, in her imagination, inside that wave lurked some unspeakable horror.

She forced herself to turn away. And when she looked again the procession, or whatever it was, had disappeared. Only bright sunlight shone on the dirt track of a road. The waving figures had evaporated into the hot air.

She turned her car around. There was no way she was going down that road. Anyway, it was highly unlikely that Carolyn was there, it was much too far for her to walk.

Unless she had been abducted, a voice in her head said.

She drove back towards the apartment looking first to one side, then to the other. This time instead of turning into her own compound she drove on.

She had only driven for a short distance when she spotted two children splashing about in the water in the creek playing with an old rubber tyre. A naked youth paddled a dugout. Hungry cats prowled creek side and stopped by some refuse or was it a carcass. Pie dogs appeared and bore down on the cats, thin, starved, yelping, teeth bared.

She jammed on the brakes.

"Carolyn!" Deborah screamed, having just come close enough to see that one of the half naked figures was Carolyn.

She threw the car door open, ran down to the creek, waded in, and caught Carolyn around the waist and lifted her bodily out of the water.

High with relief, she hugged her. "I thought you were gone. I thought you were lost. I thought someone had taken you away and I'd never see you again."

She carried her dripping wet daughter back to the car, put her into the front seat, slammed the door and drove off. She was trembling. She tried to calm herself down. She was over reacting.

"I was only playing with Omar," Carolyn said in a small voice, her eyes beginning to fill with tears. She knew that she had upset her mother, that she needed to make amends.

"Yes dear," Deborah said. She had been so worked up and then so relieved to have found Carolyn that she felt sudden drained.

She said mildly, "You shouldn't get into that water, Carolyn. You could get all sorts of diseases." Deborah regularly saw men pull up their skirts, squat down and defecate creek side. "You could get bilharzia."

"What's bilharzia, mummy?"

"It's a disease. And you get it from a worm in water like that."

When they got to the compound her distracted mother embraced Carolyn and kept repeating. "God answered my prayers."

Deborah looked at her mother and saw how feeble and vulnerable she really was. Because she had always been so strong, dominating Deborah, building into her character ineradicable complexes by smothering her with attention one day and the next forcing her to do all sorts of things she didn't want to do, always telling her she was in the wrong in her conflicts with the outside world, dominating Deborah with the strength of her personality. Her mother had been so strong. And now she was so weak. Looking at her now, it seemed really strange that all that indoctrination, all that dominance, could have come from this one small frail form.

Her mother went on piously, just as she had done all those decades ago when Deborah had been a little girl and had run away from home and the police had brought her back. "St Anthony," her mother said now, "has answered my prayers. God is looking after us all."

Deborah said dutifully, "Yes, mother."

In the matter of her relationship with her mother, she would never quite grow up; she would always be a little girl.

"Did you go to Mass, mother?"

"No. How could I go when you refused to take me?" her mother said sharply. "But I said my prayers anyway."

They went inside.

Later that evening, Deborah and David stood sipping their drinks on the roof so as to be out of earshot of her mother, Abdul, and Carolyn.

Listening to what had happened to Deborah during the day, and she seemed to have had a rough day, David was doubtful about telling her anything about finding the dead mullah's body. But he didn't see how he could get out of it, so he gave her an edited version of what had happened.

"You've done the wrong thing," Deborah said straight off, sounding a bit like CJ. "You should have kept your mouth shut."

"I would have, only Rachman came after me. He'd obviously beaten the shit out of that boy and he knew from the boy about the body in the bag. He knew everything."

"Even so, you should have denied that you saw any body. That way you couldn't be implicated. How could they prove you saw anything? The boy couldn't be considered a reliable witness. You should have denied everything. They had no proof. They weren't there, after all. My mother always told me never to tell the police anything."

"Your mother used to support the IRA, still does even though they've stood down."

"That's how she knows how to handle the police. Deny everything unless you're absolutely sure they can prove it." She softened her tone, "At least Rachman gave you a way out. You'd better take it."

"That's exactly what CJ said."

"CJ is smart. Ruthless and no doubt crooked, but smart. Anyway how can you be sure it **was** the mullah's body you saw? Are you sure?"

"I think I'm sure."

"But you're not sure you're sure. The eyes can play all sorts of tricks."

Her eyes had played tricks with her so that she wasn't sure whether she had seen a procession coming towards her on the road to the *suq* or not. She was about to tell David about this when Abdul appeared on the roof and said, "Mr David wanted on phone."

David took the call and was back in a few moments. He said animatedly, "That's the most extraordinary thing. I've just had a phone call from Sebastian."

"Who's Sebastian?"

"An old friend I haven't seen for ages."

"Is he the one sends you postcards from odd places every couple of years?"

"That's him. I knew him well when we were both children out in these parts. Now he's just rung, and guess where he is?"

"Where?"

"Over in Sinhaji Street just off the *maidan*."

"That's on this side of the creek."

"Exactly. Not only is he in Khor Fahal but he's living not far away. He's asked me to pop over for a drink. Would you like to come?"

"No thanks. I feel panned out without going out for the night. You go and have your boy talk. Only don't come home drunk."

After David had gone, Deborah stayed on the roof finishing her drink. David and his body in a bag on top of all her own troubles made her feel low. And out of her depth. She felt loose from her moorings. Maybe she wouldn't be able to handle Khor Fahal like she thought she could. Maybe she wasn't up to it. It sure wasn't turning out anything like what she had expected. Of course she had known that it would be a big lifestyle change. What she hadn't realised before coming abroad was how cut off you could feel when cut adrift from all the props of your own culture.

Suddenly the air around her resonated with a cacophony of sounds. The shops and mosques began blasting out taped messages and you didn't have to know any Arabic to feel the power of the underlying emotion in the voices that bore in on her.

Standing alone on the roof, she felt just as she had when out searching for Carolyn, menaced by a fanaticism that was reaching up to touch her.

NOEL SCANLON

CHAPTER 14

As David approached the area where Sebastian lived, the streets became more squalid. Neglect was evident everywhere: in unfinished abandoned skeletal building structures, in the general air of dirt and neglect.

It wasn't the type of place he would have expected to find Sebastian but then he had gathered from their brief conversation on the phone that it was only temporary.

Sebastian had added an air of mystery by asking him to approach his block on foot and make sure he wasn't followed, a part of the conversation he had thought it better not to mention to Deborah.

Accordingly, David parked his car in a small square some distance from Sebastian's block, nearby a taxi rank where a number of battered long-distant desert taxis stood covered with dust and sand, the sand lying inches deep inside them. Taxi drivers sat on rickety chairs at the wooden tables of a pavement cafe. A large Negroid Arab dressed in a striped shirt and a skirt of tablecloth-like material was serving them samosas which the men were grabbing with dirty sandy hands.

He hadn't met Sebastian for many years. Like Rosemary in the embassy, his path had crossed with Sebastian's here and there throughout the Middle East when they were all children of itinerant parents who were periodically posted from one country to another.

Normally, at this time of the evening, this part of the Old City would be in a state of heavy torpor, with very little moving in the sweltering heat, everything would have an air of exhaustion with even inanimate objects having had enough heat for the day.

But not this evening. This evening the area was buzzing and stirring. There was energy about rather than the customary lethargy. The bakers were baking in their old fashioned ovens; the melon vendors were hawking their wares, splitting the melons open with a long sharp knife. Even the illegal immigrants, normally dozing by the walls, were sitting up with an air of expectancy.

Amplified voices blasting out from the mosques and shops collided with one another in mid-air and fragmented.

"Avenge the murder of Mullah Hussein."

"Rise up and avenge the blood of our martyr."

What was going on here? Something had happened. The whole atmosphere had changed. Word must have leaked out about the mullah being murdered. But who could have leaked it? Certainly not him. He could only suppose that the Shi'ites had their informants among the police. Everything was leaked in Khor Fahal; or rather everything was sold at a price. That's how it must have got about. But the fact that it was out made David feel uneasy. The police would blame him for the leak if it suited them. And Colonel Rachman's threats as to what would happen to him if he talked had been pretty explicit.

Whether it was due to a leak or to some other cause, things had changed in the Shi'ite area. Whatever had caused it, there was a new sense of purpose about the place. You could feel it in the air. And he had never seen so many posters or heard so many calls from the mosques.

A piercing voice rang out from close by.

"The blood of our martyr makes us determined, despite all blows, all difficulties, to bring to the upcoming struggle, sacrifice, sincerity, faithfulness and determination."

You could discount a certain amount of this sort of rhetoric. The Arabs have a penchant for rhetoric and hyperbole, more than a penchant, they're addicted to it. But this wasn't just empty rhetoric. This was rhetoric focusing on the death of Mullah Hussein in order to incite the people.

Who was behind all this? It couldn't have happened spontaneously. Who was organizing it and driving it forward? Whoever they were obviously couldn't have any actual proof of the mullah's death. Apart from the police and the boy, he was the only one who had seen the mullah's dead body. But who needed proof? Like everyone else, the Shi'ites believed what they wanted to believe. The actual facts were by the way.

As David walked on, he was confronted with more and more evidence of what was stirring in the minds of the people. Badly daubed slogans on walls read:

RISE UP AND FREE YOURSELVES FROM TYRANNY

A SHI'ITE STATE FOR THE SHI'ITES

And in red spray paint REVENGE

When all this gets to the ears of the financial world, David thought, it will drive the Khor currency down another couple of points. He'd checked the rate on the internet just before coming out and it was still moving down nicely. The sight had given him a small thrill. At least he'd got something right.

Reaching Sebastian's apartment block which had a decrepit, decaying appearance, small boys around the entrance caught sight of David, "Who you want?" they asked cheekily, emboldened by the slogans, by the messages from the mosques, by the general atmosphere of xenophobia. "Where you going?" they called hostilely after him.

David tried the elevator.

An indicator light came on but no elevator arrived. Instead, a couple of bags of refuse came down the refuse chute and landed with a thump beside him.

"Who you want? You want the *Nazarani*?" the small boys by the door called out.

They were only children but, sure of themselves here in their ghetto, they managed to sound both threatening and sinister.

David climbed the badly stained cement stairs. The children began to follow him but he shouted at them and they hesitated, went back to keep watch.

Veiled women peeped out from doorways.

It was heavy sweaty work climbing the stairs. Turning into Sebastian's landing, the first thing he saw was panels broken in the hall door and nailed up roughly from the inside. The damage looked recent. And it looked like a planned act of violence. Or warning. It seemed a very odd place for Sebastian to be living. Why would he expose himself to the obvious dangers of this quarter? What would make him come here rather than stay in the New City?

He rang the doorbell.

There was a shuffling noise along the hallway inside and a thin man of indeterminate age whom David took to be an old servant appeared, ghostlike and fluttering. His face was dry like old parchment. One eye was blind from trachoma. With much muttering, Abood, he intimated that his name was Abood, let David in.

When he had established that Abood was indeed Sebastian's servant and that Sebastian was expecting him, David asked, "What happened to the door?"

Abood took his Arab cap off and scratched his bald pate. His body was thin and gangling in his blue *thobe*.

"Bad people. They want I let them in and, when I say no, they do this thing. Bad people. Not Allah people. I tell the mosque and they come and punish them."

As he, Abood, considered the punishment meted out, which David could well imagine was strict and cruel in this strict and cruel community, he detected on Abood's face a flicker of righteous satisfaction, a vindication of the righteous punishment of Allah duly dispensed.

Abood led him down a long passageway into a the lounge cum dining room, a spacious room sparsely furnished with a large long brown leather couch, masses of cushions about the wall and a layering of carpets one thrown down over the other; they looked like good quality tribal carpets much used and antique.

Lounging on the couch, was Sebastian, a much older Sebastian than the one he remembered, his fingers entwined with those of classically beautiful young Arab whom David guessed came from an up-country tribe, with thick kohl lines painted around his eyes.

David remembered that Sebastian had always had homosexual tendencies and these had obviously developed and flowered over the years. Still, it was something of a surprise to see such an open demonstration.

Sebastian rose now, or rather uncoiled from the couch with a grace of movement David had forgotten. The blonde young man he remembered was gone, buried in a thicker more substantial body. But the old grace was there. Despite the shabby surroundings, he managed somehow to convey an impression of smooth elegance even though he was wearing only a normal and not very clean shirt and jeans. David remembered how insouciant Sebastian had been as a youth, laughing as if the world was a place to laugh in, walking through the horrors of life on a tight rope of gaiety.

"Come in, come in," Sebastian said. "How awfully good of you to come around so quickly."

David was struck immediately by how very British Sebastian had become, no trace left of his Irish ancestry.

Abood with his long face standing there unmoved said, "Abood leave now. Abood go mosque pray."

"That's fine Abood," Sebastian said. "No problem. Off you go and pray"

Abood shuffled away out of the room.

Sebastian said, "Abood is happiest in the mosque. He croaks away all day at me with interminable quotations from the Koran, admonitions passed on straight from the mind of Allah. That's what I call him, The Mind of Allah. He looks after me though. Looks after me very well really."

"He was telling me about your front door."

"Oh that. He does fuss about little things like that."

Sebastian didn't seem to be at all concerned about the damage to his door or any implication it might have, given the strong feeling evident on the street.

"I must say it's good to see you again. You're looking well and prosperous. Rosemary tells me you're married and have a child."

So he had met Rosemary and she hadn't mentioned it to him even though the three of them had been friends as children. It was useful to know that Rosemary held things back. Given her job he supposed she was bound to be secretive.

Sebastian was saying, "Rosemary hasn't half done well for herself. Number two in the embassy I believe. How does your wife like this awful climate?"

"She was bored at first hanging around the apartment with nothing to do," David said. "But since she got a job running a woman's magazine she's fine."

"And you've come up in the world too from what I hear. Running the Trucial Bank, no less."

"I don't run it, I'm afraid. The CEO does."

"Still, you're an important man. Not a rolling stone like me."

David didn't know what Sebastian had worked at during the many years since he had last met him. He had from time to time received letters and notes and postcards from various places but these had become less and less frequent over the years. Now and then he had heard snippets, mostly from Rosemary, of Sebastian's failed attempt to make his fortune with this or that scheme that all failed for one reason or another.

Sebastian seemed to suddenly remember the boy who was standing there sulkily.

"Run along Mahmoud," he said patting him on the cheek. "Run along and I'll send for you later."

Wiggling his hips and shoulders and looking doe-like at Sebastian, the young man slid out of the room.

Homosexuality is common in all parts of Arabia. It is widespread and tacitly accepted, a behaviour which is at least partly brought about by the veiling of women, keeping them in strict purdah, segregating the sexes, leaving the women out of sight at home. All this segregation inevitably leads to homosexuality. David reflected on this and how many of the great Arab desert explorers even the great Lawrence of Arabia, were homosexual. The harsh life of desert exploration evidently had had rather more to offer that sand and dunes stretching to the horizon.

"Great to see you, after all these years," Sebastian repeated. "Great to meet someone from the old days. It was a strange life we lived as children, dragged hither and thither by one's parents. Definitely a nomadic lifestyle. I often think it's why I could never settle for long anywhere afterwards. It made me a nomad. Like the Bedouin. God how wonderful those young Bedouin boys looked. You remember them arriving in Mukulla after crossing that awful desert leading their camels.

"But what can I offer you to drink," Sebastian went on, crossing to a cupboard and taking out a half bottle of whisky. "Liquor frowned on here, of course. But I've managed to hide a small drop away from Abood's prying eyes. What do you say we polish it off while you tell me what you've been up to all those years."

It was a good whisky, single malt from a Scottish island.

"There isn't much to tell, really," David said. "I was out of work back home when I got the offer to come out here. So here I am. Good pay. Leave every year. And yourself?"

"Came out to set up a little import-export firm. Lucky to get an Arab partner and all that."

"So how's it going?"

"Fine, just fine. Until recently that is. Things were moving along at a cracking pace. Then something rather unfortunate happened. I was driving on the coast road one day when I had the misfortune to have a car accident. With one of the Sheikh's cousins no less speeding in a Mercedes coupe. He immediately got out and shot at me. Or rather shot up my car. The unfortunate thing is there is to be a court case which will of course be an absolute farce. The whole deal is done and dusted. I'm completely stitched up. The police will swear that I was driving dangerously. To back this up, they will undoubtedly produce witnesses to testify that I was in the wrong and the sheikh's relation was totally in the right. That's what would happen in the Sharia court if I were to attend. I could expect a minimum of fifty lashes and a stretch of anywhere between five and fifteen years."

Sebastian paused. He was suddenly and uncharacteristically serious.

"I don't think I could take the sort of conditions in the jails around here. I couldn't stand the heat and degradation of being cooped up in this heat with a crowd of Arab murderers and criminals. That's why I have disappeared from the scene for the moment. Removed myself. By the by, I really would appreciate it if you didn't mention to anybody where I am located just now. I'd rather prefer not to be immediately available to the police just for the moment until I work things out."

"Of course," David said. "What a terrible thing to happen. It's a pity that one of the Ruling Family is involved."

"It is indeed. I'm afraid we live in a state that is a dictatorship and a theocracy both at the same time. Rulers in the West have often tried to establish theocracies but never succeeded. Or only partially. We live under Sharia law and, as you know, to Moslems, the Sharia reveals the mind of Allah, and its function is to punish man for his sins. In Sharia, sin is a crime and a crime is a sin. A very interesting concept don't you think?"

David wondered if Sebastian was just whistling past the graveyard. He wondered what he could do for his friend.

"It should be possible to do something about your case. Does Rosemary know about this?"

"Absolutely. She'll do the best she can. It'll all work out fine in the end."

David didn't share his optimism.

There was shouting outside in the street reminding him of the febrile atmosphere out there.

But Sebastian had apparently absorbed the British ability to ignore what was happening around them, especially if it was unpleasant or dangerous. It was something David found difficult to understand and on occasion bizarre. It seemed to be a deep-seated feeling that if you ignored danger and denied its existence you could somehow lessen its impact, as if, by ignoring it, it would just go away. The British, or rather the colonial British, on occasion carried this to almost comical extremes. Like in the Hadhramut when his parents had served cocktails in their apartment above the bank, while the Hadhrami Bedouin Legion were forming into a line in the street just below and opening fire on the advancing rioters. His parents must by then have become totally British, or at least acquired a British mind set. They closed the veranda doors to keep the noise of the rioters and the shooting that followed out but, apart from that, the party went on and the events in the street below were not alluded to.

Just then there was an explosion not far away.

"That sounded pretty close," David said.

"Not really," Sebastian countered. "It was a good mile away."

A mile seemed a generous estimate to David who was thinking of how he'd get home.

"Don't you feel at all uneasy living in the midst of all this? I got a real feeling walking over here that things were about to blow. And that explosion just now seems to point in the same direction."

"I wouldn't pay one small explosion too much attention."

David wondered if this was bravura. Did Sebastian realise the danger he was in, living in this area? He surely must.

"Don't be so gloomy. Don't let one little bang upset you. Here, let me replenish your glass," Sebastian said before noticing that the bottle was almost empty. "Oh well, that's that then. I don't know how I'm going to get more supplies. I can hardly send Abood out to buy liquor. He'd be horrified at the idea. Anyway, they don't sell it in this area. It's strictly *haram.*"

They chatted on about things inconsequential. It was apparent that Sebastian had no intention of discussing what was going on around them. To David it felt surreal. Was Sebastian trying to be more English than the English themselves?

The noise of a commotion drifted up to them from the street outside.

David went and looked out through the dusty un-cleaned window on to the dingy fenced-in back yards. A few ragged children were watching and waiting. For Sebastian? For him?

A man came out of a house and two black blobs followed him a few paces to heel, women dressed in black *abbayas* that came down past their ankles.

"I think it's time I left," David said. "Deborah will be worried."

They said their good-byes and promised to keep in touch.

On his way out, David found the same youths hanging around at the bottom of the stained and dirt-streaked stairwell. A small knot of people stood just outside the entrance. They were obviously angry. Several veiled women were screaming. As far as David could make out, they were discussing the damage caused by the explosion. They turned and looked at him hostilely out of black flashing eyes as if he was responsible.

As he walked back towards his car, a boy on a bicycle appeared and rode first behind him and then in front of him, circling him and shouting abuse against the foreigner. The boy's bicycle was garishly decorated with artificial flowers on the handlebars and streamers streaming behind. As the boy rode at him screaming, his face was like a splintered mirror. The boy braked, skidded, and came back towards David ringing his bell and shouting.

Thus singled out, spotlighted as a foreigner, a non-Moslem, an intruder in this totally Moslem Shi'ite area where religious and ethnic and political passions ran high, David felt in all that heat a chilly twinge of foreboding.

NOEL SCANLON

CHAPTER 15

Deborah lay in bed restless and unable to sleep. When David had come back from visiting his friend Sebastian, he hadn't said much but it was obvious that he was concerned about something. All she could get out of him was that he was glad to see his old friend again though he couldn't understand why he was living in the middle of a poor, rundown, Shi'ite area. She had the feeling that there was more to it than that, there was something troubling him that he wasn't telling her about.

She lay awake in the hot still air and told herself to relax. But every time she thought she was dozing off, something dripped into her unconscious mind reinforcing her sense of uneasiness. She felt as if the walls of the apartment had fallen away, leaving her exposed to the shouts and screams that she heard, or thought she heard, coming from the Old City.

One thing was becoming abundantly clear. Whatever about themselves, this was no longer a place for either her mother or Carolyn to be. As her mother kept telling her. Last night while David was out she had gone on and on complaining about just about everything.

She had taken a visceral dislike to both Khor Fahal and by extension all Moslems.

Deborah put a lot of it down to the excessive heat. Her mother was feeling the heat too much and was spending a great deal of her time in her room with most of her clothes off and the air-conditioning playing on her. But there was more to it than that. She missed home. She missed her local shop. She missed her local radio station. She missed her local newspaper. She missed going to a proper church. She even missed the rain and mist.

"And as I keep telling you," her mother went on. "Carolyn shouldn't be out here. She should be back home. You shouldn't have ever brought her out. It was quite wrong of you."

Deborah didn't say anything.

"She'd be better off out of here. It's dangerous. And it's heathen."

"It's not heathen, mother, it's Moslem."

"That's even worse."

Deborah knew that her mother took every opportunity to get Carolyn alone and inculcate into her mind the religious instruction her own daughter was so lamentably failing to supply. What effect her proselytising efforts had she had no idea though Carolyn had begun coming out with some distinctly bizarre and mangled pieces of Christian mythology.

Her mother was saying, "Not that you'll take a blind bit of notice of anything I say. You never do." At this point she switched to the 'I am a martyr' option. "I'm sorry I spoke. I should have just gone on sitting alone in my room in the heat and said nothing."

Oh God. They were getting into all that again. It was like hearing an old, a very old record being played back yet again. Her mother was in one of her moods. Scenes like this brought back incidents from Deborah's childhood dominated by her mother, incidents that she had totally forgotten, or thought she had, and anyway didn't want to remember. There was a whole well of stuff back there she didn't want to tap into.

Her mother irritated her but at the same time she made her feel in the wrong even when she was in the right. She looked so weak and hard done by that Deborah felt what her mother wanted her to feel, that she was treating her own mother in a crappy manner and should start making amends.

"You're not being fair mother. You know very well that I do take account of what you say. David and I have already talked about it and agreed to send Carolyn home as soon as we can."

"I'm sorry I spoke," her mother repeated.

Deborah knew better than to say any more. Whatever she said would only make matters worse.

She lay awake now in the hot still air and told herself to relax. But instead of relaxing she was wound up as tight as a spring.

Sparring with her mother, who, as usual, landed all the best blows, hadn't helped her state of mind. The funny thing was that while their little spat had affected her, it hadn't taken a feather out of her mother who, instead of lying awake unable to sleep as she was, was blissfully and deeply asleep.

There were other things though apart from her mother keeping her awake. There had been a phone call from Margaret who said she was most concerned about her and David living in danger across the creek among the Shi'ites and then began fishing for all the information she could get about what the atmosphere was like. She wanted Deborah's opinion as to how she thought it might all develop and if things were going to get really serious. Margaret was usually detached about this sort of thing but on the phone she sounded unusually worried.

Deborah got out of bed now, went to the bathroom, then out on the balcony where she stood for sometime looking across at the creek. When she got back into bed she went to sleep almost immediately.

She came to at the sound of a faint noise she couldn't identify. Was it at the front door? It seemed to be coming from that general direction.

She held her breath and thought she heard something bump against the door. Then slide and flop down.

There was silence. No further sound.

She must have imagined it.

She was getting back to sleep when she heard a moan and a sound like someone's finger nails scraping over wood.

Honey growled. Then Poochie.

She tried to waken David but David wouldn't waken. Instead he threw his arms around her and grasped her tightly.

David could feel a movement in the bed beside him.

At the same time, he was beneath the surface of the sea swimming in the area where he had found the Mullah Hussein and the seascape around him was like no seascape he had ever seen before. When he reached the spur where he had hidden from the sharks, the mullah's body was there exactly as he had first seen it. It had been eaten by sharks but now it was back, regurgitated, reconstituted.

Colonel Rachman was there too, for some odd reason. He wanted access to his safe deposit box which contained something very valuable and he, David, had to get the key and open it. But how was he to get around Mullah Hussein, whose body was alive and animated, its rubbery lips moving as it talked to him though he couldn't hear the words.

The body of the mullah broke free and floated towards him and, although he tried to move away, he couldn't, and the dead mullah grabbed him with one flaying arm which he wound round his neck, his clutching hands colder and slimier than any fish…

Unlocking David's arms, Deborah said, "Well, if you won't bother to wake up, I'll have to go and look myself."

As Deborah opened the front door, something live and soft collapsed at her feet.

It was an Arab boy.

In the light from the hallway, Deborah could see now that the boy had been savagely beaten up. There were great red weals on his naked back where he had been beaten or whipped and blood was running on to the floor.

"David!" she screamed. "Abdul!"

Abdul came first.

"Do you know who that is?"

Abdul bent down to look. "It's that no good shanty town boy," he said with all the superiority of the tribal desert Arab and a citizen of the state.

"Well don't just stand there. Can't you see he's injured? Bring him inside. He's a human being."

Abdul obviously questioned this latter assertion but, nonetheless, he dragged the boy into the hallway. He did this reluctantly as if he was pulling a sack of rubbish along.

"Go and get a bowl of water."

"Why for?" Abdul protested. "These shanty town people, they only trouble. They no good people. This boy he just been whipped. Best thing for him."

Nonetheless, he fetched a bowl of water which he flung in the boy's face.

"Abdul!" Deborah shouted at him. "How can you be so unfeeling and cruel to a fellow Arab? You ought to be ashamed of yourself."

Abdul grinned.

"What's going on?" David asked, appearing in the hallway.

Abdul said, "It's that boy you bring fishing instead of me."

Abdul was extremely jealous of the boy being taken out in the boat.

"The boy has been severely beaten up," Deborah said to David. "He's in a terrible state. We'll have to get him some medical attention."

David took a look at the boy, then went to phone the hospital. First he was left hanging on, then he was passed from one person to another. But eventually he got them to promise to send an ambulance.

After wrapping the boy in a blanket and making him as comfortable as they could, David and Deborah went into the kitchen and put coffee on to filter.

They were drinking it a little while later, when Abdul came dashing in shouting, "The boy, he gone."

"What do you mean, gone?"

"He gone. He run away."

"Are you sure you didn't tell him to go?"

"No, no," Abdul said.

"Well, he didn't seem to me to be capable of running anywhere."

"These shanty town people always run," Abdul said contemptuously.

"He can't have gone far, not in his condition."

David and Deborah went down to the compound which they searched first and then went outside the compound and searched farther afield with their large flashlight.

Out of doors, hot, humid, dense, clammy air closed around them. Deborah had never been about the front of their building in the middle of the night like this before. She was surprised by the myriad of stealthy noises and movements: the low penetrating howl of a pie dog, the lapping sound of the water against the shore, splashing sounds out in the creek as something passed, a dugout or was it a smuggler's dhow headed out to sea?

From close-by, so close that it made her jump, came the howling of stray hungry cats fighting and foraging among the flotsam and jetsam along the littoral of the creek, their eyes floating and glittering in the darkness.

Something in Deborah's mind triggered a host of suppressed fears she normally kept strictly battened down but which squirmed out now, making her feel that there was something lurking out there about to spring at her out of the brooding darkness of the thick hot night. The night was covering up so much, hiding so much.

The sight of the way the boy who had been out in the boat when David had found the mullah's body had been savagely beaten up had shaken her.

Violence was getting a bit too close to home. A few weeks ago, even a few days ago, she would have thought the possibility of either of them being in physical danger ridiculous. But she wasn't so sure any more. The police were ruthless. And there was no one to stop them doing more or less whatever they fancied.

Deborah didn't even feel safe to be outside like this. She felt exposed. Once or twice she thought she heard a movement. Was there someone out there watching them? Was their apartment block being watched? She sensed that there was danger out there somewhere though she couldn't exactly locate it.

Still, they continued searching around in the darkness for some time before finally giving up.

There was absolutely no sign of the boy. Either someone had come and taken him away. Or he had gone under his own steam. Either way, they weren't going to find him.

Back in the apartment, they rang the hospital to cancel the ambulance. In the event, no ambulance had been sent anyway and no one seemed to have any intention of sending one. No one even knew anything about David's previous call.

After a stiff whiskey each, they went back to bed.

CHAPTER 16

———————

D avid checked the currency rates. His heart gave a leap. The Khor dinar was definitely falling faster now than before. It looked like some heavy hitter had entered the market. A speculator who had picked up on things? Or another bank covering their position? The bank was making money, he was making money. It kept mounting up all the time so long as that rate kept going south. Things were looking good.

He went on to check his mail and e-mail. As he was doing so, he had the feeling that his computer had been moved. Only slightly, but moved. Checking his desk, he noticed that his Connemara paperweight was a little to the left of where it normally was and then that everything was slightly out of position.

Someone had given his room a going over. Who were they and what were they looking for?

He checked but couldn't see anything missing. He glanced up at the walls and ceiling to see if he could see anything suspicious. But, if he had been bugged, he certainly wouldn't see it, not with the equipment they had nowadays. It mightn't be a sound bug, it might be a miniaturised camera hidden in the wall and would leave no more than a pinprick showing. Considering this, he moved the position of his computer so if there was a miniaturised camera his screen would be out of range.

He buzzed Mohammed to come in. "Who was the security guard on duty last night?"

"Hammed," Mohammed said.

"Sack him," David said decisively. "And take on extra security but only people you can vouch for. Someone was in here last night."

Mohammed looked at him with a blank expression.

"Any ideas who it might have been?"

"I'm shocked that it should happen," Mohammed said. "Really shocked."

"Do you think it could have been an inside job?"

"I'll find out all I can," Mohammed said. "If it was one of the staff I'm sure I can get a lead on it."

"I hope you can. But in the meantime ring a security firm to come over and sweep my office for bugs."

Could Mohammed have had anything to do with this? Obviously anything was possible. But he hoped not. He had to trust someone after all.

Changing the subject, David said, "I was down the *suq* last night....." He went on to outline what he had seen and heard including the explosion. "What do you make of it?"

Mohammed dragged on his cigarette and inhaled deeply.

"I think I can help here. I have some information that has a bearing on all this."

Mohammed paused dramatically. He liked these little moments when he had information that David didn't have. He liked to savour the occasion and it was only with reluctance that he yielded up these pearls.

"Up until now, the Shi'ites have been worked up about the disappearance of Mullah Hussein. And I thought there would be demonstrations and maybe a *suq* strike as a protest. But something has happened that has escalated the situation."

He leaned forward and spoke in a low voice. "The word on the street is that an Ayatullah called Ayatullah Abd Al Wahhab crossed over from Iran in secret with a band of followers a few days back."

"So?"

"The Shi'ites have found their leader. A leader who knows well how to exploit the situation. That explains the change of mood you saw in the *suq*."

"So you think this Ayatullah is behind all the carry on in the *suq*."

"Undoubtedly. Him or the people around him."

David pondered this.

"OK. Thanks Mohammed. Thanks for your assessment. Get on to that security firm right away and after that we'll see how it goes."

David got back to work. Looking over the banks leading accounts as he did every morning, there was just the usual traffic; the largest movement of money was in respect of merchants remitting money abroad in payment for goods they had imported under letters of credit. Some of them had exceeded their overdraft limits but, based on Mohammed's reports, they were good for the money.

The merchants conducted the trade of the state but for all that the largest accounts were held by members of the Ruling Family who had a finger in every pie and ran or were connected with all sorts of enterprises. These were all very wealthy people who spread their investments world-wide. Their vast fortunes were greatly swollen by the bribes, known as commissions, they all received. Sometimes these commissions were paid locally, sometimes direct into front companies offshore. In any event, if you wanted to be granted a contract in Khor, whether a construction contract or a defence contract, you had to pay a commission to the relevant minister. These could run into millions of dinars for the large multi million contracts. Smaller commissions had to be paid for smaller contracts. It was a fact of life in the Middle East and the foreign company just had to factor this element into their bid. All countries engaged in it though most of them denied it if challenged.

Having executed all the foreign exchange orders and dealt with the most urgent work, David left the office.

Half and hour later, he felt drained and wrung out as he climbed the wooden steps into a merchant's shop deep in the Covered Suq. He had heard Mohammed's views. Now he wanted a second opinion.

Bahwan was not a local but an Indian Moslem and therefore to some extent an outsider, or at least someone who could give an outside view. David had arranged generous finance for him when he needed it and Bahwan was beholden to him as a consequence.

Bahwan greeted David fulsomely and ushered him into his office overlooking the street. Dusty sunlight flooded through the little window and spilled across the expensive carpets scattered carelessly about: Persian from Ishfahan and Shiraz, Turkish from Ismir, Afghan from Andkhour, Turkistani from Bokhara.

David sat on a metal chair and lightly sipped from the cloyingly sweet tea - if he was to drink all the tea offered to him on a tour of the *suq* it would slosh about in his stomach for the rest of the day.

Bahwan sat opposite him, heavy lidded, also sipping tea. His basic features were buried in the fleshiness of his face which extended into a thick neck and obese body.

"I hear rumours," David said.

"This *suq* is always full of rumours," Bahwan said.

"Tell me about them," David said.

He knew Bahwan well and he wanted a view on the situation other than Mohammed's, a view and an interpretation of how the Shi'ites might act. However much Arabic he himself knew, he was only too well aware that he still thought like a Westerner and the Arabs take a radically different view of life from that taken by Westerners.

Uncomfortably balanced on a metal chair that creaked, Bahwan considered how much he should tell him. The chair was cutting into his copious thighs. He was only sitting on a chair in honour of David; normally he would have sat legs folded under him on a carpet.

To encourage him to talk, David told him what he himself had seen in the *suq* and what Mohammed had told him.

"Your man Mohammed is right. I fear for what will happen and what will become of me and my family. Though I have spent most of my life in Khor Fahal I am still a foreigner. And foreigners are the first people at risk in times of trouble. I fear this Ayatullah Abd Al Wahhab too much. He is a fanatic. I knew him before his exile. He was very radical even then, very extreme. And, while he was abroad, he built up a following among the people here."

"So what will happen now?"

Bahwan extended both chubby hands, turning them out as far as they would go. "Something bad. I feel it in my bones. Something very bad is on the way. I listen, listen, when people talk and I not like what I hear. Yesterday I hear one man say that, when the Ayatullah give the word, everyone rise up and start killing. The same man say they have plenty bombs, plenty ammunition hidden here, hidden there."

"The explosion last night would seem to point in that direction."

Bahwan went and checked outside to see if anyone was listening. He closed the door. He had a frightened apprehensive look about him. In that hot dusty room David could smell the hessian smell of the carpets but the room exuded something else as well. It was the smell of fear.

"Everything has been going so well up until now," Bahwan said and there was sadness in his voice. "People buying plenty carpets but now I think everything change. It was a good place but now with this Ayatullah and his followers it will become a bad place. Already I have had visits from sinister looking men asking me for funds, telling me things are going to change, everything is going to be stricter."

They both sat contemplating Bahwan's situation.

"Merchants like me have no security, no one to protect them." He looked about the room as if he was considering how he might secure his shop from the dangers that lurked out there. Perhaps he was thinking of nailing boards across the windows. But what protection would that be? "The men who called told me I had to declare myself. I was either for them or against them. And if I was for them I had to help them. I fear for myself and my family."

Bahwan sighed deeply and lowered his voice. "You must tell no one but I have decided to try to leave the state. It is a difficult decision. If I leave, I lose everything. Someone else come and take my shop, take my *godown*, take all my beautiful carpets. But, if I stay, I think I lose my life."

David felt a great sympathy for Bahwan and didn't like to try to influence his decision or intrude on his private fears.

They sat in silence sipping tea.

The smells and sounds of the street outside swamped the office. David was looking out on hung meat with hordes of flies buzzing about it. Bahwan was nervously stirring his glass of tea.

Like a flame thrower, the sun had reduced the earth to dust which rose about people as they walked. Dazzling sunlight stabbed through the rents in the hessian awning. Shopkeepers sat among sacks of rice and bales of coloured cloth and pots and pans and silver daggers and anklets and nose rings and beaten copper plaques bearing Arabic calligraphy.

Small bands of meek looking shapeless veiled figures shuffled past in sandals. Some stopped to look at Bahwan's carpets to the extent that they could see them through their veils. Others hurried on pausing at the stall that sold saffron and dried pepper and garlic, or bargained through their veils for kitchen utensils or bed linen or lengths of colourful cloth.

David said, "You blame this Ayatullah for what you think will happen?"

"I blame him and his followers. I blame him for ruining my life. It was he who sent those men to threaten me and others like me."

"And where exactly is this Ayatullah?"

"He moves about. He is hiding out somewhere in the Old City." Bahwan checked again to see they were not overheard. "I hear one man whisper to another that on the day the Ayatullah arrive he see him and his followers enter what they call the Monastery, a big area with high walls in the district of Allawi. But that you must not repeat. If they suspect me of talking they come and knife me."

"I understand. I will be most discreet."

"In this *suq* the walls themselves have ears." He went on, "All I need for my business is peace." He sighed. "But peace is so hard to find, is it not? Once I thought I had found it here but now I am afraid it is going. It is fading away. The people talk not of peace but of revolution. I am full of fear of what will happen. Already some merchants they have their shops attacked. Who is there to protect me?"

David could give him no answer to that.

As, a little later, he was about to leave Bahwan's shop, he drew back.

Diagonally across from him in an open coffee shop, a line of Arabs sat on wooden benches drinking tea, sucking it up with loud noises. On the corner by the cafe, there were fruit stalls selling kebabs, samosas, dates. The date stall was tended by a cripple. The cripple had one arm permanently bent and kept the small change in the lobes of his ears.

Sitting right at the back of the cafe and largely obscured from view was a figure that looked familiar to David. Only it couldn't be. This figure was wearing an Arab *kheffiah* and was in deep conversation with a man David didn't recognise, an earnest looking man wearing an Arab cap. In response to some remark his companion made, the man turned full face. The glow of the furnace used for baking even in this heat fell on his face.

It was Sebastian.

CHAPTER 17

The boy knocked as instructed on a large ornate double door set in a long high wall in the Monastery grounds in the Old City. The location had been passed on to him by a man, a stranger, who had approached him while he was lingering on a wooden bench in an outdoor *chaikhana* nursing his wounds and bruises from the brutal beating up he had suffered at the hands of the police. His back was still mangled and he walked with a limp. The stranger who had been watching him for sometime told him this was a place where he would be safe, a place where he would be welcomed, a place where he could fulfil his destiny.

After he had run away from the apartment block by the creek where the man with the boat lived, he had wandered until he came on a deserted fisherman's hut where he had taken shelter for the night. The palm shelter was old and collapsing, no more than four stakes driven into the ground and patched with palm that had come loose. There was the stale smell of fish from the sardine catches which had been laid out to dry on the sand. But the boy didn't notice the smell. He was out of reach of the police.

The trouble was he couldn't chance going back to his shack in the shanty town out by the Three Palm Oasis in case he was arrested again. At the same time, he couldn't stay for long in the fisherman's shelter. When the sun came up, he had virtually no protection from the sun and none from the heat. He lay all day without food or water. That night, driven by thirst, he slipped out of the hut to search for water. As he approached what he thought was a well, he was driven back by a pack of pie dogs. At first there was only one but their number kept increasing as other dogs kept coming out of the darkness. One more vicious or more desperate than the others ran at him and fell back only at the last moment when he kicked out. They had gathered into a pack. The pie dogs were just as thirsty and starving was he was. He couldn't blame them for trying to attack him but he had to run to save himself.

Shortly after he had escaped from the dogs he found some stagnant water in a shallow pool and drank it. It would probably give him a fever. But he didn't care any longer.

Back in the hut, the lash marks on his back, the kicks to his ribs, were more painful than ever. It was then he decided that to survive he had to chance going back into town.

He hammered on the big double doors again now and suddenly a small door set within one of the huge doors was opened by a man in a white *thobe* with a long black beard. He gave the man the password he had been given by the recruiter who had approached him in the *chaikhana*. The man motioned him inside.

The boy found himself in a courtyard completely cut off by the high wall. All around the courtyard, men dressed in black and all armed with rifles talked together animatedly.

He was led into a small room where young men, some boys as young as himself, were gathered around listening to the words of an older pale-faced man who could have been a teacher or a mullah.

As he sat and listened to the man who was reading and teaching from the Koran he gradually relaxed. The teacher didn't pay any particular attention to him. With the other youths, he listened to the man's words with rapt attention. He was attracted to the man; he felt the draw of his charisma.

He had entered a *madrasi*.

Later on food was brought, simple food, and the boy who was starving was given his share with the others. The others asked him about his marks and bruises and how he had got them and he told them his whole story and how the police had beaten and tortured him and everyone sympathised so that he began to feel at home, that this was the first place in all his life that he had been welcomed. Afterwards, they all went to the mosque.

The boy's induction had begun.

CHAPTER 18

When David drove into the parking space outside the palace where the *majlis* was to be held, most of the slots were already filled with chauffeured air-conditioned limousines, the chauffeurs standing in little knots gossiping. David parked beside Andy Wilson's Lexus. CJ had asked him to represent the bank at the *majlis* and he had arrived late to shorten the waiting time before the Sheikh's arrival. The first thing he noticed was the number of armed police around. There was always some security but today there was a lot more than usual.

Meantime, Sheikh Suleiman Bin Himyar Al Yas's motorcade was sweeping through the streets and palm-lined avenues of the New City, speeding towards the palace where a crowd was standing in the hot sun awaiting his arrival. Many had been there for hours. The Sheikh's bullet-proof stretch limousine glinted bright red in the sun and the pennant that flew had as its emblem a silver dagger on a red background.

The Sheikh was dressed in a long stiff white *thobe*, a diaphanous gold-bordered cloak and white head cloth held in place by a five cornered headdress. His face was chubby and, at first glance, he looked soft and benign, almost cuddly, an impression heightened by the glasses he wore. But, as those whom he had eliminated, those he had swept out of his path, would have attested, there was nothing whatever benign or cuddly about him.

This was a man who pursued power with absolute single mindedness. He had got to his present position through cunning and intrigue. When he saw that the West were dissatisfied with the former Ruler, his elder brother, Sheikh Jilyani Bin Himyar Al Yas, he began working behind the scenes making contacts and putting himself forward as an acceptable alternative. To help things along he had undermined Sheikh Jilyani by having many of his key supporters murdered. It had required a plotting mind to get all this arranged in strict secrecy while making sure that none of it could be traced back to him and that the struggle for power was kept so well hidden that on the surface everything was calm and all the proprieties adhered to. It had been essential that he could go on offering his full support and allegiance to Jilyani even as he was murdering his supporters and negotiating with the West to replace him.

It was a two-way deal. The West wanted the oil and rapid development and Sheikh Jilyani stood in their way. Suleiman promised to deliver oil in the manner the West wanted it. He undertook to sign all the deals that Jilyani had held up. He promised rapid development of the oil fields.

In return, all he wanted was to be Ruler. The West agreed and made the whole transition not only possible but smooth. It had all worked out very neatly, with satisfaction on both sides. And, not only that, it was all achieved without the real story ever reaching the Western press who settled for a press release presenting the abdication and the whole transfer of power as due to a deterioration in Jilyani's health.

Since then, as the oil output had increased yearly, Sheikh Suleiman had reigned over the state with absolute power in his hands alone. Among those of his relatives left alive there was no one to threaten him. The crown could rest easy on his head. He had everything under control, even the *Ulema*, the religious, whom he flattered and rewarded handsomely for their loyalty.

Of course there had always been the problem of the Shi'ites but they had been quiet for a long time now. He had kept them quiet by brutal force, by excluding them from power and wealth, by buying out any of their leaders who could be bought and imprisoning or assassinating those who could not. The system had worked perfectly. Until now. Until the unfortunate death of this troublesome Shi'ite mullah, a death that had resulted from Chief of Police Qassim being over zealous in the execution of his duties.

Before coming out this morning, Sheikh Suleiman had spent an hour in his residential palace, he had four palaces in all, reviewing this threat to security which had just recently arisen. There were alarming intelligence reports that something was brewing in the Old City.

On foot of the intelligence reports handed to him, he had given orders for the arrest of a long list of Shi'ites who were on Chief of Police Qassim's files as agitators or possible terrorists. To this list had just that morning been added the name of Ayatullah Abd al Wahhab. It was unfortunate that such a man had managed to slip into the country despite all the attempts the government made to secure their borders. If this Ayatullah became active, he would have to be got rid of. Better still, he decided then and there as he was being driven along the beautiful immaculately kept avenues of the New City, he would have Al Wahhab hunted down and disposed of as quickly as possible before he could cause any trouble. He would tell Qassim to see to it.

The Sheikh's cavalcade swept down the wide avenues, accompanied by outriders in front and behind.

As he entered each boulevard the police on duty blew their whistles, the motor cycle outriders sounded their sirens and the sheikh's chauffeur, a long standing retainer, drove swiftly along the wide sweeping roads past the lines of palms and juniper, aloes and eucalyptus and the mile long beds of myriad coloured flowers.

On phone instructions communicated from the police department, the driver suddenly altered his route and drove down Medina Street instead of Ma'ala Street. This was part of the extra security decided on at that morning's meeting.

As the Sheikh's bullet-proof car swerved into Medina Street, a youth on a motorbike following behind took out his mobile and called a number.

The couple in a room high up on the seventh floor of the Sheikh Yeslam building took the call at the same time as they saw the cavalcade swerve away, out of range. They had been sent on this mission by the Ayatullah. For months before this assignment they had been indoctrinated at the *madrasi*, had pledged themselves to the cause, had offered themselves as martyrs or, in the case of the girl, as a *shahida*. Such a sacrifice was not required on this mission though it would be on a later assignment.

As the cavalcade sped away now, they stood helplessly behind the Venetian blinds of the big glass window as their target drew farther and farther out of range. The man, a rocket propelled grenade in hand, remained peering down into the street below where the Sheikh's cavalcade should have passed. The girl in black and veiled got to her feet and began quickly packing everything away. She had volunteered as a *shahida* as a means of atoning for the dishonour she had brought on her family through committing adultery. Death as a *shahida* would restore her family's honour. The man said, "We will try again. Our opportunity will come."

The cavalcade swept up to the palace steps where the reception party had been lined up for the past hour sweltering in the sun. David watched as the Sheikh's personal bodyguards stood to attention, each man equipped with a gold mounted sword and dagger as well as side arms. The head of the bodyguard opened the car door and Sheikh Suleiman Bin Himyar Al Yas stepped out. Chief of Police Qassim, in a uniform adorned with numerous medals, saluted and the Sheikh's entourage slowly mounted the steps on which deep pile carpeting had been spread all along the front of the palace.

Everybody began to file in behind. Everybody, of course, was male. There is no place in a *majlis* for any female.

David, entering the palace, felt like he was stepping into a deep freeze compartment. So powerful was the air-conditioning that the sweat immediately cooled and chilled on his skin.

The original concept of a *majlis* was that the sheikh of the tribe would sit in his black goatskin tent, or, as in David's childhood memories, in the clay-floored room of an ancient fort with reed matting on which retainers sat about and passed the *hookah*. But things had moved on. The building in which Sheikh Suleiman Bin Himyar Al Yas's *majlis* was being held was the ground floor of a towering marble palace. The whole ground floor was covered in one single carpet with the tribal design of the Al Yas tribe.

The Sheikh and his retinue mounted the steps of a dais built at the end the great hall. The dais by elevating the Ruler did away with the accessibility of the old desert *majlises* where any tribesman could bring his petition to the head of his the tribe, a place where feuds and personal problems were ruled upon. But that concept was in the past. In the present setting, the Ruler was anything but accessible.

Sheikh Suleiman was elevated, the power centre around whom lesser mortals swirled. He held himself aloof and let members of his retinue conduct any business that needed to be conducted. Occasionally, he chatted to the higher-ranking members of his retinue who sometimes summoned a leading merchant or even a banker to approach on matters of business. At the *majlis* were leading merchants and foreigners who held senior positions. Everybody wanted to be close to the nexus of power, to sit close to power, or at least to be close to the men who were close to power. A substantial number of people were here, not to petition the Sheikh directly, but to petition someone who had his ear or had the ear of someone who could approach him.

Here contacts were made and deals set up. Not the big deals, of course. The arms deals, the oil deals, were negotiated in strictly private audience.

Still, there were plenty of opportunities at a lower level. Many substantial contracts would be negotiated by the lucky few before the *majlis* ended.

The reps working the hall feverishly represented everything imaginable: construction companies bidding for contracts, computers companies, supermarkets chains, every facet of the great western consumer market extending from the utilitarian to the luxury market of fast cars, perfumes, haute couture (despite the veiling of women), diamonds. There were reps of one sort or another for every conceivable commodity seeking to get a foot in the door of this highly lucrative market in a state with great spending power.

David kept clear of the reps; he got more than enough of them in the bank. He did the rounds of the merchants though. This was a ritual made easy by the formality and length of Arab greetings which were usually sufficient in themselves without any elaboration. Contact had been made or maintained.

"Salaam aleikum"
"Aleikum asalaam"
"Massalkheir."
"Keif Halak,"
"Tayyib alhumdil'allah."

His duty done, David gravitated towards the ex-pat community. A newly arrived executive of an industrial company was complaining about the bureaucracy, the awful climate and on and on. The man seemed to thoroughly dislike Arabs and Arabia. A lot of Westerners did. And yet there were plenty of takers for jobs out here. And would always be so long as people could salt enough money away.

Making the rounds, David chatted to some friends from the British Embassy and he had the feeling that they were more guarded than usual in what they had to say. The thought crossed his mind that the embassy knew something that he didn't know. Something was going on. The police had approached him when he had arrived in the car park and spent a long time going over his documents. Someone had gone over his office presumably looking for something. In the *suq* he kept having the feeling that he was being followed. Perhaps it was time to watch his back.

Here in the *majlis,* he sensed the same subtle change in the atmosphere that he had noticed in the Phoenix bar. Despite the impressive glittering palace and the outward manifestation of confidence, he sensed that there lurked a certain unease, he wouldn't put it higher than that. But it was there.

He felt it most strongly among the expats who, even in the isolation of their compounds, had picked up a whiff of danger and were sniffing the air like gazelle at a water hole that sensed a predator approaching.

The Arabs didn't betray their feelings so easily but there was some unease there too. Undoubtedly they knew about the trouble brewing in the Old City. Their position in the world where for so long they had been super rich and financially super powerful had once made them feel invulnerable. But that invulnerability had been cracked long ago and now they couldn't be sure of security even in their own state.

"How's it going?" asked Andy Wilson materialising out of the crowd. David ran into him at almost every function he attended. They had a lot in common by virtue of the similar banking positions they filled. "Bloody awful scrum today. Seems to get worse all the time."

"How's Margaret?" David enquired.

"Fine, fine. Looking forward to end of tour. Only a few more weeks now."

"That's right. I'd forgotten you were on your way out. Almost on the plane."

"Margaret says it's none too soon. Never really took to it here. It's just not her scene."

"I can understand that. Any news on your next posting?

"Didn't I tell you? Almost certainly Singapore. I was expecting it mind you. As compensation for sticking it out in this shit hole. I just hope we get out before anything happens. What do you think of this Ayatullah fellow they're all talking about?"

"Not a lot. Except that he was expelled from here years and years ago."

"Head Office seems to have got a whisper about him from some source or other. They urge caution."

"They could be right. The word on the Arab street is that he has been plotting his return during his years of exile."

Andy made a face, "I don't envy the bloke taking over from me, he might have a difficult row to harrow. Still, our outfit has survived a lot of mullahs and ayatullahs in our time in the Middle East. So I'm sure we'll survive whatever comes along. Could be uncomfortable though. Have you done anything special about security?"

"I've increased the number of guards. That's about it."

"I don't suppose you have much to worry about being an Arab Bank.

We've already stepped up security about as much as can be done. Erected steel shutters, all that sort of thing. And installed a lot of gadgetry from CCTV to a whole lot of fancy new electronic stuff for which we are paying an absolute fortune. I don't put much faith in any of it though. Let's face it, there's no way you can make a bank in the middle of an Arab city bomb proof or even attack proof. It just isn't possible. The fact is we can install all the fancy gadgetry we like but in the end we have to depend on the local police to protect us if there's trouble. To tell you the truth, if we didn't have our posting further east, I'd consider packing Margaret off home to her mother's."

"Deborah's mother is out on a visit," David remarked.

"Then get her out of here pronto. Probably the rumours going around are a lot of hot air and nothing will happen. But, then again, the whole fucking Middle East might blow up. Though hopefully not before I get out of here. Have you ever worked in Hong Kong?"

"No."

"That's where we were on our previous posting. Spoils you for anywhere else. Fantastic nightlife. We had lots of friends there, lots to do. I hope Singapore is as good. In any event, it's bound to be better than here."

David looked about the magnificent *majlis* hall.

"Yes, I suppose so."

"No offence. I know you like the place here. Though I can't understand why."

"I suppose it's because I have lots of childhood memories. A lot of associations."

"Indeed. But look what the bastards did to your father. A bloody outrage that. I don't suppose you have any more word on the body after all the passage of time."

"No," David said. "No word at all."

"Fucking bastards."

The Sheikh in his gold-bordered robe was descending from the dais and everyone drew back as he left the *majlis* surrounded by his retinue. There were, David noticed, even more police than when they had come in.

Another banker friend who had joined them said, "They're certainly stepping up security. Not that it would be any harm if they shot the fucker on the way out. They tried to before as you know. One of the bodyguards took a pot shot. Barely missed too. Pity."

NOEL SCANLON

CHAPTER 19

Far away from the glitz of the *majlis* in the New City where so many people vied for even one word in the ear of the Ruler, an old man wearing a white *thobe* and brown cloak, a thin stooped figure, whose eyelids drooped, his face deeply indented around his aquiline nose, went to a window in the upper floor of the decrepit palace known as the Summer Palace and looked down on the palace grounds which were covered in blown sand.

Times had changed. But not for the old Sheikh. His mind dwelt on the past. For him time had frozen, stopped in its forward movement a long time ago.

The Summer Palace was in a corner of the country near the Jebel Akhdar, the only substantial mountain in the state. It was on the edge of the great desert. There was no oil or indeed any activity in this desolate area. The Summer Palace was surrounded by mud walls and in the grounds there was a subterranean well that provided water for the household.

The man, under his white head cloth and black head-rope, looked ancient. Only his eyes were alive and sharp as he looked down on an old gardener who was pottering about in the dirt. He was a palace guard who doubled as a gardener just as another palace guard doubled as a cook. The guards were there to guard the man looking down from the window as well as to imprison him. They changed from time to time in case they should be suborned. But the old man always knew which among them were employed to be his jailers.

The man at the window was Sheikh Jilyani Bin Himyar Al Yas, Ruler of the state until he had been deposed by his plotting and conniving younger brother. He had never understood why his brother hadn't had him assassinated which would have been the normal course of events and was something he had fully expected. Perhaps there had been outside restraint.

Away back then, he had been warned that a coup was planned but he hadn't acted soon enough or decisively enough to forestall it. He had under-estimated the cunning and ruthlessness of Suleiman whom he had always trusted and never expected to move against him. Suleiman who had been a troubled and troublesome boy had gone against the rule of the clan which always recognised and honoured the oldest brother. Suleiman had broken that tradition for the first time in the tribe's history.

At least his life had been spared though he had had to swear not to interfere in or take any part in the politics of the state ever again and he was not allowed to travel. He had to stay out in this remote place and never enter the city.

In a way, being deposed and removed from high office had been something of a relief to the old ex-Sheikh.

He had been a tribal leader and had led his clan honourably and to the best of his ability over a long lifetime. But things had moved on. After the discovery of oil, it wasn't a tribal leader of his type the powers who had begun to exert more and more influence in the state wanted. They wanted a younger man, and he was no longer young. They wanted a more malleable man and he was far from malleable. He didn't embrace change. In fact he impeded it. He was unimpressed by the offers of great wealth. He was not the man to take on the modernisation of the state. He had had only a Koranic education and had never felt the need for more, he had all the savvy needed to be head of a tribe at a time when leadership and integrity were highly valued and formal education was non-existent.

But when oil was discovered, he never really came to grips with the implications of the sudden access of wealth that began to pour into the state. He had no great desire to deal with the heads of foreign oil companies, with foreign captains of industry. He had refused to sign the deals he was asked to sign. He was stubborn and obdurate. He was accused of holding the state back.

When the decision was taken to depose him, assassination would have been the normal procedure. He was glad to have been left with his life and with no more than a few bullet wounds as a result of the resistance he had put up.

After a time, living in isolation in the decrepit Summer Palace, cut off from all state activity, it dawned on him that he quite liked his new lifestyle, remote and simple as it was. The truth was that by nature he didn't much care for a lot of ceremony or even a lot of company, certainly not of the kind available in the New City. He was given to introsp[ection?]. And to religion. He was a profoundly religious man in the old sense [of] spirituality, not in the new sense of using religion as a justification fo[r] violence and murder and mayhem. His life and his religion were highly disciplined and severe and spartan as had the life and religion of his forbears for many centuries. He was a man who accepted that whatever happened to him was the will of Allah.

The old man had a strong sense of history and of his place in it. He had a strong sense of his historic roots.

For thousand of years his forbears had wandered over these deserts. They were descendents of the tribes who, in the seventh century, surged out of Arabia to conquer the world under the banner of Islam. They conquered the richest part of the Roman Empire and the whole of the Persian empire until their rule extended from the Pyrenees to the Atlantic, from the Indus to China, spreading Arabic, the language of the Bedouin, creating civilizations across the world, all inspired by an idea, a new religion.

Dr Mahesh, the Indian doctor assigned to look after him came into the room. "Ah, you have eaten your curds. That is good. Now I give you injection."

The old sheikh put his hand to his side where the pain kept recurring. "No injection."

The Indian doctor gave him a sly smile. "I have given you one sedative though."

"I haven't taken any sedative."

"Your Highness has. It was in your curds."

The old sheikh turned. He looked gaunt, his head a skull on which the skin had loosened, falling away. But he still retained the dignity and authority of a tribal leader. He had presence and a certain charisma though he was too detached and haughty to really care what view others took of him.

"You are a knave, Mahesh. When I was Ruler I would have had your head struck off in the *maidan*."

The Indian knew that many heads had been severed from many bodies in the *maidan* over the centuries but he also knew that the old sheikh had a certain liking for him and any way depended on him to keep him alive. Dr Mahesh said, "There is news from the city that a mullah has been murdered. An Ayatullah who was banished has returned. Trouble is expected."

...ply. He cared nothing for what happened in the
... planet.

...an doctor who was always bringing him gossip
...t not be true. He knew that Mahesh, like most of the
... pay of his brother and thought it most likely that the
doctor would poison him one day when the order to do so came. But that
neither bothered him nor affected their relationship in any significant way.

"I have decided that today I will ride out into the desert. Tell Abu Assad
to make the necessary arrangements."

"Your Highness's health is too poor. You are too frail. You are too old."

Mahesh was thinking of the possibility of the old man making an escape
attempt though it seemed unlikely at this stage. How could such an old
man escape? He could hardly walk, yet alone ride on a camel across the
vast treacherous desert between here and the city. Still, this was a time of
danger and tension. And thinking of the consequences to himself if the old
sheikh should happen to escape, Dr Mahesh went on protesting.

The old man didn't even hear his doctor's protests. Already his mind
was on the great desert where he had spent so much of his life. He loved
the openness, the memories, the desert brought him.

"I will go into the desert," he said. "And I will hunt for bustard."

A few hours later, a small group of tribesmen gathered in the courtyard
of the Summer Palace sitting cross-legged on mats strewn with date stones.
Jet black loin cloths covered the tribesmen's sinewy bodies and their long
hair stood out from their heads setting off their large wild eyes, their
flashing white teeth. The falconers among then carried their birds on a
leather strap on their wrists. The camels were couched. They had already
been watered and saddled. It was time to go.

After an hour's riding, the small party of riders were into the Rub al
Khali, for the Summer Palace was located on its borders. Here the surface
of the sand was rippled by the breeze. The ridges were formed from the
heavier darker grains and the hollows from the lighter paler grains, gold
and silver, orange and red, pink and yellow. Ahead in the distance lay
dunes several hundred feet in height rising from the desert floor.

Out here, the old sheikh was happy, despite the indignity of having been
forced to accept a second rider on his camel, a young boy who
inconspicuously steadied him in the saddle. Without the young boy, there
were times when he would have fallen off. He was too old to be out riding.
But he was happy to be in the desert. It was his terrain.

He thought to himself. All that was best in the true Arabs, the tribal Arabs as he had known them, their dignity, their generosity, their endurance, their sense of themselves, had all come to them from this desert, this harsh, barren, beautiful, testing, dangerous place.

It was the old sheikh's firm belief that the Arabs should never have left the desert. They needed the desert which had made them and shaped them. They needed the discipline and hardships of the desert. It was in the desert they had found their fullest and truest expression.

This land he now rode slowly over was their place as it was his. It nurtured their souls as it nurtured his.

When they left the desert, when they migrated to the towns and cities, and for money turned their back on the desert life that had gone on for so many generations with all its ethos and customs and culture, the tribal Arabs cut themselves off from their roots. They became bloated with food and wealth and power. They became corrupted and altered irrevocably.

They became wealthy, but their souls withered away.

That is what he, as Ruler, had foreseen and opposed from the beginning, this removal of a people from its roots and culture. He had seen the great riches oil had to offer dangled before him, not as a great boon, but as a great danger.

He thought then, and still thought, that, far from benefiting the Arabs, oil would destroy them. And that is what was coming to pass.

The old sheikh thought these thoughts as his old bones were jolted by the movement of the camel. He felt his age. His mind wandered back in time.

As young man he and a few companions riding racing camels had crossed this desert land of Arabia from Salala to Mukulla, from Abu Dhabi to Buraimi arriving there after all their dates and goatskins of water had run out. These and many others like them were long hard journeys in deserts that cover more than a million square miles and on these journeys there was no room for any error; when you aimed at a well that was a pin prick in a trackless desert you had to hit the mark, there was no room for error for without replenishing your water skins you could not survive. In his youth, though, he had thought nothing of it. Now, after only a couple of hours, he called a halt and some of his men released their falcons, those magnificent predatory birds that went zooming over the desert in search of prey, while others lit a fire and began to make coffee.

Dismounting stiffly, for his bones ached, the old sheikh walked a little apart from his companions, one of whom he knew would one day kill him.

He felt happy. He looked in rapture at the dunes, nearer now. He could not conceive of anything on this earth more beautiful than this harsh barren landscape. He hoped that when Allah called him, it would be to a place of brilliant coloured sands just like these. But meantime he was happy to be left waiting for that call.

If, at this moment, a rider on a camel were to materialise out of the dancing shimmering air and offer him to be Ruler again he would not have accepted. And indeed he had had such an offer only the other night. Isolated and guarded as he was, he still had clandestine visits from with the city.

People came secretly to the Summer Palace, riding across the desert at night, risking their lives if they were caught, though the bribes they paid lessened the chances of this. They were the emissaries of members of the family who hated the present Ruler, people who had suffered at his hands, people who had had loved ones eliminated or tortured, people who had their own ambitions and wanted the present tyrant gone, wanted to seize his power for themselves, people who were planning and plotting, people who wanted him, old as he was, as a figurehead behind whom they could manipulate and pull the strings.

He wondered for a moment what would happen if he were to give his assent.

What if he decided to take his revenge after all these years? It would be a sweet revenge. But he quickly put such foolish thoughts out of his mind. He no longer wanted revenge. He had long since lost his appetite even for that.

The old sheikh had to pause for a moment to steady himself. The pain in his side had returned despite, or perhaps because of, Mahesh's medicine.

He waited until the pain had eased. Then, with slow deliberation, he turned towards Mecca. And, the limitless silent sands his prayer mat, he began to perform his prayers, chanting to himself in a weak voice,

"*In the name of God, the Compassionate, the Merciful. King on the day of reckoning.*" He prostrated himself. "*Thee only do we worship and to Thee we cry for help.*" His voice was growing stronger and clearer. "*Guide us on the straight path.*" He looked across to the distant sand dunes. "*The path of those to whom thou hast been gracious, with whom Thou art not angry and who do not go astray.....*"

CHAPTER 20

When Deborah arrived early at her office she found Aisha in tears, her glasses off, sobbing at her desk in the empty office.

"What's wrong? What's happened?"

Wiping her eyes, Aisha told Deborah what was wrong.

She had so far managed to fend off suitors she strongly objected to marrying. But that state of affairs couldn't go on forever. Now crisis time had come. Her family had produced yet another suitor except this one came with the warning that she had been obdurate for long enough. This time her father was insisting that she accept this man.

Aisha wiped her eyes and adjusted her headscarf. "He got so angry with me when I tried to argue with him. He shouted at me that he had spent so much time and money negotiating with the family of this man who has a secure job in the civil service. He asked me why I keep refusing everybody. He told me I had refused once too often and that this time I must accept."

Deborah had known that this was going to happen sooner or later. It was inevitable that it should.

"Is this man so bad?"

"He is awful. He is old. His wife just recently died and he needs a young wife to replace her. He is very orthodox, very religious. He will demand obedience. Already I have heard him say that he would not tolerate a wife of his working. He thinks like the *Taliban*. If I marry him I would have to give up my job and stay always in the house."

Deborah liked Aisha who had a real talent for her work, an intelligent and studious girl who would have had real prospects in any normal society. But here wasn't normal.

"It is hateful for me to leave my home to be under the control of this man who would, I think, be very harsh. I lay awake all night imagining living in this stranger's house ruled over by his old mother, confined for day after day, year after year with no contact only with other wives confined just like me. I would sooner die."

Deborah tried to advise her, to console her. But what could she do? This was a strict paternalistic society with its own rigid rules and traditions. She offered what support she could. Her father might change his mind. The man might not turn out to be as bad as she anticipated. And, if she really hated the idea of marrying him, why didn't she herself suggest someone else and try to persuade her father to accept him. Weren't there boys her own age she at least knew by sight even if she had never socialised with them which wasn't possible in her society where, if a girl was caught in the company of a man not a relation, she would be compromised, ostracised, branded, rendered for ever un-marriageable.

Even while she offered suggestions, Deborah knew that they were meaningless and useless for an Arab living by the strict codes Aisha had to live by.

Aisha had just left her office when the phone rang. She picked it up thinking it was her mother. Instead, a female voice said softly but venomously, "We are ringing you to warn you off trying to introduce immoral western women's propaganda into the pages of *Al Jameela*. That is a dangerous thing to do."

"Who's that?" Deborah asked, stunned.

"We are the Party of God. We stand for the Khor Moslem women's values. You are not wanted here. You or your depraved western values. Pack your bags and go. If you do not go by tomorrow there will be a body-bag waiting for you."

There was a pause. Then another female voice whispered, "We are digging your grave."

The phone clicked off and Deborah sat there in shock at these threats dropping out of the ether into her ear, into her brain. She tried to put them out of her mind but instead they kept echoing in her head as if being run on a loop. Who were these people ringing her? Did they really mean what they said?

She looked at her desk. Lying scattered about on it was a collection of photographs complete with captions left there the night before by the magazine's male photographer. These photographs hardly varied from issue to issue. They had to be of the Ruling Family and there were only so many ways you could photograph His Highness arriving in the country when he was greeted by a line of his aides or leaving on a visit abroad which looked much the same, same tarmac, same plane, same cloak and headgear.

She felt upset by the phone call but at the same time defiant. She would defy them all and bring out an issue the way she wanted it. She started to put it together. Sorting through the material to hand she picked out an interview with a visiting delegation of women called Women's Rights International that had been lying on her desk for some time. The report had been critical of the regime in Khor Fahal. Oblique but still critical. That was the type of thing she wanted. There were quite a few pieces she had held back on until now. But now she was going to publish them and to hell with the consequences.

Later in the day, Deborah was visited by Eileen Hisham. Eileen was highly unusual in as much as she was a young Irish woman married to an Arab Shi'ite from the Old City. Though raised a strict Irish Catholic, she had converted to Islam when she met her husband, a Khor Fahal national, in UCD, married him and had come back to Khor Fahal to live in his family house. As far as Deborah could gather, her husband, Safwan Hisham, had turned out to be an extreme Islamist and Eileen seemed to have not only absorbed his views but to have herself become an Islamic activist.

She dropped in on the magazine office at regular intervals seeking publication of material she had written. It was all so extreme that not only could Deborah not publish it, she was afraid even to keep any of it in the office it was so inflammatory.

Nonetheless, Deborah quite liked Eileen or at least admired her pluck and courage. Also Eileen gave her an intimate insight into the life of the Shi'ite community in the Old City, something that wasn't at all easy to come by given that they were a closed community and suspicious of strangers. Eileen could be a valuable source if she didn't contradict or argue with her too much. Eileen was highly opinionated and averse to contradiction. She tended more to hand down indisputable truths from on high, which for her, of course, meant from the Koran.

She now threw a pile of papers on Deborah's desk and, as was customary with her, launched into a rant against the government and against the Sunni Ruling Class.

Deborah, somewhat in awe of Eileen's total conviction, how could anyone be so totally convinced about anything, watched her as she spoke. She was dressed in the traditional manner, her body covered completely in a long loose drab dress and, of course, covering her head with a cowl of the same material. Any trace of the western make-up she might once have worn had disappeared from her freshly scrubbed face from which the rosiness of the Irish skin had faded to be replaced by the sallowness of the locals.

"It's an outrage what the government are doing to us in the Old City. It's an outrage. It's repression. It's against all international law. The world out there ought to know what's going on. The world out there has got to be told about it......"

Deborah marvelled at the passion of this small but very sharp and fiery Dublin girl. She was sure that if she hadn't been here protesting the repression of the Shi'ites, she would have been with Amnesty International, or joining in demonstrations against globalisation or against killing the whales or saving the earth from global warming, or joining the tree people to climb trees and chain herself to a branch.

If Eileen had made it into politics, she would have been in the Green Party though she might have been a bit too extreme for them. She was an unstoppable firebrand. It seemed to Deborah that it didn't much matter what the cause was, the point was that there had to be wrongs to be righted. And the particular wrongs she was out to set to right were those endured by the Arabs or more specifically the Shi'ites in the state. That's what energised and motivated her.

"The world has to be told about what's going on. People have to be informed. Pressure has to be brought to bear. Otherwise they will begin to murder our leaders one by one just as they've already murdered Mullah Hussein."

Deborah noticed her use of the word our, and took it to denote complete identification with the Shi'ites. As far as Deborah could gather, Eileen, like all the other Moslem women in the state, lived a very confined life though Eileen would not accept any criticism even of this, taking it to be a personal insult. Deborah had to be careful what she said or she'd fly at her. She had once offered a mild criticism of veiling and confining women and Eileen had taken off aggressively.

"Why are Westerners always going on with this stupid criticism of the way Moslem women are veiled? As if it was the be all and end all of our life when it's actually only a minor issue. In any event, we are treated with a fucking sight more respect than Christian women are. The way Westerners bleat on and on about our dress code is only an excuse to make us look peculiar and alien so that they can the more easily go ahead with doing what they really want to do, which is to suppress us and imprison us and torture us or rather get the western supported dictators kings and sheikhs who have sold their souls to the west to do their dirty work for them......"

Were Eileen's extreme views due to the enthusiasm of the convert or the fierceness of her own uncompromising nature or a mixture of both? Despite all her preaching, it seemed to Deborah that the Arab women could hardly be portrayed as getting a good deal. They were, like Aisha, stuck in a highly paternalistic structure in which the attitude to women was pure medieval. She didn't express these views though because, any time she had, she had been subjected to a more prolonged tirade.

"It's all there," Eileen said indicating the sheaf of scrawled on paper she had thrown on the desk. Deborah had read some of her previous material and been horrified by its content.

"Why haven't you published any of what I've brought you yet?" Eileen now demanded.

"I'll try and get some of it into the next issue which I plan to be a real bombshell. It'll be more radical than anything previously published in the state. That is if I can manage to get it past the editor in chief, the Sheikha."

"Fuck the Sheikha. She's just a lackey of the government. Who cares what she thinks or says?"

"Unfortunately she's in charge."

"Why don't you stand up to her?"

"I'm going to. But it'll probably get me the sack."

"Don't let her sack you. Refuse to go. Stage a sit in."

"Get real. I'd be forcibly ejected if I tried anything like that."

"Then let them eject you. It'd make great publicity. So are you going to have the guts to publish my stuff?"

"As I said, I'll use some of it." She'd have to be careful though that she didn't end up in prison as a result. She went on, "But you're in the wrong place. Whatever I try to do, *Al Jameela* is only a woman's magazine. Why don't you try the newspapers?"

"You think I haven't tried them."

"And?"

"What do you think? They're all run and controlled by the government.

They're only propaganda machines. They threw me out. And told me that they'd arrest me if I kept bothering them. They said they'd have me deported if I set foot in their buildings again. So you're my only hope."

"I'll see what I can do," Deborah said, "But don't expect too much." To change the subject she asked, "How are things in the Old City?"

"Hotting up. Why don't you come around and see for yourself."

"I'd love to."

"OK then. Come on Thursday. I'll show you the other side of life in Khor Fahal."

CHAPTER 21

David again climbed the badly stained cement stairs to Sebastian's apartment.

On the way over he had noticed a number of police motorised patrols along the main roads of the area, young policemen in the backs of their vehicles gripping their rifles tensely. But there were no patrols here. These alleyways were too narrow for a vehicle to get into.

He felt exhausted from walking through alleyways where the poor and the illegal immigrants lay comatose, their limbs awry. Out here it was hot as hell, wringing sweat from his body until he felt like a limp rag.

At the entrance to the block he had, as before, been surrounded by a band of ragged boys in dirty t-shirts. Were they the same ones who had been here last time? They chanted with a mixture of hostility and curiosity, "Who are you? What you want? Where you going?" The elevator was still out of order and there was an even larger pile of black refuse sacks in the entrance hall.

He knocked on the door with the broken panels. No attempt had been made to mend it. For days he had been trying to contact Sebastian by various means but without success. Presumably this was because he was lying low and keeping well clear of the police. The whole situation bothered David. It didn't quite add up. If Sebastian was lying low then why had he seen him out drinking tea in a public cafe in the Covered Suq opposite Bahwan's shop disguised as an Arab?

He had enquired about his import company, Gulf Enterprises, and had traced it to a small office in a large block in the Mansoor district but when he called by he found the office closed. He then tried to contact the Arab partner Sebastian had mentioned but every time he rang him all he got was an answering machine.

He had also tried to enquire into the accident that had got Sebastian into all this trouble, the car accident involving a younger member of the Ruling Family. But the police told him that they didn't disclose any information about matters of that nature to a third party and put the phone down. Even Mohammed, who normally had his finger on the pulse, hadn't picked up anything about it. Such incidents were common enough, members of the Ruling Family shot up cars, purely out of pique, on a regular basis. But, when they did, the incident circulated, became part of the day's bulletin of *suq* gossip. Yet Mohammed had picked up nothing about this particular incident.

David was worried about his friend. He might well be hiding from the police but did that require him to live in what was so clearly an area hostile to foreigners. There was something odd going on here. Why had he come to live in a place as obviously dangerous as this? Sebastian hadn't come clean with him and he wanted to find out what was really going on.

After the third knock, there was a shuffling noise along the hallway and Abood peered blearily out of his one good eye. On his face was a look of the deepest melancholy which seemed to be Abood's normal expression.

"Is Mr Sebastian in?"

Abood considered this as a philosophical question that required much inner thought and consideration. His face was even paler than before. And he looked thinner. He didn't appear to have eaten since David had last seen him. The dryness of his lips and the hoarseness of his voice coming out of a dry throat indicated that he was both fasting and abstaining from water. Abood was certainly born into the right faith. He was a natural for the suffering, and self abnegation, and self flagellation which Shi'ites impose on themselves. Eventually Abood decided on a reply, dragging it reluctantly from the recesses of his brain.

"No. Not in."

"Will he be out for long then?"

Another long pause.

"He no tell Abood."

"Did he go out alone?"

"No. He go with friends."

This was hopeful.

"European or Arab friends?"

"Arab. All Arab."

"He goes out a lot?"

"Yes. And his friends they are coming here. They stay talking talking all night." He added, "But Abood go bed. Abood go bed early."

"So Mr Sebastian has plenty of friends?"

Sebastian had always had an almost magical capacity for attracting people. Of both sexes

"Yes," Abood said. "All night they are keeping me awake." He paused. "They talk very hot, yes very hot." He added, "They no like government."

"I see," David said. "And have you any idea when Mr Sebastian will be back?"

"No," Abood said, beginning to edge the door closed, looking as if he might collapse before he achieved this task. But the door clicked closed solidly enough leaving David looking at the damaged panels.

After leaving Sebastian's block, David, deciding to take a short-cut back to his car, turned into a narrow walkway where the intense heat with its syrupy humidity was trapped and magnified. Everything sweltered. The whole scene was faded and blurred, so that it seemed that he was seeing it through a hazy cracked mirror. In this teeming, dirty, richly layered slice of life, this fading sepia picture, stabs of sunlight haloed an upturned face, fell on veiled women huddled inside doorways watching.

When he was well into this walkway, men began suddenly to appear as if from nowhere, pressing forward, carrying him with them in a tense excited tide which caught him and held him and carried him along, his feet barely touching the ground. More and more people poured out of the side alleys to swell a crowd that seemed to be imbued with one purpose.

As the route twisted and turned, David soon lost his bearings. He had no exact idea where he was. He regretted having taken what he had thought would be a short-cut but he couldn't turn around and go back. He was caught and held in a vice like grip by the moving throng of people. The route twisted and turned now one way, now another, sometimes turning back on itself in a loop until he was completely confused as to where he was going or even in what direction. Where were all these people headed? What were they so excited about?

He tried to manoeuvre himself to the side but his efforts had no effect. The crowd had sucked him in and held him tightly in its fist.

After a period of time and countless twists and turns the walkway unexpectedly debouched into a *maidan* or square closely surrounded by tall houses. Here he was deposited like a piece of flotsam thrown up by the tide.

The *maidan* was already packed with people. What looked like some sort of public meeting was in progress. On an improvised stage a number of black turbaned men were seated. Behind them heavily armed men lurked, guarding and protecting the man who was addressing the quickly augmenting crowd.

The speaker looked frail but animated. As he spoke, he seemed to vibrate with the intensity of his oratory. He quivered in the heat, now small and thin, now large and powerful. Both from Mohammed's description and the comments all around, David knew this to be Ayatullah Abd Al Wahhab. Quite by chance he found himself caught up in the mad scary brew of extreme Islamists.

The impassioned voice of the Ayatullah was declaiming in a high reedy voice, "*You have been bled by the greed of the Sheikh and his family who daily grow wealthier and fatter while you,*" he stabbed his finger, "*you grow thinner and thinner.*

"*Oh Shi'ites, follow me and I promise you victory against evil, victory against those who have oppressed you and betrayed the Arab cause. Follow me and with the sword of righteousness we will cut a swathe through the ranks of our enemies....*"

David realised that something extraordinary was happening here. It wasn't just that Ayatullah Abd al Wahhab was a skilled orator. It wasn't even what he said. David frequently heard this type of rhetoric when he tuned in to the various radio and TV stations in the Gulf. It wasn't what he said; it was the power he projected. It was a power that obviously overwhelmed his listeners.

Language has always been a powerful force in Arabia, a powerful tool in the hands of an orator who can wield it and this man knew how to wield it. He knew how to appeal to the dreams and aspirations of his listeners. He knew how to make them feel special, apart. He knew how to get inside their brains. But there was something else. There was something creepy, something subterranean, something dark going on here.

As the Ayatullah spoke, a cloud of darkness seemed to gather around him and enshroud him. And some mysterious power emanated from him

David could feel its power coming at him through the hot air.

"*Rise up oh Shi'ites.*"

"*Revenge the death of the Mullah Hussein.*"

"Let blood be spilled."
"Let the blood of our oppressors be spilled."
"Let the blood of the traitors be spilled."
"Let the blood of the infidel be spilled..."

A great cheer went up. David felt a bolt of lightening run through the crowd as the words of Ayatullah Abd al Wahhab were mainlined into their arteries. The Ayatullah had become an all powerful force, a great black bird swooping on the crowd, wings outstretched, encompassing them, herding them, drawing them up towards him.

He had become a leader, a messiah, a man with extraordinary and supernatural powers. There was, so people said, lots of evidence of this.

This was heady dangerous stuff ringing in the ears of the poor and deprived people still crowding into the *maidan* from all directions.

The people stood with upturned faces as if they were hearing a voice from on high. They were spellbound. They were back in the time of chaos before things began to take shape. They had been reduced to swirling atoms and were being reshaped as the Ayatullah wanted them to be. They were being reformed. Reborn.

"Pick up your swords and thrust them into the bowels of the evil ones."
"You are special."
"You are the chosen ones of Allah."
"If you fight for Allah every one of you will enter Paradise."

The people sighed. How sweet were the Ayatullah's words. How heady they were to the people listening. They lived in poverty. And here was the Ayatullah offering them a way out. The Ayatullah was offering them not just material wealth. But Paradise itself.

Ayatullah Abd Al Wahhab was on an emotional high. He held the crowd in the palm of his hand. He could feel the power he exerted over them. The sweetness of it hummed and sang inside him. His listeners were putty in his hands as he injected more emotion into what was becoming a supercharged atmosphere.

"Do not be afraid of death."
"Death is pure."
"Death is the highest, fullest expression of life."
"If we dedicate ourselves to Allah many of us will die."
"But in death, victory will be ours...."

David could feel shivering waves of emotion sweep through the people all around him as Ayatullah Abd Al Wahhab led this crowd into a realm that is inaccessible to reason or logic or refutation, a Paradise which every man, every boy in the crowd could gain access to by rising up, by taking up the sword.

David was awed by the power of this frail man, amazed, though he probably shouldn't have been, by how readily people were indoctrinated, their minds dominated and taken over. How ready they were to embrace the prospect of death.

This man was drawing hate from the recesses of their minds. He was licensing them to kill without committing murder, to have all their actions absolved and sanctified and glorified if they wielded the sword of Allah. They were the Righteous Ones, the Chosen Ones. They were chosen by Allah to serve. They would be born again. Reconstituted. The gates of Paradise would open before them.

"You are the Heroes."

"You will avenge the death of our martyrs."

"You are the heroes who will do this….."

The electricity running in the crowd touched David and he was burnt by it. At the same time he felt a cloud of darkness enter his own mind and begin to drift about in there. He felt fear creep up his spine. Physical fear. But fear too that some dark force emanating from this man was trying to break into his mind and replace what was in there, change the chips, reset the circuits.

He couldn't stay here. He had to get away. He began to look about for a way out. But more and more people had come in behind him. He tried to move backwards to get to an exit but, instead, was shoved further forward. He was trapped in the mob. Fear breathed down the back of his neck.

Something strange, something very odd indeed was happening in this *maidan*. Sweat ran down his spine, wrung from him by heat and by fear. For how long could he block the messages slamming into his brain?

The Ayatullah was in full flood now.

"Ali, blessed be his name, was a martyr."

"Many Shi'ites have been martyrs."

"Many of you will become martyrs."

"Who among you will be a martyr?"

A great cry of people offering themselves as martyrs rose from the crowd. And the chilling thing was that they meant it. When the Shi'ites said that they were prepared for martyrdom, that is precisely what they meant.

Looking around, David saw what he thought was a familiar face in a group of young Arabs. For a second he thought it was Sebastian. But it couldn't be. Not down here at a subversive meeting like this. But the man turned so that he saw his full profile. It was Sebastian.

Ayatullah Abd al Wahhab was screaming,

"We have many enemies."

"We have enemies in the west and we have enemies here in this state."

"They have sent spies here and they are right down there among you."

"There are traitors among you."

"Catch them and kill them."

"Tear them to pieces, tear them limb from limb."

People began to look at David hostilely. He could smell their sweat, feel their tenseness, their suspicion, see the workings of their minds. If they were looking for enemies they had one right here.

Here in this place you had to carry the right mark, have the right chip embedded in your brain giving out the right signals. He was giving out the wrong signals. Everything about him declared him to be a non-Moslem, a *Nazarani*, not one of them.

Mobs coalesce into a single entity that rejects any foreign body. And he was a foreign body. Mobs are human beings reduced to their most basic, their most savage.

He was shoved from behind. Then jostled. He was a foreign body, a dangerous outsider. He was afraid to look in their eyes. Were they going to attack him? Kill him? Behead him? Hitch his body to a vehicle and drag it through the streets? Suspend it from the Old City gate?

A few feet to his right, a man went berserk, screamed, tore at his *thobe*. His eyes wild, he began lashing himself with a club.

With the crowd momentarily diverted, David decided to go for it, make a break. He shoved and butted his way until he was almost clear. But the crowd wanted to hang on to him, to swallow him up, to digest him. Spurred on by a rush of adrenaline, he worked himself loose, extricated himself from their grip.

David ran.

In the hot, cloying, sticky atmosphere he ran as fast as he had ever run, sucking searingly hot air into his lungs. Running down that narrow walkway, the shadows cut dramatically across his path, dividing it into dazzling sunshine and deep shade. On one side the facades of houses towered over him. On the other a long white mosque wall reflected the sun's intensity, bouncing back the light.

The mosque wall stretched ahead, over ten feet high and smooth. There were no turnings off. Ahead of him an old man being led by a small boy tapped the wall with his stick.

David looked behind. A gang of youths came around the corner. Were they coming after him? Of course they were. Who else? And still the words of the Ayatullah pursued him. Ayatullah Abd Al Wahhab preached death. He embodied it. He presented death as the greatest expression of self, a dark ritual but an exciting one. Death was the gateway to paradise. Death was the gateway to eternal life. It was only by dying, dying for Allah, that you could be born again.

David tried to run faster but couldn't. A rock hit him on the back. Another hit the mud wall just above him making an indent in it and flaking off pieces that fell in the dust before the stone clattered to the ground at his feet.

He sidestepped into the mosque doorway and paused there panting, his shirt sticking to his skin.

He hesitated before entering the mosque. A mosque area is sacred and as a non-believer he wasn't supposed to go in. He opened the door fearing to see the usual lines of robed men kneeling on their prayers mats, touching the ground with their foreheads.

There was nobody there but the old blind man and the boy. Both ignored him chanting in high reedy voices, one youthful, one aged, *"Bismillah-ir-Rahman-ir-Rahim. Al-Humdu-illah. Rabb-il-alamin."*

David crossed the mosque, found a door on the far side, and plunged into a labyrinth of empty alleyways.

CHAPTER 22

D avid and Deborah drove west towards the brightness and order of the New City and the apartment block where CJ was holding his party.

They drove through avenues that grew wider and wider and better cared for, all tree-lined in this arid rainless desert state, all drip fed by expensively produced water from the desalination plant. It all somehow seemed improbable and impermanent, a foreign implant in a desert that was essentially barren. One day the desert would turn hostile and reclaim the area where the New City had been built.

David had mentioned what he had seen in the *suq* earlier that day to Deborah but only briefly and sketchily. He didn't want to frighten her. She was already worried enough about her mother and Carolyn and the rumours that had begun to circulate as to what might happen to the expats if there was real trouble.

In any event he hadn't yet got his head around the possible significance of what he had seen and heard. In retrospect the whole scene in the *maidan* seemed unreal even surreal, as if it had happened on a different planet, in a place far removed. A world apart. And yet that world of militant Islam was only a few short miles away. Its ominous threat still hung around in his mind, Ayatullah Abd Al Wahhab's voice booming out and making the crowd crazy. David kept seeing the madness, the hatred in the eyes of the people as they glared at him. The whole scene, the atmosphere, the claustrophobia, the pledges of martyrdom, went round and round in his head.

In the compound of CJ's apartment block their car was taken and parked by one of the uniformed servants who populated the compound. This was CJ's pad in town, a penthouse suite in a twenty-storey block, one among several such blocks in a prime location.

NOEL SCANLON

They walked through a garden tended by teams of gardeners, among blooms of tropical plants never intended to grow in these desert climes. Water murmured from fountains, water shone a clear blue in the underwater-lit swimming pool.

Rising swiftly and smoothly and at great speed in an elevator that seemed to be jet propelled, they were met by a smiling white uniformed beturbaned Sikh major domo with a military bearing and shown into CJ's vast, sunken, lounge.

The chattering, smoking, drinking crowd in the lounge was a mixture of some of the usual crowd to be found in the Phoenix Bar with a sprinkling of others including some high-ranking government officials. There were also special dignitaries among whom David recognised Chief of Police Qassim, and Colonel Rachman. There were no reps here, none invited. This was strictly social. Arabs invited were confined to the more westernised ones, those who wore lounge suits and travelled extensively abroad.

They were greeted by Cynthia who was acting as hostess with CJ hovering in the background drinking a glass of Guinness. Cynthia looked elegant, lived elegantly. Sometimes she lived in this penthouse apartment with CJ. But her status was ambiguous. CJ was a married man with a wife back home, a family man, or so he represented himself. Cynthia just happened to be here helping him out. She disappeared every now and then for long periods, no one knew where. It was said that she was wealthy in her own right.

She moved out of the maul now to greet David and Deborah.

"David, Deborah," Cynthia said, advancing towards them, and kissing them on both cheeks. "How nice of you to come. You're so far away over on the other side of the creek. I can't imagine why anyone would want to live over there."

She beckoned and two Indian servants appeared gliding silently, silver trays in hand.

As they selected their drinks, Cynthia turned to Deborah, "We must meet for coffee one of these days. I've been meaning to get in touch but it's so hard to fit everything in. And you're such a busy working girl running that magazine. I really must get my hands on a copy sometime. But it's all such a mad social whirl out here..." She went on in this vein, cool and controlled, poised and patronising and sure of herself.

Cynthia moved on and David and Deborah, who knew most of the people there, circulated, moving from one group to another, picking up a fresh drink, selecting small eats from the silver trays laden with smoked salmon, caviar on biscuits and king prawns and pieces of lobster on sticks and an array of cheeses and dips.

The conversation was light and urbane. Though the colonies were long gone, this type of party, apart from the setting, had changed remarkably little from those David had glimpsed as a child with people attending a drinks party almost every night of the week moving on to a dinner party if they were on the A List, continuing drinking if they were on the B or C List. All these years later it had much the same basic format.

But, for whatever reason, tonight David was seeing all this from a different angle, almost as an outside observer. He had a feeling of unreality, as if everyone at this party of the elite, including himself, was acting a part rather than being themselves. He had the feeling of being in some parallel world which was exactly the same as the real world, only not quite. There was this slight sense of dislocation. He had long had the perception that deep down expats, from whatever decade, had the conviction that real life was taking place somewhere else. However lavish their present lifestyle might be, the real world was elsewhere.

David joined a group where Tommy Graham, a Scotsman and a surgeon from the Al Khalifa hospital, was holding forth. "Times they are a changing. Instead of getting the usual women stabbed or axed by their uncles or brothers to clear their family honour, the work I'm doing in the operating theatre these days is for the most part digging bullets out of young men and stitching up their wounds. I'm not allowed to express political opinions, it's in my contract, but I can't help noticing that there's an extraordinary increase in the number of young men who have taken to shooting one another. I'm saying nothing and you can draw whatever conclusion you like from that..."

Catching sight of David, he paused and turned to him. "Oh there you are. He drew him aside. "Is it OK if I call to see you after surgery tomorrow? A little bit of business."

"Of course," David said. "No problem."

"Good," Tommy said, turning back to the group, "Good."

After he had done the rounds several times, in the end David found himself with Andy Wilson and another banker. It always worked out that way at these dos. The bankers ended up together.

"How are things?"

125

"Fine."

"Did you see the closing rates? The dinar is starting to plunge. Of course, given the general state of the Middle East it's only to be expected."

David didn't comment on the state of the dinar. They, the bank that is, were doing very nicely indeed out of his forward selling orders. At last calculation they were up a few million. CJ was quite chuffed about it when he eventually told him.

Andy went on, "The market could still go the other way of course. Just as suddenly. My fellow tells me he expects it to recover. There'll be a rebound when the speculators pull out."

"There could be," David said. "But I wouldn't bank on it. I think it's politics not economics that's driving the currency market. By the way, I stumbled on what looked like a political gathering this afternoon. There was a lot of shouting and screaming. All the usual rhetoric. But more so if you know what I mean. It was really quite scary. I felt trapped. I thought for a while I wasn't going to make it out of there."

"Good God, I don't know why you go to these places. I wouldn't be found dead in them. But then you speak the lingo. Never learned more than a few words myself. Can't stand the sound of it. The bank threatened several times to send me on a course but I always managed to get out of it. I've no intention of learning how to write backwards. At least in Singapore they can't tell me to learn Arabic.

"No. But they might ask you to learn Chinese. And from what I hear that's even tougher."

"Maybe. But at least in Singapore we won't have people like these bloody Arabs who are liable to martyr themselves at any time. Fucking lunatics with their suicide bombs. I can't even begin to imagine what goes on in the minds of people like that."

"At least you're getting out. Everything fixed up?"

"Absolutely. Got our Exit Visas today. All packed and ready to go."

Deborah was chatting to Margaret, Andy's wife. Margaret was talking about her new posting. "I'm really looking forward to it. From what I hear the bank house is really superb. And the bank is giving us a good allowance for refurbishing, and I intend to go to town, new curtains, new decor, the lot. Andy reckons the take-over will take the best part of a month, it's a big office out there and he'll be in charge, quite a step up for him. I've been in contact with the couple we'll be taking over from and they seem really nice. They'll show us the ropes; throw a few parties to introduce us, that sort of thing. And at least you can be sure of some decent servants. Have you got rid of that fellow of yours yet?"

"Abdul? No, not yet," Deborah said. "Did I tell you my mother and Carolyn are going back home."

"I'm glad to hear it. This is no place for children. Of any age."

They drifted apart. Deborah had a word with various expat acquaintances, people she didn't know well but she recognised them as they recognised her, they were all in it together out here, a long way from home. They sought each other's company. They were all pleasant and urbane. They were skilled in social intercourse; they had plenty of practice being invited out most nights.

But tonight Deborah sensed that something was different, something had changed. She had the feeling that, despite all the conviviality, everyone was on edge. They certainly seemed to be drinking more than usual. The liquor was disappearing off the silver trays with great rapidity.

Cynthia moved about among them, an accomplished hostess with a quick word for each group. People tended to drift towards others of their own kind. Bankers talked to bankers or embassy people. The Arabs kept mostly to themselves with their glasses of plain water laced with gin. CJ was chatting to Chief of Police Qassim who was beaming genially. It was hard to believe that this man, ostentatiously sipping his orange juice, was really responsible for the disappearance of so many people as well as for torture and unknown atrocities.

Deborah drifted out on to the enclosed balcony, and looked down. Far below, the heat throbbed, the traffic whispered past and out there on the other side of the creek, *suqs* were blasted by noise and churned with emotion. But here they were far above all that. The apartment was cooled by a powerful stream of air-conditioning making the temperature in this hot Middle Eastern state pleasantly cool. Here one was protected from the world outside. A triple glass wall kept out the heat. Kept out the flies. Kept out the smells. Kept out the outside world, none of whose nastiness could intrude here. Or could it?

From this great height she looked out on the dark sea of the Arabian Gulf to the east, the open desert to the west, and upwards towards myriads of stars, so many of them in the clear middle eastern sky.

Deborah became aware of someone standing beside her.

She turned and saw Zayid Sharif standing there. Behind him, turbaned servants lurked like shadows in the doorway ready to do his bidding.

Zayid Sharif owned the magazine she edited. And the office block in which it was located. Also numerous other properties. He was the local partner in a whole plethora of multinational companies. He was one of the leading merchants in Khor Fahal. He had risen from comparative poverty to become a multi millionaire.

"Our editor, I believe," he said advancing towards her. "I have heard of your good work on the magazine. I have been meaning to call. But my time is all taken up I'm afraid. Still, I hope in the future to take more interest in *Al Jameela*."

Zayid Sharif was dressed in a silk lounge suit. He wasn't good looking but he wasn't bad looking either. He had the self confidence of a man who always got what he wanted. He was obviously westernised in a much as he had come to the party and he hadn't dressed in Arab dress. Also he was actually addressing a woman in public, something no strict orthodox Moslem would have done.

"I see you are looking out at our wonderful city. Unfortunately I have to spend much of my time abroad but when I come back I am most happy."

He came and stood close beside her. She didn't know why but he made her feel uncomfortable.

Zayid Sharif took out a gold cigarette case and lit a Russian cigarette. As he exhaled he said. "I have been thinking about our little magazine. I have plans for it. I would like you to come to a meeting at my villa to discuss policy. Tomorrow night. Ten pm."

Then he was gone, the waiters, or were they bodyguards, following him.

Deborah, looking in at the party humming along, felt cold. She had no doubt at all that if she went to Zayid Sharif's villa she would be the only guest there. She had seen his villa in passing; David had pointed it out to her. It was lavish as only an oil rich state could make it. Lavish and ostentatious with its colonnades and extensive grounds. There had been henchmen on duty at the gate and in the grounds. She couldn't possibly go. But what excuse could she make? This was Arabia where the male reigned supreme. And a man like Zayid Sharif, a merchant prince, had a degree of power undreamed of back home. He could do what he liked and neither law nor state would touch him. She'd have to tip toe her way around this one.

From inside now came the sound of a commotion. Not the commotion of a party but something else.

Deborah went back in to see what was going on. There were a number of armed police in the room.

Colonel Rachman was saying, "Quiet please. We have a bomb alert."

There was a moment of shock as danger, real live danger, reached in to touch and chill them. In their darkest moments they had thought of the possibility of drive-by shootings, of attacks in the malls, of lone hooded gunmen shooting expats in their offices, of vehicles loaded with explosives being driven into expat compounds. But not of a bomb at a party.

"I want all of you to leave this building. Now. As quickly as you can. In an orderly manner. And by the stairs."

"Under no circumstances are you to use or even approach the elevators."

NOEL SCANLON

CHAPTER 23

David and CJ sat in a corner of the Phoenix Hotel bar. The guests from CJ's party had all dispersed. Deborah had gone home with Andy and Margaret who had offered her a lift. Cynthia had gone on to a late dinner engagement, or said that was where she was going. CJ and David had come to the Phoenix Hotel bar.

The way CJ told it, the police had received a tip-off on the basis of which they had evacuated the whole apartment block. The special bomb disposal unit had located a bomb with a timing mechanism ticking away hidden in the stairwell outside CJ's apartment.

"The bastards!" CJ exclaimed, "trying to blow us all up! The funny thing is that, just before the warning, Qassim was telling me that they were on high terror alert on the basis of intelligence coming in that a terrorist act was going to be carried out somewhere in the New City. Apparently they'd been picking up chatter for days. Though nothing specific. Nothing they could exactly pin down.

"I'll tell you one thing though, Qassim is dead keen to get whoever was responsible and God help any poor bastard he picks up. Sleep deprivation, freezing, burning, hooding, immersion until suffocation, white light, constant sound. You name it and the Khor Fahal police are into it." The prospect of what might happen to the bombers if caught gave CJ evident satisfaction.

David told CJ about what he had seen and heard in the *maidan* and about Ayatullah Abd Al Wahhab and how weird an effect he had created and how he had incited the crowd.

"Probably inciting them to place that bomb outside my apartment," CJ said.

"I'm sure the bomb wasn't intended for you," David said. "What seems most likely to me is that the bomb was intended for Qassim. It would have been known he'd be there. Lots of people have scores to settle with him, lots of people would like to see him out of the way."

"I don't know," CJ said doubtfully.

"Come on," David said. "It wasn't intended for either you or the bank. Qassim was far and away the most likely target. And your party gave them the opportunity. "

"Maybe. But, if that bomb had gone off, we'd all have gone with it. I'll tell you one thing. I'll never spend another night in that apartment again. And I'll never invite Qassem to a party again either."

CJ paused reflectively, sipping his pint.

"Looking back on it you can see that it all started with that fecking mullah. The one you saw in the black bag being eaten by sharks. When I heard about that I said to myself, 'Something's starting here.' It's a pity you ever found him."

David had a flash of the body of the mullah writhing eerily underwater. "I wish I hadn't. But my seeing him didn't kill him. My seeing him had no effect on anything." He was going to add that if the police themselves hadn't killed the mullah, as everyone now assumed they had, there would most likely have been no bomb or any other trouble for that matter. But he thought better of it and said instead, "Tell me, that time I found the body, did the police really consider framing me?"

"More than likely. It was certainly an option. You were there. On the spot. You found the body. And nailing you would have given them an out. It's been done here before."

"So why didn't they?"

"Who knows?"

David reckoned that CJ was holding something back. CJ always held something back. He was one cute bastard.

CJ said now, "I'm not so sure you're right in thinking the bomb was intended for Qassim. It might have been. But then again the banks are an obvious target for terrorism. And having such good relations with the Ruling Family, holding so many of their accounts, puts us right there in the cross hairs.

"And there's something else. If the Shi'ites are serious about making trouble, they will need funds. And how do they move funds? Through banks. That makes banks a good place for tracing terrorists. Qassim has worked that one out and he's asked me personally to check see if there have been any big movement of funds that might be for the purposes of buying arms. I'd like you to look into it first thing in the morning. But do it on the quiet. You can't trust anyone in there. You don't know who they're working for. You can bet your life that those terrorist fanatics have a man in place in the bank. You can bet your life on that."

David remembered the going over his office had had. Who had been behind that? And what had they been after? He almost told CJ about it but held back.

As they chatted, CJ went on drinking steadily. He had been drinking steadily, Guinness and chasers, for hours. He seemed to have an enormous capacity for it. The combination of the bomb scare and the liquor he had consumed had made him mellow, put him into a sentimental and communicative mood.

"What I'm going to tell you now, I'm telling you in strict confidence. After all this has died down, I intend to get out. I'm not going to be rushed or dictated to by the bastards who did the bomb, but I'm getting out shortly anyway. I've been thinking about it for years and I took the decision last time I was back home. I promised Mary I'd retire. Apart from anything else, my doctor tells me my blood pressure is up, my cholesterol is up and my liver isn't great. He puts it all down to stress. It all comes from working too hard in this atrocious climate and taking all the responsibility I have to take."

What CJ was telling him didn't surprise David. Many, indeed most expats, thought and talked endlessly about getting out, going back home, making elaborate plans for their retirement, but, according as their salaries and prosperity increased, they kept postponing retirement from year to year. They were held by their increasing salaries and perks. Maybe they'd stay on for just one more year to have enough to pay off the mortgage. Or trade up. Or pay for that villa in Spain. Or, as in the case of CJ, make another few million. They were all, however much they complained, held by golden handcuffs.

CJ was saying, "I've been thinking about it for years and that incident just now doesn't encourage me to postpone it much longer. Christ, if the police hadn't got there in time, we'd all have been blown to smithereens with people gathering up the bits and pieces like those Jewish volunteers do in Jerusalem. It's not my idea of how I want to go. Anyway, I've always intended to spend my retirement back in the old sod, well away from this fecking heat and the mad bastards that seem to be around these days. It's not like it used to be in the old days. The type of Arab around nowadays has changed. They've got nasty. The present lot aren't a bit like the old Arabs used to be. They were men of dignity, men of their word. Christ, when I came out here first we used to do business, substantial business deals, purely by word of mouth, not a document signed. And I was never let down. None of them ever reneged on a deal, not one of them. This place was so safe that you could leave the door of your house wide open and you'd never be robbed. Your house was safer here than back home. You know that from when you were out here yourself as a kid with your dad...."

David knew what he meant.

As a child in the Bank House in Mukulla in the Hadhramut his family had never had to lock a door. It was about as peaceful as you could get, even though the Bedouin tribes who regularly came to Mukulla, an old Arab town with a town gate, were invariably armed, small men, hardened by their desert nomadic lifestyle, wearing loin cloths and carrying daggers. But they weren't perceived as a threat of any sort. Far from it.

"Yes, I know what you mean," David said agreeing with CJ.

"Well those days are well gone. They're gone a long time ago. Look what the feckers did to your father. Which shows there were some bad eggs even back then. When I offered you the job I thought you'd more than likely turn it down given what happened.

"I've had a good run of it," CJ went on. "I'm not pulling out right away, but the time isn't far off, that's why I brought you out. To be my successor. I'll be happy to go. I've had a good run of it here. I've even managed to put a few bob in the bank."

You can say that again, David thought. Not to speak of his property in Ireland or his string of thoroughbred horses that Mary looked after.

"I've made a few bob. Enough to get by. But I've worked hard for it. And I've never really got used to this climate. I've always looked forward to going back to the lovely moist mists of the west of Ireland ...."

CJ had had enough drink by now to begin to grow really maudlin.

"I have a little place outside Westport.....

The little place, David knew, was an estate of several hundred acres, with a substantial house that had once been the manor house.

"... I have a nice little place. And do you know what I miss more than anything out here? A night out in the pub. There's a local nearby that serves the best pint of Guinness in Ireland and you sit there by the fire sipping it at your ease and what could be better than that. It's not one of those new style pubs, those great barns of places they have in Dublin. This pub has never modernised, it's the genuine article. And it has traditional music once a week; it gets some of the best musicians in the country. Fiddle players come from all over to play sessions there. Great craic. Best fecking little pub in the world....."

CJ was in full flow now and pretty well unstoppable. "There's a beach near our place. And there's nothing finer than putting on a pair of boots, taking the dogs - Mary loves dogs you know - and walking there right beside the Atlantic with that lovely misty rain in your face and those waves, green and white and black and the smell of seaweed and the odd seal popping up to take a look at you. That's living. Instead of being baked to death in this fecking oven they call the Middle East. No wonder the people out here are so crazy. They've all had their fecking brains burnt out of them...."

David couldn't help reflecting that, if this was how he truly felt, why was he here and not there. If he had wanted to be an Irish landowner in the West there was nothing stopping him. Instead of being a multi-millionaire out here with his luxurious office suite, his city apartment and his villa out among the ranch-style bungalows, the pretentious neo-Georgian mansions with colonnades and pools and walled gardens, out there among the dwellings of the ultra rich and the sheikhly families.

David doubted that CJ had any real intention of retiring. It was more than likely just the drink talking. He was finding it hard to reconcile this present manifestation of CJ with the hard-nosed businessman he had to deal with everyday. Maybe his brain had been affected by the bomb scare. Or maybe he was being genuine to a part of himself that was normally repressed. Maybe this was a dream he had always had but was afraid to put to the test, aware in the back of his mind, that like all dreams, it would evaporate when you tried to make it a reality.

David wondered how Mary, who had got used to running the estate over the years and who had established a quite well know stables, would appreciate CJ's return. Did Mary know about Cynthia or all the others Cynthias there had no doubt been?

David had been subjected to this type of sentimental talk before on nights out with CJ when he had said much the same things as tonight and a lot more. The general pattern, when he got drunk, was that he'd be all over you but sober and as sharp as a button the next morning without any apparent recollection of a word he had said the night before. In David's judgement, CJ was too fond of the power he exerted and the money he was making to give it all up just like that. Despite his protestations he'd likely still be here till he dropped.

CJ ordered up another pint apiece. "I've never told you this before but another reason I gave you the job was because of the raw deal your father had. Have they ever told you anything about what happened to him?"

"Only what was in the papers."

David had made some enquiries about his father since he had got here. He had called at the police station to find out if there is anything new only to be told that the file was closed. He had got absolutely nowhere.

"I know you've been making enquires....." CJ said.

So the police leaked. As he might have expected.

".....So I thought I'd look into it myself on your behalf. And the word from the top is that the file is technically still open but there have been no leads or developments in years.

"The police take on it is that your father's bank the Eastern offered a reward but no one ever came forward. Their information is that there were two groups involved in the kidnapping. One group would have taken the ransom money but another more fundamentalist group, the SPA, wouldn't. There was a row between them. Your father was shot when fighting broke out between these two factions. That's the police's best take on it."

CJ put his hand on David's shoulder. "That's as near as you'll ever get to the truth. Do you mind if I ask you something?"

"Go ahead."

"How do you stand the sight of them, how can you walk down the *suq* after what they did to your father?"

"I don't know. Because it wasn't the people in the *suq* who did it, I suppose."

David had never really analysed his feelings in this regard. But it came to him now that what had happened to his father actually gave him a link to the place. It gave him a connection. A permanent connection. When he walked the *suqs*, he was walking where his father had walked.

"Do you forgive them?"

"I don't know. Not really."

CJ looked at the waiter bringing two more pints, "I don't believe in forgiveness. I'm a good Catholic but that's one tenet of the faith I don't believe in. I go for the ancient law. An eye for an eye."

CJ took a long draught of his new pint.

"After that bomb scare and what you've seen yourself in the *suq*, I'd like you out of your present apartment as soon as possible. I'll close the deal on that villa and you can move into it right away.

"The sooner you and Deborah get out of that kip you're living in on the other side of the creek the better. It's getting too dangerous over there."

NOEL SCANLON

CHAPTER 24

From the beginning the boy enjoyed the security behind the high mud walls of the Monastery. He enjoyed the good regular food. Compared to conditions in the shanty town and the precarious hand to mouth existence he had always led, he was on easy street.

In here he was out of danger. He didn't have constantly to listen for the sounds of a police raid. And the marks from his last beating were quickly healing.

He was accepted in here. He sat with the other boys and recited from the Koran and listened to the teacher whom he learnt was also a warrior who had fought in Afghanistan and Iraq. He had taught in *madrasis* in various countries. He had taught and inducted large numbers of willing Moslems. The boy scarcely noticed that he was being watched and groomed, his thoughts, his movements, his beliefs monitored.

At first nothing was expected of the boy other than to listen to what the *madrasi* taught, which was an absolutely literal interpretation of the Koran and Moslem law that did not allow any shades of meaning or alternative interpretations.

Allah had written or rather dictated the Koran and what he said he meant. If you wanted to know what God's law was you studied the Koran and did precisely as it instructed. Everything for the disposition of life had been recorded there for all time including all present human inventions and those to come.

But the Moslem faith, the teacher explained, required a great deal more than that. The Moslem faith demanded certain things from its adherents. In fact it demanded rather a lot. It demanded total dedication. It demanded a clean pure soul. It demanded that true believers be prepared to sacrifice everything including their own life if called upon to do so. If called to *Jihad*.

The boy was not surprised when it became clear that something might be required of him in return for the comfortable life he was living. No one had ever paid such attention to him before and he was flattered.

Over time the boy got to explore the Monastery, its decrepit buildings and the surrounding area that was much larger than it appeared from the outside. He wandered about, up and down long dark passageways that seemed to go on and on. He was never sure what he might encounter at the end of any passageway. And there was something very strange here. Each time he explored it, the building seemed to have changed. This was one of the many aspects of the Monastery that he couldn't begin to understand. But he accepted it as part of something that was magical and beyond his comprehension.

At the same time, the teaching in the *madrasi* had moved on. The warrior teacher, or *taliban*, who at times recounted his exploits while fighting with the *Mujahadeen*, taught that the survival of all Moslems was being threatened by the Christian crusade. He and the other *Mujahadeen* had made great sacrifices to defend their faith, to ensure their place in paradise and the eventual defeat of the hated crusaders who threatened their survival.

Men of his generation had made great sacrifices and now they called on the younger generation to play their part, to study, to volunteer to go on to the training camps, and for those who were worthy, to become martyrs.

The teacher explained what it was like to be a martyr, to be a suicide bomber. There were other paths to be followed but this path was the highest and most worthy. And, for those who volunteered, it had the greatest rewards.

To become a martyr you had to be a very special person. You had to want to be with God. You didn't want any more of this life with all its suffering. You wanted to be happy in God's presence.

People asked what would it be like after you pressed that button on the pack that would be given to you to set off the explosives.

The first thing to understand was that there would be no pain. The teacher emphasised that, no pain at all. Your body would be blown into small pieces but there would be no pain. Because, instantly, in the same second you pressed the button, you would enter Paradise.

Imagine the glory of it. The bright shining light. A clean sunny place very different from the shanty towns and alleyways of this place. No more troubles. No more worries. No more harassment. No more suffering. Just perfect peace and pleasure.

The boy listened and, though he wasn't aware of it, he was being indoctrinated, his mind was changing. Thoughts he had never had before when he had to spend all his time foraging for food, begging or stealing with no thought for anything else, began to enter his mind. The voice of the teacher probed his brain. He began to see the world differently. He began to feel, for the first time in his life, imbued with a sense of purpose.

Then, one day, the chief teacher of the *madrasi* took him aside and told him that he and a few selected others would be brought to meet the Ayatullah himself.

Ayatullah Abd Al Wahhab was not always in the Monastery. He came and went. He never stayed in any one place for long for security reasons and, when he was in residence, he was heavily guarded by a squad of men with rifles and machine guns and rocket launchers.

When the students were escorted into this area, the Ayatullah was sitting on the floor with his back to the wall at the far end of a room which was lit only by oil lamps so that only a faint light flickered on his face which was largely in darkness.

From the moment he entered the room, the boy knew that the Ayatullah was watching him closely. He experienced the full force of the power coming from this man who sat perfectly still. Later he learnt that all the others had the same experience.

Strong men who came into the presence of the Ayatullah found themselves unable to retain control of their minds. They lost the power of speech. The Ayatullah infused them with his spirit, took over their minds.

It was primarily the eyes that caught the boy's attention, that mesmerized him. The eyes, when the boy looked into them, were black deep sunken eyes that glowed with some eerie light. He felt himself drowning in them.

At first he tried to avoid looking. But he couldn't resist. He wasn't strong enough. He had to look. And, when he did, he was sucked in and lost himself in there.

He had heard other boys whisper that once you looked into the eyes of the Ayatullah, who after all was an reincarnation of the Mahdi and knew all the secrets of the after life having died and come to life again, when you looked into those eyes, you felt your mind, your whole being, begin to alter, to be reshaped, to be born again.

And so it was with him. From then on he was no longer in control of his own mind. The Ayatullah sat in there in a corner of his mind directing him, instructing him, guiding him. And the teacher began telling him he saw something special in him, that he saw a great and glorious future ahead of him.

The boy was made to feel not only wanted and appreciated but important.

And, as time progressed, his mind became more and more fixated on that glorious future, a future that held out the certainty of eternal life, a life that went on forever and ever in more fabulous comfort than that which he enjoyed at present in the Monastery.

The boy paid more and more attention to what the *taliban* preached and waited for the glorious day when he would fulfil his destiny, when he would be martyred and all those promises would be fully realised as he entered through the gates of Paradise.

CHAPTER 25

Davis sat in a small outdoor cafe on the waterfront of the old neglected and little used harbour in the Old City, a harbour that had been superseded by the huge new modern harbour in the New City. The cafe he sat at was a fisherman's cafe with a battered old refrigerator, bare wooden tables and benches.

He had had a message conveyed to him in a distinctly roundabout way asking him to meet Sebastian here. There was something decidedly mysterious about Sebastian's behaviour. He was in hiding and yet, despite this, David had seen him in a cafe opposite Bahwan's and even more surprisingly at the meeting in the *maidan*. Odd. Definitely odd. And hardly the actions of a man who was lying low. He had rung Rosemary at the Embassy and she had surprised him by confirming Sebastian's story both regarding the import-export agency and the car accident. But she refused to elaborate in any way whatever even though he had pressed her.

David was both intrigued and worried about his friend. As a boy they had shared numerous adventures in what were pretty exotic locations. Sebastian had been a little on the wild side. As a child, he had lived in a world of fantasy and David had the impression from what he had heard of his various schemes since that he still did.

David was concerned about him. He was living in an impoverished and highly volatile Shi'ite ghetto. Surely he could find a better place to stay even if he had to avoid the attentions of the police.

After CJ's revelations about the death of his father, David had hoped to lay to rest, to kill off, the horrific imaginings that had been embedded in his brain for so long, imaginings surrounding that awful event which in a way he had come to Khor Fahal to confront. He had been disappointed last night when he'd had yet another of these nightmares that had plagued him ever since his father's disappearance in this state. As usual in his nightmare a warder led him along dark shadowy corridors. He could hear screams coming from the cells all around and he walked and walked for what seemed like miles until the warder threw open a door and there inside was a man, bowed and emaciated. He could never see this form clearly. Always the form began to turn towards him, but, just before he could see his face David, in his dream, turned and ran and ran back down those echoing corridors pursued by unbearable screams, the screams of his tortured father.

He had woken up sweating. He had to stop these nightmares. Now that he knew how his father had died, that he had been shot in crossfire, he had no need to speculate in his dreams. CJ had told him as certainly as could ever be known how his father had died and he accepted that was as near the truth as he'd ever get. He had sat up in bed telling himself that if he concentrated on the facts, if he kept reminding himself that he had reached closure, that would be the end of his obsession.

While he waited for Sebastian now, David sipped his glass of sugary tea and looked out to sea.

The old harbour hadn't changed much since the days when the British had sailed past on their way to India and the Honourable East India Trading Company. At that time there was a proliferation of harbours like this surrounded by small settlements built all along what was then known as the Pirate Coast. Mostly the harbours were hidden in lagoons, protected by sand bars that made them difficult of access with few and narrow approach channels. In front of them lay coral reefs and behind them a great desert inhabited by bands of wandering nomadic tribes of Bedouin.

The harbour today was much as it had been in the days of the pirates. It was used only by small craft which for the most part were similar to those that had been used for centuries. Dugouts scurried to and fro. Heavily laden *dhows* and *bellums* were off-loading sacks of rice. Men ran up and down the gangplanks bent under their loads.

There was the heavy smell of fish being landed from small fishing vessels, a smell that brought David back to his childhood when he would escape from the supervision of his ayah, his mother being out as she was most mornings taking coffee in one or other of the European houses or playing *Mah Jongg*. David would come to this harbour, then much busier than it was now, and he would sit and dream and watch the dhows and the teeming life of the waterfront just as he was watching it now.

It was somewhere near here that, as a child, he had watched the new bank safe being off-loaded. He had followed it in the bank's Land Rover, the driver driving with his hand on the horn watching the pedestrians, the veiled women with lucerne balanced on their heads, the donkey carts, the camels with their mincing gait, all making way for the bank car.

No sooner had the bank, the first ever in the area, opened for business than a crowd of women dressed in white for the *Haj* who had been squatting outside waiting for the door to open were herded in, filling the bank with a heavy odour. They were lined up to make their thumb print and collect the money that had been remitted here for the completion of the rest of their journey.

David, absorbed in his memories and the waterfront scene, took no notice of the man wearing a *thobe* and *kheffiah* who sat down at an adjoining table and ordered a glass of tea in guttural Arabic.

He was startled when the man came over, sat beside him, and Sebastian said, "I hope you're not going to go on ignoring me. I can see you're away in another world. Dreaming about the past?"

"Something like that," David said. "You might have let me know you'd be in Arab dress."

"I find it better not to make myself conspicuous."

"So I see."

"I thought the waterfront might bring back memories. It's the only place that has hardly changed at all. Since we were here as children that is. It's wildly nostalgic don't you think?"

"Absolutely."

"The old fort is still here too of course. Do you remember the time we sneaked in there and tried to get a look at the prisoners in those awful holes in the ground where the old Sheikh used drop his enemies and let them cool off for a decade or so. And we did get in too. Until we were thrown out."

David remembered the incident well.

They had both been told never to go near the dreaded Fort Jalali where the Ruler's prisoners were held, members of other tribes with whom he was feuding. Naturally this was the place where Sebastian just had to get to see. So, one day when he and Sebastian were wandering along the shoreline among the fiddler crabs, they left the beach and climbed up the rocks to the old Portuguese fort.

The fort was surrounded by massive walls but, after hiding for ages, they managed to slip in when the gate was opened to allow a lorry in. They made for where they knew the prisoners were incarcerated and remained hidden until a warder came along, pulled back a wooden construction that covered a huge hole in the ground and began to climb down a wooden ladder.

They waited a moment then crept forward and found themselves looking into a deep pit, the warder's lantern a glimmer going down and down into darkness.

When their eyes got used to the darkness after the intense brightness outside, they could just make out, huddled down there in the blackness, shackled to the wall, thin desperate looking creatures who never saw light except when the covering was pulled back like this and food brought down to them. They had been tried and condemned in a Sharia court and they were confined in that hole in the ground at the Ruler's pleasure.

While they were looking into that deep pit with their eyes agog another guard came up behind them, caught them and handed them over to the British officer in charge who had them escorted home to their parents.

Not long after that incident, they were both sent home to boarding school, their parents having decided they were getting too old to be left wandering around Khor Fahal and needed some discipline. But, at the time, what David had seen down that dark hole had impressed itself deeply in his mind. What terrible things had those wretched prisoners done? How long would they be left down that hole in the ground? For months, years? Could you live down a hole for years? Were they beaten? Were their hands chopped off? He never did get to see those prisoners again and not seeing them except as vague shadowy figures allowed his image of them to grow and grow in his mind and it was no doubt these images that had fed his nightmares about his dead and disappeared father.

Just days before he was sent back home to school, he met the officer in charge of Fort Jalali. He was helping to hand around small eats at one of those cocktail parties where his mother wore her long dress and the men wore cummerbunds and white shirts and bow ties and drank a lot of whisky and talked in loud voices. The man he was offering small eats to was talking in a booming voice about Jalali and something the man said made him realise that he was the man in charge of the Fort. And he found it exciting and macabre to think that, less than a mile away, this officer was in charge of all the men who were shackled in that hole in the ground so close to Bank House.

"Do you remember the man who threw us out eventually?" David asked Sebastian now.

"I do indeed. Major Grimes. He ended up in the Hadhrami Bedouin Legion and was shot in the head by a legionnaire when asleep in his tent while out on patrol around the wells where the camels were watered. Jalali is still there though. But the atmosphere is quite gone. No prisoners, no shackles, no guards."

"What are you doing out here, Sebastian?"

"Running my company. This time I really do expect to make my fortune. I have already secured some good business. Once this accident nonsense is over I'll soon be on my feet."

"When I couldn't contact you I called around to your office. There didn't seem to be a lot going on there that would make your fortune."

"Ah, I see. You've been checking up on me."

They sat at the rickety table with their glasses of sugary tea while in the hot steamy air a dhow pulled in and its fenders scraped and slapped against the side of the wharf with the rise and fall of the water, a creaky boat with a thunder box in the stern, a boat of ancient structure, out of date, out of time.

Sebastian sipped his tea and stared out at the wharf.

"Did you know this is where the gold smugglers still leave from? It's the last bit of romance left. Smuggling dhows still go out like they always did. Three or four at a time. Only one carries the gold. The others are to confuse the Indian customs launches."

"I know," David said. "They buy their gold bars from me."

There was a loud meowing and they both looked down to the strip of beach by the pier. The meowing came from a horde of hungry cats foraging among the flotsam and jetsam along the littoral. David's mother used to feed, or have the servants feed, stray cats. She used say they kept the rat population down. One of the cats he and Sebastian were watching was a ginger tom and David wondered if it could possibly be a descendant of the ginger tom cat they had left behind all those years ago.

"Sebastian, what are you really doing here?"

Sebastian considered before replying, "I shouldn't really be telling you this but believe it or not I'm employed by a British Intelligence Agency. I've been with them for a long time now. I had failed at all my enterprises until they took me on and saw something in me no one else had. Having knowledge of Arabia and Arabic was a great point in my favour. I am fluent as you know. And I know a few dialects. You'd be amazed how few fluent Arabists with knowledge of the terrain are available for recruitment.

After all these years I'm considered something of an expert on the Arabs and the Middle East. I lecture on the subject back home. Within the organisation of course. Not in public...."

As Sebastian talked, David watched a high wave sweep inshore and as it washed up against the pier, he could see garfish caught in it as if in a tableau, thousands and thousand of garfish.

"I'm sorry about the cover story," Sebastian said. "But it was necessary. There's a lot at stake here right now."

David was surprised by what Sebastian had just revealed but not entirely so. At the back of his mind he had suspected something like this. And he knew immediately that Sebastian was speaking the truth. It all fitted together, the way he had behaved, the difficulty in contacting him, the various unlikely places he had sighted him. It all made sense. Sebastian wasn't making this up. This was deadly serious. He was an agent for MI6.

"The life suits me," Sebastian was saying. "I have to move around a lot but then I always did. The work gives me a niche in life."

"Not a very comfortable niche," David said, thinking of the location of the apartment he lived in, the dangerous looking youths hanging around, the way people looked at you with hostility in that area. "I'd sooner you than me."

"I fit in here," Sebastian said. "I merge into the place."

"Why do you do it? It has to be a dangerous occupation."

"I don't know. I'm not particularly patriotic. And I'm certainly not particularly brave."

In David's book he was extremely brave, but he said nothing.

A few fishermen carrying a kingfish came to a nearby table. They ordered kebabs and chapattis. Though they were out of earshot, Sebastian lowered his voice.

"There's one or too small things I'd be obliged if you would check out for me. Things are hotting up. There are a number of cells I am keeping my eye on. The leaders have in the last few days taken to moving around all the time, sleeping in a different location every night. Like Saddam Hussein used to do. There's one small favour you could do me. You know Safwan Hisham?"

"Who's he?"

"He's the husband of your wife's friend Eileen. He's one of the prominent Shi'ite leaders. Any information on his movements would be useful."

David didn't fancy the idea of asking Deborah to spy for MI6, but said nothing.

Sebastian got up. "Well, I'll have to be getting along. I've a lot on my plate. Before I go, may I offer a word of warning. Be careful how you go. You have decidedly shady characters on your staff. And we have information that all the banks are being watched. We don't know exactly how things will develop. But shall we say it'd be best to keep a keen eye out."

Then he was gone, swallowed up by the people on the quayside, just another Arab *thobe* and *kheffiah*.

And David was left staring at the dhows off-loading. The chapattis had come to the table nearby and the men were munching them hungrily. David could almost taste the charcoal taste they had from the open fire kept up despite the terrible heat.

CHAPTER 26

As Deborah drove to office next morning, the increased security and police patrols reminded her of how the bomb scare at CJ's apartment block had shaken everybody. Up until now, there had been rumours, speculation, reported incidents that couldn't be verified and all well away in the depths of the Old City. But the bomb in CJ's apartment block brought terrorism right up close. Right in your face. The bomb had been of sufficient strength that it would not only have blown them to pieces but would have demolished a fair part of the block had it gone off.

On the phone to the oil camp compound last night, her friend Sally had told her there was something approaching panic out there. Orders had gone out that no one was to leave the compound unless on urgent business. The oil company employees had little contact with the Arab world at the best of times. Now none of them was leaving the compound at all. They were holed up and self-sufficient. Security had been stepped up, with more watchtowers, more armed guards, and more surveillance cameras than ever.

When Deborah got to the office it was buzzing with excitement.

Aisha wasn't in and the mail was thrown on her desk unopened. She had hardly sat down when one of the girls came rushing in, her eyes bright with excitement

"The Sheikha is in," she said breathlessly. "When we came in this morning she was already here."

Deborah was taken aback. The Sheikha hadn't come in for so long that her sudden appearance like this was a bit of a shock.

A little later the same girl was back. "The Sheikha wants to see you right away."

Deborah sat in Sheikha Sharifa's office waiting for her to take note of her presence. Ignoring people was a trick the Sheikha had evidently learned from the males of her race. Perhaps it was genetically inherited.

Deborah had never been inside the locked doors of the Sheikha's sanctum before and looked about her curiously. Unlike the rest of the floor, it was large and luxurious and well equipped, although it seemed most unlikely that the Sheikha had any idea how to operate all the state of the art technical paraphernalia on her jumbo size desk.

An old woman, obviously a servant, sat on the floor just inside the door, ready to do her mistress's bidding. A private secretary sat at a small desk in a corner, her head down, working. That, with her driver lounging around outside in the corridor, seemed to comprise the Sheikha's entourage.

Deborah wondered why the Sheikha had suddenly appeared. What did her presence in the office now portend?

The Sheikha was wearing a dark grey ankle length dress. She wore no make up. Her expression was severe. Her black *abbaya* lay on the chair beside her reminding Deborah that the Sheikha was a strict ultra orthodox Sunni Moslem.

Without any of the usual Arab preliminaries, she got down to brass tacks straight away. "Up until now," Sheikha Sharifa said in a distinctly imperious voice, "I have been neglecting my duties as editor-in-chief." She paused. "However, I am now about to assume them in full."

Wasn't it odd, Deborah thought, that in a country where the women were abused and virtually locked up, that, at the same time, it could produce a strong domineering matriarch like the Sheikha? And this woman had power. Her power derived from her being a cousin of the Ruler.

"A national magazine is a most important forum and it is essential that it should present Arab society in the correct light and guide it along the correct path."

The Sheikha went on, "There have been complaints about many of the articles you have run in *Al Jameela*. They have offended the dignity of the Arab woman."

"I haven't had any complaints," Deborah protested. "On the contrary I have had lots of women write in to say how delighted they are with the magazine."

"That is not my information. The magazine is becoming radical and subversive, aimed to destroy the roots of our Arab society."

"Nonsense," Deborah said and she could see from her reaction that the

Sheikha wasn't accustomed to being addressed like this. "We are only a woman's magazine. We haven't the power to change Arab society. And, anyway, all the new material I have introduced has been on matters of concern to women not only in Khor Fahal but worldwide."

"I'm not concerned with women worldwide. I'm concerned with this state. I want a different approach. His Highness has graciously consented to contribute a message through *Al Jameela* to the women of Khor Fahal who need guidance and reassurance of His Highness's continued concern for their welfare."

You could hardly get more pretentious than that. Still Deborah had a fair idea where all this was headed.

The Sheikha put on a pair of steel rimmed spectacles. "I've been looking at your layout for the next issue,"

How had she got that? Who had photocopied it and brought it to her?

The Sheikha was saying, "I want it scrapped and rewritten."

"Why?"

"Because it's subversive."

"Subversive of what? Everything in it is well researched and any views expressed are moderate by any normal standards. And anything we quote are the considered views of well known, well recognised, international bodies."

"I won't tolerate international bodies interfering in this state. I want your layout scrapped and rewritten. Even the cover gives the wrong impression. It's disgusting. It's licentious."

"That's ridiculous," Deborah said thinking it would be a laugh if she did run a licentious cover and briefly imagined the reaction from all those fanatical *Muttawa* and the like if she did.

The Sheikha went on, "I have myself chosen a suitable substitute."

The Sheikha handed Deborah a photograph of Sheikh Suleiman bin Himyar al Yas, the Ruler, be-robed, hawked nosed, intolerant, autocratic and regal. It was the same photograph as was already plastered up everywhere, on every street, in every office, every shop and most homes.

"I'm going to reclaim *Al Jameela* for the Arab women. It will be more Arab, more expressive of the Arab concept of the world."

"I can see that," Deborah said, unable to keep the sarcasm out of her voice as she pointedly handed the photograph back. "It's your magazine and you can do what you like with it. But not with me as editor. Unless I can run the magazine the way I want to, I'm out of here. One thing I would remind you of though is that I have built up the circulation from almost nothing to a hundred thousand. Not a bad record."

Sheikha Sharifa looked at Deborah's short-sleeved shirtwaister and bare head with disapproval. "Circulation figures are a western concept. It is the ideas the magazine projects that really matter. And, in future, I want these to be in accordance with the Moslem philosophy of life. I made a mistake in being persuaded to appoint a non-Moslem woman as editor."

The old servant woman lumbered up from the stool and poured tea into a small glass which she offered to the Sheikha only. The Sheikha sipped her tea and reached for some sticky cakes. You could see she was keen on sticky cakes.

"If you want to resign, that is up to you. But, if you wish to stay, it will be along the lines I have indicated." The Sheikha licked her fingers and put down her teacup decisively. "Think about it and inform me of your decision."

The audience, for that's what it really was, was over.

Back in her office, Deborah looked at the great pile of correspondence on her desk revealing the predicament of her veiled Arab female correspondents. Nothing was going to result from any of their pleas. The Sheikha would regard it all as subversive and go after the writers if she could get her hands on their letters. She must remember to shred them all.

That was that then. All her efforts had been a waste of time. The Sheikha had been sent in to take over. Because of the present political situation which seemed to be hotting up? Because someone had decided that the magazine could be used for propaganda purposes? Who knows?

What difference did it make what the reason was? The Sheikha had all the power and she had none. It was as simple as that. The Sheikha had well and truly scuttled all her plans. Up until now she had planned to bring out an issue, even if it was only one issue, the way she wanted it. It had been at the back of her mind to arrange to have it printed by private printers, the firm David employed for bank work, and to keep it secret until it hit the news stands. Would that still be possible? No. It wouldn't work. Not with the influence the Sheikha and those who backed her had in the highest echelons of government.

So that was that then. A pity. It would have been a gesture on behalf of all the women in the state who had no voice at all. But it probably wouldn't have changed anything. It had been fanciful to think that, as an outsider, she could have any effect whatsoever on Arab women or their outlook or status in this state or any other.

The events of the last few days had brought home to her that there was an awful lot going on around her she didn't understand, or at least understand at any depth.

Up until now, she thought she had at least some insights, that she was getting a line on what Arab women thought, their role in society and the home. She was getting at least a glimpse of how their minds worked. But she was beginning to doubt that she had any real insights into the thought processes of either the Arabs or the Arab women. She only thought she had. The bomb scare had made her realise that there was a great deal about Moslem society that she didn't know and didn't understand, a great deal going on beneath the surface that she didn't have any real awareness of.

So what to do now? Since there was no possibility of getting *Al Jameela* out in any form acceptable to her, there was obviously no point in continuing with her work editing material for the next issue. That would be pointless.

She spent the next couple of hours clearing up and shredding. Then headed home.

NOEL SCANLON

CHAPTER 27

Back home, and after a brief word with her mother, Deborah locked herself in the room she used as an office, turned on her computer and settled down to work.

She had contacts with a western newspaper with whom she had worked and who had more or less undertaken to publish anything she sent in particularly if it was exclusive or topical or gave a view of the Arab world from the inside.

While focused on *Al Jameela* she hadn't pursued that option. Now she would. From the ease with which the words seemed to come she realised that she must have been working all this material over in her mind for some time.

She wrote:

Here in the Persian Gulf in the strategic oil-rich Gulf state of Khor Fahal which presently pumps three million gallons of oil a day and has large oil reserves there is growing tension between the Sunni and Shi'ite communities.

There has always been tension in the state between the Sunni Rulers and the largely Shi'ite population but these tensions were stepped up recently when a Shi'ite mullah was arrested in his mosque and subsequently mysteriously disappeared.

The government claim that the mullah was deported to Iran and is safe and well there. The Shi'ites allege that the cleric never left the state but was murdered with the approval or participation of the government itself.

As of now the situation remains unresolved.

The disappearance of the Shi'ite mullah and his alleged murder has inflamed the people and this incident may well be exploited by a radical cleric who has recently arrived on the scene.

Ayatullah Abd Al Wahhab was expelled from the state many years ago for his radical and revolutionary views. He went to live in Iran. There he lay low, all the time building up his base in this state which he has now re-entered in order, so informed sources speculate, to lead the Shi'ites in a rising. If this eventuates it would present a new and potent threat to the stability of the state.

The Ayatullah is a radical fundamentalist. And fundamentalism is the rallying call in the Arab world just now. With its appeal to the dispossessed and the disenfranchised, it is the biggest threat for decades to the Rulers of this whole region....

Deborah was interrupted by her phone ringing. It was Margaret.

"Are you alone?"

"Yes," Deborah said. She was about to tell Margaret about the Sheikha taking over but she didn't give her the chance.

"Good," Margaret said. "Because we don't want anyone listening in. Andy has been passed some information from the highest level which I can't tell you about right now over the phone. But the way things are shaping up, and especially after that bomb scare in CJ's, we all have to be very security conscious."

"I suppose so."

"I don't want to frighten you. But, on the advice he's had, before he goes out every morning Andy checks under the car for an explosive device attached to the underside. That's what he's been advised to do. Perhaps you and David should do the same. You're not in a good security area over there, Deborah, that's what Andy thinks, and I know the embassy take the same view. It's such a pity you're so far away."

"We're not very far away."

"You're on the wrong side of the creek, Deborah. You're among the Shi'ites and it's the Shi'ites who will make trouble. I think you should seriously consider relocating."

"The bomb scare wasn't on our side of the creek. It was on yours."

"But it came from your side. You should seriously think of moving out."

"We are. Probably within days if CJ keeps his word. He has promised to get us a villa more or less straight away."

"That's good. Because Andy thinks that things aren't going to get better, they're going to get worse. Did I tell you, he's forbidden me to go near the Old City? Or even cross the creek. I know that sounds terrible but he says we can't take any chances. Not now when we have our transfer out of here."

"That's very sensible."

"These things count, Deborah," Margaret went on earnestly. "One's life may depend on them. Europeans are always targets in these situations. Especially with these Moslem extremists who are so vicious and unstable and up to doing anything. I'm telling you all this because you're my best friend, Deborah, you do understand that, and I don't want anything to happen to you."

Deborah muttered her appreciation.

"Now I have to run."

The phone clicked off.

Deborah turned back to her computer.

She typed.

A fundamentalist Islamic wind is blowing across the whole Arab world.

It is a wind that threatens to blow all the present Gulf Rulers away.........."

NOEL SCANLON

CHAPTER 28

Deborah was out of bed and on the balcony at dawn. This was Friday. This was their day off, their Sunday, and she was determined that, no matter what, they would get out and away from all the tensions building up around them.

She had absolutely made up her mind to resign the editorship of *Al Jameela*. She would miss her job but there was no way she could stay on. No way. Not when it was clear that, if she did, she would have to follow the Sheikha's imposed agenda.

In any event, she really needed to be back in the apartment to be close to her mother and Carolyn in these uncertain times. Carolyn was being affected by what was going on around her out here, no doubt about it. She was beginning to have nightmares and had begun asking some decidedly awkward questions. One that she kept bringing up was the boy who had collapsed at the door. Deborah had thought she was in bed at the time and knew nothing about it, but apparently she had been woken by the commotion, crept out of her bedroom, witnessed the whole scene, the badly beaten up boy, the bloodstains on the floor, the lot. She wanted to know what the boy had done and who had beaten him up. It was impossible to know how much she understood but one thing was for sure and that was that she shouldn't be exposed to any of this at her age.

But this was Friday. And here by the creek, in contrast to the general unease, everything was peaceful, or at least seemed to be. It was quiet and still. The sun rose and, spilling across the sky, touched with colour the sandbank and the creek and the dhows at anchor. And, farther away, it touched the domes of the mosques and a roofscape where shrouded shadowy figures were beginning to rise from their string beds.

A stealthy movement on the adjoining balcony made Deborah turn just in time to see Yasmin disappear, her headscarf pulled over her face.

They had planned to get away early, but Deborah's mother held them up. First she wanted to change her dress and then she couldn't find her tablets and then she mislaid the book she was reading.

Almost from the moment her mother had landed in Khor Fahal, Deborah had felt guilty about a holiday which, right from the start, didn't live up to any of their expectations due largely to the intense heat and the new strange surroundings. She had known from day one that she had made a mistake in bringing her out. But, with the bomb scare, Deborah's misgivings had moved up a gear. There was no question but they would have to get her and Carolyn out of here. David was doing his best to get the necessary Exit Visas but there seemed to be some snag he was trying to sort out. Just as soon as he did, her mother and Carolyn would be on the next plane out.

This picnic was a sort of farewell treat.

"Are you sure it's safe to go out?" her mother asked now. They had told her nothing about the bomb scare at CJ's but she had probably picked up something about it from Abdul even though they had warned him that if he breathed a word about the bomb to her mother he'd be out on his ear.

"Of course it's safe. What can happen out on that dead calm sea?"

"I don't know," her mother said doubtfully. "But I wouldn't be surprised at anything that happened in this place. I'd just as soon stay in my room and read my book. I don't like the sun. My skin won't take it. I keep getting a rash."

"That's why we're bringing a sun canopy for you and a big straw hat," Deborah said encouragingly.

David was getting irritable and tense at having to wait and the two dogs were already panting with the heat. Everyone kept shouting for Abdul who seemed, as usual, to have disappeared when he was wanted.

After much coming and going, they were all packed and ready to go and then they were out driving towards the sea.

David hadn't taken the boat out since the day he had discovered the mullah's body.

As he drove along now, there was the usual soft whispering of waves on to the sandbank across the creek. He carefully steered his way through the narrow streets and alleyways set in a jagged line, the wooden shutters of the houses still mostly closed. Little laneways ran down to the creek that lapped against the houses on the front.

He was quite relieved when they reached the Fishermen's Mosque without incident. The mosque looked normal. According to Abdul, there was a new mullah. He had thought there might be a police presence but there wasn't.

Unhitching the boat and running it into the sea, he half expected the boy to appear, though there was no way the boy could know he would be here at this particular time and, anyway, he was most likely in a police cell.

Out at sea, David gave a sigh of relief. It felt good to be out here away from the land and in a different element.

David let Carolyn help steer the speedboat while Deborah and her mother sat in the bows under the sun canopy. They were headed for a cove along the coastline. Carolyn was enjoying herself. She had been kept in a lot recently and she found that irksome. On her insistence, they had brought Honey and Poochie who didn't normally get to go in the boat.

David eased the gear lever forward. They moved out into the bay and the warm wind struck their faces as the bows rose and they shot forward at speed.

He felt glad to be out here on the flat Arabian sea where they were away from it all. Away even from any sign of human habitation. The villages that extended along the coast had been left behind and were growing more and more distant, smaller and smaller, until the brown of their structures merged into the brown of the coastline. Beyond them the desert stretched undulating whitely to the village of Ajman which appeared to be sinking in a sea of sand, its ancient fort just discernible above the waves.

The outboard engine throbbed, the coastline slipped by, and they were speeding past dazzlingly beautiful deserted beaches.

David tried to relax, waiting for the wide sea to work its magic, for his mind to be emptied by the motion of the boat. The trouble was, it didn't seem to be working its magic today. Not yet anyway. Not even when Carolyn spotted a shoal of dolphins. Not even when a flying fish landed in the boat.

The boy had contorted his body to catch a flying fish. Where was he now? Was he even alive? He had looked bad that night slumped in their hallway. David had since thought of contacting the police, but hadn't. It would have been ridiculous to complain to the police since it was almost certainly they who had beaten the boy up in the first instance.

It was beautiful out here he kept telling himself. If he were to dive overboard right now, the underwater world would be as wonderfully colourful as ever. But would it? What was down there in the deep water?

What horrors were hidden down there? The mullah for sure. David could see him clearly, his robe floating behind him, his mouth open in a scream which could be heard through all that water.

"Can't you go slower," Deborah's mother complained. "You'll capsize the boat if keep up this speed."

"OK, OK," David said, easing back on the tiller. What had he been doing opening the throttle until they were skimming over the waves at a dangerous speed. He'd had a blank moment just then. His mind had gotten away from him. He hoped the others hadn't noticed. Or seen what was down below them in the depths. He eased back some more. "It won't be long now until we can go ashore," he said cheerily.

"Look," Carolyn said, pointing as one of the shoals of following dolphins leaped out of the sea and regarded them, sentient, intelligent, aware of them.

"Look mother," Deborah said with forced enthusiasm. "Look at all those lovely little coves. And we can land at any of them. You choose."

"They all look the same to me."

A few minutes later, Carolyn, with David's assistance, was steering the speedboat ashore. At the last moment, David reached back and raised the outboard so that it didn't scrape bottom.

They had stopped in a few feet of water.

"I hope you don't expect me to get into that water," Deborah's mother said.

"Of course not," David said. "I'll carry you. Just get up on my back and hold on."

The mother rather liked being carried by a big strong man. It perked her up.

Ashore, David erected the big awning. He propped it up with two poles and tied it to a palm tree. He had selected this spot because it had a little oasis of vegetation and a lagoon just back from a sandy beach.

Deborah carried the folding chairs from the boat. David fetched the cold-box and the books and settled his mother-in-law in the shade.

The dogs had jumped out of the boat into the water and swum ashore. They shook themselves now. Then began to run around wildly. In a release of pent up energy, they stalked and rushed about growling and pouncing on one another. Their eyes were round and brown and compressed into little points of excitement. They were running wild, caught up in some fantasy of their own. Or did dogs have fantasies? Did they, like humans, see the world through the prism of their imagination? Humans are supposed to be the only animals capable of imagination. But who knows? Who can tell?

"Anyone fancy a drink?" Deborah asked a little too brightly.

She carried her mother a glass of fresh lime and set it beside her chair while Carolyn ran off to have a swim.

David, his feet in the hot sand, opened a beer and sipped it. Sitting there on that remote Arabian beach gave him the feeling of wide open empty spaces. Being on the rim of a vast and almost totally unpopulated desert gave him an awareness of the mystery and adventure that has always drawn people to the wilder parts of the earth's surface.

From where he sat, he could see in the distance the desert rolling endlessly to the horizon. All his childhood he had seen the desert as wildly romantic. The desert Bedouin were his childhood heroes. He had seen the Bedouin as daring, heroic adventurers venturing into the great desert with their camels, existing on dates and camel milk and a little dried fish and coffee made with brackish water, small thin men cheerfully pitting themselves against the hazards and hardships of that beautiful cruel desert.

As a small boy David had stood at his window in Bank House in Mukulla in the Hadhramut looking out excitedly as a Bedouin camel caravan arrived from the desert interior and entered the Camel Park. The camels moved in a long single file, each tied loosely to the tail of the one in front of it. A group of men walked beside the caravan and outriders accompanied it. Their black hair was long and greased. They carried daggers and rifles whose stocks were reinforced with animal skin. They were a young boy's dream.

David opened his eyes now and the image of the Bedouin vanished just as the Bedouin themselves and their way of life disappeared a long time ago when they had swapped the abstemiousness of the desert for the squalor of the coastal towns and cities. Not only the Bedouin but the concept of them as romantic figures was a thing of the past. It had always been a western concept anyway.

The desert became romanticised in the nineteenth century and there began the west's love affair with a concept of the desert that reached its apogee with T.E. Lawrence, all flowing robes and camel riding and English endurance and indigenous tribes sharing their fly-blown dates, and killing a camel or a goat to feast the stranger, wildly romantic figures as they rode their camels across the barren deserts of Arabia performing incredible feats of endurance. It was a concept that embraced the freedom of the desert and the poetry of emptiness, an emptiness that was awe inspiring and mysterious, the sweep of those great open spaces inducing a mystic spirituality.

It had been there. In the mind. As a perception. A construct. For decades and decades.

But the discovery of oil and the move to the cities and the west's changing view of the Middle East put paid to all that. Romantic Arabia was dead and gone. Buried by the onward march of modernisation, of relentless progress following on the discovery of oil in the very desert wastes that had been for so many centuries barren, desolate unheard of and unwanted.

Deborah was rubbing on suntan lotion. Then spreading a towel on the sand, she stretched out on it in her bikini.

Over them arched the blue dome of the Middle Eastern sky. The surface sand on this remote beach was white and dazzling and sun-reflecting. A light offshore breeze for the moment warded off the excessive heat that would shortly make them feel torpid and languid.

"This is the life," Deborah said brightly, trying to convince her mother and herself that this was the place to be, that they were all having a great time.

"Sure is," David said, with equally false brightness.

David was wondering if his memories of his childhood were true memories at all. Or an embellishment of memory. Did the mind play tricks with the past, with all our pasts, editing, cutting out the nasty bits, throwing a false warm nostalgic glow over the rest?

Deborah's mother dropped her book and dozed off, her mouth open. Deborah lay in the comforting balm of the sun.

David opened another beer. He was beginning to relax a little. Out here his tensions seemed less important, less immediate.

Carolyn called from where she was paddling in the sea.

David got up and went towards her.

Watching her, he felt protective. How precious and fragile she looked. "What is it?" David asked, the beer can in his hand.

Fiddler crabs scuttled about, their burrows stretching all along the beach. "Look," Carolyn said, pointing at a dead cormorant lying in a pool of oil.

"Why is it dead?" Carolyn asked.

"Oil," David said. "Oil killed it."

Bending down he burrowed a little into the white sand under his feet and his fingers struck a globule of crude oil.

"How did the oil get here?"

"I don't know. There must have been a spillage." There had been massive oil pollution after the first Gulf War but that was long past. This must have been some tanker cleaning their tanks out to sea. Unless it was a pipeline sabotaged?

"Come back and I'll get you a cola from the cold box."

They all had drinks. You lost liquids rapidly in this heat. Even if you took salt tablets they didn't replace the other minerals you lost.

They settled down again, stretching out by the lagoon in the heat, the sun, the blue sky, the light breeze coming off the sea.

Suddenly Poochie barked. Poochie had exceptionally sharp hearing even for a dog.

"What's that dog barking at?" Deborah's mother asked.

"I don't hear anything," David said automatically.

Nonetheless, he listened and heard, with a feeling of foreboding, the distant sound of a vehicle. He sat up, suddenly alert. It was unusual to hear any mechanical sound on beaches like this, accessible only by sea or by driving across a seldom used desert track. Which is what this vehicle seemed to be doing.

They all sat up and watched the cloud of dust move closer.

David said, "Probably just people out for a picnic. Like ourselves."

He said this reassuringly. At the same time he checked on the handgun CJ had given him the night before and insisted he should keep with him at all times, 'I don't trust those fuckers. Not any of them. I don't want to lose you just out of carelessness.'

David hadn't wanted to take the gun. It felt odd in his hand. He was a banker. Not a gunman. But CJ had insisted he take it.

Should they go? Or should they stay? The decision was taken for them. The men in the Jeep had already spotted them and were speeding up until they were hurtling towards them at breakneck speed. To make a move now would just make them a target.

The battered Jeep was driven by a young man who appeared to be no more than seventeen years or so old, and the others crammed into the back didn't seem to be much older. Why were they in such a hurry to get here? David didn't like the situation. He didn't like it one little bit. There was so much incitement being pumped into people's minds down the *suqs* and laneways of the Old City that impressionable youths like these would feel licensed to do things they would not ordinarily have done. Nasty, perhaps lethal, things.

There was something else that set the alarm bells ringing. They were all dressed in black shirts and jeans and wore green headbands, the uniform of the Ayatullah's Mujahadeen. And men in uniform, any uniform, become more dangerous by the very act of putting the uniform on. The uniform bestows a sense of power and a cloak of anonymity. The uniform gives the wearer license to do what he likes to those he has power over.

"Get ready for a quick get away," David said to Deborah sotto voce.

"Oh hell," Deborah said, pulling on her beach robe. Her movements were quick and nervous. She too had been alerted to danger.

David stood up.

"What's going on?" Deborah's mother asked, putting down her book.

"Nothing," David said, calling to the two dogs who had started to run towards the Jeep barking. He had to shout at them before they turned and came back to him.

Arabic music blared from the Jeep's radio.

Instead of choosing a spot well away from them, as Arab males out for a beach picnic would have done in the ordinary way, they pulled up right beside them. The youths jumped out of the Jeep and began to strut about. They all carried daggers or weapons of one sort or another. One of them carried a Kalashnikov, the possession of which put an extra strut into his step.

Looking into their eyes, David realised that they were wired. They were high on something. Drugs? Qat? Islamic fundamentalism? What difference did it make? The end result was the same.

"What do they want?" Deborah asked. "Ask them what they want."

David spoke to them softly in Arabic, offering the time-honoured greetings to which any Arab would normally respond. The Bedouin he had been remembering certainly would have. But this was a different Arabia. A deeply embittered Arabia. These boys didn't give a damn how well he spoke Arabic. They couldn't care less. They didn't even care what he thought, whether he was friend or foe. He was white. He was an infidel. What more did they need to know?

"What do they say they want?"

"They don't." David doubted very much if the youths themselves knew what they wanted. They were bitter. They wanted revenge. For wounded pride. For suffering. For their life of poverty and repression, a life without hope. High on the Ayatullah's rhetoric, their quick moving eyes were seeking action, violence, relief.

One of them suddenly snatched Deborah's mother's book which she gave up only after a tussle; she wouldn't be bested by one of these young brats if she could help it. The youth looked at the cover which depicted two young people embracing and threw it in the sand and stomped on it. They all screamed with hysterical laughter.

"What do you think you're laughing at?" her mother said. "Give me back my book straight away. It's out of the library."

They ignored her and began searching through the picnic basket, examining everything, opening the sandwiches and, when they saw the meat filling, began arguing as to whether or not it might be pork. One of them snatched the suspicious sandwiches and threw them in the sand. And another of them turned the volume of the music up even higher.

The thin under-nourished bodies of these youths vibrated to the Arabic music blaring from the Jeep. They vibrated like tuning forks.

There was that jumpy look in their eyes that was just a word, a wrong move, away from violence. David could feel their volatile anger just waiting to be ignited, to flare up. It wouldn't take much to push them over the edge. The situation was delicately poised.

If he did the wrong thing, he had no doubt they would kill him and his family. Just as a diversion. Why not? They all had knives. Business-like knives sharp enough to sever a head.

What should he do?

Should he confront them?

It would be pointless to be attacked and killed just because they had come on a picnic, just because they were in this particular spot at this particular time. But then lots of people die in an equally pointless manner. Still, it would be madness to do anything that might bring their deaths about. On the other hand, to do nothing and still be killed would be even worse.

David waited tensely for something, he didn't quite know what.

Suddenly, one of them kicked over Deborah's chair and laughed hysterically. David looked into his eyes and saw the look of someone who was about to snap.

The boy crushed the chair with his foot.

Anger came to David suddenly and unexpectedly. He welcomed it. It changed the situation. Anger drove out all other emotions and gave him adrenaline-driven energy and aggression.

The dogs seemed to sense his change of mood and reared up trying to get loose to defend their patch.

Poochie broke free.

The boy with the gun fired at the dog who yelped as if mortally wounded and bolted towards the sea with lightening speed, bleeding.

That was it. They would be next.

David whipped out the Glock automatic CJ had given him and fired. The bullet struck the boy with the Kalashnikov on his right arm and the weapon shot out of his hand.

There was a scream of pain. The boy fell to the ground. He writhed about. His screaming seemed to split the air. It even startled a seagull that was floating overhead. The sand was greedily soaking up his blood

CJ had said as he handed him the gun, 'If you get into any trouble, don't hesitate to use it. If they threaten you, shoot the fuckers. They're dangerous. Kill them before they kill you. The world will be better off without them.'

As David hustled Deborah, her mother and Carolyn towards the sea and the boat which the dogs were already swimming towards, he kept firing randomly at the youths who, for the moment, seemed to be nonplussed, not to fully comprehend what had happened.

David was horrified by what he had done, horrified at the pain and damage he had inflicted on another human being.

Life is so fragile, so precious, so tentative, struggling to survive on this planet hurtling through space, a lonely form of life on a lonely planet, life so rare that it is nowhere else to be found not on any of the myriads of stars, how can we treat it so casually?

They had crossed the hot burning sand abandoning their picnic, the food Deborah had prepared, the cold chicken and salad, the bottle of wine, the cold box, the chairs, they left them all behind as they plunged into the sea, Deborah helping Carolyn, and David again carrying his mother-in-law on his back, pale and frightened and, for the first time he had ever experienced, completely lost for words.

They tumbled unceremoniously aboard. With the speedboat bobbing up and down, it was a lot more difficult to get on board than it had been to get off, but they managed it and pulled the dogs in with them. Poochie turned

THE GULF

out to have been only lightly grazed. David shoved off, lowered the engine and started it.

As they roared away out to sea Deborah's mother said, "Some picnic."

Several of the youths had come after them but the boy who had picked up the Kalashnikov from his wounded comrade didn't seem to have much idea of how to use it. He was slow to get off his first shot which hit the water well to the side of the boat. Hatred he had in spades, but not much, if anything, in the way of training in firearms. The others were carrying the wounded youth to the Jeep.

As David gunned the engine and they zoomed out to sea, a couple of ineffective rifle shots landed in the water behind them.

In reaction to what had just happened David found himself shaking all over. He was shaking so badly that he found it hard to steer the boat.

He thought about the youths and how they had reached some place where their lives and the lives of others were so devalued in their minds that they were ready to kill or be killed. Such as they had the making of suicide bombers ready to blow themselves to pieces, scattering their bloodied body parts here and there in the street, on the hot sand. That way at least, after their death, someone would take some notice of them, they would have a last speech and video and a degree of notoriety even if posthumous.

Looking back from well out to sea, the Jeep and the figures beside it were small and insignificant against the great sweep of the desert back of them. They had been so menacing close up. Yet they looked so harmless and ineffective now seen from the sea.

But they weren't harmless. They were part of a movement that was sweeping the Middle East.

And another, more disturbing, thought occurred to him. What he had done was likely to have consequences; he had after all shot one of them. If the youths didn't know who he was, they wouldn't be long about finding out.

171

NOEL SCANLON

CHAPTER 29

David, at work in his office next day, was still deeply horrified by what he had done. When CJ had forced that revolver on him he had taken it reluctantly and had had no intention of using it.

But he had used it. He had wounded one of those youths, if only in the arm. It could have been a lot worse. He could have killed him. For some reason, he hadn't yet told CJ about the incident. He had fired in self defence and CJ wouldn't blame him for doing that. But something, he didn't know what, held him back from confiding in CJ.

What he had asked CJ about was the villa he had promised and when they could move in. But what CJ had to tell him on that front was disappointing. "I was on to the contractor only this morning and it isn't ready for occupation just yet. They're waiting for some vital parts for the air-conditioning system to arrive from London. I told him to get his finger out and have the parts flown out immediately. I'm sure he got the message. I expect him to have the villa ready within the next few days. So you can go ahead with your arrangements to move."

David believed that CJ would do his best but, at the same time, he felt somehow let down. Still, he didn't expect a few days would make any difference one way or the other. Where they were living now might turn out to be as safe as anywhere. On the other hand it might not. The big question was, would the youths in the Jeep identify him? If they did, it wouldn't make much difference where he was living. If he was wanted by militant Islamist extremists, they'd come after him wherever he was and, if they did, it would be curtains.

The immediate question then was what he could do about security. Both here at the bank and at home. All he could do was take on more armed guards to operate around the clock. And, from here on out, he himself would have to be careful and watch his back at all times.

Meantime, he had better get on with his work. And the first item on the agenda was to take an overall look at the accounts as CJ had asked him to do.

As he displayed one account after another on the screen, he noticed a definite increase in the movement of money. Not a deluge. But an increase. There was nothing necessarily wrong with that. In Khor Fahal there was no law against the transfer of money in to or out of the state.

What he was looking for was large and abnormal transfers of funds. He was familiar with all the accounts and most he could flick through quickly. The majority were held by merchants who needed bank finance to carry on the state's trade. In any of these accounts it would be was possible to conceal the transfer of funds by the use of falsified invoices but he reckoned most of the transfers were legitimate and straightforward trade.

He began pulling selected accounts for closer scrutiny. He was trying to trace dubious transfers of money. What he was looking for was large movements of money that had no obvious explanation and which could have been used for the purchase of arms.

After trawling for an hour he had a short list. These accounts had had large withdrawals in recent days to cover remittances abroad to Teheran, Beirut, Cairo, and Damascus. Any of these movements of funds could be payment for arms to be shipped to Khor Fahal.

He mulled the matter over in his mind. If arms were being purchased on a substantial scale for use in the state, there had to be a money trail. All financial transactions leave a money trail. It was only a question of identifying and tracking them down. Given time, he thought that he could. He was on to something here. But it would take time to follow up.

He was in the middle of his investigations when Mohammed rang up. He had sent Mohammed out to the passport office and told him to stay there until he got Exit Visas for Carolyn and his mother-in-law to fly out. Since he knew that the state bureaucracy was at the best of times both slow and corrupt, he'd given Mohammed a wad of money to oil the wheels.

"How's it going, Mohammed?"

"Not good," Mohammed said. "They have tightened up. Anyone at all leaving the state is coming under the closest scrutiny. They are being very difficult. They ask for forms to be filled, we get them forms filled. They ask for photos, we get them photos. Now they ask for your mother-in-law's No Objection Certificate for coming into the state, something they have never asked for before. I have paid them well above the normal rate but I am still having trouble. Today I put heavy pressure on my contact and he admitted to me that there is a list."

"What sort of list?"

"A list of the names of people whose cases must be referred upwards to higher authority before their Exit Visa can be granted."

"So?"

"My friend, and this is private, he would lose his job for disclosing such information, told me that your family is on the list."

"God almighty," David said, shaken.

"What do you want me to do?"

"Stay where you are. We'll have to find a way around this."

"More money might help," Mohammed suggested.

"All right. I'll get more money over to you. And hang on until I make a few phone calls."

One way or another he would have to get those Exit Visas or Carolyn and his mother-in-law would never be able to leave the state.

NOEL SCANLON

CHAPTER 30

"Have you got the Exit Visas?" Deborah asked David over the phone.

"I have it in hand," David said. "Mohammed has been around in the passport office all day. He's running into some difficulties though."

"What sort of difficulties?"

"They're vetting all applications like they never did before. Not only are they turning applications down, but they have put a number of applicants in jail. It's all about heightened security."

"Are you telling me my mother is considered to be a security risk?" Deborah asked.

"Of course not. In your mother and Carolyn's case it's probably just a bureaucratic hitch. First they said the passport photographs we sent in were the wrong size. When we put that right they said they wanted to see the original of your mother's No Objection Certificate. She should have that there in her room."

"I don't know if she has."

"Of course she has. The No Objection Certificate was her permission to enter the state."

"Then she would have handed it over on entry."

"No. The immigration authorities just stamp it and hand it back. But now they need it as proof that she has a right to be here."

"Of course she has a right to be here. If she hadn't, they wouldn't have let her in."

"You're applying logic. But logic doesn't apply to any government bureaucracy let alone one out here. If they want to, there is no end to the objections they can think up."

"But why would they want to think up objections?"

"What Mohammed thinks is behind it is that they're gearing up to prevent a lot of people involved in anti-government activity from leaving the state and this has made it difficult for everyone trying to leave. Things have become much tighter. Even bribes don't seem to work. They're doing everything by the rule. Their rule."

"But surely that wouldn't apply to my mother?"

"You wouldn't think it would. But what Mohammed picked up from a contact on the inside is that they have a note from Sheikha Sharifa claiming that you were about to publish seditious material contrary to the welfare of the state until she prevented you by her careful oversight and vigilance."

"What a lot of rubbish. Are you trying to tell me that Carolyn and my mother can't get out of this state because of articles I was going to publish in *Al Jameela*?" Deborah asked furiously. "That's totally unfair. It's unreal. I thought that bitch could be spiteful but not that spiteful." The thought occurred to her that, if her mother and Carolyn couldn't get out, her own chances would be zero. "So what official reason do they give for the delay?"

"They don't give a reason. They don't have to. It's entirely at their discretion."

"So what's the present position then?"

"The present position is that we're trying as hard as we can to get around their objections. But I think this will need more than that. It'll need the intervention of someone higher up. I've spoken to CJ and he's agreed to contact the Minister in charge."

What CJ had actually said was, 'What does your wife think she's fecking around at? You should have more control over her. If she writes any more of that liberal rubbish, it'll not only do you and the bank harm but stop her mother ever getting out of here. Why can't she behave like all the other women and be content going to morning coffee and playing *Maj Jongg* and keep her nose out of things political.'

David said to Deborah now, "The first thing is you must find your mother's No Objection Certificate and send Abdul over with it as soon as possible. Meantime we'll keep the pressure up from here."

Deborah put the phone down. She was disturbed by what David had told her about Sheikha Sharifa contacting the passport authorities. It was only now it was hitting her and she felt a wave of guilt. Could there be more to this than she had realised. Eileen had brought in an enormous amount of material that was certainly seditious. Could whoever was spying on her in the office have got her hands on some of it and brought it to the Sheikha. But surely that couldn't be held against her. She hadn't published a word of it and didn't intend to.

"Who was that?" Deborah's mother asked coming into the room.

"David. He's trying to get the Exit Visas today but he's finding it hard to get them."

"Exit Visas! What's an Exit Visa for?"

"It's something you must have to get out of the state."

"I've never heard of anything so ridiculous."

"Don't worry about it. We'll get it for you. Only first we need your No Objection Certificate."

"What's that?

"It's a certificate giving you permission to enter the state."

"I never knew I had one."

"Well you do, and now we have to produce it."

"Was it in English or Arabic?"

"Arabic."

"Then how in the name of God would I know what it was?"

"Never mind. I'll search for it."

After going through all her mother's things, Deborah located the No Objection Certificate being used as a book marker and sent Abdul off with it post haste in a taxi.

After Abdul had gone, her mother said, "You should get rid of that boy, I don't like him around the place. He's far too familiar and cheeky."

"It's only his manner."

"Well I don't like his manner. He says things to try to frighten me. He keeps talking about violence and trouble in the streets."

All day Abdul had been complaining about the difficulty and danger of shopping in the *suq*. 'You cannot buy anything. All shops close tightly and shopkeepers hide inside. I see one shop try to open but these men come and beat the owner.'

Deborah's mother was saying, "I wouldn't trust that fellow an inch. I think he's probably a terrorist"

That was a bit extreme. Even for her mother.

"Why do you say that?"

"I caught him in my room yesterday."

"He has to go in there to clean."

"Then why was he looking in the drawers of the dressing table?"

"Was he now. I'll speak to him about that."

"And another thing, he was shouting down from the balcony to a gang of youths this morning. I didn't like the look of them. They looked dangerous to me. They were all probably terrorists. Like him. "

"Did they do anything?"

"Not that I saw. But they looked as if they wouldn't need much encouragement. They looked very like those louts on the beach who attacked us and nearly killed us. Would have if David hadn't had that gun with him."

Her mother was still incensed by the incident on the beach.

"I keep seeing gangs of dangerous looking men driving by shouting and screaming. I feel they're going to attack me. I'd like you to get me a handgun. A Glock, like David has. That way I could take a few of them out before they raped and strangled me."

"You don't have to worry about being attacked. You have my word that you'll be out of here within a day or two. And David has hired more security both for the bank and here."

"What sort of security?"

"An armed security guard who'll be out front at all times."

"I'd sooner have my own gun and defend myself."

A little later the phone rang.

It was Margaret.

"My servants have gone missing." She sounded upset.

"All of them?"

"Yes. All of them."

"That's extraordinary. Any idea why?"

"I have no idea."

"Is anything missing?"

"That's the curious thing. They don't seem to have stolen anything. But they've taken all our keys with them. Which gives them access to the apartment. That really worries me."

"Did you report all this to the police?"

"Of course. They didn't seem to be frightfully interested."

"At least you're in a secure area," Deborah said encouragingly. "You're in the most secure area in the state, Margaret. Apart from the oil camp, that is."

"There is that. Still and all, Andy is going to have all the locks changed and the security on the building increased. What's the position on your side of the creek right now?"

"It seems to be quiet enough. Abdul says there's a strike in the *suq*."

"A strike?"

"Abdul was down there early this morning and that's what he says. All sorts of rumours are flying about. All the shops are closed and barred. Apparently enforcers are making sure they stay that way. Apart from that, everything is normal. Except that my mother is frightened every time a Jeep load of youths drives by. She's on the warpath since the trouble we had last Friday when we went for our picnic."

"What happened? You never told me. "

"Didn't I tell you? I thought I had."

Deborah described what had happened, the trip in the boat, landing on the beach, the sudden and unexpected appearance of the Jeep load of youths wearing black bandannas and threatening them with a Kalashnikov. "We had to get out of there fast. Beat a hasty retreat"

For some reason, Deborah didn't feel inclined to tell Margaret that David had shot at and wounded one of the youths. She was cautious about mentioning it to anyone. To do so would spread the word around, get to the wrong ears, do more harm than good.

"That's frightful," Margaret said sympathetically. "These people are beasts. But you're all right?"

"Absolutely," Deborah assured her. "It was just a bit scary at the time."

"Has David done anything about your security?"

"Indeed he has. He's arranged for an armed guard to be outside the apartment block here around the clock."

"That's the least you would need. When are you moving to your new villa?"

"There's some hold up. But CJ is putting pressure on the contractors and he'll get it all fixed up within a few days."

"I'm glad to hear that. But keep on to him, make sure he does what he promises. Because the signs aren't great. I don't know if I told you, but firebombs were discovered in several department stores this morning. It's not public knowledge. The police have hushed it up, but Andy thinks it's a sure indication of more trouble. And that *suq* strike sounds like it could escalate.

"By the way, the embassy is advising everyone to maintain the highest level of personal security, to keep a low profile, to be especially vigilant in places popular with foreigner nationals such as hotels, restaurants and shopping malls."

"That sounds alarming."

"It does, doesn't it. We're beginning to get ourselves organised over here: where to rendezvous in case we have to evacuate. No one expects it'll come to that. But there have to be plans laid and people organised, just in case. The embassy is putting a whole information sheet together. I'll pass the details on to you as soon as they're finalised. If I can get them to you, that is. It's such a pity you're on the wrong side of the creek, Deborah."

"You wouldn't think that if you were here. I have never seen the place look quieter or more idyllic," Deborah said looking out the window. Clear, pure sunlight shone on the still water of the creek. In the glorious clarity of the Middle Eastern sun it all looked so good, so tranquil, so appealing.

"Well let's hope it stays that way. Ring me if anything happens. Ring me anyway."

"I will.'Bye."

"'Bye. Look after yourself."

Deborah had put the phone down before she realised that she had forgotten to ask about Margaret's transfer to Singapore.

CHAPTER 31

On the morning of her mother and Carolyn's departure, Deborah was preparing her mother's breakfast. Even with air-conditioning they were bathed in hot air.

David had finally got the Exit Visas after they had produced the No Objection Certificate, CJ had made the crucial phone calls and more money had passed hands. 'Thank God for corrupt officials,' David had said.

As Deborah served her mother her cereal, she asked, "Did you sleep all right last night?"

"Yes, dear," her mother said. "After I said my prayers. I slept all right but I was woken this morning by an awful din from the mosque. It started earlier than usual, I'm sure it did. Don't those people ever get tired of screeching? But I shut the noise out and went to sleep again."

Had she really slept as well as she claimed, Deborah wondered. She had noticed her mother's light on during the night and she was up and dressed with everything neatly packed and ready in her suitcase by six o'clock.

The night before her mother had made a number of long distance calls to her other children arranging to be met, enquiring about her grandchildren and their illnesses, about her poodle, Mitzi, and how she was, chatting on and on about the wonderful holiday Deborah had given her and how much she had enjoyed it.

"Did you sleep well yourself, dear?"

"Not terribly," Deborah admitted.

No, she had not slept well. She had hardly slept at all, tossing and turning in bed. If the authorities, as appeared to be the case, had threatened not to give her mother and daughter Exit Visas because of her work with *Al Jameela* what would they do when and if they saw her up-coming articles in the Independent? She could only hope none of them read the

Independent which would hardly be their paper of choice given it was the Arabic press the Arabs were really into around here. Still, she'd feel more relaxed about everything when she got her mother and daughter safely away, at least she wouldn't be putting them at risk over whatever she might write.

All this had kept churning around in her mind as she'd tried to sleep.

"You want to put your trust in God," her mother said. "Put your faith in Him and He'll look after you."

Her mother hadn't mentioned the Glock again. Maybe God was a better bet.

"Yes, mother."

Her mother had barely touched her cereal and had put her egg aside.

"Don't you want your egg?" Deborah asked.

"I'll just have a cup of tea. I don't like to eat much when I'm travelling." She paused, "I hate going home and leaving you here in this awful place. You should never have come out here. It was all a mistake."

"Not at the time it wasn't. There was absolutely no trouble of any kind when we came here."

"All the same, I think David took a wrong decision. In my opinion, what you should both do now is leave. Right away."

"David can't just up and leave what's a brilliant job just like that. But if things deteriorate and the embassy advises us to, we'll certainly leave."

"I meant to tell you," her mother went on, "That security guard pointed his gun at me yesterday and I thought he was going to shoot me. It looked as if he might. And it made me think. If someone kills me here before I get to the plane where would I be buried? Can you answer that? Where would I be buried? Would I even get the last rites, not to speak of a decent Christian burial? I don't want to be buried in these heathen parts. I want you to promise me that you'll fly me back to Ireland and bury me in my own plot."

"Yes, mother, I promise."

At that moment Carolyn came in followed by the dogs. She didn't want anything to eat either and, when Deborah insisted, only played with the cereal in her bowl. Earlier that morning, Deborah had found Carolyn on the veranda brushing Honey and Poochie and whispering goodbye to them. She had stood watching her fondly for a moment. She'd miss her and Carolyn would miss the endless bright sunshine. But she had to go. It was impossible to tell how much she took in. But she had seen too much violence already to be good for her.

"You'll look after Honey and Poochie, won't you Mum?" she said now.

"Of course I will."

"You won't just leave them to Abdul to look after. Abdul doesn't treat them right. He kicks them when he thinks no one is looking."

"Don't worry. I won't let Abdul touch them. I'll look after them myself."

Carolyn had abandoned her breakfast. No one wanted anything to eat. Everyone wanted to get going.

On the road to the airport, with David driving and Carolyn with her gran in the back, given that there had been so much trouble getting the Exit Visas Deborah was afraid that more obstacles would be put in their way even though they had all the valid papers required.

She had the feeling that if she couldn't get her mother and Carolyn out today, she'd never get them out. She felt really apprehensive and screwed up about what might happen and what she would do if they were turned away. And if they were, it would be all her fault.

They crossed the bridge and entered the New City. After a few miles they turned off at a roundabout and on to the airport road.

There were far more people on this road than Deborah had ever seen before. On foot, in cars, and in taxis. She had the idea that they were all rushing madly to get out of the state before something awful happened. But perhaps that was only in her mind. In her present emotional state she was exaggerating everything.

She was over sensitised to all the hustle and bustle about her, to the noise that seemed to have been turned up a few decibels. While actually, objectively viewed, everything was probably normal.

But was it? It wasn't really. What had happened on the picnic wasn't normal. Being threatened and shot at wasn't normal.

No. Things weren't normal. Nothing had been normal since that morning when David had gone out in the boat and found the body of the dead mullah.

When they reached the airport, the whole area was chaotic. David tried to park near the entrance but couldn't and had to drive all the way around again. Cars and taxis crowded the parking lot and people kept driving round and round looking for somewhere to park. Eventually, David found a space distant from the main buildings and, even then, another car tried to slip in just as he was backing into the space. There followed a heated argument with an Arab man and his family. Tension was high, arguments were breaking out all over.

David lifted the luggage out of the back. "There's an awful lot of luggage here. I don't know if you'll be allowed to take all this."

"Of course we will," his mother-in-law said emphatically. "As it is, I've hardly got presents for half the people back home. I haven't got anything at all for Mrs Sutton who is looking after Mitzi and she's bound to expect a present from Khor Fahal."

Buying presents from the long list Deborah's mother had produced at the last moment had led to arguments and a lot of running around trying to get what she wanted.

David carried what he could of the baggage and Deborah carried or wheeled the rest as well as taking Carolyn by the hand.

When they finally got to the airport terminal building, it was jam-packed so much so that it was difficult to penetrate the swirling crowd of anxious, fearful and aggressive people.

David recognised a number of influential leading merchants who evidently had had no problem in obtaining visas for a foreign trip. Obviously word had got around and they had decided that this was an opportune moment to travel out of state. If there was any chance of trouble, better jet out to Beirut or Cairo or London or Paris or Frankfurt and come back when it was all over. That was precisely what had happened during both Gulf wars. There was a big rush for five star hotels in neighbouring countries, a rush headed by the Ruling families with most leading government figures and wealthy merchants not far behind.

The merchants were easing their way through the crowds, waved through by officials and surrounded by their own private security.

There was, however, a great mass of others, not so wealthy or privileged, people who had no influence and, in the case of many of them, no Exit Visas. They had come to the airport to try to get on a plane anyway. They were impelled by rumour and by their own well developed presentiments and perceptions which told them that they were in danger. These people were arguing and shouting frantically at officials. Some of them were on the edge of hysteria. People were screaming that they had to get out, that they had been threatened, that their lives and their families' lives were in danger if they didn't get out straightaway.

The armed airport police controlling the crowd treated these people roughly, restraining them and, in cases, handcuffing them, dragging them away and throwing them into the backs of vans. David was surprised to see Bahwan among them evidently having trouble with officials and tried to make contact with him but was carried away in the crowd. He remembered his call to Bahwan's shop and how desperate he looked. He hoped he managed to get away.

People kept shoving Deborah and David from behind as they tried to get through the maul to the check-in desk. They were engulfed in a scrum of people, in the boom of announcements, in the screams and arguments going on all around them.

Once in the checking-in area, they joined a long queue that moved painfully slowly while armed police stood by with aggression stamped all over them. At the check-in desks every Exit Visa was scrutinised with great care and every name was checked against a list. The airport staff appeared to be looking out for specific people. When someone was turned back, presumably because their papers were not in order, the police moved in quickly to arrest, cuff them and lead them away. Right behind them a man was pulled out of the line, protesting, waving airline tickets, shouting and demanding the seats on the plane that he had bought and paid for and was entitled to. But to no avail. He was hauled off to the wagon.

When their turn came, the check-in clerk kept looking from their visas to the list and back again. Then he glanced up at them scrutinizing them. He seemed to be uncertain about what to do. He got up and left his position to consult a superior.

They had no option but to stand there sweating and waiting for his return. It didn't look good. It looked like they were going to be turned back. CJ had got them the visas but their names must still be on the list of those banned from travelling.

"What's wrong mummy?" Carolyn asked.

"Nothing dear."

"Then why are we waiting? I don't like it here. I want to go."

"So you can. In just a moment."

At this point David caught sight of the badge pinned to the shirt of the official the clerk was consulting. The badge read Ali Dawoud. That was the name of the man Mohammed had bribed on his behalf. David waved, the man waved back and then came over and shook hands with him.

Dawoud and the clerk went into a huddle behind the screen. After a short whispered consultation, the clerk bowed to his superior's instructions, stamped their papers and handed out two boarding passes. Once again David thanked God for the rampant corruption among state officials.

"Come this way please," Dawoud said, as he led the way to the security check.

This could have been a long and laborious process but Dawoud brought them to the head of the queue.

"I understand you would like to see your daughter and mother off."

"I'd appreciate that."

"No problem."

Within moments, they and their hand baggage passed through the metal detector channel and they were into the comparative calm of the departure area.

Dawoud shook David's hand and said, "Have a nice flight."

Then he was gone.

"What a nice man," the gran said. "He can't be Moslem. I'm sure he's not Moslem."

"Of course not," David said dryly.

As they walked on into the departure lounge, he glanced back at the melee at the security check where everyone was being told to take their shoes off and travellers who caused a beep as they passed through the metal detector channel were led away to be frisked and have a hand held metal detector run over them or in some cases strip searched. A man was protesting that he had an implanted heart pacemaker and the metal detector rays would cause a fibrillation which might fatally affect his heart. But no one took any notice.

They walked on to their assigned departure gate and David went off in search of coffee.

Deborah's mother turned to her and said, "I should have worn something lighter. The heat is killing me." Just as they were leaving the apartment, she had decided to change out of her light blue dress for something heavier and had taken so long about it that she had nearly driven David up the wall already in the car waiting and conscious that they had to leave plenty of time to get to the airport given the likely congestion on the roads.

"It's hot here," Deborah said. "But it's going to be cold when you get off the plane. You're best dressed the way you are."

David came back with the coffee and the news that the flight had been delayed.

"For how long?"

"They say for an hour."

"What's the delay for?"

"They don't say."

"There's probably a bomb on board," Deborah's mother said.

"Don't be ridiculous," Deborah said sharply. "Look at how tight the airport security is."

"I don't know," her mother said. "These Moslems are always putting bombs on board planes and blowing themselves up and security doesn't stop them."

"Stop that nonsense," Deborah said sharply. "You'll frighten Carolyn."

What really annoyed Deborah was that she herself had been thinking the same thing, the thought implanted in her mind by Abdul who, as they left for the airport had said, 'A friend tell me too much trouble at airport. Those terrorists try smuggle bomb on plane yesterday. This man he work at airport as cleaner and he know everything happen there.' "Shut up," Deborah had said, silencing him.

Now her own mother was on about bombs on planes.

"Come on," Deborah said to Carolyn, "we'll go to the duty-free and buy some nice things."

In the duty-free, Carolyn said, "I don't want to go on the plane. I want to stay here."

Deborah pointed to a selection of children's books, "Which of these would you like for the journey?"

"I don't want to go."

"Of course you want to go. It's getting hotter and hotter out here and it'll soon be far too hot for little girls. Besides, you've been complaining about not getting out to play, about being kept in the house."

"When are you coming?"

"Soon, darling."

"I'm afraid they'll shoot you, mummy."

"I think we'll take this book," Deborah said adding it to the bottle of Baileys Cream she had bought for her mother. "Who on earth put that ridiculous idea in your head?"

"Abdul," Carolyn said. "Abdul says they're shooting people in the *suq* and soon they shoot all foreigners."

"Don't take any notice of what Abdul says. He only makes these things up to frighten you. Nothing bad is going to happen."

"They shot at us when we went on the picnic and daddy had to shoot back."

"Yes, well, that was unfortunate and very unusual. I think we have enough here," Deborah said. "Let's check out and go back to gran."

They sat drinking cups of coffee, waiting for their flight to be called. Time seemed to go very slowly, to crawl along.

Then, suddenly and unexpectedly, their flight was called and time wasn't going slowly at all. It had speeded up. It was going too fast.

Deborah hugged her mother and Carolyn goodbye.

"Ring us as soon as you arrive."

"Why don't you come with us, mummy?" Carolyn asked tearfully.

"We'll be coming soon," Deborah said.

"Promise you won't stay if there is more shooting like Abdul says."

"I promise," Deborah said. "Any trouble and we're off. Now be a good girl and go with your gran."

Watching her tearful daughter walk away from her, so vital and alive, she was overcome by an overwhelming surge of relief that she was getting her out and away from whatever might be coming down the line. She hadn't wanted to leave her mummy and daddy for the first time and it was going to be tough on her. But it was better that way.

Waving to Carolyn and her mother, Deborah was surprised by the strength of the wave of emotion that swept through her. She hadn't realised how much in her subconscious she had all the time been worrying about their safety. She would miss both of them terribly. But now at least they would be safe.

CHAPTER 32

Deborah was sitting on a narrow balcony four stories up in the heart of the Shi'ite quarter of the Old City. Beside her sat Eileen, who was wearing, as ever, her *abbaya* with a scarf on her head.

Now that she was freelancing, Deborah was excited by the journalistic opportunity to break a story and file an exclusive. But if she was going to write with any authority about the Shi'ites, she had to spend time in the Shi'ite quarter. Eileen's invitation gave her a wonderful opportunity to assess whether the situation was going to escalate into something really serious. With her mother and Carolyn safely out of the state, she felt freer to pursue her journalistic instincts.

Behind the veranda where Deborah and Eileen sat was a poorly furnished room with only a few sticks of furniture and lots of cushions on the floor around the walls on which a number of women were sitting. In-laws? Neighbours? They were all Arab, some quite young. The younger women were sewing what looked like banners. They talked excitedly with frequent gestures. The older women sat on mats, leaned on cushions. There was a threadbare carpet on the floor. A strong smell pervaded the room, the smell of heat and sweat and cooking and spices. There was constant loud chattering. A young girl was going around offering glasses of tea with cardamom and heavily laced with sugar.

Deborah didn't know who any of the women were except that the old woman who watched her with a sly hostile look was Eileen's mother-in-law. There were lots of children running around, three of them Eileen's, though Deborah wasn't quite sure which ones.

There was a feeling of overcrowding and communalism and noisiness coming not only from Eileen's flat but from the flats all around from where came the loud sounds of Pakistani music, women calling to their children, beating carpets, some even cooking out of doors. In this block and all the blocks around it, a communal life was conducted, with severe overcrowding, often six and seven sleeping in one room. It was a situation where there was very little privacy, where everyone knew what everyone else was doing, where rumours spread like wildfire.

What Deborah was beginning to find out was that life, even for suppressed Arab women living in harshly restricted circumstances, was a great deal more complex than seeing them like black bundles in the *suq* would suggest. Although they appeared to have no rights, the women were often strong, even dominant, in the home, transmuted into bossy matriarchs who exerted great power within the family circle. She had been taken aback by how raucous and high-spirited these down-trodden women could be.

Eileen had taken her out on to the narrow balcony because the women in the living room were constrained by her presence.

The block where Eileen lived had, at ground level, a completely secluded courtyard cut off by high walls. It had a wrought iron gate with a metal panel. This metal panel had a small window grate or peephole cut in it. All the apartment blocks had similar courtyards so that, as you approached them, the long continuous high walls and similar metal gates, none of which had any marking or number, made it difficult to locate any particular house or apartment unless you knew the area well. Deborah had lost her way several times coming here. From outside the walls, the strong impression she had got was of private lives, hidden lives, mostly of women, lived behind high walls in crumbling houses.

A dusty palm tree grew in the centre of this courtyard which was obviously much used, with tables and chairs scattered about. Children were playing in the courtyard raising dust, their shrill voices rising as they argued over whatever game they were playing.

But just outside the walls all around lay a quarter with a general air of neglect.

Sitting out on the balcony in this Shi'ite area within the ancient wall, Deborah found it difficult to believe that she was in the same country, or even in the same world, the same planet as the people who sped about the New City in their limousines and who lived in luxury apartments or in villas in the suburbs where CJ was getting them a villa. But when?

From the balcony where she and Eileen sat was a good if restricted view of the whole area.

Eileen was being her usual ebullient self. She never seemed to be down.

It seemed never even to occur to her that the circumstances under which she lived were both deprived and highly unusual. She didn't seem to notice. It seemed as if her passionate convictions buoyed her up and blinded her to the obvious squalor of her surroundings.

Deborah was telling her about how the Sheikha had come back and taken over the running of the magazine.

Eileen's reaction to this was to say, "You should have done more while you were there and had the chance. You should have published the material I brought in to you. It was good authentic material telling of the suppression of the Shi'ites. The world has to be informed of the atrocities being carried out against the Shi'ites here in this state, one way or another..."

Deborah wasn't going to get dragged into an argument with Eileen. It was amazing really. Eileen was still young, well comparatively young, lively, and attractive. If you could get to see her properly that is. Back home she'd be wearing cut-off jeans, a t-shirt that didn't reach her belly button and no bra, showing off her body, and she had a good body to show off, socializing, mixing in whatever social milieu she found herself. She'd be involved in some sort of social or environmental work, maybe even politics. What a difference there was between her life here and the life she would have had back home in the ordinary course of events if she hadn't, quite by chance, met and fallen for a foreign student who happened to be Moslem and Arab.

As they sat there on the balcony in the heart of the walled city, Eileen went on and on excitedly. As she did so, Deborah became gradually aware of people arriving in the streets and alleyways below, of an underlying buzzing and stirring. People began to come out on to their balconies. There was a general air of expectancy.

"What's happening?" Deborah asked. "The people seem to be expecting something, waiting for something."

"You bet. They're waiting to be addressed by Ayatullah Abd al Wahhab who's scheduled to broadcast shortly from the mosque. We invited him in and we are honoured to have a man of such learning, wisdom, experience and inspiration among us to lead us. He has inspired us all already just by his presence."

"This is an important day. Things are coming to a head," Eileen said excitedly. "The time has come. The people are going to rise up and take ownership of the state in which they are a majority. They are going to get rid of that corrupt Ruler and his even more corrupt and vicious sons."

Deborah noticed how pale and pasty-faced Eileen looked, only the oval of her face showing, framed as if in a painting from the seventeenth century, pale almost to translucence. She wore no cosmetics. Though she lived in a land of almost endless sunshine, the type of climate European tourists paid highly and travelled far to enjoy for a week or a fortnight, her skin was never exposed to the sun.

She was saying now, "Things have been building up for a long time. The corrupt bastards who rule this place grab all the oil money and squander it. While the Shi'ites starve, all those brats of princes are abroad breaking every law in the Koran, gambling in casinos and behaving like dissolute pigs while the Ruler poses as a Moslem leader. It's disgusting."

Eileen spoke with the sort of passion that must have imbued the people who carried out the various Irish risings against the occupying British. Except that that all took place a long time ago in a cold misty boggy land far removed from this place.

"The Shi'ites have been waiting for this day for a long time."

Right enough there was a real buzz of excitement in the air. There were a lot of people on the move in the streets down below and more and more were coming out on to their balconies.

"This is fantastic. There's going to be a huge crowd listening, not just the people around here but from all over. It's being broadcast over our own short wave radio which we've set up just within the last few weeks.

Eileen was exultant. She was all hyped up. "This is it," she kept telling Deborah. "Now we have a real leader the revolution can begin."

The way Eileen told it, the Shi'ite leaders had been deeply involved in arranging for the return of the Ayatullah. They had travelled to Iran and accompanied him when he had crossed the border back into Khor Fahal.

Ever since, squads of men crossed that border every night. These men were fighters. They had been battle hardened in Afghanistan, in Chechnya, and there were new younger fighters who had been active in Iraq. There were among them even some Europeans, converts to Islam, and Eileen hinted but wouldn't elaborate on one ex-IRA man who had come over to train the gallant fighters in bomb making techniques that had been successfully employed in Northern Ireland.

"We have a saviour to lead us."

Eileen's eyes glowed, making her pale-framed face look somehow beatific. She looked more like a nun who had just seen a vision of the

Blessed Virgin than someone in the middle of a Shi'ite ghetto where it was shortly likely to become highly, even lethally, dangerous.

"This is going to be the turning point. This is going to build up. There is going to be a rising. There's going to be an *Intifadah*. There's going to be a *Jihad*."

Eileen uttered the word Jihad reverentially as if it was something to be highly desired rather than something that could only bring death and destruction and probably defeat to her husband's people, the people she had adopted.

"That sounds very extreme."

"It's a very extreme situation. Something has to be done."

"But can you succeed? What if the *Jihad* is defeated?"

"It's not going to be defeated. We have right on our side."

Deborah didn't like to tell her that being in the right, if they were in the right that is, would have no effect on the outcome. It never had.

"That's what you hope. But the fact is that all previous risings were put down."

"It's going to be totally different this time."

"What's going to be different about it?"

"This time we have a leader. This time we have experienced fighters coming to support us. This time we are bringing in arms. There's a consignment due to arrive any day now. This time we will have our suicide bombers. This time we will win."

"Or maybe you'll lose. You always have in the past. Aren't you afraid?"

"No. Not a bit."

"But what about your children?"

"They have no future as they are."

"Then what about your husband? If he's involved and they arrest him what will happen to him?"

"He is gone to be with the fighters. None of the fighters will be taken alive. If necessary they will martyr themselves."

Deborah was shocked. Did Eileen really mean this? Deborah herself had strong views about all sorts of things, but she couldn't think of anything she would be prepared to give her life for.

"But what if the *Intifadah* fails?"

"Then we all die. But we are all dying slowly anyway. The Shi'ites are allowed no life in this state. So none of us has anything to lose."

How could Eileen, who had been raised a Catholic in Catholic Ireland, how could she have become so completely Moslem? How could she achieve such total identification, her husband ready to die for Islam, or his version of it, and Eileen herself no less committed, how was such a total change possible?

And she didn't seem to have got much of a bargain. It was difficult to see what was in it for her. Certainly not on the materialistic level. It couldn't be a lot of fun living with that mother-in-law and all those deprived relations in a shabby apartment here in a ghetto in the Old City. You'd certainly need a lot of rhetoric to convince yourself you were doing the right thing by being here.

Deborah wondered if Eileen's views were due to the enthusiasm of the convert or the fierceness of her own uncompromising nature or a mixture of both.

Suddenly there was a tremendous burst of noise as a number of mosques began blasting out an auditory barrage.

This went on for a few minutes and was followed by total silence. Then a voice rang out loud and clear.

Deborah listened intently but had no real idea what the Ayatullah was saying; she had some colloquial Arabic but she wasn't up to this fast spoken emotional oratory. What she was able to pick up was that the Ayatullah was having a visible effect on the crowd.

Eileen was well into it though.

Deborah asked. "What's he saying?"

Eileen gave her a resume of what was being said. She told her it was difficult to translate exactly, that what was being said in Arabic didn't sound quite the same in English, it had none of the resonance of the original. But, in general, the Ayatullah was calling on the people to rise up, to avenge all the wrongs that had been done to them, to seize the opportunity presented to them by the arrival of the fighters from across the border.

Deborah made notes. She had a good memory but notes would help and she'd type up a record as soon as she got home. It all seemed to her to be highly inflammatory and a bit over the top. But there was no doubt that the message was being heard loud and clear. Every time the Ayatullah paused, there was thunderous applause. If the Ayatullah was there to arouse feelings, to fan the flames, he was doing an excellent job.

Eileen whispered, "Isn't he terrific?" rather like as if they were at a pop concert and she was an avid fan of the performer.

"We are privileged to be here at this historic moment."

She at least seemed to have no doubts about what she was involved in. She was obviously delighted by the way things were shaping up. She was in her element.

But where was her husband, Safwan Hisham? David had asked Deborah to keep an eye out for him and find out what she could about him, but she had only seen him briefly once and would only recognise him if she saw him in context. He wasn't in the flat, she was pretty sure of that. Several men had slipped out as she arrived but she had no idea if he was one of them. Was he one of the men moving about in the street below, the ones in black t-shirts? She didn't like to pry too much, but she had the feeling that he was prominent in the Party. If so, was Eileen not afraid of her husband being arrested, of their lives being ruined? Apparently not. Whatever the rights and wrongs of what she believed in, Eileen seemed to have no fear.

The voice of the Ayatullah had increased in both volume and intensity.

"What's he saying now?"

"He's calling for volunteers. He's calling for fighters," Eileen said her eyes shining.

To Deborah this all sounded dangerously inflammatory stuff, an incitement to hatred and violence, but it was obvious that it was having its desired effect. You didn't have to be down there in the crowd to feel the heightened atmosphere.

The balconies were crowded. The alleyways between the houses were crowded. A lot of children had left the courtyards and were now running around excitedly among the crowd. Looking down, Deborah saw that more and more men had appeared, a number with their faces covered.

One word that Deborah was able to understand was repeated over and over. The word was *shahid* or martyr. It was a word that she thoroughly disliked. It had a chilling ring to it. It conjured up in her mind young people blowing themselves to pieces as suicide bombers and taking as many as possible with them when they went.

Again it all came back to the concept of self sacrifice. The Christian monks of old used flagellate themselves and wear hair shirts to subdue the sins of the flesh. But these fundamentalists went a lot further than the medieval monks; they actually killed themselves.

Deborah had never seen a crowd worked up like the people in the streets below were worked up. She had read that men in a mob were human beings reduced to their most basic but she had never witnessed anything quite like this before.

She wondered if she could chance a photograph. She had brought a small camera with her. But it might be risky to use it. People in this area were particularly sensitive to cameras and could turn violent if they saw one being used.

Then one of the women in the room called out and Eileen went in to see what she wanted and quickly and surreptitiously Deborah, turning aside and going to the left edge of the balcony, snapped off a dozen shots in quick succession. Then hid the camera away.

The Ayatullah's voice rolled on and the chants of, "Ali, Ali, Ali," grew louder.

The awesome intensity of emotion being whipped up seemed to Deborah to be away beyond anything rational.

A man came forward from the back of the crowd. People were making way for him. He was carrying a chain and his eyes were glazed. He swung the chain and began beating himself across the back.

The crowd cheered.

The man lashed his back with the chain, gradually reducing it to red pulp.

Someone handed him a sword.

The man dropped the chain. Gripping the sword in both hands, he struck himself in the middle of his forehead. Blood gushed out.

Deborah had seen enough. She felt sick and was afraid she was going to vomit. Self- inflicted violence might send the crowd into ecstasy, but it sickened her. She moved back against the wall and averted her eyes.

Standing there, she thought she heard a burst of gunfire.

Eileen came running back on to the balcony screaming in fury, "The fucking pigs of police have moved in. They're shooting unarmed people."

A youth came running and panting into the courtyard below and Eileen shouted down to him, conducting a heated exchange in Arabic.

"What's going on?" Deborah asked.

"The police have sent in snatch squads and the people have started stoning them and the police are shooting back."

"Who do they want to snatch?"

"Who knows? It could be anyone. They come with lists. But they're not too fussy, anyone who gets in their way will do."

"What happens to the people they lift?"

"They beat all hell out of them and then let them out or, if they're on the lists, they throw them into a network of prisons they have all over the state. You must have heard of them, they're infamous torture chambers. Once you go into one of them, you'll never come out again."

The voice from the mosque had stopped and the crowd below was rapidly dispersing to the sounds of gunfire.

Eileen was more fired up than ever.

"The *Jihad,* the *Intifadah,* has started! The Rising has begun!"

Thinking of her own situation, Deborah asked, "How am I to get back home?"

Eileen considered this. "I'll see about it." She shouted into the room, summoned one of the children. A girl who looked about ten years old or at any rate hadn't reached the age of puberty and the necessity of being veiled came running in.

"This is my eldest daughter Fatima," Eileen said.

"Hello Fatima."

Prompted by her mother, Fatima said, "You are welcome."

Eileen spoke at length to her daughter giving her instructions, then turned to Deborah. "Fatima will lead you to your car."

"Don't you think we should wait a while?"

"There is no necessity," Eileen said. "The police have retreated taking their prisoners with them. There is no longer any danger."

Deborah wasn't entirely sure of this but she followed Eileen who led the way downstairs and out into the courtyard. Deborah pulled on her black cloak. Opening the metal gate Eileen said, "May God go with you."

Fatima set out, sure-footed and nimble, and Deborah followed, a little uncertainly, down through a confusing jumble of alleyways littered with rocks and stones but almost empty of people now. It didn't seem to Deborah to be the best of situations but the little girl seemed perfectly poised and sure of herself, something of her Irishness coming through in her bold defiant looks and bearing. She was carefully groomed, her black hair combed and oiled, her dress brightly, even extravagantly, coloured and patterned, bought from an Indian cloth merchant and sewn at home.

Fatima walked at a quick pace, her small sandaled feet treading the uneven surface with a sure grip, glancing back constantly to see if Deborah was keeping up and waiting for her when she wasn't, delighted with her task but serious about performing it correctly, negotiating a maze of trails.

As they passed along, sounds issuing from the cracks in shuttered buildings, voices raised, radios thrumming, the smells odoriferous in the heavy heat, Fatima kept well away from the main streets until suddenly they emerged into a *maidan* which Deborah recognised as the one where she had parked her car.

Deborah tried to put together a sentence in Arabic and when this wasn't very successful thanked the little girl in English, searching for some notes in her bag, wondering whether she could chance offering them to the child, Arabs were so proud and so much on their dignity, and Eileen might be offended if she found out, but in the end the girl put her hand out and the money quickly disappeared into her clothing in a way that brought home to Deborah that the family were poor, probably very poor.

She watched as the little girl moved quickly and nimbly away down those dangerous alleys and wondered what sort of life lay ahead for Eileen's half Irish, half Arab little girl who had already vanished from sight into the maze of laneways.

Deborah turned and walked quickly towards her car.

CHAPTER 33

David stood at the door of Sebastian's flat. He had knocked several times but there was no reply. It looked as if no one was in.

The phone call which had interrupted his morning's work had been short and sharp. An Arab voice said, "I am speaking on behalf of your friend Sebastian. He is in trouble. Big trouble. His life is in danger. You must come to his place now."

Then the phone had gone dead.

David had carried on signing letters, passing overdrafts, making notes. But he couldn't concentrate, couldn't focus. Unheeded by him, figures flickered on the computer screen.

Whose voice had that been on the phone? It had sounded familiar. Or he imagined it had, though he couldn't place it.

He had been unsettled since their trip to the airport. It was obvious from what he had seen there that already people were panicking and trying to leave the state. And that could only mean that they were fearful of what would happen to them if they stayed.

The increased security he had taken on in the bank should be a help, but you could never be one hundred per cent sure of anything when it came to security. You could cover the obvious things but be attacked in some completely different manner. Surprise and innovation were always on the side of the terrorist. The terrorist chose both the time and the target. With the ethnic mix among the staff in the bank, there were without doubt spies placed there by various interests ready to pass on any information they could get their hands on.

Some of the staff he knew he could trust. But there were others he had doubts about. There were some among them who would back a revolution if one broke out and might well do so actively but there was no way of identifying who they were. He had no way of knowing who was on whose side. His father had been in much the same predicament all those years ago in Aden when he suspected and was even informed by a friend in British Intelligence that half of his staff were either making bombs in the bank basement or throwing grenades at selected passing vehicles in the street outside in the afternoons after the bank closed.

Sebastian had told him when they had met in that cafe on the waterfront to take care. Since then he had been extra careful about whom he allowed access to his office, but still he wondered if it was possible for someone to have found out that he was passing the names of account holders with suspicious recent transactions on to CJ who promptly passed them on to the police. If someone found that out, he could expect that there would be consequences. How could he protect himself? The answer to that was that he couldn't do any more than he was doing. All he could do was wait for something to happen without knowing what or even from where it would come.

Deborah had told him about Eileen revealing that their organisation had an ex-IRA explosives expert out from Ireland working with them, instructing them in the manufacture and detonation of mortars and bombs of the type that the IRA had developed and used so effectively in both Northern Ireland and the UK.

At the time, he had considered if he should pass this information on to Sebastian. But he hadn't. For some reason when Deborah had told him about this mysterious operative it flashed into his mind that this could be Sebastian himself.

Why had he made that connection? Probably because Sebastian was Irish, at least nominally. Was this a leap too far? Could Sebastian really be posing as an explosives expert? It was something he'd better keep out of. In the shadowy world where Sebastian operated no one was what they seemed to be. What a world of mirrors and fantasising he must live in.

Leaving all that aside, Sebastian was his friend and when he got that phone call telling him Sebastian was in trouble he didn't see that he any alternative but to respond.

David went on banging now on the door. Smells drifted up from below. Noises came from the other apartments: Arabic music, the smell of food cooking, and, drifting in from the street, the voices of people arguing, shouting. His banging was beginning to cause people to look out from their apartments and eventually made him stop. This was not an area where

David wanted to make himself at all conspicuous.

While walking towards the apartment, he couldn't help noticing the blown up posters of Ayatullah Abd Al Wahhab pasted up everywhere. Wherever you turned, there he was staring at you out of his black eyes, giving the impression that he not only physically dominated the area but was also hard wired into the minds of the people, controlling them from inside their brains. Since the Ayatullah's arrival, the whole atmosphere of the Old City had changed so that he now sensed a deep underlying tension and watchfulness.

As he was about to give up and leave, there came from the landing below the sound of footsteps and laboured breathing. Someone was coming up the steps towards him.

Abood came around the corner, longer faced and more sepulchral than ever. As he laboured upwards towards him, David asked,

"Anyone at home, Abood?"

"Abood not know. Abood not home for days."

"Why is that?"

"Trouble," Abood said. "Too much trouble. Trouble with strike. Trouble with people in the streets. Too much trouble. So I go to mosque to pray. Abood praying nicely nicely until police come into mosque and cause too much fighting."

Abood was shocked and horrified at the very idea of the police going into a mosque let alone fighting breaking out. His thin stooped figure registered his horror.

"Mosque is for Allah. Mosque Allah place. If police go mosque, Allah get angry. And when Allah get angry, trouble, too much trouble for everyone."

"So what happened?"

"People they begin to fight with police. Too much shouting. Too much fighting. Then police they start to shoot."

Abood adjusted the Turkish cap on his head, raising it slightly to reveal its bare billiard baldness.

"Police they seal off mosque and I am having to sleep there. All locked in, no one allowed leave until now. No water. No food."

He shook his head in melancholic contemplation of the inexplicable vicissitudes, follies, violence and viciousness of human nature which had detached itself from the law and from the mind of Allah.

Abood searched for his key which was tied with string under his *thobe*.

He opened the door and David followed him into the apartment.

What they were met by was total chaos. The main room they stepped into was devastated. What furniture there was had been broken into small pieces. The bottles of whisky Sebastian had secreted had been emptied on the floor and the bottles smashed. The cushions that had been about the wall had been ripped to pieces and the stuffing torn out of them and scattered about the room. It looked like someone had gone berserk in here.

David called out Sebastian's name but there was no reply.

Abood shuffled ahead of him down the length of the dining room and, as he did so, a square of the false ceiling collapsed releasing a great cloud of dust that totally enshrouded Abood who didn't even attempt to wipe it off. Perhaps he regarded it as further evidence of Allah's anger. There now adhered to his face and blind eye and blue *thobe* a thick coating of dust.

Still calling out Sebastian's name, David went into his bedroom. Here too everything had been broken. The bedclothes had been flung across the floor.

David picked up the bedclothes and was putting them back on the bed when he spotted a large stain on the sheets. A red stain. Blood. It had to be blood. There was blood on the sheets. And there were bloodstains on the wall where someone had been thrashed and beaten against it.

Sebastian had been severely beaten up and assaulted in this room. Looking about the room more carefully now he saw clear signs of it everywhere.

The only construction that David could put on all this was that Sebastian's cover had been rumbled. Someway someone had discovered that he wasn't what he said he was, that he was in fact working for MI6. So they had come and taken him away. What they were doing to him right now didn't bear even thinking about.

"Come here, Abood."

Abood came into the room. David showed him the blood, pointed out where there had been a scuffle.

"Blood. You see that blood."

Abood stared at it out of his one good eye.

"Is that not blood?"

Abood shook his head slowly, his yellow face creased, his melancholy deepening. He was lost in contemplation of the utter folly of mankind.

"Yes yes. Blood. In the mosque too much blood. Police come around corner and shoot quickly, quickly. Everybody run. Everybody hide.

Abood run. Abood hide."

"And you were in the mosque all night?"

"Yes, yes," Abood said. "Police not letting anyone out."

"And Mr Sebastian, he was here when you left?"

"Yes, yes. Mr Sebastian here with Mahmoud." Abood made it obvious that he did not approve of Mahmoud. "Mr Sebastian ask Abood to buy food on way home from mosque."

"But you didn't come home."

"No. Not come until now."

David continued to have a sinking feeling in his stomach. He said, "It looks remarkably like Mr Sebastian was seized, put up a struggle, you can see the blood for yourself, and taken away. Would you agree with that?"

"Maybe. Maybe Allah punish him. He drink too, too much whisky. He keep that Mahmoud. He do bad things. Maybe Allah want punish him."

Abood saw the hand of Allah everywhere and in all things. He looked self-righteous now and prim, yes prim, as he contemplated the chaos of the flat and Sebastian's moral degradation. Of course all westerners were morally degenerate to a greater or lesser extent. But evidently Sebastian registered in the upper scale of degeneracy. And in Abood's concept of how the world was ordered, the consequences of this were always severe. As surely as night follows day, sin is always followed by retribution. If Sebastian, or anyone else, commits a sin, and in Koranic terms a sin is a crime and a crime is a sin, the religious and secular being indivisible, then they have to be punished. But could Abood's concept of right and wrong, of crime and punishment, of good and evil, include conniving in, being part of whatever had happened to Sebastian?

Could Abood be an informer and collaborator in a plot against Sebastian? Being into suffering could, after all, cut both ways. If you were prepared to inflict suffering on yourself, might you not be willing to inflict it on others? Had Abood betrayed Sebastian? Rather than helping him, he might well have brought in the people who thrashed the apartment and assaulted him. He might have stood by and watched it being done. His story about being confined in the mosque might well be a concoction.

They went back to the dining room. Abood bent forward and, in this manner, generated just enough energy to propel himself without lifting his feet so that he slid ghostlike along the floor. He didn't look either threatening or dangerous in any way.

205

David began to cough. "I can't see properly with this dust. Open a window.

Abood did so reluctantly.

David went to the window and looked down. Had he been followed here? Were the people who had beaten Sebastian up and taken him away waiting for him outside? Had Abood been sent up to see how things were and to give a signal to those below?

Abood moved slightly and David said, "Get away from that window."

He was looking to see if he could spot anyone loitering outside. There were people about but not many. There wasn't the usual crowd sitting at the pavement cafes. There were no old men playing trick track. The taxi rank had disappeared. In the distance teenagers were piling stones on the pavement.

Who had rung him and why? A friend of Sebastian's? Or an enemy? Or someone tipped off by Abood? Had he been lured here? Had he walked into a trap? Was Abood a loyal servant? Or a traitor implicated in whatever had happened to Sebastian?

From a nearby apartment there came over a crackling radio the voice he had heard haranguing the crowd in the square: the voice of Ayatullah Abd Al Wahhab. The voice brought back to him the feeling of claustrophobia he had experienced when hemmed in in the *maidan*. He began to feel the same sense of claustrophobia here. The Ayatullah's *Mujahadeen* were on their way to get him. They had him trapped in here. He felt dizzy with the thought of the danger he was in. He had to get out of here without delay.

David abruptly left the apartment through the wrecked main room and ran back down the dirty stained stairwell. He could smell the smell of human sweat. He could hear the sound of ascending footsteps, then laboured breathing. An old woman in an *abbaya* passed keeping close to the wall. Apart from that, he reached the bottom of the steps without encountering anybody.

He moved quickly away from the block, glancing behind to see if he was being followed. But he didn't seem to be. It didn't seem to have been a trap. If people were waiting for him they would move in on him now.

He kept moving fast past shops that were mostly boarded up. There were signs that there had been fighting in this street. Empty cartridge shells, burned out cars, debris. A burst water main flooded the side of the road unattended.

There had been fighting here, and there was going to be more. There was a quietness and at the same time a sense of expectancy. The slogans and posters that had been pasted up on the shops' shutters were uniform in their calls for everyone to join the Jihad to get rid of the Ruler, give the Shi'ites their rights. And everywhere there were garish posters of Ayatullah Abd Al Wahhab. His posters and staring eyes were everywhere, a ubiquitous, mesmerising presence.

David came to where teenagers were piling stones into heaps. They were being joined now by others wearing black shirts and green headbands, the improvised uniform of the Ayatullah's *Mujahadeen* in Khor Fahal. They were hauling blocks and barrels and old tyres and an old car to the end of the road. They were obviously going to build barricades. They were going to cut off this area inside the ancient walls.

Would he be able to get out?

Blaring from transistor radios, from tape decks on every side came the Ayatullah's voice, turned up full volume, calling on the people to rise up.

He had been foolish in coming here in response to an anonymous phone call. On the other hand, what else could he have done? Ignore the call, refuse to come? That wasn't on. He had to try to do something for his friend.

David hurried along the street trying to move inconspicuously but aware of the eyes, the sideways glances of the men and women he passed and who looked down from their windows and balconies.

He turned down a narrow street towards where he had parked his car. The Ayatullah's voice boomed out along the street, leaping from one transistor to another.

Some *Mujahadeen* youths began to follow him. Was this spontaneous? Or had they been given a signal? Was the whole episode, right from the phone call, a way of setting him up?

He tried not to hurry, tried not to show any of the unease he felt.

The youths went straight to his car. Obviously they knew which car was his. They had gathered around it by the time he got there. David tried to look innocuous, casual, as he approached, but, try as he might, he felt conspicuous. By reason of his size. The colour of his skin. Everything about him.

He should have stayed at work at his computer in the office. He wasn't good in this sort of situation. But he had to help Sebastian if he was in trouble. Now that he had seen the situation for himself, he would try to get the help of the police. And he would ring Rosemary at the Embassy as soon as he got out of here. If he got out of here.

He felt blinded by the strength of the sunlight. The whole scene with women leaning over balconies, men coming out of alleyways, was beginning to move away from him, to blur, to become insubstantial and wavy in the heat haze.

"Is this your car?" demanded a *Mujahadeen* youth, thin boned and not very strong looking, with eyes lit up by fanaticism.

The youth reminded him of those boys on the beach. Could he be one of them? He tried to remember what they had looked like, what the boy he had shot had looked like, but couldn't. Their faces were all a blur in his mind.

David didn't reply.

"We want it," the youth said.

"Want what?"

"We want your car."

"Keys," an older man demanded imperiously. And when David didn't respond, repeated, "Keys, keys."

"Certainly," David said. Or did he? He wasn't quite sure if he had said anything.

The leader of this *Mujahadeen* group was bragging, "Last night the police come, but we were expecting them." He had begun in a normal voice but now he was screaming, "Our fighters stone them and drive them out of our territory. The police shoot. Some of our fighters are killed right here. They are martyrs. They are in paradise. That is their blood there on the pavement. Look at it, *Nazarani*. Look at it."

The *Mujahadeen* surrounding David, menacingly closer now, pointed proudly to several little piles of stones on the pavement. Each pile marked a bloodstained spot. Each bloodstained spot had become a shrine.

"Look, *Nazarani*. Don't turn your eyes away."

David jumped at the sound of a shot ringing out. For a split second he thought someone was shooting at him.

Where had the shot come from?

There was a commotion just down the road where men were breaking into a store, beginning to carry things out. The attention of the youths threatening him was momentarily diverted.

"I just want to get some things out of the car," David mumbled.

He inserted the car keys, swung the car door open. Even as he did so, he thought of how foolish he was in trying to defy people like these.

But, having begun, he had to continue. He jumped into the car. As he slammed the door to, its heavy metal caught the hand of one of the *Mujahadeen*. This was a disaster; this was violence on his part. But the adrenaline was pumping through his body, priming him for action.

He started the engine. At the sound of the engine, the youths, whose attention had been on the shooting and looting down the road, realised what was happening. They caught hold of the car and began trying to overturn it.

David was committed now. He had to get away. Or be killed.

He scraped the gears before ramming it into second. But the youths around him, thin and scrawny beneath their black shirts, had surrounded the car and were hammering on the windows.

How was he to get away without hitting one of them? Which would really seal his fate, if it wasn't sealed already.

He let the clutch out, swung the car violently. To avoid being struck, one youth jumped right up on to the car bonnet. David ignored him and the youth on the bonnet threw himself off .

As he screeched away up the street, the *Mujahadeen* youths threw rocks after him. Glancing in his rear view mirror, he was startled to see a face close-up, the face of someone clinging on to the back, a face belonging to one of the group who had surrounded him, a face distorted and screaming.

David swerved, throwing his unwanted passenger crashing into the roadway.

He drove on unaware that he was grinning.

CHAPTER 34

Getting out of his car outside the police station, David knew that he might not be doing the wisest thing, but he was so upset by what he had just seen in Sebastian's bedroom with the obvious likelihood that Sebastian had been abducted and was right now being tortured and possibly killed, that he was left with no alternative.

He pushed his way through a crowd to the reception desk but was told to sit down. After a long period of obstruction and being told to wait, he lost his cool.

"This is something that has to be dealt with. Now," he said to the constable at the desk. "My friend has been assaulted. There is blood all over the place. He was beaten up in his apartment and abducted from it. He's gone missing. He may well have been murdered. This is a matter for the police to investigate urgently."

"You will be attended to as soon as possible," the constable said in a way that made David pretty sure nothing, or nothing much, would be done at least in the immediate future. "But we are very busy just now. We have many matters to deal with."

"You may well have. But if you won't do anything I want to see the officer in charge."

This appeal to higher authority didn't have any effect. He was still left waiting in an area packed with people trying to trace missing family members who had recently been arrested, probably in the various police raids, and secure their release or at least establish where they were being held and why. It was pure bedlam. There were various police stations and prisons and their relatives could be held in any of them. Mostly they were told that if they came back tomorrow there would be lists and they could all get to study the lists.

After keeping up constant pressure on the constable, David was eventually led along a passageway past cells and into a small interview room where the sergeant in charge lounged behind a large desk and studiously ignored him while he went through files and papers on his desk.

At last the sergeant gave him his reluctant attention. "So what do you want to see me about?"

"I told the constable at the desk. He wrote it all down."

"I'm afraid I don't have what he wrote down. He needs that for his files. Besides I want to hear the story from you. So, let's start at the beginning. I will need full particulars." The sergeant pulled out a notebook. "Your name, address, place of work, identification and residence permit."

"I don't carry my residence permit with me. But you know very well I couldn't be working in a bank here if I didn't have all the correct papers."

"If you want our help you will have to comply with our regulations."

David gave him his name and address which, for some reason, he had a feeling he already knew.

The sergeant wrote slowly and laboriously in Arabic script.

"Now the missing person's name and address and place of work."

While this bureaucratic game was being played out, David tried to suppress his annoyance. He recounted how he had gone to his friend's flat, knocked for a considerable period of time but without getting an answer. Finally Abood had let him in. As soon as he stepped inside the door he was confronted by an apartment that had been systematically and deliberately ransacked.

At this point the sergeant who was obviously determined to put him down and assert his authority, asked him for a full list of the items damaged.

"What has that to do with anything? What has a list of contents to do with someone being beaten up, abducted and probably murdered?"

"That's for me to decide."

This came over as a threat. It gave David the feeling that he was being treated as a criminal, the one under suspicion, rather than the real criminals who had taken Sebastian.

The sergeant went on asking desultory questions that gave David the impression that he wasn't being taken seriously, that the policeman didn't grasp the seriousness of what he was reporting. Instead of getting a description of the crime scene, what witnesses there might have been or even rushing out to secure the crime scene, the sergeant seemed to be taking little or no interest in what had happened.

Instead, he went on to ask questions about Sebastian in whom he seemed to have developed a great interest. David tried to steer him back on to the crime that had been committed but found himself being slapped down.

Eventually David lost his cool. "Why are you asking questions about my friend and not about his abduction?"

The sergeant heaved himself about in his chair and eventually said, "I'm questioning you about this man because he has a record. He is wanted by the police for a crime he committed. Do you know anything about this?"

David considered and decided that it would be better not to lie. "I know that he was involved in a car accident, if that's what you mean."

"Why didn't you tell me that before?"

"Why should I? It was only a car accident."

"Did you know that he was summoned to appear at the Sharia court but didn't turn up."

David considered his reply again and said, "Yes."

The sergeant moved forward in his chair resting his heavy arms on the desk and pounced. "So you were withholding information which is a serious offence in this state. Why didn't you tell me straightaway that your friend had committed a crime and was wanted by the police?"

"He didn't commit a crime. He was involved in a car accident."

"In this state having a car accident and injuring persons and property due to dangerous driving is a serious matter that usually results in the offender being jailed." He sat back in his chair adjusting his belt with its holstered pistol attached.

The sight of the gun gave David a flash from the past. A walled town. A massive main gate which, when closed at sunset, trapped everyone inside. A long stone archway where a policemen with a bayoneted rifle stood guard. Behind him in the police compound, crude iron shackles hung from pegs in the wall. In the compound the lock-up with one small barred window aperture. A terrified looking prisoner gazing out from the window, gripping the bars.

"The fact that you were assisting a criminal to evade the law and did not give us your full co-operation from the outset changes the whole situation." He went back through his notes. "Now I have some questions for you. Why were you visiting this man since you have admitted you knew he had committed a serious crime and failed to appear in court? What were you visiting him for? Were you visiting him to assist him in his criminality?"

213

By this stage David was convinced that this man knew more about the whole situation than he let on. Had the station been contacted and given instructions by another police department during his long wait outside?

"Well?" the sergeant prompted.

"I was visiting him because he's a friend of mine. There's no law against that is there?"

"And why were you visiting him today, in the middle of the day during working hours? Did you have any particular reason for going there at that time?"

"Someone rang me and told me I had to go there, that my friend was in danger."

"Who rang you?"

"It was a voice. I didn't recognise it."

"Male or female?"

"Male."

"Language spoken?"

"Arabic."

What was this policeman after? Was this all a cover-up? Was it the police themselves who had beaten up Sebastian before arresting him? Were they now holding him in custody? But how had they found out where he lived? There was something very odd going on here.

As far as the fat policeman's attitude was concerned, this could well have a simple explanation. It was quite possible that the sergeant was resentful that neither the constable nor himself had been bribed. He had made a mistake in overlooking the necessity to always bribe policemen. It was something he should have done in the first instance and, if he had, it might have made everything easier for him.

But this seemed like too simple an explanation. Somehow he thought there was more to it than that.

He realised now that he should never have come here on impulse like he had. Suddenly he didn't like the situation. He wanted out.

But he couldn't get out. He had to spend the next hour in the police station answering questions about Sebastian, the same questions over and over, then telling this sergeant over and over what he had seen and trying to insist that it be investigated.

When the questioning was all done and the sergeant could think of nothing else to ask and told David he could go, David asked, "So do I have your assurance that the matter will be investigated?"

"It will be investigated in due course?"

"What does 'in due course' mean?"

"It means as soon as possible."

As David made his way out through the crowded waiting room, a number of women dressed in black were screaming and wailing, obviously highly distressed and emotionally disturbed as they pulled their hair and beseeched the police to tell them where their loved ones were. There were various prisons with various degrees of notoriety throughout the state, the most infamous one being out in the desert where prisoners still wore leg shackles in the old style and no one ever escaped.

Back in the bank, he was hardly in the door when CJ phoned down.

"What's this I hear about you calling into Manama police station and giving the police trouble?"

It certainly hadn't taken long for the word to get to CJ.

"I did no such thing."

"That's not what I hear. What I hear is that you called around to the Manama police station and tried throwing your weight around."

"That's rubbish," David said.

"But you did call there?"

"Certainly I did."

"So would you like to tell what this is all about?"

"I called to report a case of suspected murder."

David paused.

CJ prompted, "Go on."

David told him the story just as it had happened. When he had finished he said, "So I went and reported the matter to the police. What's wrong with that?"

"Nothing. On the face of it. But it would have been better to refer to me first. Things are never what they seem here. Look at the trouble you got into over that dead mullah. I told you to keep clear of the police."

"But I had to do something. Something terrible happened in that apartment. Sebastian was abducted and may well have been murdered by now. You will have to help me have it investigated."

"You say he may have been murdered. But you have no evidence of that. From what I hear from the police, your friend is a wanted man. He seems to be a shady character. God knows what he was up to."

"So the police rang you."

"The Chief of Police rang me," CJ said pretentiously. "He's taking an interest in the matter himself. So you needn't worry about it. I want you to drop the matter straight away."

"But how do I know the police will do anything?"

"I have the Chief's word that the matter will be looked after."

"I'm not happy with that," David said.

"I'm afraid you'll have to be. There are incidents all the time from young men coming out here and getting themselves into trouble. In the case of your friend, there seems to have been something very odd going on. Maybe he was assaulted like you think he was. Maybe he's in police custody which is where he should be. He may even have been abducted like you think. Either way I'm not interested. I have no interest in him whatever. What you have to learn to do is mind your own fucking business and don't keep sticking your nose into what doesn't concern you. You're paid to do banking not feck about like some private dick."

"He was a friend," David said. "I knew him when he we were both children. His father was on posting here at the same time as my father. We used knock about together."

"The fact that you knew him as a child means absolutely nothing at all."

"It means something. It means we go back a long way."

"It may well. But what do you really know about him in the here and now?"

David considered whether or not he would confide in CJ but decided against it.

"Not a lot."

"You're better out of it then."

"I have to try to help my friend if he's still alive."

"That's all better left to the police. You did what you could. You reported what you saw to them. It's a matter for the police now. It's got fuck all to do with you. I don't employ you to set the world to rights. I employ you to run the office and that means keeping your eye on the ball, keeping your focus where it should be. On bank business. Not running about concerning yourself with all this other crap."

CHAPTER 35

Deborah was sitting at her computer, the dogs lying at her feet, adding to and amending the draft of her follow-up article which she was hoping to e-mail to the Independent as soon as possible.

I paid a visit yesterday to the apartment of a friend married to an Arab and living in the heart of the Old City in a largely Shi'ite quarter.

Sitting on the balcony with my friend, I had a view of the nearby mosque and the surrounding streets. In the room behind me the women of the house were making flags and slogans. All the talk was of the return of Ayatullah Abd Al Wahhab whom the people regard as a saviour sent to lead them.

The Ayatullah rarely appears in person but, while I sat there on that balcony, a great crowd of people gathered, crammed on balconies, on the streets and in the alleyways to hear a speech and a message from the mosque delivered by the Ayatullah himself. In a highly emotional and inflammatory speech and to frequent applause from the people in that poor neglected Shi'ite area, the Ayatullah called on the people to rise up, to act decisively and act now when a great opportunity was presented to them.

He mentioned the arrival of fighters who had come from other Arab countries to support them several times. If his claim that fighters have come into this state from outside is true, it could be a matter of great significance. It is something that has never happened in the history of Khor Fahal. If armed Islamic groups come in here from other countries, or are already here, that could profoundly affect the course of events.

The Ayatullah's words were dangerously inflammatory. They were an incitement to insurgency and were received with what I can only describe as rapture.

He worked on the crowd until their passions were at boiling point. At the end of his speech, he called for young men to come forward to be trained as fighters and martyrs, a call that drew an instant response from the crowd, young men pushing forward in their eagerness to offer themselves.

At the same time a man down in the crowd began to self mutilate, strike himself first with a chain and then with a sword.........

Deborah wondered if she should leave this last passage in, or would it be too gruesome. She wished she'd turned her head away earlier when that man had begun lashing himself with chains. The image seemed to have implanted itself permanently in her mind. She decided to leave the passage out and continued with some historical background.

The present situation in Khor Fahal comes from a combination of a general feeling of resentment throughout the Middle East, the mixture of Sunnis and Shi'ites in the state, the Shi'ites being numerically greater, and the recent upsurge in Moslem fundamentalism all over the Middle East.

Whether the Shi'ites respond to the rhetoric of the Ayatullah or whether they reflect on past history and the terrible consequences of their previous failed attempts at insurgency when so many Shi'ites were shot or imprisoned, it is impossible to tell. But my strong feeling, from what I saw and heard from that balcony in the heart of a Shi'ite ghetto, is that the emotion among the Shi'ites has reached such a fever pitch that insurgency is liable to erupt at any time.

Deborah paused for a rest and to gather her thoughts. She felt suddenly tired, a draining away of vital energy. The decrepit air-conditioning in their block gave little or no alleviation of the heat which was really beginning to bite now. She checked the thermometer. It was 140 degrees.

Arabs didn't seem to be too bothered by this sort of excessive heat, after all they had had centuries to acclimatise, but, for her, the heat at this temperature combined with almost one hundred per cent humidity was unbearable. The combination of heat and high humidity was like a paralysing drug. It anaesthetized the mind. Almost before a thought formed, it dissipated into vagueness.

She got up, fetched an electric fan and put it on her desk to move the air around. They were waiting for the word to move to their new villa which would have a highly effective modern air-conditioning system. In anticipation, she had begun packing their personal possessions into boxes.

The bank would arrange to have the first lot moved to the villa tomorrow and they could follow the day after.

Despite the heat, Deborah typed on for another few paragraphs but found it impossible to continue. She kept having to wipe her hands which were wet with perspiration and were slippery on the keyboard.

That morning, she had been chatting over the phone with Sally whose bungalow in the oil camp had perfect, state of the art, air-conditioning. But, when she rang her, Sally wasn't taking any comfort from that or from the oil company's private beach and numerous facilities. Sally, who had always been so laid back, was laid back no more.

"We're like prisoners in here. We're not allowed to leave the compound under any circumstances. That and all the new security patrols and watch towers and CCTV and god knows what, makes you feel like you were a prisoner in a prisoner of war camp.

"I can't sleep with all that's going on and the children are having the most terrible nightmares. The telly doesn't help what with all the horrific images you see on it from all over the Middle East. They shouldn't be allowed to show such terrible gory images of bodies torn to pieces by bombs and the bits scattered everywhere. They never show anything nice. They seem to show nothing but horror. It just goes on and on. There's no let up.

"I've stopped the children looking at it, at news programmes anyway. The cartoons are all right. But even without the telly, the oil company itself keep putting out so many warnings and having so many fire drills and what to do in this or that circumstance that they're terrifying the life out of everybody. Every night I expect the terrorists to launch an attack. And I'm convinced they will. Those terrorists all have mortars and all sorts of armaments these days. Nobody is safe."

Deborah tried to tell her that she was in the safest and best guarded area in the state. But Sally wasn't impressed.

"I've told Bob that I've made up my mind. I'm going back home with the children. I'm not going to become one of those corpses you see all the time on the telly. I think Bob should come home with me, but he says he won't. His job is here. I tell him his life is worth more than his job. But he's too conscientious to take any notice. And he's mad keen to pay off the mortgage on our house back home by the end of his contract out here..."

Sally went on and on....

Deborah turned her computer off and went out. She called into *Al Jameela* office to collect a few things. There were a few of the girls there but nothing seemed to be going forward in the way of producing another issue of the magazine. The Sheikha wasn't in and her suite was locked up again as it had always been. Maybe that was all to the good, a confrontation with the Sheikha certainly wasn't going to help anything. The girls who had come in weren't doing a stroke, just gossiping and giggling.

After collecting some items from her desk, Deborah left and driving past the Phoenix Bar decided to take refuge in its powerful air-conditioning. There were very few of the usual expats to be seen. Perhaps it was too early in the day for them. She sat on a bar stool and ordered a long cool drink with ice.

There were a number of international press people in the bar. Several of them drifted over to her for a chat and to see what they could pick up from her about the local situation. They in turn were able to tell her what had been reported in the Arab press - *Al Hurriya* and a few others had reported trouble in the Old City without going into any detail or giving any specifics. Was it, they asked Deborah, going to develop into something big, something worth covering or was it all going to fizzle out in a few days as it had on previous occasions? Deborah told them that their guess was as good as hers.

Most of the press people in the Phoenix had been sent to Khor Fahal before to chase some report or other of a shooting or a riot or whatever, but so far none of the incidents had ever developed into anything worthwhile. It had all been a waste of time. They were hoping something big would happen this time.

She knew one of the reporters, Lina Tabbara, a Lebanese woman who reported out of Beirut and who drew Deborah aside and bought her a drink. Deborah told her more or less what she knew. Except for a few things she held back. And she refused to speculate as to what might happen. After all, her opinion might turn out to be way off the mark. One thing was for sure, if anything serious went up, there would be a flood of reporters arriving in a matter of hours.

On her way out of the Phoenix Bar, she was waylaid by Don McIntyre who was on his customary stool. Don had stayed on past retiral age. He had stayed on away too long. He was, as usual, totally smashed or headed in that general direction. The heat was getting to him as it was to everyone and there were patches of prickly heat all over his face and neck. His eyes, squinting through the cigarette smoke, were bleary and heavy with alcohol. He was the ex-pat who had spent longest in the Gulf, far longer than he should have.

"What's the news?" he asked.

"This and that," Deborah said.

Don waved towards the reporters drinking at the other end of the bar. "There must be something going on or that lot wouldn't be here."

"Just rumours," Deborah said.

"You'll tell me if anything bad is coming?"

"Sure," Deborah said.

"I should have got out years ago. Instead of the life being leached out of me in this killing climate."

"Why didn't you?" Deborah asked.

"Didn't what?"

"Get out."

"Laziness. Inertia. Because I got good money here and no one would employ me back home. If I had a home. Which I haven't had since the wife left me all those years ago."

Don beckoned to the bar man to replenish his drink. "I came back tour after tour even though I hate the place. And look at me now. Totally buggered. Totally fucked up.

"But don't mind me," he went on, pouring his chilled beer. "I'm just bitter. I loathe this place. I loathe the Arabs. And I loathe myself. Have a drink."

"No thanks," Deborah said. "I've got to be getting along. See you."

CHAPTER 36

D avid's phone rang and went on ringing demandingly. Most of the calls were from expats. They were scared about their money and what might happen to it. Scared too for their own physical safety. One or two mentioned specific incidents - a stone thrown at them, dirty looks in the streets. One had had his car rammed. One had been attacked by hooligans. All felt that there was a breaking down of law and order. They were beginning to keep to their houses. They wanted to know David's opinion on what was likely to happen, were things going to get more dangerous or were they going to settle back down into the way they had always been. It was odd to hear the fear in their voices as he sat at his desk in the safety and calmness of the bank. It underlined the contrast between all that uncertainty and apprehension and unrest out there. And in this office, peace and quiet. An oasis of calm. Or so it seemed.

But he resisted the inducement to talk politics. He wasn't going to be drawn into a political discussion. He stuck to advising them on their accounts. He stuck strictly to finance. Just as CJ had told him to.

In answer to their queries, he just opened his mouth and professional moneyspeak poured out. He was glad to do so. He was glad to immerse himself in the safe, familiar world of banking. That way he avoided the dangerous realities out there. He kept to the solid high ground of finance where everything was gloriously clear and unambiguous. Or reasonably so.

David listened to caller after caller. They wanted advice, but even more they wanted reassurance. That their money would be all right. That the precipitate fall in the dinar, and the dinar was still falling, wouldn't continue until it had wiped out years of hard graft and savings out here in this heat.

Though many had funds in different currencies, they all held fairly substantial dinar holdings and, even if they didn't, their salary was in all cases expressed in dinars. So the fall in the value of the dinar was a matter of concern. Money was, after all, why they were out here and its accumulation all they had to show for all their work and effort. They had escaped from the UK climate, escaped from income tax and exchange control and all such horrors. Here they were in the Middle East doing very nicely for themselves, squirreling money away, tax free money. And they wanted to be reassured that they weren't going to lose any of it.

Most of the callers were financially well off and reasonably financially sophisticated. They knew all about growing their money, keeping up to date with the tax havens. They knew all the dodges, legal and semi-legal and illegal, to enable them, even when they returned home to the UK, to go on avoiding tax for ever and ever amen. But still they were worried.

"What should I do? Should I sell all my dinars now? Or should I hang on, wait for a recovery?" That was the refrain, the question they all asked.

"That's up to you, that's your decision," he told them. "If you decide to get out of dinars that's no problem. Though of course you will have to take a hit on the exchange rate. A considerable hit."

"How can I come to a decision if I don't know what is going to happen politically in the state. What do you think will happen?"

"I don't know, it's not my field. Perhaps the embassy could tell you."

"Don't be ridiculous. Embassies are past masters at using a lot of words to say nothing. They never commit themselves on anything. No. What I want to know is what you think. You have a lot of experience of these parts. Could the dinar collapse completely?"

"I can't foretell the future," David said. "But a total collapse of the currency is highly unlikely. So far, rumours of unrest among the Shi'ites has brought the value of the currency down in the markets and, in my opinion, will continue to do so as long as those rumours persist. The currency is likely to be weak in the short term. Perhaps even the medium term. But the dinar is backed by the oil reserves of the state which are vast. Long term, whatever the fluctuations, the currency should recover eventually."

But they weren't happy. They wanted more reassurance. They wanted certainty in an uncertain world.

"That's in normal circumstances," they countered. "But what if these Shi'ites do really start a rebellion. What happens then?"

What David felt like saying was, 'What happens then is you lose money.

But there is also the strong possibility that you might lose your life. Which would be a lot more serious. So maybe that's what you should be thinking about and never mind the money.'

What he actually said was, "At the moment there is pressure on the currency, mostly of a speculative nature. I would expect a technical adjustment in due course and that might be a good time to sell your dinars if that's what you want to do. If you are really worried, you can always convert into another currency right now and take the loss..."

"If I do convert what investments would you recommend?"

"What I'd recommend would be a spread of currencies in offshore accounts: 70% in safe low interest accounts, 20% in a spread of stocks, leaving 10% to put into something more speculative, perhaps an offshore equity investment in the Asian market through one of the offshore unit trusts. That's the area of future growth: China, the Asian Pacific region, Hong Kong, Singapore, Malaysia, that whole region of the world, but particularly China. Cheap production costs. For a long time now multinationals have been transferring operations to that area and closing factories in high cost Europe and America, a trend that can only accelerate............."

Would this babble of talk cover over the dangerous pitfalls opening up all around him?

David had a flash of standing in Sebastian's apartment after he had found the blood stains splattered on the bedroom walls and looking out the window and wondering if he had walked into a trap, if they were already on the stairs, coming to get him. He hadn't stopped thinking about Sebastian, about what had happened to him since that moment he had found the empty apartment.

Who had taken him? His first presumption had been that it was the Ayatullah's *Mujahadeen*. But could it have been someone else?

Despite CJ's prohibition, he had rung the British Embassy and tried to get on to Rosemary but hadn't had much luck with her. Up until now, she had been very friendly but, all of a sudden, he had difficulty in reaching her. When he rang she was always unavailable; all he got an answering machine.

When he did eventually get to speak to her she was in a hurry, had a lot on her plate, was overdue at a conference. But he insisted and she took time to listen.

She heard him out without interruption.

"I'm shocked at what you have told me. It's all very disturbing. You were right to report it to the police. Leave it with me and I'll get on to them and make sure they pursue it vigorously. We can operate further up the chain of command than that sergeant who gave you trouble."

David said, "From the first time I visited Sebastian I sensed that he was in danger. Now I'm afraid that the worst has happened. I'm afraid that he's been murdered."

"Why do you say that?"

"Because they blew his cover. Oh yes, I knew what line of work he was in. I knew he was in danger. I knew he was posing as...."

"Hold on a moment," Rosemary interrupted. "This is an open line we are talking on. Anything you say over this line may be overheard."

"I appreciate that. But I'm worried. And I feel implicated. I feel guilty. I feel I have to do something."

"Of course you do. I understand all that. Believe me we appreciate you reporting what you saw to us. And you have my word that I'll be on to it straight away. I'll see that it is attended to at the highest level. Meantime, though, it will be better for everyone if you don't do or say anything about this. Don't breathe a word about it to anyone. Loose talk could be extremely dangerous. It could well put lives at risk. Do I have your word on that?"

"If you put it like that, I suppose so. But if I can't talk over the phone, I insist that I meet you."

"OK. Just as soon as things are clarified, I'll be in touch. You'll be the first to hear of any developments."

"Promise."

"I promise. But now I really have to run. They're waiting for me."

The phone went dead.

David felt glad that he had got on to Rosemary at last but somehow felt dissatisfied. No doubt her concern was genuine. But he wasn't sure that he entirely trusted her despite their long friendship. He was sure she had some connection with MI6 and it was they who should have been looking out for Sebastian. It was their responsibility to look after him, look out for his welfare. It was they who employed him, they who had brought him out here, set him up, put him in that apartment. They were responsible for whatever had happened to him. And, if he was dead, it was they who were responsible for his death. They couldn't just walk away from that. And he wasn't going to let them.

The phone calls kept coming in. And David kept talking his moneyspeak on and on. Eventually, when it looked like the calls would never stop, he refused to take any more.

With no calls coming in, David's fingers moved quickly over the computer keyboard executing customers' orders, giving instructions for money transfers all over the world.

David's fingers worked the keyboard. Though he was in what was until recently a remote part of Arabia, he was in touch with the worldwide financial world. He was locked into that great super communications highway that girdles the globe, bounces off satellites.

He was safe in his little bubble in here and he wished he could stay in it forever. He wished he could walk right into the world of virtual reality.

But he knew that he couldn't, that he would have to face all the problems and dangers that were gathering outside.

NOEL SCANLON

CHAPTER 37

In the middle of the following night the Shi'ite mosques began to broadcast, not the call to prayer, but a call to arms.

Lights went on all over the Shi'ite areas of the Old City and the New City as people got out of bed, came out on to their balconies. Fighters who hadn't already left their homes and gone underground left hurriedly now as the call boomed out. Men gathered in the dark pools of shadow at the corners of alleys, squeezed into nooks and crevices, lowered themselves into the tunnels they had been digging for weeks now.

Ayatullah Abd Al Wahhab's voice, greatly amplified, rang out. He had already prepared the people for this. They were ready for whatever upheaval was about to take place. There was a feeling in the air that something of great import was about to happen.

The police had begun a series of co-ordinated raids and the call was going out to the people to fight back.

In Eileen's apartment, there was a fever of activity. All the women were up, most of them hadn't gone to bed for days, sleeping on the floor in the main room. There were no men in the house. The men were long gone. Eileen and several other women were out on the balcony listening to the Ayatullah.

The amplified voice screamed, *"We are being attacked. This is the night the police plan to slaughter us, to wipe us out.*

"Even as I speak, they are breaking into our homes. They are defiling our women. They are stealing our goods. With arms supplied by the west, they are beating and humiliating and killing our people.

"You must fight back. You must report to and follow the commands of your local leaders. If you do that we will prevail. We must prevail. For Allah is with us... "

Fierce hand-to-hand fighting was taking place in the alleyways which the police would normally have avoided, preferring to patrol from vehicles with machine guns mounted on the back from where they could easily wipe out any resistance. But the fighters refused to come out into the streets. They kept to the alleyways that were too narrow for the police vehicles to enter.

If he was to clear the area, Chief of Police Qassim, who was supervising all this, realised that his men would have to go in on foot. He had already sent in snatch squads who had managed to seize a dozen or so men. All prisoners taken were rushed off to the infamous police headquarters, where they would be interrogated, deprived of sleep and tortured in the many and various ways developed and refined by Qassim over the decades. Few of the prisoners would ever see the light of day again.

In the past, when the Shi'ites had attempted risings they had put up a certain amount of fight and made an awful lot of noise but, when Qassim had put the pressure on, they had collapsed easily enough. After all, the Sunnis had the power, the Sunnis had the training, the Sunnis had a large supply of up to date western weapons. The Shi'ites were poorly and lightly armed. Taking them on in the past was a one sided encounter with only one possible outcome.

Because of his past experience, Chief of Police Qassem was surprised at the resistance he was now encountering. The word coming back to him was that a number of his men had been led on and on, deeper and deeper into mazes of alleys where they found themselves trapped. They were surrounded and in danger of being wiped out. The Shi'ites were exhibiting a discipline they had never shown any sign of before. He sent more men in. And the same happened to them.

The police deep in these alleyways were raked by small arms fire from both sides, from ground level and from the buildings on either side.

Desperate for cover, his men tried to find openings to squeeze into, but this wasn't easy. Most buildings were private houses and were surrounded by high walls and therefore impregnable.

Screams pierced the air, a cacophony of different explosions and detonations, the cries and moans of the wounded.

The police fought back but found themselves completely surrounded. As soon as they put their heads out they were shot at from all sides from protected and entrenched positions. Where there had been no one a moment before, men began to emerge from the tunnels they had dug.

Qassim's primary objective had been to seize Ayatullah Abd Al Wahhab and a number of squads were assigned this task. No one knew for sure where he was and the police intelligence turned out to be faulty. On the basis of this inaccurate intelligence several buildings were earmarked. The first to be raided was the Monastery. But the squad assigned found that they couldn't even get into the grounds. They had brought equipment for scaling the walls but there were fighters on top of the walls directing a hail of fire down on them.

Over all the gunfire and fighting, the voice of the Ayatullah rang out. It could be heard everywhere.

"Praise be to Allah, we are resisting the onslaught of the oppressors. They are falling before us.

But some still resist. And some of these are Shi'ites. Some of you among the police are Shi'ites. You joined the police to feed your families. You joined the police to survive.

Now is your chance to redeem yourselves. By joining us. By serving the cause of your people. By joining the martyrs who have laid down their lives this night for the cause.

Lay down your arms. Refuse to fight and slaughter your own people.

You are one of us. You are Shi'ites. Join us. Lay down your rifles. Do not fire another shot.

In some squads there are many of you. Take your fellow policemen prisoner. Guard them until our men can get to you.

Join us and you will be honoured. Join us and all fighting will cease. Join us and the victory will be to Allah…."

The force of the Ayatullah's words penetrated the mind of those among the police who were Shi'ites. Always susceptible to rhetoric, the Ayatullah's powerful insistent message bored into their brains and inflamed them.

The Shi'ites in the police had heard many stories about this Ayatullah. They had heard that he was a reincarnation of the Imam Yahya. They had heard that he had died several times but always came to life again. They had heard many stories about his supernatural powers.

And now they heard his voice and felt him entering their brains and taking them over. Or that is what they imagined happened. At least it was the story they told.

The first Shi'ite policeman to throw off his uniform and join his fellow

Shi'ites was a young and recent recruit. Others quickly followed. The word spread.

They changed sides. They joined the insurgents and were embraced by them. Cries of *'Allah al Akhbar'* rose up to the skies.

In Eileen's house there was jubilation. All night the children had been coming and going with news of the battle. Leader of the children had been the sure-footed and nimble Fatima, certain of her way among the jungle of alleys where any stranger would be quickly lost. She was wildly excited. Her mother's excitement and jubilation had transmitted itself to her. She ran in among the fighters, squeezed into crevices, ducked and hid when she heard gunfire. And, several times on her outings, she saw, standing on a corner, a figure in a black cloak, a figure she was sure was the Ayatullah himself, even though at the same time his voice was booming out over her head, lapping through the air in great waves. Which seemed strange. But then it was probably magic, for it was well know that the Ayatullah could do all sorts of magical things.

She wondered whether or not she should tell her mother who she had seen. She thought not. It was a secret she would keep to herself.

CHAPTER 38

During the night David awoke briefly to hear distant shots, vehicles revving, and the faint sound of shouting and screaming, but fell asleep again.

At breakfast, he asked Abdul what had been going on during the night.

"Police go into Old City, plenty police," Abdul said, and added with satisfaction, "They shoot plenty Shi'ites."

David didn't pay too much attention to Abdul. He always wildly exaggerated everything.

All the same, he paid particular attention to what was coming out over the radio. The government radio station was reporting that there had been a number of minor incidents the night before but that didn't add up to very much. He tried to get on to CJ but couldn't get him. He would have to go into the bank, see what the position was, and take it from there. If there was going to be trouble of any sort, he needed to be in there to organise things and tell the staff what to do.

On the way in, everything seemed normal. In fact it was somewhat quieter than usual with less traffic on the road. When he got into the bank, he was taken aback to find it almost empty. Normally, at this time, everyone would be in and at their desks. But today there was only a small huddle of people standing around aimlessly. And the air-conditioning didn't seem to be functioning as well as it normally did. Certainly the temperature was way up.

Phones were ringing unanswered all over the place. He went into his office and had just sat down when Mohammed came in.

"Where are all the staff? What exactly is going on?" David asked.

"Haven't you heard?"

"All I've heard is the government radio reporting some minor incidents."

Mohammed nervously lit a cigarette. "There's a lot more to it that that. There's a lot of confusion. Nobody knows exactly what happened last night. But the word on the street is that the police tried to lift the Ayatullah and immediately fighting broke out throughout the Shi'ite areas."

"I thought I heard a commotion in the distance right enough. So did they get the Ayatullah?"

"No, they didn't. Instead, they were ambushed in the alleyways. Then Al Wahhab appealed to the Shi'ites among the police to join him and it seems that quite a few of them did, taking all their weaponry with them."

David was beginning to get worried. He hadn't expected this. "That doesn't sound great. Where does that leave the police force?"

"It leaves them short of manpower."

"So what happened last night was really speaking a police mutiny?"

"You could put it like that."

Almost exactly the same thing happened in Aden after his parents had left. The Arabs in the armed police force mutinied and killed twenty six British troops and took over Crater. To avenge the death of the troops, the dashing and hugely popular Colonel Colin Mitchell led the Argyll and Southerland Highlanders into the hell hole of Crater to retake it. The whole revolt was an ugly and bloody affair.

Mohammed kept nervously re-adjusting his *kheffiah*.

"What are the police doing about all this?" David asked.

"They say that Sunni officers and the men loyal to them are guarding all the key installations. But I don't know. I haven't seen many of them around. There's a general scare on and nobody really knows what's going to happen. Quite a few of the larger merchants have already left the state."

"Surprise, surprise. Anyway, what we have to do is look after the bank. How many staff are in?"

"Very few. Some of them rang me, and I've been on to others. They all want to come in but a lot of them are afraid to. It's difficult for them. Some of them live in strongly Shi'ite areas. They want to stay with their families to protect them. They're afraid that, if they leave, something bad will happen. Some of them told me they had heard that the Ayatullah's *Mujahadeen* have formed paramilitary groups trained to penetrate the New City and slaughter Sunnis."

"You're not serious."

"That's what the people are saying."

This might all be gossip or at least an exaggeration. But, even so, it was a bit shattering. And yet there had been signs. Quite a few signs if you added them all up. There had been signs ever since that fatal day when he had come upon the mullah's body

"All right," David said. "I don't suppose we can expect all staff to come in in the circumstances. But why aren't the security guards on duty? They're supposed to be here twenty four seven?"

"There were a couple here when I arrived," Mohammed said, "but they were hours and hours over the time when they were meant to be relieved. So I let them go." He went on, "Maybe the relieving security were told not to come in. Maybe they were intimidated. They might even be held hostage."

Things were a lot worse than David would have believed possible. But he had to deal with the situation as he found it.

He considered for a moment. "What I want you to do is close the bank, tell the staff who have come in to take the day off. Tell them we'll be in touch, probably tonight and, if not tonight, then tomorrow. Tell them to await instructions. Then see if you can do something about the air-conditioning."

"I've already tried but it seems there's an outage. Maybe the lines have been disconnected. Or the power plant disabled. The auxiliary unit has cut in but it's not working very effectively."

"In that case just see if you can contact the service people. Though I doubt if they'll do anything right now.

"After that what I want you to do is make sure all the shutters are down and secured properly." The shutters were the most modern and effective available on the market and were built to withstand quite a lot.

Mohammed left and David started making a list of what he needed to do to preserve the bank records, assuming a worse case scenario. Obviously the bank records couldn't be allowed to fall into the wrong hands. He had an odd feeling of deja vous. He had a feeling he had been in these or similar circumstances before. Then remembered where and when.

When things were at their worst in Aden he, as a small boy, had been with his father when he had driven down from Ras Marshaj to the bank in Crater to destroy the most sensitive documents before the insurgents, as they were called then, or terrorists as they would now be called, could get them. It was then only a short time before the evacuation of the all European civilians from Aden and his father was going in to the abandoned bank in order to destroy the codes, the telegraphic cyphers, the private correspondence, all of which he kept in his safe. Fearful but excited, he had helped his father shred or burn the lot to ashes.

Banks had changed a lot from those days but, even though nowadays everything was computerised, still, much the same sort of things needed doing. He was mulling all this over in his mind when the phone rang.

It was CJ. "I'm sorry I haven't been able to get in, but I've been held up here on business. What's the exact position in there?"

"Hardly any of the staff have come in, not even the security, so I think it's best to leave the bank closed for today."

"I agree," CJ said. "There's no point in opening until we see how things go."

CJ and David discussed the situation, at the end of which CJ said, "I've already been on to Chief of Police Qassim. Even though he's a bit short handed just now, he's promised to send patrols out to keep an eye on things in our area. I'll ring him again and get him to send a squad of his boys to mount a guard on the bank just as soon as he possibly can. They'll have orders to shoot all rioters on sight, so that should fix that. And don't worry; it'll all work out in the end. Anyway," CJ went on, "you should be used to this sort of situation. You've been in similar circumstances often enough before."

It was true. The situation in Khor Fahal now was very similar not only to Aden but to various situations he had been in before.

CJ was saying, "These things are always exaggerated out of all proportion. I don't expect much to happen, certainly not anything Chief of Police Qassim can't handle. Though, mind you, from the bank's point of view, if the worst comes to the worst, we have nothing much to lose. All our funds are out of the country. In fact with those forward currency contracts, and I have to congratulate you there, with those contracts coming up, we'll come out of it well ahead of the game. I've been following our position closely and we're now up forty million give or take. If this whole shagging state exploded we'd lose little or nothing. Except of course the building itself. And not only is that insured but it's written off on the balance sheet. So don't worry about anything. There may be a bit of trouble in the streets but a mob on its own will achieve fuck all."

"Thanks for your optimistic assessment," David said dryly. It really was a bit rich for CJ away out in his luxury villa sitting by the pool with a

236

drink in one hand and a phone in the other, well away from trouble, telling him who was in the middle of it not to worry if there were mobs outside in the streets Any minute now he'd be telling him not to panic.

"Whatever happens don't panic," CJ went on. "Meantime what I want you to do is to get that place closed up as tight as a duck's arse. When you've done that, I want you to secure what records you can. You'll have to do it on your own, I'm afraid. Don't get that fucker Mohammed to help you. Maybe he's trustworthy but then again maybe he's not. Who knows? He could well be playing both sides. He could be bought - they can all be bought. Better do it all yourself."

They spent some time discussing how this might be done.

"When you've finished all that, I want you to get the hell out of there. If anyone gets in your way drive at them. Or preferably over them.

"Now as far as your accommodation is concerned, you should be safe enough down by the creek just for tonight. You have armed security guards there, I believe?"

"We have two dodgy looking characters, one for the day and one for the night."

"Good. What I want you to do when you get home is get all your packing finished. I'll send transport to move all your stuff into the new villa tomorrow and I suggest you both come with it. It doesn't matter that the villa isn't completely ready, it'll have to do. I'll send a police escort should that be necessary. I'll ring you later to let you know the arrangements. And good luck."

After speaking to CJ, David sought out Mohammed.

"There's no point in your staying on here," he said to Mohammed. "I'll be able to handle the rest myself. I'll give you a ring later on and let you know what the situation is. Just leave the back door open for me to get out. Then you'd better get home yourself."

Mohammed left hurriedly.

David went out into the main banking hall. It was eerily empty. Several large signs in both Arabic and English read 'You are under continuous closed circuit television scrutiny'.

There was the sound of shouting from outside.

He went to the window to look out. People were beginning to appear in Bank Street in some numbers.

The wind was picking up and the scene was becoming obscured by the edge of a dust storm that was blowing in from the desert. Swirling dust was blowing along the street making the crowd that was beginning to gather swirl and sway in the dusty air, mirage like.

David turned away.

He had work to do.

CHAPTER 39

Deborah was working on her computer in her study with the door closed and the air-conditioning on when the dogs jumped up and began barking insistently and clawing at the door. They had been nervous for days, particularly Poochie who had acute hearing and could hear distant noises and bangs a human couldn't.

Deborah opened the front door and the dogs dashed madly down the stairs and out into the compound barking as Abdul came bursting into the apartment, his thobe torn, his face bleeding. He was speaking fast in Arabic. Deborah couldn't make out a word he was saying.

"What is it Abdul?"

"The boat," he said. "They take it boat. Come I show you."

Deborah followed Abdul out on to the balcony just in time to see the back of their Dory speedboat on its trailer disappearing from sight.

"Was the garage door closed?"

"Yes yes. Closed. They break it open, wheel out boat and hitch trailer to their pick-up truck. Abdul tell them not their boat. But they point their guns at me and laugh. "

At the memory of what had happened to him he got so excited and worked up, screeching at the top of his voice, his Arab cap tilted over his forehead that she wasn't able to make out half of what he was saying.

Deborah interrupted him, "Calm down and tell me what happened. Who stole the boat?"

"Those no good Shi'ites. Robbers, thieves. I know them. I see them down the suq and in coffee shops. Now these robbers say they Ayatullah men. They need boat to carry arms for revolution. I tell them in the Koran it say do not steal but when I tell them this they beat me good."

He indicated where he had been struck and indeed there was a bloodied gash on his head.

"You're injured."

"No no," he assured her. "Abdul very strong for pain."

Deborah remembered the guard. "Where was the guard in all this? He's here to protect us and our property. And I know he was somewhere around. I saw him earlier this morning."

"They shoot him. They shoot him nicely." Abdul said.

Deborah was shocked. She couldn't believe what she was hearing. What sort of savagery was this?

"I don't believe it."

"Yes yes. He shoot at them so they shoot back and hit him. Plenty blood. Look, you can see it blood on ground." Abdul pointed to where down below there was a dark moist stain on the dry earth.

"So, if he was shot, where is he now? We have to get help"

"He gone," Abdul said.

"What do you mean gone?"

"Those Shi'ites they throw him in truck and take him away." Abdul went on, "Why not you give me gun. Then next time these Shi'ites come here I shoot them."

"There's no gun in the house."

"You must have it gun. Everyone have gun. Give me money and I go suq now and buy it gun."

"I don't think so Abdul. But we have to do something. If they killed that man it's murder."

Deborah went inside, picked up the phone, and dialled the emergency number. She asked for the police, she wanted to report a robbery and a shooting. What she got was a torrent of Arabic, none of which she understood.

"Abdul. Abdul. Come here." She handed him the phone. "Tell me what they're saying."

There were now two torrents of Arabic, one at the other end and one at her end. After a long time, Abdul put the phone down.

"What did they say?"

"They say they very busy. They say too many reports coming. They say they investigate. They say they call later."

Abdul became suddenly animated. "Look," Abdul said pointing, "Those Shi'ites gone mad, *majnoon*. Look. They all marching on New City. Thousands and thousands of them."

Deborah looked and, right enough, in the hot quivering air, she could see a large crowd of people coming from the direction of the Old City in cars, on scooters, walking. From this distance they looked like little stick figures headed for the bridge. Those of them who had guns regularly discharged their weapons into the air.

"What are they doing?"

"They go kill the Sunnis. Take over the country. Make Ayatullah Abd Al Wahhab Ruler. Then they ban all liquor. They ban all music. They ban all prostitutes. They ban all fun. They make it like Taliban."

Abdul was no doubt exaggerating grossly as was his wont. All the same, there were a lot of people on the move.

Were the Shi'ites really on the march right now just as Eileen had predicted? Looking down the road, she tried to see more clearly but the wind was blowing dust into the air and making the scene obscure and dream-like.

Abdul was saying excitedly, "Look, those Shi'ites they starting fire, big fire."

"Where?"

"Look. Over there."

Deborah looked where Abdul was pointing in the direction of the Old City and, right enough, saw a lick of flames, hardly discernible in the bright sunlight.

"You know what building they burn? Police barracks. Look. Burning nicely."

It did indeed look as if the revolution or at least some kind of insurgency had begun. Al Wahhab had released forces in the minds of the people and this was the result.

Deborah went back inside and dialled the bank number. The phone in the bank kept on ringing but no one answered. Did that mean that David was in some other part of the building or that he was on his way home? She tried his mobile but it was turned off. She couldn't contact him. She felt a stab of fear.

On impulse she rang Eileen's number. Eileen would know what was going on, help her to interpret what she was hearing and seeing, give her a line on what was the intent of the crowds on the road, if this really was a rising or just another demonstration.

But Eileen's phone too just rang and rang. And no one answered it either.

Wanting to get in contact with someone, she dialled Margaret's number.

Margaret would know more than she did about the position on the other side of the creek.

A strange voice answered the phone, a strange man's voice.

"I must have the wrong number."

"This is Mr and Mrs Wilson's apartment."

Deborah was taken aback. "May I speak to Margaret please?"

"She's not available at the moment, I'm afraid."

"Not available! I'm a close friend and I want to speak to her."

"I'm sorry, but she's not available."

"Who am I speaking to?"

"I'm a member of Mr Wilson's staff."

What was a member of Andy's staff doing taking phone calls in their apartment? If Margaret wasn't there, one of the servants always answered. Then Deborah remembered that the last time she had spoken to Margaret she'd told her that her servants had gone missing.

"Can I ask what you're doing there?"

The man said stiffly, as if her call was an unwelcome intrusion, "I'm looking after their apartment."

"Why can't they look after it themselves?"

"They're not here."

They must have gone. Their transfer to Singapore must have been brought forward a couple of weeks. But surely they wouldn't have gone without saying good-bye. Unless they'd tried and couldn't get through.

"Have they gone to Singapore already?" Deborah queried.

"Unfortunately not."

"So where have Mr and Mrs Wilson gone to?"

"I have been instructed not to give out any information. I've been instructed not to disclose anything as to their whereabouts."

Deborah was losing patience. She wasn't going to be talked down by some junior assistant of Andy's who'd got too big for his boots. She told him so. She explained who she was and who her husband was.

Relenting, the man said, "I'm only doing my job. But if, as you say, you're a close friend, I suppose I can give some indication."

"Go ahead."

"There's been an accident."

"What sort of accident?"

"An explosive device detonated under Mr Wilson's car early this morning as he was getting into it to go to work."

Deborah remembered that, after Margaret's servants had gone missing and there had been mention of firebombs in stores, Margaret had rung her to warn her to be careful. Hadn't she said something specifically about looking under one's car every morning?

"Was Margaret in the car?"

"No. Only Mr Wilson and his driver."

"Was Mr Wilson injured?"

"I'm afraid so."

"How badly?"

"Actually, his position is quite serious.

"Was he killed?

"Yes."

The man put the phone down.

Deborah rang back immediately to find out where Margaret was but the phone had been taken off the hook.

NOEL SCANLON

CHAPTER 40

S tanding in his office, David, considering what he should do first, quickly decided to start with the computer room in the basement.

The basement computer room had high security and he could access it only by using his swipe card and the code for the electronic locking system which made it accessible only to himself and a very limited number of staff.

This room was normally kept at a low controlled temperature but as he stepped into it now it was beginning to heat up.

He stood surveying the main computer surrounded by a lot of other high tech paraphernalia. This was the server computer to which those in the banking hall were all linked, being really only work stations or monitors able to access controlled amounts of data.

He crossed to the tower, extracted its hard drives and carefully carried them up to his office. Hunting about, he found a roll of bubble wrap, wrapped the hard drives in the bubble wrap and put them in his own office safe just for now.

He thought about the vault and main strong room with all its cash and gold bullion. But there was nothing he could do there. It was secure enough anyway. With its massive steel construction it was proof against pretty well anything, even a fairly substantial explosion.

Next he went out into the passageway and took CJ's special private lift that served only the third floor. The normal lift stopped at the floor below.

David stepped out into an extensive area, a whole floor which accommodated CJ's suite and a small number of work areas. A lot of work had gone into making this floor secure. There were CCTV cameras all over the place. A small number of specially selected staff who worked on this floor had, in the first instance, been recommended by Mohammed and then checked out by the police department before being even allowed to enter its precincts.

All that worked perfectly well, indeed the bank had an excellent security system for normal circumstances and there had never ever been any difficulties security wise. But these weren't normal circumstances. With the defection or intimidation or kidnapping or whatever of most of the security guards everything could be at risk. Some of the staff undoubtedly did have good reasons not to come in; their lives could be at risk. But there were others who could well be members of, or acting for, the *Mujahadeen*.

It was up to him now to secure the most important data. And fast.

He punched in the code on the door pad and entered CJ's suite. He then accessed CJ's private sanctuary with a further keypad code.

CJ's office was luxuriously furnished. His large teak desk was heavy and ornate with framed photographs of his wife Mary, his house back in Ireland and his much-prized racing horse, Black Storm, which was trained in the famous Coolmore stables in Kildare and had come second in the Sheik Mohammed hurdle at Leopardstown some months ago. Opening off the office was a reception area for important customers. There were tapestries on the walls, couches, brass Moroccan occasional tables on wooden legs, Arab chests and ornamental coffee pots. It was, of course, less luxurious than the fourth floor, but luxurious nonetheless.

Considering what was to be done here, David crossed to CJ's well stocked-drinks cabinet. He helped himself to a generous scotch without water, not the best thing in this heat, but he felt he needed it. As he did so, he heard, or thought he heard, a movement in the hallway outside. He stood listening. There was just the whisper of a footfall. Who could it be? It certainly wasn't CJ who was at home in his villa and, with CJ absent, his staff, if they had ventured in at all, would have left with the others. With the fourth floor also empty, as far as he knew, there was no one in the building apart from himself.

He dashed to the door and, as he opened it, he just glimpsed a figure rounding the corner. Before he could get there, the lift door had closed and begun its rapid descent. He punched the buttons to no avail.

He thought of pursuit but there was no point. There was no way he could get down the stairs before the intruder had not only reached the ground floor but left the building. The fact that he had gained access to the suite at all meant that he was in possession of the code relevant to that day, which indicated either a senior staff member or someone colluding with a senior staff member. In any event, the way he had sneaked out made it pretty clear that he was up to do good.

Back in CJ's office, David checked on what was happening down in the street below. The crowd was growing in number. At first sight it had seemed just a disorganised mob but he could see now that it was being directed and marshalled by the Ayatullah's *Mujahadeen*.

There wasn't a lot of time. Coming away from the window, David crossed to the small private computer room in CJ's suite. It was the same as the basement computer room only on a smaller scale with the server computer in this case linked only to the few workstations on this floor. From here, the Ruler's private accounts and those of most of his senior ministers were administered.

David repeated what he had done in the computer room. He extracted all the hard drives and brought them down to his office.

Then he came back up to the third floor and had a look at CJ's private computer. This was a stand-alone. It had no links anywhere. It couldn't be hacked into. And it couldn't pick up any viruses. It also contained the most sophisticated technology in the bank. Its hard drives were divided into an accessible part and a virtual part. The virtual part was the mystery hard drive where the most vitally sensitive and confidential materials were hidden. This was the part of the hard drive where the secret, off-record accounts and transactions of Sheikh Suleiman Bin Himyar Al Yas and his most senior ministers were stored.

David didn't know all the contents, but he had a fair idea. Here were the accounts of the secret bribes or commissions paid to the state for the granting of oil contracts and major building contracts. From these accounts multimillion-dollar transfers were made to offshore jurisdictions and to various investments world wide. There was a lot of information stored in there that would be highly dangerous if it fell into the wrong hands. In certain circumstances and in the wrong hands it could not only cause enormous embarrassment to a number of states but threaten the continued rule of the Sheikh himself.

Deciding what he could do, David picked up CJ's computer with both hands. It was heavier than he had expected. The temperature was rising all the time – the stand-by generator either wasn't functioning properly or had been sabotaged. He felt like opening a window but, if he did, he would only have let in hot dust-laden humid air. As he carried the computer away, he was perspiring so much that his hands were slippery on the computer casing and he was afraid of dropping it.

He glanced at his watch and was surprised at how much time had passed. Given the scenes he had glimpsed from time to time on the street below, he didn't have any time to spare. If anything, he had stayed longer than he should.

Carrying the computer, David left CJ's office, pulling the door to. He checked in the other offices. There was no one there.

Taking CJ's lift, he stopped off at the ground floor, went into his own office and put CJ's computer on his desk. He went to his own safe, opened it, and collected all the hard drives he had put there when he had taken them from the basement computer room.

His safe was a top quality OK safe but not good enough for present purposes. In present circumstances it would act as a decoy for anyone who might get this far. They would waste quite a lot of time trying to crack it open.

Next he went to the right hand corner of his office and rolled back the Persian carpet. He measured a distance in and with his envelope opener pressed at a certain point activating a hidden electronic remote control button.

A section of the floor swung back. He took a flashlight from his desk and went down half a dozen steps to where a small fire proof, blast proof and bomb proof safe of six inch thick steel was set in mass concrete. He operated the top combination lock with his code and the second combination lock with the code CJ had given him earlier. The safe opened. He put all the hard drives he had collected into the safe, went back and fetched CJ's stand alone computer and put it in the underground safe too.

He had just closed the underground safe and pulled the Persian carpet back in place when he heard the sound of the basement lift coming up. He froze. The lift door opened and he could hear the slapping sound of feet on the marble of the main banking hall. He got to the door in time to see a masked figure disappearing out through the back door.

What the hell was going on here? Was the masked man the same man he had glimpsed upstairs on CJ's floor? Or was he an accomplice? Were either or both of them bank staff, even senior bank staff? They certainly knew their way around.

He went to the lift the masked man had just emerged from and took it down to the basement. There was a smell in the lift, a smell he couldn't quite place. The door to the safe deposit area was open. This was clearly where the masked man had been.

He went into the safe deposit area and looked up and down the rows of safe deposit lockers. They were used by customers for all sorts of purposes: keeping documents, bundles of private papers, stacks of share certificates. But also gold. And sometimes stashes of cash.

His eye stopped at locker number 10031, the door of which was slightly ajar. He knew that locker. He had brought its owner here only a few weeks ago. The locker was hired out to Bahwan, the carpet merchant, the man he had seen at the airport trying to flee the country.

He pulled the door open. He did a double take, not believing his own eyes. The locker was empty.

Except for a bomb.

The masked man must have been down here placing a bomb. But how had he obtained access to the locker? Mostly likely he had got the key from Bahwan by force.

David stood back and studied what was in the locker. Bombs, even crude ones, were something he knew very little about. He could do with some advice and instruction right now. But none was available. He had no idea how much havoc a device like this would make when it went up, and he didn't want to know. That sort of thing was more in Sebastian's line. In his cover as a bomb expert he'd certainly be expected to know about bomb making. He wondered with a pang where Sebastian was now. What had happened to him? Was he dead or alive?

But he mustn't think about all that now. He must narrow his focus to what was in front of him.

The device he was staring at in the locker consisted of strips of plastic explosive about a foot long and a couple of inches wide taped to several short lengths of flat wood. A detonator tube had been inserted into the plastic explosive and this tube led through a hole into the timer unit.

He gingerly prised open the top of the timer unit which contained the timer itself and a twelve volt battery.

One strand of fuse wire had been soldered on to the positive terminal of the battery and the other strand soldered on to the negative. This double stranded flex then came out of a hole drilled in the side of the box. An electric charge from the battery would ignite the detonator in the plastic explosive which would then explode.

All very simple. But what he saw on the face of the timer would have made him break out in a sweat if he wasn't sweating so heavily already.

The timer was operated by a spring slowly unwinding. The timer face clearly read twenty-seven minutes and it was falling steadily down towards zero.

In its present state, the circuit was open. But it was gradually closing as the spring unwound. When it wound down to zero, the circuit would close and the detonator would be ignited by an electrical charge from the battery.

A feeling of horror and dread lodged in the pit of his stomach, and there flashed through his mind a kaleidoscope of the innumerable TV shots he had seen of explosions going off leaving mangled and dismembered bodies in their wake, tossing body parts randomly here and there.

But his sense of self-preservation took over, concentrating his mind wonderfully.

He had to defuse the bomb.

If his reading of the situation was right, what he had to do was extract the detonator tube from the plastic explosive, pull off the wires soldered on to the battery terminals and the whole device would be as dead as a dodo.

Or so he hoped.

But what if his reasoning was all terribly wrong? What then?

Maybe the most sensible thing for him to do was to get out of this safe deposit room and run like hell.

His teeth were gritted and his hands were visibly shaking as he yanked the detonator tube out of the plastic explosive.

He paused for a second.

Had he done the right thing? If he hadn't, then his next breath would be his last.

He waited for the explosion that would end everything, but the safe deposit room remained silent except for his own accelerated breathing. He left the dismantled bomb in locker number 10031, wondering what sort of damage that quantity of plastic explosive would cause were it to go off, how much of the bank would it have destroyed.

He closed the safe deposit locker room and, as he exited, locked the safe deposit vault.

Taking the lift up to the main floor, he rang CJ from the empty banking hall. The phone went on ringing until the recorder cut in. He left a message. It was CJ's responsibility to take it from there.

He left the building by the back door that gave on to the car park.

CHAPTER 41

At last, after numerous attempts, Eileen's phone was answered by the little girl Fatima who either couldn't or didn't want to speak in English. She had put the phone down and left Deborah hanging on.

Deborah was still devastated by the news of Andy being blown up. She was sure he was dead, that was clear from the tone of the man she had spoken with. She knew he was dead but she had difficulty in taking it in. Andy was the last person you would think of this happening to. Both he and Margaret had been so careful. They lived on the right side of the creek, in the most secure area. They kept well out of harm's way. Margaret had even told her that Andy had forbidden her to cross to this side of the creek under any circumstances whatsoever.

What would Margaret do now, her whole glittering future left dangling there, uninhabited, unfulfilled? Deborah wanted to commiserate with her but couldn't get through to her on the phone though she had tried numerous times. The best she had been able to do was to send her an e-mail.

As she hung on for Eileen, she remembered the scene when she had visited her in her apartment and, sitting out on the balcony in the middle of the most deprived and staunchly Shi'ite area of the Old City, she could hear in the background the chatter of Arab women. Were those same women still sewing banners or had they moved on to something else, something more lethal? The photographs she had taken that day had turned out remarkably well in catching the moment. She had sent them as e-mail attachments to her article and she wondered if any of them had been used.

At last Eileen came on the phone. Deborah was wondering how she might get something more substantial from her than the usual rhetoric. But she needn't have worried. Eileen didn't need any prompting in order to impart valuable, eyewitness, on the spot reportage. She was unstoppable.

She was hyper.

"The revolution has begun," she burst out. "What sparked it off was when the police attacked us in the streets and in the mosques last night, firing indiscriminately. They forced us to fight in self defence and that made us put our plans for action into immediate effect."

"What sort of plans of action do you mean? I've been watching people heading for the New City. Are they going to demonstrate or what?"

"They're going to take over the city. The revolution has begun."

Deborah was shocked by Eileen's certainty. She had rung Eileen to get a line on what was going on. But she hadn't expected anything as sensational and scary as this firm confirmation from someone right there in the depths of the Old City that a revolution had actually begun.

In parallel with her feeling of apprehension and dread at the thought of an uprising, her journalistic instincts had been aroused. Her journalistic nose told her that she had a scoop here.

Eileen was saying, "Our fighters are on the move and we already hold the bridge. Where are you just now, Deborah?"

"Here at home."

"Then you must be able to see what's happening."

"I can see some movement on the bridge. But is it true that the main police station in the Old City has gone up in flames?"

"It sure has. Those of the police who were Sunnis have scarpered. They weren't going to hang around to suffer the wrath of the people. Almost all of the Shi'ite members of the police force came over to us after the Ayatullah himself addressed them over the loudspeakers. They were won over by his passion, by his conviction. Listening to his inspired words they broke ranks and came over to us......."

Deborah could well imagine the scene. She had, after all, herself witnessed the effect of mob oratory from close up. She hadn't yet completely shaken off the memory of the hysteria it had engendered or the image of that crazy man mutilating himself with chain and sword.

"It was a great historic moment." Eileen was saying. "We are going into battle with an inspiring leader...."

"How do you see this working out then?" Deborah asked. This exulting was all very well for Eileen. But what about ordinary expats like herself and David? What was going to happen to them? "David went in to the bank this morning. Will he be able to get home?"

"Not unless he gets out pretty smart. Some of our best fighters are on their way to hold the bridge."

Eileen launched into her usual list of all the Shi'ite grievances. They certainly had grievances. But did they have the ability to actually confront and win against the Sunnis who had held power for so long and were so well entrenched? Without doubt, Eileen was exaggerating their capabilities.

She was saying, "We are well armed. And more on the way. We have support..."

Deborah wondered where Eileen's husband was and what part he was playing in all this, but didn't like to ask. She let Eileen fire away. She had heard it all many times before. But suddenly, in the middle of it, with Eileen in full spate, Deborah's ears pricked up. She could hardly believe what she was hearing.

Eileen was saying. "Did you hear about the Ruler?"

"No."

"We got him."

"What do you mean you got him?"

"An assassination attempt was made this morning by a young Shi'ite martyr who sacrificed his own life."

"Was the Sheikh killed?"

"No, but he was wounded."

"When you say wounded, how badly wounded?"

"We don't know. But he was whisked away to hospital."

"How come I haven't heard anything about all this?"

"Of course you haven't heard about it. How could you? All you hear is government propaganda."

"There was nothing about it on the radio"

"Of course not. The government wouldn't allow such news to be broadcast. They suppress anything they don't want to get out. Eventually, if the Sheikh recovers, they will probably issue a denial that the incident ever took place. But what I'm telling you is true," Eileen added triumphantly, "It signals the beginning of the end of the Sunni regime in Khor Fahal."

Deborah had her story. And, without doubt, she'd be first with the news this time. Provided she got her despatch off straightaway before the other journalists got wind of it when they'd be on to it like a pack of wolves. That meant she'd better get moving and have her piece e-mailed before there was a power cut. Power cuts were common on this impoverished side of the creek.

So, immediately Eileen rang off, she began to put her piece together. Deborah wrote.

I am informed by a reliable informant that an attempt has been made this morning on the life of Sheikh Suleiman Bin Himyar Al Yas by a suicide bomber who blew himself up on the palace steps. The Sheikh survived but was injured and is now in hospital. His condition is unknown.

Deborah paused. Could she fully rely on Eileen's account of what had happened? Eileen was after all a long way from being an impartial reporter. She would undoubtedly exaggerate Shi'ite plans and successes. She would have to try to confirm Eileen's account.

She rang around looking for confirmation that a failed attempt had been made on the Sheikh's life, but got nowhere. The government ministries all made a flat denial. All of the Arab embassies denied any knowledge. And the British Embassy spokesman she got flatly refused to say anything on the record.

She tried the hospital where a number of special suites were reserved at all times for the senior members of the Ruling family but the hospital would not confirm that the Sheikh had checked in.

So that was that. She firmly believed that what Eileen had told her had some substance and that some sort of assassination attempt had been made. On the other hand, she could get no confirmation or corroboration of any such thing having happened. She reviewed the possibilities. Given that she accepted that an assassination attempt had been made, the Sheikh might have been seriously wounded. Or he might have been only lightly wounded. Or he might be suffering from shock. Or he might have escaped any injury.

So what to do? She decided to use what Eileen had told her but she'd qualify it heavily and stress that her report was uncorroborated. And she wouldn't lead with it.

She deleted what she had written and began again.

A revolution, or at least a rising, began in the early hours of this morning in this oil rich state of Khor Fahal here in the Gulf.

As I watch from my balcony on the Shi'ite side of the creek I can see large numbers of people spilling across the bridge that spans the creek. Among them are armed members of the Ayatullah's Mujahadeen.

They are headed towards the New City. My contact within the Shi'ite community tells me that their fighters are on the move and will attack the Sunni strongholds. They claim that already they hold the bridge across the creek linking the Old City to the New City.
She paused.

My source claims that early this morning an attempt was made on the life of Sheikh Suleiman Bin Himyar Al Yas by a suicide bomber who blew himself up on the palace steps. I must stress that I have not been able to obtain official confirmation of this assassination attempt which is vigorously denied by the government. Nor would the hospital confirm or deny that the Sheikh was under treatment. Nonetheless, I place a good deal of reliance on my source and am of the opinion that an attempt of some sort was made on the Ruler's life this day.

An incident for which I do sadly have official confirmation is that the British manager of the Standard Chartered Bank, Andy Wilson, was killed this morning by a bomb placed under his car and detonated when he got into it to drive to work.

The events beginning to unfold today are the culmination of the long standing tension between the Sheikh and his government and the more radicalised Shi'ites under the leadership of the fundamentalist cleric Ayatullah Abd Al Wahhab who recently entered Khor Fahal to organise this rising of the Shi'ites who are, to a large extent, excluded from both power and representation....

When she had finished writing and e-mailing her article Deborah went out on to the balcony and looked down the road. The glare hit her in the eyes. The heat and humidity were extreme. Objects were dancing in the heat haze.

She wished she could get on to David. From what Eileen had just told her things were going to be get very unpleasant.

She had intended when she had finished her piece to get on with the packing but she couldn't bring herself to until David got home.

She watched out for David's car, paying particular attention to any car that turned on to their road. She kept phoning the bank but got no reply, no one lifted the phone. The bank must have closed. David must have closed up or someone would have answered. He must have closed the bank and be on his way home with his mobile switched off.

Several times she spotted a car that was the right colour or the right make and she was sure it was his. But each time she was disappointed.

Honey and Poochie sat looking at her disturbed because they thought that she was disturbed. Occasionally Honey would raise a paw and touch her questioningly.

CHAPTER 42

D avid edged the car out of the bank car park and, entering the mayhem on the street, joined a long line of slowly moving cars.

The street was filling up with a Shi'ite mass demonstration crowding the pavements and spilling well out on to the road. They were carrying flags and they were shouting slogans. The atmosphere was alive and highly charged. It looked like a situation that could easily turn ugly. You could feel its strength, its potency, its energy. Filled with this screaming crowd, Bank Street was scarcely recognisable as the street he drove along every day.

Bank Street, the financial centre of the state, normally exuded a solid and impressive atmosphere. The buildings dominated. They stood for wealth and affluence. Their marble facings glinted back the light of the sun. In deference to this show of wealth and power, the street itself was normally quiet and subdued with the swishing sound of the smoothly gliding limousines of the wealthy and ultra wealthy, their white robed occupants hidden by the tinted glass, the uniformed chauffeurs solemn, reflecting the status of those they drove.

Everything reflected the status of a street that was fast becoming one of the financial centres of the Middle East. Here in these banks, as well as the oil money, was lodged a fair share of the international money that moves around the world with every shift of the financial winds, money that seeks as few onerous taxes and as high a degree of discretion and secrecy as possible.

But the street David was driving cautiously along now was something else. Instead of the usual quiet respectful atmosphere with the silence broken only by the rich and powerful as they alighted from their limousines with their sycophantic entourages, what he found himself surrounded by was a screaming horde of Shi'ites chanting, displaying banners, firing shots in the air, a ragged crowd wearing every kind of clothing, t-shirts and jeans and Arab caps and thobes. In among them was a scattering of men in police uniform and carrying arms, obviously Shi'ite police who had deserted.

The demonstration was being led by *Mujahadeen* in black shirts and green headbands. They made the demonstration look both political and organised. They were the cheerleaders who harangued the people and told them what to do.

The crowd was beginning to press against his car on either side. CJ was always calling Shi'ites feckless. But it seemed to David that the bugging of his office, the placing of the bomb outside CJ's apartment and the more recent one in the safe deposit vault was all far from feckless. To the contrary, they seemed to him to be highly organised. And just now looking at them out on the street, demonstrating, he hoped that was all they intended to do, demonstrate.

As he moved along in the line of traffic, he kept his car windows closed, trying to keep out the noise of the screaming crowds. He was able to lock out some of the sounds but what he couldn't lock out were the memories that those sounds, sounds deeply burnt into in his mind, evoked. Some were recent memories. Some from the long ago. All stalked on the edge of his consciousness and jumped out now, stimulated, resurrected by the scene he was driving through: the youths about to attack them on that isolated, cut-off beach, the boy he had shot, the shock of seeing Sebastian's blood on the wall of his bedroom. David struggled to clear his mind and concentrate on his driving, on the here and now. But, try as he would, the demonstrators crowding in on him on either side, gave him a terrible feeling of having seen it all before, not once but many times.

What was wrong with the Middle East? What was it that seemed to condemn it to an endless cycle of violence? It was like as if this part of the world was on a wheel of violence that just went round and round and round, endlessly repeated.

By now, hemmed in by the mob, he was only able to move at a walking pace. How had all these people got here so quickly and in such numbers and apparently unopposed? They were, after all, the Shi'ites, the poor, the largely uneducated, dismissed by those in power. Up until now, the police had always seemed to be comfortably in charge. Why weren't they in charge now? And, apart from the normal police, where were the much feared and highly reputed Special Armed Police accustomed to dealing ruthlessly with this sort of thing.

He soon found out where the armed police were. From behind him, they began firing off tear gas from positions they had taken up. Clearly, the ordinary police had been taken off guard by the sudden massive influx of Shi'ites who vastly outnumbered them.

The initial shots carried canisters of tear gas which added to the suffocating atmosphere and enveloped sections of the crowd, making them cough and splutter.

David entered one of these areas in which clouds of gas lay inert in the hot windless air. Everything was indistinct and vague. The crowd outside looked like ghosts. His eyes began to sting and water. Tear gas had seeped into the car. He began to feel odd, to feel queasy. He covered his mouth and breathed as shallowly as possible.

Then he was through the tear gas cloud and moving on.

A loud noise made him start involuntarily. What was it?

There was no mistaking what it was. Shots were being fired, gunfire as opposed to tear gas canisters was coming from various positions.

Bullets zinged overhead.

David ducked. His hands sweating on the steering wheel, he tried to get out of range. There was another volley. No rubber bullets just the plain old live ammunition.

Looking in his rear view mirror, he could see that the latest shots were coming from one of the windows of the Middle Eastern Insurance Corporation building. The SAP up there were firing directly into the crowd.

"That'll do it," David shouted out loud, though there was no one to hear him. "That'll really get things going. That'll put the show on the road."

He knew that he would now inevitably be exposed to the heightened anger of the crowd in the street. Clearly, they would be out for blood and he hoped it wouldn't be his. He knew that, as a European, he would be seen as an enemy. He might even be seen as an American which meant that if he was killed he would also be mutilated and probably dragged along behind a truck.

When the crowd looked at him, all they saw was a European man alone in a car. No one in that crowd he was trying to nose the car through gave a fuck what he thought. They weren't going to stop and ask him what his opinions were, discuss with him the pros and cons of their present situation viz a viz the ruling Sunnis, engage in an exchange of opinions, weigh matters up, think before acting. What they would do was kill him first and ask questions later.

Heavier fire opened up from the end of the street. Looking around, he could see that the police were firing from behind lorries they had positioned to block exit from Bank Street. As the bullets thudded into it, the crowd stopped.

It sighed, like a wounded animal, then erupted in a kind of maniacal hysteria, a whole river of men panting and sweating, their faces distorted, their mouths open as they screamed, dazed and crazed, charging towards where the firing was coming from, oblivious to the bullets.

He kept his head down and edged forward as fast as he could.

Blood had been spilled. The first spilling of blood was like firing off a starter's pistol. The mob reacted to it as to the off signal. Ready. Steady. Go.

As they surged forward, the crowd picked up the bloodied bodies of those who had been shot. Gory exhibit number one. Gory exhibit number two. And so on. They carried them with them, raised above their heads like trophies.

Crouched inside his car, David knew that, with these deaths, the situation had changed, and changed utterly. The crowd had their martyrs. They had their brand new martyrs. The effect was electric. It was as if they had collectively received a blood transfusion.

He was getting seriously worried. A slow moving car isn't a whole lot of protection when you get down to it. A car might be a powerful missile when speeding along a highway. Starting and stopping, hemmed in by a hostile crowd - he'd have to call them hostile - a car, with its breakable windows, doesn't offer all that much in the way of protection.

To save his life he had to get away, get out of this area. He was already out of Bank Street which had by now become Sheikh Mahmoud Boulevard, a high class shopping area with all the large department stores where all the well known international names were represented, Dior, Gucci, Valentino, Versace, Armani. Here were the malls where the wealthy shopped. This street was wider than Bank Street. He needed to get moving but even in the wider street the lanes normally reserved for cars had been taken over by pedestrians who shouted at him, sometimes hitting his windscreen with their banners. He had to drive slowly, careful not to hit and injure anyone. If he did, it would be curtains. They would literally pull him limb from limb.

If only he could get up speed, speed would help him get away. But with the line of cars and with the street full of people, he was forced to stay in first or second gear, to crawl along.

Since the shootings, the crowd in the hot throbbing air were driven by rage. Their rage empowered them. They surged forward, energised. They didn't care if they were shot, if they died.

They had about them that air of fatality, that sense of waiting to suffer which he had discerned in Abood. Abood wasn't violent, didn't approve of violence. But, even so, he was in some odd way wedded to suffering and accepting of, almost welcoming, it.

It was obvious that some deep vein of masochism ran through these people in a way that was incomprehensible to the western mind. And, in its present and immediate application, it was perfectly clear that however many casualties they suffered, they would keep going.

David kept his head down in the hope of avoiding attention.

There was a lull. The shooting had stopped at least temporarily. It looked like the police, confronted by the sheer weight of numbers, had withdrawn or relocated.

Suddenly he spotted an opening.

He didn't waste any time in availing of the opportunity. He knew it was a once off chance. He knew the opportunity wouldn't last for long. He seized the momentary space, the sliver of time given to him and floored the accelerator. He moved up through the gears and, the more he got going, the more quickly people jumped out of his way.

He was travelling at speed down the Sheikh Mahmood Boulevard when, to his horror, he saw a stretch limousine coming straight at him down the wrong side of the road from the opposite direction. The insignia painted on its side meant that it belonged to the Ruling Family, but it was now being driven wildly and inexpertly by a bunch of youthful joyriders who had obviously highjacked it.

David was mesmerised by the sight of the limousine being driven right at him, a highjacked limousine on a wild ride, the ragged joyriders in it laughing, excited, drunk with the speed they were travelling at. As the wildly driven limousine bore down on him, blood pounding in his ears, he wrenched and pulled on the steering wheel until with a terrible crunch and jolt, he mounted the pavement, bouncing along with two wheels elevated and two in the gutter.

The oncoming limousine shot past him and suddenly swerved out of control. It crashed into a lamppost just behind him. Its wild ride over, some of its occupants were thrown out on the street, some crushed against the lamppost.

David bounced his car off the pavement back on to the road and drove on. He swerved down a side street. Then another side street. And so on, each new street now with a smaller and smaller and less threatening crowd.

A short time later, by a winding, circuitous route, he came out on to the bridge.

Here on the bridge things were surprisingly orderly. There was a high degree of control. Shi'ite ex-police, some still in uniform, were supervising the erection of barricades. A squad of men were lowering themselves on ropes and examining the underside of the bridge. Were they going to blow it up? He didn't think it likely, at least for the moment, after all they needed the bridge to get into the New City, but maybe they were making a survey, even planting charges for future use. Anything was possible.

David got across the bridge before the erection of the barricade was completed and, although a cordon of insurgents looked at him doubtfully, they let him through.

He was well off the bridge and on his way home when, unexpectedly and randomly, a rock hit the car with a clatter and a breaking of glass. He didn't see where it came from or who had thrown it. The rock shattered the back window and landed on the front seat beside him.

He put his foot down and roared along the creek road towards home.

CHAPTER 43

T hat evening Deborah and David sat in the lounge feeling cut-off and isolated, a feeling not helped by an electricity outage that left them without lights, fridge, air-conditioning or telephone. They sat listening to the noises of shouting and shooting coming from not all that far away. The guard who was due on duty about now hadn't turned up which wasn't that surprising considering his predecessor had been shot. But it did leave them without any protection.

It was clear from what Eileen had told Deborah and from David's experiences driving back that, if not exactly an uprising, there was mayhem on the streets and if someone didn't get a grip on the situation soon anything could happen.

Even though CJ had just that morning said he'd be sending transport and an escort to move their possessions to the new villa next day, in present circumstances, it was obvious that, as long as the whole area was in bedlam and those insurgents stayed on the bridge, there was no way any vehicle was going to get across from the New City or visa versa for their personal possessions or for anything else.

That left them completely cut off. It also meant that there was no point in getting on with the packing. All that would have to be put on hold. The new villa would have to wait, at least for the moment. It was all very disappointing and a bit crushing, but what could they do about it.

An awful lot seemed to have happened since David had gone to work that morning. A single day seemed to have changed pretty well everything and David even began to wonder if, given the sudden turn things had taken, they had made a wrong decision in choosing to live here on this side of the creek at all. But there was no point in going down that road. They were where they were and they had to make the best of it. Or, as his father used say, 'We're where we are because that's what happened.' Which was a complete practical and philosophical explanation of any situation you might find yourself in.

When, later, they went out on to the balcony with their drinks, Deborah told David what she couldn't hold back on any longer, the death of Andy Wilson, blown up by a bomb under his car. Her words dripping into the air seemed to tighten and darken the atmosphere around them. All the other happenings of the day were bad enough. But Andy being blown up by a car bomb was something more personal, more close up. And a lot more devastating.

In the ordinary way, they would have gone across to the New City to do what they could and give Margaret support, but, in present circumstances, that just wasn't possible.

They would have liked at least to have rung Margaret to commiserate but they had no phones. The landline was dead and their mobiles had gone down with the burning of the police barracks where the aerial was located.

They reminisced about Andy and Margaret and the pleasant evenings they had spent together, and how very close they had been to getting away to Singapore. Margaret had started the packing long ago, and, in her efficient way, had most of it done, the suitcases no doubt lying there on the bed in the spare room ready to be closed up. It didn't bear thinking about.

As they stood there mourning Andy's death, it was that time of evening when the sun begins to set, and the Middle Eastern night falls swiftly like a guillotine. It was poised now in a moment of expectancy. Suddenly the sun plummeted as it only can in these parts. It ducked quickly behind the Old City. There was a brief orange glow as the buildings yielded up their whiteness. Suddenly it was dark. Just like that.

Standing in the sudden darkness, they both felt as if they were on the edge of something, that something of great import was under way, something that looked bad for them in their present situation.

It was beginning to look like they might be getting close to exit time though, unfortunately, they had no idea how they could get out of here in the event that the bridge, which had been swallowed up in the darkness only occasionally illuminated by headlights and flashes of gunfire, remained closed.

They felt very much alone in a foreign place. However fast and painless it is nowadays to jet abroad from your home place without any real sense of having travelled at all such is the speed of transit, there is still, when living in a foreign culture and especially in times of danger, a deep sense of displacement, of disassociation.

There were several postings when David's parents had been in much the same circumstances as they were in now. That is, they had to exit in a hurry. His parents had had to leave, they and all the other foreigners suddenly exposed to what had been fomenting all the time in the minds of the people around them and of which they had been apparently blissfully unaware. No one had expected their lives there to be cut off so quickly. The Arabs were a nice people, really, pleasant, courteous and dignified in an old-world way. And his parents weren't even British, weren't colonial oppressors. Being Irish, they were supposed to be the oppressed, weren't they, historically speaking? Still and all, you had to admit they were as colonial as anyone else in their mentality, if colonial was the right word.

His parents' lives and the lives of all the other expats had been a privileged life, but with a price, the price of exile in a hot foreign land. They imagined their life to be secure. But, suddenly, they were blasted by hatred. Shot at. Bang. It was all over. Finished.

David had learned early in life that we live in an uncertain changing world in which nothing is fixed or permanent. Nothing at all.

They watched the bridge.

The barricade David had seen under construction was now completed and reinforced with another one behind it. They could just about follow this activity in occasional bursts of illumination when headlights were trained on the barricades.

The power remained out, the telephones remained out, Abdul had gone out and hadn't come back. So they stayed late on the balcony drinking, while the sounds, shouts, explosions, gunfire and the roar of a crowd, drifted up to them through the hot air like pieces of a jigsaw that they were not quite able to put together.

The only news available to them was what they could get via the transistor radio David kept to his ear, translating the Arabic broadcasts for Deborah's benefit. A radio station in the Old City had been seized and taken over by the insurgents who broadcast the Ayatullah's speeches, repetitive and full of rhetoric. The government station from across the creek either played music or reported a small demonstration and assured the populace that everything was under control, to stay indoors and not to panic.

Deborah opened a tin of tuna and made up a snack with the left over spinach tart from the night before. With the power off, the ice in the cold food compartment of the fridge was already melting and forming a pool of water on the kitchen floor.

When they had finished their snack they went to bed. There didn't seem to be anything else to do.

Going to bed didn't turn out to be such a great idea. They could still hear the sounds of disturbances which built up unsettling images inside their heads.

At least Deborah had something to console her. They had acted promptly in getting her mother and Carolyn out of the country. Her mother had telephoned her earlier saying she had seen Khor Fahal on the TV. It had given her a real shock and she kept telling Deborah to get on a plane right away and come home. She tried to allay her mother's fears saying that they were going to move to a safe area next morning. After her conversation with her mother, she got to speak for a few minutes to Carolyn who was excited about a kitten her gran had got her and was blissfully unaware of the situation her parents were in.

Still, she just couldn't get to sleep. She couldn't turn her mind off. Without the air-conditioning, it was overpoweringly hot. How did people exist without air-conditioning in the old days? Eventually she drifted off into sleep and into dark nightmarish dreams. She didn't know how long she had slept for when she thought she heard a noise in the apartment. But perhaps it was only an echo of what had been in her dream.

She must have been tossing and turning - the sheet that covered her was twisted into a long coil. She had a memory of darkness, a trapped feeling as if someone had taken a pillow and placed it over her face.

David was sound asleep. The apartment was deadly silent without the constant hum of air-conditioning.

Groping, she pressed the bedside light switch. Nothing happened. She had forgotten all about the power cut. She felt about for the flashlight.

Deborah went to the bathroom. Coming out of the bathroom, she heard what sounded like some sort of activity down below. Looking out, she saw a straggle of people moving along their road, past their building, something she had never seen before at this time of night. Had some of them come into their compound?

She opened the front door of the apartment. There was a miaow and Mr Tom the compound tomcat rubbed up against her. She went to the fridge and poured some milk into a dish.

She climbed the back stairs on to the roof and looked down into the compound. She thought she saw shadows moving about down there, but couldn't identify any of them, pin them down. It was only her imagination, she was getting jumpy. She watched until she was reasonably sure that the compound was empty.

She wandered about the roof under a myriad of stars. Although there was only the faintest whisper of a breeze coming off the creek, it felt better up here than trying to get to sleep down in the apartment. Before air-conditioning, in the hottest days everybody slept at the highest point they could find which was usually the roof, and the air did seem fresher up here with the smell of the sea on the breeze. It felt a lot better out in the open, not only because it was cooler, but because there was a lull in the sound of gunfire that had been disturbing her since she had gone to bed.

Deborah went to the balustrade and, under a bright moon, the scene was idyllic. It was strange how the mayhem of the streets and this idyllic scene could co-exist so close to one another, one scene with man at his most violent and vicious, the other still and peaceful. To cap it all, an ancient looking dhow came sailing down the creek. The dhow was out of the past. Painted on the still water, it slid slowly along, its Arab crew silhouetted in their white robes, ghostly and silent, insubstantial, ethereal, from another time, the breeze in the brown of its sails the breeze of eastern mystery and adventure.

But that image lasted only for a minute. It burst like a soap bubble as her attention was brought back to the compound below where, this time, she was sure she heard a movement. The darkness began to resolve into images.

Or was she imagining things?

No, she wasn't.

Dark shapes were moving about down there. But when she tried to identify each shape, it merged back into the darkness. She was beginning to think that she must be imagining things, letting her imagination run away with her, when a light flickered. Then went out.

Muffled voices drifted up from below.

The dogs in the apartment began to bark. Something untoward was happening down in their apartment.

Deborah began to run across the roof, down the stairs, stumbling and falling in her haste. Hearing noises, she went quietly around the side to the kitchen door. She edged the kitchen door open a few inches. There was someone moving about in there. She could hear voices in Arabic, see the flashing of torches. She stood listening with her hand on the door.

They were being burgled, was that what was happening? That's what it sounded like, men arguing about what they should steal.

Remembering what had happened to the guard earlier in the day, she decided not to take the risk of bursting in and having herself shot unnecessarily just to save a few household items. People were always saying you should never confront burglars especially if they were armed which they were likely to be.

As she stood there listening, she heard people leaving the apartment and going down the stairs.

She edged the kitchen open, not turning on her flashlight until she was pretty sure all the intruders had left. The first thing she saw was that the front door of the apartment stood open.

In the lounge the furniture had been thrown about and knocked over. The TV was gone, the CD player was gone. Drawers had been pulled out and their contents emptied on to the floor. It looked like they had been burgled by passing youths encouraged to raid houses following on the start of the revolution.

"We've been burgled," she called to David as she approached the bedroom. David was probably still asleep, had slept through it all. It took a lot to wake him.

There was no reply.

In the bedroom she shone her flashlight around. He must be in the bathroom. But David wasn't in the bathroom. Nor was he in any of the other rooms.

He must have gone out. He must have heard the burglars and gone after them, a stupid thing to do, given that they were probably armed.

She went out on to the balcony calling out to David not to do anything silly, to take care, everybody knew that the worst thing you could do was to confront intruders.

David didn't reply. Instead, as if in answer, an engine revved up right outside their gate. In the road outside the headlights of a vehicle were turned on and she could see shadowy figures hustling someone into the back. She could just make out the heads of men crammed into the back seat before the car roared away. It was an old battered car, probably stolen, and somehow she knew that David was in that car.

The car's headlights briefly illuminated the creek, then quickly disappeared at speed.

CHAPTER 44

Curled up in the boot of the car, David thought he would suffocate. The gag tasted foul in his mouth and he was afraid it was going to choke him. He was gagging on the cloth that filled his mouth, bulged out his cheeks. His body jerked in spasms and he felt nausea begin to rise up in his throat.

He knew he mustn't vomit. If he did, he would choke on his own vomit. His tongue at the back of his mouth seemed to be large and swollen. His whole body was shuddering, his heart jolting about dangerously.

Then he regained control and began to breathe slowly through his nose. But there was so little air in the boot of the car that he couldn't get enough into his lungs and what he did inhale was thick and musty and smelling of something in the boot. Oil rags maybe.

He tried to brace himself, to steady himself but, whatever position he tried, his head kept bumping on the floor of the car, and with his hands tied, he couldn't do anything about it.

He had been asleep when they'd burst into the bedroom. His first assumption was that what he was dealing with here was casual looters, inevitable when you thought about it. Law and order, which had previously been rigidly maintained, brutally maintained, had broken down. So he supposed that what you could expect, at least in the short term, was chaos.

And he was right to the extent that the apartment was looted - he had seen items being carried out. But he quickly realised that the looting was not the primary motive. It was just opportunistic. These men had been sent for a purpose. And he was the purpose.

He was pulled from the bed, thrown his shirt and trousers and told to get them on quickly which he tried to do but apparently not quickly enough. They began slapping him around. Even though he wasn't of a fighting or aggressive nature, David resisted, kicking out. He was incensed at being treated like this by a gang of masked hoodlums with their *kheffiahs* pulled across their faces to hide them.

Resisting hadn't turned out to be a great idea. All it did was give them the excuse to rough him up even more, which was probably what they had intended to do anyway. By resisting and even landing a few kicks here and there gave them sanction, so to speak, to set about him in proper order.

One of them pulled his head up while several others punched him in the face and about the body.

David knew in a vague way that he should clench his body to resist the blows but there was no way of knowing where the next punch would come from. When they had knocked him to the ground, he did remember to draw his knees up and tried to roll up into a ball and get his arms over his head to protect the most vulnerable parts of his body. Which did to some extent protect his vital organs.

Fortunately, his assailants were only wearing sneakers. None of them was wearing strong shoes or boots so that it wasn't easy for them to do serious damage. He worried about broken ribs though. His rib cage felt very painful. His attackers had been nothing if not enthusiastic. They obviously enjoyed what they were doing. It wasn't often, after all, that they got their hands on one of the hated *Nazaranis*.

When he was lying more or less still, his wrists were grabbed, pinned back and tied, a gag was stuffed in his mouth which someone then taped so that he couldn't scream or cry out. Then he was supported under each armpit as they dragged him down the stairs whispering and arguing among one another while the dogs went mad barking.

A car was waiting outside the compound gates. He was blindfolded, then bundled inside the boot which was slammed closed, very nearly catching his fingers.

The car pulled away taking off with a crack and a bang and a lurch. He could feel that the driver had his foot down but it was apparent from the sound of the engine that what they were using was an old banger with a limited capacity for speed. David could hear and feel the clanging of the loose exhaust and smell its fumes which he couldn't avoid inhaling.

He could also hear his captors arguing, the sound dribbling into the boot. Everybody in the car seemed to be screaming at the driver to get on with it and drive faster and the driver was arguing back. There didn't seem to be a whole lot of discipline. They were all overexcited and overwrought. There was also an argument about stealing the TV and whatever else they had stolen. The man who appeared to be their leader was furious at this. Looting wasn't part of the plan. It wasn't part of instructions. And they should have kept to instructions.

His face on the floor and the smell of exhaust fumes in his nostrils, David concentrated on protecting his head which had already taken a few bad knocks as he was bumped about. The journey was mercifully short which was just as good because, if it had gone on for any length of time, he was sure that he would have expired from carbon monoxide poisoning if from nothing else.

The shortness of the journey, together with the fact that they had taken a sharp left, made him certain that, when the car suddenly skidded to a halt, they were somewhere in the Old City.

He could hear his kidnappers getting out of the car.

He hadn't seen Deborah in the bedroom when he had been so rudely awakened. Where was she? Had they taken her before him? But, if so, he would surely have woken up.

After a short delay, the boot was opened and he could hear a babble of excited voices. Fingers poked at him as if to see if their capture was for real, like as if they were fishermen and had just landed a kingfish so popular in the local fish market.

The fingers poking him reminded him, irrelevantly, of his mother's visit to the harem of the Sultan of Mukulla when she was surrounded by a babbling excited crowd of wives and concubines who had poked her all over, felt her clothes and pulled her skirt up to see what she was wearing underneath. Strange the odd connections the mind makes, a line crossed here, an electric impulse jumping a synapse there. And hey presto you have an image from the past.

Voices in Arabic told him to get out, but he was so dazed he wasn't able to move as quickly as they wanted. Impatient hands grabbed him, lifted him out and again supported him on either side while they half carried him down steps and along a passageway, accompanied all the time by the sound of voices arguing.

There was a pause evidently at a door and a lot of fumbling before they got the key to turn in the lock.

He was shoved into a room with his blindfold still on. He could smell stale air and cigarette smoke. He was still handcuffed and there was a jangling noise while a chain was clamped to one ankle.

A thin reedy mocking voice said in English which indicated that they didn't know he spoke Arabic, "This nice hotel. Arab boy bring you tea. What time you like morning tea?"

Everyone giggled at such a display of wit. One of them kicked David in the ribs and said, "Why the West love the Jews and hate the Arabs? We are followers of Ayatullah Abd Al Wahhab and we will drive all you filthy infidels from our land. Just like you drive Moslems from their lands and destroy their homes and kill their women and children." This was followed by more kicks.

After his gag had been removed, David was left alone in darkness. He wondered how much damage had been done. He was bleeding from a cut on the back of his head, a warm trickle of blood ran down his face, but he had the feeling that were was no vital damage.

There was pain though. Pain and darkness. Pain in his head which when he lifted it surged towards his eyes. Pain in his ribs. The sound of his breathing seemed unnaturally loud. As was the beating of his heart pumping blood around his body and seeming to push it into his ears.

Still, at least, it was still beating.

CHAPTER 45

D eborah felt scared as she shone her flashlight around the chaos of her living room, on the knocked over side tables, the broken glass of the glass coffee table top, the empty stand where the television set had been.

She blamed herself for not having acted faster, for wasting valuable time waiting outside the door thinking that the men in the house had been burglars. They hadn't been burglars. They'd been a lot worse. They'd been kidnappers. David had been forcibly abducted. Just as his father had been in very similar circumstances. And his father had never been seen again, not even his body had been recovered.

Although she was trembling from shock, she tried to remember everything she had seen. It might be important. But she had only glimpsed the kidnappers in the car, and then she couldn't see them properly the way they had their *kheffiahs* pulled over their faces. There was something frightening about men masked like that. It had all the power of the unseen threat, the one that doesn't fully show itself, the one that grows and grows in your imagination.

These featureless men had abducted David. Would they have taken her if she hadn't chanced to be outside the apartment at the time? And if they had, what would they have done? Would they have raped her? Wasn't that what people like that were supposed to do?

But she wasn't thinking straight. She hadn't been abducted, David had.

What was she going to do? She didn't have any experience to guide her. Of course everyone knew that the first thing to do was to dial the emergency numbers and report the matter to the police. That is if you were back home not out here in the Middle East in the middle of the night during a revolution with the landline and her mobile out.

She felt she should do something but she didn't know what. Her mind was confused by her imagination which was conjuring up all sorts of possibilities, one worse than the other. She could see behind the masks of the men as they sped away, cruel, evil or was it just fanatical faces.

Where was Abdul? She hadn't seen him for ages. He sometimes disappeared for short periods though not usually without saying anything. Wherever he was, he certainly wasn't in the apartment. Somehow, in her mind, Abdul's face became confused with the ones she had conjured up of the masked kidnappers.

Could Abdul be one of them? Could he have been implicated in what they had done? She could see him opening the door to let them in. Plenty of stories circulated among the expats of Arab servants even those who had been loyal for many years suddenly turning on their employers and cutting telephone lines and locking European women up in rooms.

Whether Abdul had anything to do with this or not, David had been forced from his bed, dragged down the stairs, and taken away. She had to pull herself together and try to do something.

Her neighbours? Would they help her? Of course they were Arabs and she had no real idea how they would react to a request for help especially in the middle of the night. At least it was worth a try. It was somewhere to start.

She ran to Yasmin's apartment, first ringing the bell until she remembered it wouldn't work without electricity, then hammering on the door.

Would Yasmin want to help her or see her as an infidel, someone to be shunned? She recalled her first encounter when Yasmin had been confused and embarrassed at being addressed at all, quickly pulling her veil across her face. Still, she was the only woman in the block Deborah had even a tentative relationship with. Yasmin occasionally sent her Filipino maid with a little gift, a special sweetmeat she had bought in the *suq* or a packet of tea. They had had some sort of communication despite the language barrier.

There was still no answer to her hammering. Then she remembered Eileen saying that a lot of Sunnis had got out while the going was good, that they weren't going to hang around to suffer the wrath of the people. And she remembered that Yasmin's husband had a good position in one of the ministries, which meant that he was almost certainly Sunni. That explained the lack of response then. Yasmin and her husband had already left.

It was the same in all the other apartments including Dr Rashid's who lived above them. There was no response from inside. Just silence. Had they too gone away, left for the safety of the New City before the bridge had been cordoned off? Or were they in there all the time, but wouldn't open the door to her? She did think that at one or two apartments she heard a faint noise inside and, once or twice, felt that eyes were looking out at her through the spy hole in the door.

Eventually she had to give up. There was no response anywhere.

She told herself that the occupants were probably just as frightened as herself and were afraid to open the door. After all, there were likely to be looters roaming around now that there was probably no one to impose law and order on this side of the creek. And they would be especially nervous in the dark. If any of them were there, she couldn't really blame them for not opening their doors to a knock in the middle of the night.

Unless of course they were in sympathy with the uprising and wanted nothing to with an infidel with a problem.

In retrospect, locating on this side of the creek hadn't turned out to be the best decision they had ever taken. But that was with hindsight. At the time, locating here seemed the right thing to do. How were they to know that a revolution was going to suddenly erupt like this?

And they certainly hadn't ignored the possible dangers. They had agreed with CJ to move to the new villa. In fact, if things had gone as arranged, they would be moving the next day. She shone her flashlight on the bags she had already packed. If only they had had another day, they'd have been out of here. Just as Andy and Margaret would have been away to Singapore if only they'd had another few days. But they didn't have another few days. Time had run out and Andy was blown up.

Was there any possible way of her getting across to the other side even at this late stage? She'd have to look into it further tomorrow in daylight.

Everything would be different if she could be with the Europeans on the other side of the creek. They would be able to help. They would have themselves well organised by now. After the first rumours of possible trouble, Margaret had told her about plans they had begun to make for an emergency and had even given her updates on how they were going to gather into groups with leaders, what numbers to ring in an emergency and, if the worst came to the worst, where to gather to be evacuated. And, if she was over there, the expats would give her back-up and help her find out who had taken David and why and do all they could in trying to locate him.

But she wasn't on the other side of the creek, she had no way of getting in contact with the people over there and couldn't attempt crossing the bridge till daylight.

She was alone and she wasn't used to being alone. Being alone put a different spin on things. It left everything up to her. Being alone like this was lonely and frightening and could lead to disaster if she didn't get a grip on herself and stop her imagination running away with itself, conjuring up the most awful scenarios fed by all she had seen and heard and read about women caught in similar circumstances.

CHAPTER 46

Feeling along the wall, David tried to determine how restricted his movements were. Following the chain with his fingers, he found that it was secured to a ring in the wall. So he wasn't going to be able to move much. He could just about get to sit on the hard dried mud of the floor with his back to the wall.

Still suffering from the shock of being kidnapped, he tried to take stock of his situation.

On the positive side, he hadn't been shot as he could easily have been. He'd only been roughed up a bit. He was still alive though in a situation where that condition was by no means a given.

Had they taken Deborah too? The very idea made his blood boil. It was only with a great effort he prevented himself from lunging away from the wall, the only effect of which would have been to do himself an injury. He forced himself to sit still and calm down. Respect for women is deeply ingrained in Moslem culture. The odds were that they wouldn't have taken Deborah. In general they didn't kidnap women, given very few famous exceptions. Anyway he couldn't let his mind go down that route.

Deborah was safe. He had to take that as a given. The whole logic of it was that it was him they wanted.

The next question was why kidnap him in particular rather than somebody else?

Was his kidnapping planned or haphazard?

Had it merely been an opportunistic and casual action? Or did it have the sanction of someone in authority among the Shi'ites?

On balance, all things considered, far and away the most likely thing was that his kidnappers were part of the Shi'ite uprising under the general direction of the Ayatullah.

Someone chose to snatch him in particular. But why? He wasn't a person of any political importance, or indeed of any importance at all. So why kidnap him? A thought struck him. Andy's car had been blown up as he was getting into it. And Andy had worked in a bank.

He worked in a bank. His father had worked in a bank. Was that why he'd been kidnapped? Several banks had been blown up around the Middle East in recent times. Banks were becoming an attractive target and presumably that would extend to bankers. On the other hand, his reasoning might be completely wrong. He could have been kidnapped, not because of his position in the bank, but for a different reason altogether. For instance, it could have been for a personal reason. By someone who held enmity against him. An image jumped into his mind. The picnic. The Jeep approaching. The youths walking arrogantly around. And the screams of the youth he had shot and whose blood he had seen seeping into the sand as they had roared away in the speedboat. Could it have been instigated by him?

The thought made David shiver. If that was the case, then he had no chance of survival, none whatever. Revenge would be exacted. The image was so terrible that he concentrated to dismiss it from his mind. Or at least banish it to the outer regions. He could not allow such a negative image to take over his brain or he was finished. He forced himself to breathe in and out slowly. He held off a panic attack. He grew calmer.

He forced himself to think of other things. He thought back over the morning he had spent in the bank securing the bank records in an impregnable safe. Was the bank still in the state he had left it in, empty but secure? Had CJ done anything more to secure it? Had he got the squad of police promised by Chief of Police Qassem to protect the premises? Had he gone in to see the position for himself? Or had the Shi'ites consolidated and been able to hold their position in Bank Street?

And, if they had kidnapped him, not because of himself but because of what he represented, what did they intend to do with him?

His mind strayed back to Deborah. His gut feeling was that she had not been kidnapped. Assuming that she wasn't, how would she cope? Could she handle a situation like this on her own?

She was on the wrong side of the creek, cut off from everyone of her own kind. Her Arabic was pretty inadequate. Meantime, she'd be alone and under extreme pressure. What would she do? Would she be tempted to go out in the streets, which would be the wrong decision? Or would she be sensible and stay indoors? That would be her best course of action. To go out at all would be extremely dangerous.

As he considered all the possibilities of this uprising for everybody and the disaster it had already dealt the Wilsons, David's body moved restlessly, twisting this way and that in an effort to find a bearable if not comfortable position propped up against the wall with his legs stretched out on the mud floor. Eventually he drifted into an uneasy sleep.

And he was a small boy again with his friend Sebastian in Fort Jalali, the old Portuguese fort where the enemies of the state were held. And suddenly, inexplicably, he and Sebastian were down in that deep hole to be abandoned there for years and years. And he could hear all around him the rattle of the prisoners' chains deep in that hole in the ground. Their screams rang out in his dreams.

And, mingled with their screams, was the sound of his father howling.

NOEL SCANLON

CHAPTER 47

Deborah became aware of the dogs whimpering and scratching at the kitchen door. As soon as she opened it, they burst out jumping up at her, barking, nuzzling her, joyous at their release, demanding attention.

They were thirsty, so she went to the fridge to get them a drink. Although the power was off, the bottled water was still reasonably cool though, if the outage lasted much longer, everything she had in the fridge would begin to go bad.

She poured herself a glass of water and poured the remainder of the bottle into the dogs' bowls. She stood in the kitchen, the flashlight casting a pool of light over the dogs lapping up their water.

She considered her position.

David had been kidnapped. Would they come back for her? Why not? What was to stop them? She couldn't help imagining the same shadowy people who had taken David coming back to the apartment and seizing her.

Just then, she thought she heard noises outside, saw shadows. They had taken David and now they were waiting out there for her. And these people were dangerous, they had already murdered Andy.

There was no way she could stay in the apartment for the rest of the night on her own. Her space had been violated. This violation changed her whole view of the apartment. It looked different. It felt different. It didn't even seem like the same space; something essential had been leached out of it. It was like as if the old apartment had been spirited away and replaced by a virtual computerised image that had no substance. Whatever had given the apartment its atmosphere, its attraction in a particular time space continuum had vanished. It had been desecrated and she wanted out of it.

"Come on girls," she said to the dogs when they had finished drinking.

"We're going up on the roof."

She pulled the cushions off the couch and, followed by the dogs, went up on to the roof.

She had once thought it would be pleasant to spend a night in the open on the roof in the great Arabian outdoors under the canopy of the stars, listening to the lapping of water in the creek. It was something she had often intended to do but never quite got around to. Now that it was being forced on her, it didn't seem that great.

She looked about the roof for a protected corner to lay out her cushions and chose and area where the stairs emerged on to the roof and a low protective wall had been built. But there was a mattress there already, a tatty mattress. Whose was it and how had it got here? She had never noticed it before.

She moved away and found another corner and laid out her cushions. Honey and Poochie slumped down beside her, putting their paws on her and looking at her out of worried, soulful eyes, then snuggling up behind her.

Where was David? Where had they taken him? And why? The question went round and round in her head until it had worn a groove, but she didn't have any answer.

Since there was nothing else to do, the best thing was to settle down and get some sleep during what was left of the night. There was one advantage to being up here out of doors, she had less of a feeling of being trapped. At least she could hear anyone coming up the steps.

She had expected it to be cooler than indoors but there didn't seem to be much difference. She felt sticky and uncomfortable. It was intensely hot even now during the night. The hair on her neck was glued to her skin with perspiration. And she was not, as she had once visualised, under a canopy of stars but a canopy of solid heat which was about to descend on her and choke her. Or so she imagined.

Before they had come for him, she and David had been insensibly dreaming together down there in the apartment under their single sheet with no premonition of the dangers gathering around them. The intruders had struck unexpectedly and savagely, breaking into their lives and shattering them.

The abduction, although it had taken only a matter of minutes, had changed everything.

What could she do?

She couldn't go back down to the apartment and, even if she did, there was nothing she could do from there. And she certainly couldn't go out alone into the darkness and chaos and gunfire she heard coming from the Old City and the area around the bridge. To do so would be suicidal.

She had no means of calling for help or even of letting anyone know that David had been kidnapped. In a world of instant communication she had no way of communicating with anyone. At first light she'd do something even if it were to try and cross the bridge on her own.

Meantime, all she could do was settle down as best she could and pass the night where she was without giving her mind over to what might be happening to David and warding off the imagery of all the kidnappings she'd seen on television, some with the most gruesome and horrific outcomes. It didn't bear thinking about.

Clearly what had happened was the revolution had begun just as Eileen had told her it would. She had all the confirmation she needed that her newspaper report was correct on that score. She wished she hadn't. She wondered how much of the rest of Eileen's predictions would turn out to be true. Would all this turmoil turn out to be the great historic moment Eileen had declared it to be? Did the Shi'ites really have the support of armed groups from outside the state? Had an attempt been made to assassinate the Ruler as Eileen claimed?

The transistor she had brought up with her kept pouring out a flood of Arabic but, without the language, it was no good to her, it wasn't imparting any news to her. It was only an irritating noise and, in the end, she turned it off.

She tried hard to get to sleep but couldn't. She was kept awake by the constant sound of gunfire and shouting coming from the distance. These sounds gave her no real idea of the situation but they did bring home to her that she was really quite close to a crowd of fanatical fundamentalists all fired up by something she didn't really understand.

Deborah tossed and turned on her cushions in the hot night full of noises.

She eventually abandoned her attempts to sleep and got up. She went to the balustrade and leaned on it. There was suddenly a quiet moment as if there was a lull in the fighting. She turned and looked in the direction of the beach where they used take the boat out. It had only been a few weeks ago but it now all seemed in a different era, a different country. It was a completely different aspect of Arabia.

Back before her mother had come out on holiday, they used spend every Friday morning skiing behind the boat, swimming in clear water with long lines of rollers breaking far out, sitting sunbathing as the speedboat bobbed at anchor. Or walking to a small lake just off the beach where flamingos moved with long-legged delicacy or stood and fished, darting their S shaped necks downward before they rose orange-winged into the sky. That's why they had come to live on this side of the creek - the proximity of the best beach and a place to launch the boat and the old world ethnic atmosphere which, up until now, she had so much preferred to the harsh soulless high rises.

But those bright images and even the views she had held then no longer seemed valid. Everything had changed.

She turned, startled by the sound of footsteps. Someone was coming up the stairs. She tensed. She looked at the dogs. They hadn't reacted; they were still asleep. Maybe it was only her imagination, but she had the strong feeling that whoever had been on the stairs had come out on to the roof and was watching her from the darkness. But she couldn't see anyone.

She stood taut and apprehensive, waiting for whoever it was to make a move, make a sound, declare themselves. But nothing happened. Nobody appeared.

Finally, she went back to her cushions and lay down. She turned and twisted fitfully, damp with perspiration, conscious of being in the open unprotected and conscious too of what must be going on not far away from her. She was afraid to go to sleep.

But despite her efforts to stay awake, sleep descended on her like a guillotine, sudden and unexpected. But it was not restful sleep, it was not oblivion. Faces floated in the air above her watching her, ready to swoop. Some of the faces wore masks which they pulled off to reveal a face that wasn't a face at all but something grinning and evil looking out at her from glowing red eyes.

Noises penetrated her mind, the distant murmur of shouting and screaming and chanting. A menacing black river of people, bound together in a bond of xenophobia and hatred and a lust for revenge, and something else, something dark and hidden and evil was headed towards her.

A darkness was spreading out from the Old City in waves until it reached where she lay twisting on her cushions. This darkness was no ordinary darkness. It was dense and thick, packed closely together with an impenetrability through which no light could filter. This darkness was stygian. It was absolute and all embracing. It lay heavily on her, pinning her down. It was a darkness that was cloying, a darkness through which unspeakable horrors moved.

NOEL SCANLON

CHAPTER 48

———————————

Sitting with his back to the wall, chained and blindfolded, horrors that were normally dormant and inactive in his mind came to life. David had walked through the mirror into the nightmare, plunged into dark places.

He was in Death Wadi. Death Wadi formed a great natural amphitheatre and was the location for executions which were the normal method of punishment in that town. The prisoner, shackled and chained, was being walked to the centre of the amphitheatre, a raised circle of hard packed sand where a group of officials were gathered. In the centre of the circle the executioner stood, tall and swarthy, his black skin glistening in the hot sun, resting on the ground in front of him a tribal sword of the sort used on camel raids and in battle. Two officials blindfolded the prisoner and a member of the sheikh's household dressed in white robes led the prisoner to the marked spot. The black executioner jabbed the sword into the man's stomach and, as he jerked his head upwards in reflex, the executioner severed the man's head cleanly and swiftly with one clean strike so that, freed from its body, it rolled on the ground while blood pumped from the decapitated, headless and twitching torso.

The severed head rolled to the edge of the raised circle, hit a declivity and began to roll down the slope towards David. The man's torso had toppled over but was still alive or at least moving. The arms and legs lashed about as the headless body went into contortions until finally it went slack.

David jolted awake. For a moment he was in shock, his spirit in a cringing, shrunken state from what he had been watching which, as he came to, began to recede, became more and more blurred by the second, fading away into a dull feeling of apprehension and a foreboding of horrors past and horrors to come.

Gradually, by an act of will, he overcame or at least controlled, or partly controlled his fear. But he was shaking and trembling. The atmosphere of his dreams was still with him. He was afraid to surrender himself to sleep again and what terrors further dreams might bring.

He had no idea what time of night it was or for how long he had slept. His face was raw from rubbing it against the wall in an attempt to release the blindfold. He felt extremely thirsty, there was little or no saliva in his mouth. He was stiff and sore all over from the manhandling and then from having to sit up all night on a bare mud floor chained to the wall.

But at least his nightmare was over and his brain was beginning to clear. What a fantastic thing the human brain is. What a fantastic capacity it has to recover, to wipe out the darkness, to re-balance, to re-invent itself. David was almost himself again, the night over, the day breaking, his brain sorted, ready to face whatever circumstance he found himself in.

Still he was apprehensive. Why was he chained here? What was to prevent these people who held him from murdering him, even from beheading him as they had the man in the *wadi* - that image had sprung back into his mind - at any time, if they felt so inclined? Why had they kidnapped him? What did they want from him?

He remembered the day his father had been kidnapped, and the terrible legacy of that one senseless act, his mother never recovering, spending decades in a home not recognising anyone. His father had been kidnapped while driving home from work, nobody really knew why, no one had ever found out why. And while what CJ had found out might be the truth or near to it, no one really knew for certain how he had died.

Was the same fate or something similar, going to happen to him?

He began to hear muffled sounds. Shortly afterwards, the buzz of people talking and moving about drifted in to his cell, then the Call to Prayer rang out from quite close-by.

His first impression had been correct. He was somewhere down the *suq* in the Old City. The sounds coming faintly to his ears now were definitely *suq* sounds. That was good, better than being held away off in some remote place.

He sat monitoring the sounds around him. The activity overhead told him that he was in a two-storey house. There was the sound of footsteps up and down the stairs and, a little later, there came wafting to his nostrils the strong pungent smells of cooking and of coffee being brewed. No one came near him but someone was bound to come in time.

What a sudden and complete change the situation he found himself in now was from the banking life to which he was accustomed. In normal circumstances, before the uprising, he would shortly be going to work in the bank in comfortable and secure conditions, booting up his computer, surveying the mass of information it offered. But the revolution or attempted revolution had changed everything.

Had he rendered safe everything of importance in the bank before he had left? He thought he probably had.

He wondered what was happening on the outside. He wondered what Deborah was doing. How would she react? She was a capable, resourceful woman. But would she be too impulsive? Would she take risks that she shouldn't take? He hoped she wouldn't try and cross the bridge. Her best course of action would be to lie low and, if she did, she had a good chance of being left alone in their apartment which was after all in a quiet backwater. But somehow he didn't think she would.

There were footsteps outside and his door opened.

A voice said in English, "I am Ahmed and I bring you breakfast."

David waited while he heard a tray being placed on the floor. He waited to be untied but nothing happened.

"I can't eat unless you untie my hands and take off the blindfold," David said.

"Blindfold not possible," Ahmed said. "But hands possible." As he untied David's hands, he said, "You like my English?"

"It's very good. Where did you learn it?"

"Ah, that I am not saying. Eat breakfast."

David rubbed his wrists to try to get the circulation back. Feeling about, he located a tray with chapattis and a mug of what from the smell was obviously coffee. He wasn't at all sure that he could grip anything properly so he started on the chapatti first on the basis that if he dropped it it wouldn't be as big a disaster as dropping a mug of hot coffee.

"This is very nice, Ahmed."

In reply Ahmed said, "Why do the Westerners, the Crusaders, wish to kill all us Moslems, wipe us out?"

David was taken aback. "I don't think they want to wipe out all Moslems, Ahmed. That's an incorrect concept you've got there." The chapatti was freshly made and tasted great. The smell of the coffee was even greater.

Reverting to his native Arabic, Ahmed said, "Oh they do. They very much wish to wipe out all Moslems. It is a Christian crusade. We must fight back to defend ourselves."

David sensed that he was entering an area of danger here. He could hear it in Ahmed's voice. He reminded himself that this mild-spoken man was a Shi'ite and a member of a kidnapping gang. He reminded himself that the Shi'ite mind was still shaped by the murder of Ali the son in law of Mohammed in the year six hundred and fifty six, the massacre of Hussein in Karbala, and other historical events.

That was the corner this young man was coming from and such a person would not be easy to influence or persuade, such a person was very set indeed in their world view. Ahmed's views wouldn't shift one iota whatever David said. That was something he had to accept.

The best thing he could do was to try to form a relationship, a linkage with him. On the positive side, Ahmed was prepared to engage in conversation. He talked, he asked questions, he was curious and that was good. If he could keep him talking, he might even find out why he had been kidnapped, and what they intended doing with him.

Ahmed was saying, "The Christians wish to wipe out all Moslems, in Iraq, in Chechnya, in Iran, everywhere. And all the time the Israelis kill Palestinians every day, they bomb them, they shoot them, they bulldoze their houses, they put them behind big wall like animals. Israelis and Americans they very bad people. They kill from air. They sit away up there in the sky and the pilot he press button and bang, thirty Moslems dead. They look. They laugh. For them, they not people. They only dots down there. Puff, they are gone. They not count. America count only American bodies. Muslim bodies not count. Puff they are gone. Blown to bits...."

David heard sentiments like this all the time. They were broadcast from every Arab radio station, printed in every Arab paper. They throbbed in every street in the Middle East, these deeply embedded convictions, this blazing sense of injustice, humiliation and lack of power, compounded not a little by the fact that their own states were largely run by oppressive tyrants and dictators.

But David knew he couldn't argue with his captor without bringing disaster on himself.

"I can see that that's a point of view, Ahmed, and I see how you might arrive at it, but I think it may be a little exaggerated."

David had the bizarre feeling that he was having a debate as in a debating society when he was blindfolded and chained to the wall and

Ahmed as a member of the group who had kidnapped him would undoubtedly kill him without the slightest qualm if he was given the order to do so.

"Allah is on our side."

David had wolfed down the chapatti and was holding the coffee mug with both hands. "Of course he is." Allah was on the Moslem side, and the Christian God was on the Christian side, that's how it was. That's how it has always been.

"You are Christian?" Ahmed asked.

"I suppose you could say that."

"Then you are corrupt."

"Materialistic maybe. But I wouldn't say corrupt."

"All Christians are corrupt. But the Shi'ites are not corrupt. The Shi'ites do not compromise."

"In the end, we're all human, Ahmed. We all compromise. If only a little."

"No, no, no," Ahmed burst out angrily. "You must not say such things." His voice now was hard edged and threatening. "We Shi'ites never compromise. We choose death before compromise. We are prepared to sacrifice our lives for our beliefs. How many Christians are prepared to sacrifice their lives? Tell me, how many Christian are prepared to be martyrs?"

David didn't like the turn things were taking. He was beginning to see that Ahmed had another side to him altogether. A dangerous side.

"Not very many come to think of it."

"None," Ahmed shouted. "There are no Christians willing to be martyrs," he added contemptuously. "The Christians are cowards. They are sick. They are morally bankrupt. They are destined for oblivion."

David said nothing. His instincts told him to stay quiet. He would have liked to have observed that western civilisation is the best we have. And a good deal better than the alternatives. But he knew that to express these views might cause Ahmed to flip, might cost him his life. He had, after all, no way of fighting back if he was attacked.

Ahmed suddenly said, "That is a very nice watch you are wearing." This sudden change of mood pointed up the man's unstable volatility.

"It is, isn't it. I'm very fond of that watch myself. But I tell you what I'll do, I'll make you a present of it, Ahmed, just to improve your opinion of the corrupt and perfidious West."

"Thank you," Ahmed said solemnly taking the watch off David's wrist.

"I can see you're a highly intelligent man, Ahmed. And I can see we could have a most interesting philosophical conversation here. But before we get down to that, do you think I could get to use the toilet?"

"All right," Ahmed said. "But first it must be I put handcuffs on your hands."

David's excursion to the toilet which wasn't in the basement but up a stairway and into a room with a long drop that stank, gave him some idea of the layout of the house.

When they came back to the cell, someone else took over from Ahmed, someone rougher and stricter who silently chained David closer to the wall and tightened the blindfold and refused to engage in any conversation.

Sitting back in his cell, he set himself the task of listening to every sound and trying to interpret it. Who was mounting the stairs, who was going along the passageway and so on.

David concluded that the building in which he was being held had a courtyard to the front, probably leading into a laneway or street. As far as he could deduce, he was imprisoned in the basement of a building with a courtyard off one of the side *suqs*.

CHAPTER 49

Deborah was awoken by the sun shining on her face as she lay on her cushions on the roof. For an instant, she didn't know where she was. Then her awareness of herself, her situation, the tail-lights of the car accelerating away, the steps on the stairs, the night noises, the gunfire, all came flooding back.

She jumped up and went downstairs. But there was no welcome for her there, no atmosphere to embrace her. The apartment was not welcoming. It had a feeling of total absence.

She walked towards the bedroom in the hope that a miracle had taken place during the night, that David had been released and been brought back home. Of course she knew perfectly well that his sudden or even early release was extremely unlikely. It was far more likely that he would be held until the kidnappers had made their demands. Then, if their demands were not met, they would kill their hostage as they always did and post a video on the internet filming his death, she could see it now, the figures with balaclavas standing hooded at the back, the Arabic lettering with the translation underneath. Unless a miracle happened. Her mother believed in miracles, the miracles at Knock, at Lourdes. Perhaps she could come to believe in them too.

But there was no miracle here. The bedroom and the whole apartment was empty, and more than empty. It felt lonely and desolate. Life had departed from it.

As she stood there, she could feel the heat gathering force, hanging heavy in the rooms, the whole apartment closed up tightly so that it was hot and claustrophobic.

Despite all this, Deborah determined to face the day with optimism or at least to try. She opened the windows, let the light in. The sun was up and shining fiercely outside.

She began to gather up the pieces of the glass top of the coffee table that had been shattered and righted the side tables that had been knocked over.

The dogs, unusually subdued, nosed about trying to identify the strange smells. They were obviously picking up the scent of the intruders of the night before.

She checked Abdul's quarters. He hadn't come back. There was no sign of him. He must have taken off and left her. He must have been one of them all along.

In the kitchen she shook cereal into a bowl, took a carton of milk from the fridge which was fully defrosted now, a large pool of water in front of it. Everything was beginning to go off and would have to be thrown out. The milk had gone sour so she mixed some powdered milk in water and ate her cereal standing up. She wasn't able to finish it so she emptied what was left into the dogs' bowls, added milk to it, and went to try the apartments again.

She was taken aback when, this time when she knocked on Yasmin's door, a solid substantial door with a dead bolt and a spy hole, it was opened immediately as if someone had been lurking behind it.

Yasmin's Filipino maid, Maria, opened the door. Her face was pale and strained. She kept the chain on, opening the door only as far as she had to. Maria stood there with her head bowed; a slight self-effacing girl brought all the way from Manila to be a servant to the wealthy Arabs of the Gulf. "Can I speak to Yasmin please?" Deborah asked.

"She not here," Maria said without raising her eyes.

"Her husband then?"

"He not here either," Maria said in such a way that Deborah felt that someone had instructed her not to speak, not to give anything away.

"Where are they? When are they coming back?"

Maria hung her head and was silent. She had closed down. Her face was implacable. She was going to obey whoever had told her not to talk.

Deborah felt like grabbing the girl and shaking some information out of her. But she had already lost. Even her tone had frightened this Filipino girl who was accustomed for years now to being a non-person, a shadow, less than a shadow.

"Gone. Gone," the nervous girl suddenly blurted out. "Gone, Gone. All gone," she repeated as she slammed the door.

Deborah brought the dogs down to the compound to give them some exercise. She had had no luck in any of the other apartments. Waiting while the dogs ran around now, she checked out the block. There was no one on the balconies and all the blinds were drawn. The block looked deserted. Either it was empty or, if anyone was in there, they were keeping very quiet indeed.

As she was about to bring the dogs in, a truck suddenly appeared from the direction of the Old City. In the back, a group of fighters were standing up firing off shots randomly in the air as they came towards her.

Before she could stop them, the dogs had leaped over the compound wall and were racing at the truck, barking, attacking the wheels. That had always been a problem. It was a habit she could never break them off and was the reason why she always exercised them well away from traffic. Given the chance, they would launch themselves suicidally at cars, trucks, whatever they perceived to be invading their territory. You couldn't stop them. It was in their blood. They were territorial animals.

Deborah screamed at them to come back but they ignored her. Then she stopped. One of the men was taking pot shot at her pets. She stood rooted to the ground, horrified. Then she ran out on to the road waving her arms and screaming at them to stop. Laughing at her, the men raised their clenched fists and shook them in her direction, their faces shining with excitement. One of them pointed his rifle at her and shouted, "Bang bang," and laughed.

Honey had given up chasing after the truck but Poochie continued to follow it, a blur of black and white streaking along with that graceful movement that made her seem to fly through the air as if her paws never touched the ground, as if she was back on her native hillsides rounding up sheep. There was the crack of a shot and a yelp. Poochie turned around moving slowly now and obviously in pain. She was shot. Again.

Deborah ran towards the dog who leapt into her arms, blood running down the side of its head. Poochie began licking Deborah's face and trembling spasmodically. The blood dripped on to Deborah's jeans as she carried the dog up to the apartment, followed closely by Honey who kept barking sharply in protest and circling around her.

Mr Tom, the compound cat, came in and sat primly watching Deborah as she did her best to clean and disinfect the wound. She was afraid the side of the skull might have been blown away and that her fingers would encounter a gooey mass and sink into Poochie's brain. But, luckily, the wound was only superficial though part of the dog's ear had been blown away. As she patched her up as best she could, Poochie licked her hand and gazed up at her with supplicating, trustful eyes.

When she had dressed the wound she went in search of tablets. She found an old bottle of antibiotic tablets she had got months ago from the vet and gave them to Poochie wrapped in cheese. She also gave her a tranquillizer and, after taking them, Poochie relaxed and fell asleep.

Deborah was nervous about taking the car out of the compound, more especially after what had happened to Poochie. But it looked all right out there, not in any way dangerous. In fact there were fewer people than normal on the road that ran past their apartment block. In the bright sunlight the atmosphere was that of a quiet backwater.

So she backed the car out and headed off.

At first everything seemed as it had always been. But once she got past the roundabout and the turn off to the Old City and was on the main road to the New City the whole atmosphere altered. There was a lot more activity than usual. There were far more people on the road than she had ever seen. Cars, pick-up trucks, SUVs and captured police Jeeps, were moving in both directions.

She began to have a sneaking feeling that she was doing the wrong thing. This wasn't the time to be out driving around. It was dangerous to be out. But she couldn't go back now. She had to go on. She had no choice. Whatever the risk, she had no alternative but to try to get across the bridge.

She deliberately hadn't let herself think about what she was going to do, weigh the pros and cons. If she had thought too much about it she wouldn't have ventured out at all. Better jump off the diving board than stand there thinking about the cold water you're going to plunge into. She hadn't even taken a conscious decision to get in the car. She had just done it automatically, knowing that if she thought too much about it, debated it in her own mind, she might weaken and decide not to chance going out at all, just stay in the apartment and do nothing.

As she neared the bridge, the road became more and more congested with cars and lorries, all blowing their horns, all packed with people shouting and gesticulating, some of them unarmed, but some of them not only armed but shooting off bursts into the air at random. There was so much traffic on the road that she had to slow down. Gradually, she had to drive more and more slowly until she was stopping and starting in first and second gear.

A few miles later and, just as she was getting close to the bridge, a large truck that had been obscuring her view pulled in to the side and she found herself approaching a throng of women. They were in full *purdah*, heads covered, long skirts to the ground, moving along in a black undulating mass. They presented an extraordinary sight. A great sea of black clad, black veiled women. The whole scene looked like some gigantic set from some outdoor operatic performance. They looked so absolutely photogenic that Deborah, for a second forgetting the danger she was in, wished she had a camera to photograph them.

Many of them were carrying banners. All of them were shouting slogans. They were supporting the men who had taken up arms against the government. Released from their houses, they were venting their emotions in intense and prolonged outbursts.

She should have felt some connection, some solidarity with these women whose rights she had championed as best she could in *Al Jameela* and whom she had thought she had come to learn and understand something about through the letters and poems that had poured into the magazine in such profusion, some of them extremely explicit given that all these women lived in a society where they were airbrushed from existence, condemned to a domestic life dominated by a harsh patriarchal system, virtually treated as slaves.

But Deborah got absolutely no echo of any of this from these protesting women. The cloistered neglected downtrodden women of the Moslem world had been transformed. They had become something else again. They were vehement and aggressive as they shouted their slogans. Yet they had to be, if not the same women, at least from similar backgrounds to those who had written in to *Al Jameela* and whose outpourings had so affected her. But she felt no sisterly connection with these street protesters. Instead, she was beginning to feel decidedly apprehensive of them.

Suddenly she was swallowed up by this mass of black clad screaming and ululating women. As she drove on she was in among them and forced to slow down to a walking pace. With the women all around her she found it difficult to move forward at all.

And these women certainly weren't friendly. They weren't kindred spirits. In fact some of them began to strike the windows and sides of the car with their placards. They shouted at her. Emotion had carried them away, released inside them some kind of manic energy.

Or so it seemed to Deborah as she felt herself shrinking, wishing for invisibility.

Trapped in her car, like an animal in a stiflingly hot glass cage, she had the feeling that she was about to be burnt up not only by the rays of the sun but by the rays of hate that were emitted by the women closest to her. She was pinned to her seat by all that hatred.

Then everything ground to a halt. The front of the women's protest had reached a series of barricades manned by fighters with hand held rocket launchers. There seemed to be a debate going on as to whether to let the women pass the barricades or not. Nobody seemed to be able to come to a decision. Everything had come to a standstill and it looked like it would stay that way for some time.

Deborah realised that there was no way she would be allowed through the barricades. If she got that far she would most likely be arrested and thrown in prison and that wouldn't get anyone anywhere. She had been wrong to think she had any hope of getting through to the New City.

The best thing she could do now was to go back. But how could she? There was total gridlock on the bridge and no way she could possibly turn the car. She was held in place like a fly on a pin and might be there for a very long time.

She began to panic as more of the women surrounding her car began striking the doors and windows with their banners.

She had to get out of this vehicle. She couldn't bear to stay trapped in it. But she couldn't get out. She was completely hemmed in. She couldn't get out, she couldn't turn back, she couldn't move an inch in any direction. There was total gridlock on the road. No one could move. Horns blasted, people shouted. She and a whole mass of people and vehicles had ground to a halt on the bridge in the soupy deadening heat.

One woman's face was jammed up flattened against the window of her car, only inches away. The woman's face was distorted. The women surrounding her car were probably good wives and mothers, but, right now, they looked as if they were out for the kill, and the person they wanted to kill was her.

Just then the crowd of women around her car was joined by a mob of men who thrust the women aside and began to attack the car in earnest. The car began to rock. No doubt about it. They intended to turn it over.

She tried to get out. But the doors were locked. She fumbled to unlock them but couldn't as she was being thrown from one side of the car to the other now as it rocked wildly.

The car right in front of her was a new Mercedes driven by a fat prosperous-looking merchant with a group of women in the back. The man was arguing and handing money out, trying to bribe his way through. The crowd's interest in the Mercedes and in the money being handed out momentarily distracted them, drew them away from Deborah's car.

Deborah fumbled at the car door, her sweaty hands slippery on the handle, and this time she managed to get it open. She scrambled out.

As she edged away into the crowd, she noticed that the man in the Mercedes had handed all his money out but apparently that wasn't enough to save him.

He was ordered out. And then shot. Just like that, casually, as if they were shooting a dog. The merchant slid to the ground and lay there.

Deborah moved farther into the crowd, anonymous looking in the black cloak and veil she had quickly pulled on, putting distance between herself and her car, disassociating herself from it. She moved away, leaving the vehicle to whoever wished to have it.

Keeping well covered, the veil and cloak pulled tightly around her, she eventually got off the bridge and began the hot long arduous trek back to the apartment.

NOEL SCANLON

CHAPTER 50

Later that day, David's cell door was suddenly thrown open and the room seemed to be filled with people.

"Come. Come," they said excitedly, dragging him to his feet and unchaining him. "Quickly. Quickly."

What was happening? Were they releasing him? Or were they taking him to a place of execution.

He was marched out of his cell, down a passageway, then up a flight of stairs and into the open air and a cacophony of sound.

"In, in," they said, and there was tenseness as well as excitement in their voices.

Hands raised him, lifted him into the boot of a car.

The car engine started and they shot away with a screech of tires. The car, as far as David could make out, was full of men. It was the same ordeal all over again with the same fear of suffocation except that this time he wasn't gagged. He again concentrated on bracing himself in such a way as to protect his body as much as possible from being thrown against the metal sides.

They drove at speed or so it seemed from his position in the boot, taking numerous turns on to different roads.

Jolted about in black darkness, he wondered where they were taking him and what was going to happen to him. He tried to visualise the scene outside. Were there people still marching, still demonstrating? He listened for gunfire but didn't hear any.

The car slowed at a checkpoint and he had the sense that this checkpoint was on the bridge. He could hear voices outside challenging. The men in the car called out, "We are *Jihadis*. We are *Jihadis*," and, following some exchanges, were allowed through.

After a time, the car stopped suddenly, bumping his head.

He expected the boot to be opened immediately but this didn't happen. They just left him where he was while they stood about arguing and waiting for someone else to arrive. He called out to try to attract attention but his voice was muffled and nobody heard or if they did didn't take any notice.

Time passed and he had the feeling that if they left him here for any length of time they wouldn't need to bother executing him, if that was their intention, he would die anyway. But just as he was about to pass out, the boot was opened and he could breathe properly again. Hands reached in and dragged him out.

"Hurry, hurry," they urged. "Hurry, hurry."

David didn't know whether they were addressing one another or him. As far as he himself was concerned he was incapable of hurrying anywhere without being able to see where he was going. Besides, his heart was still thumping in his chest and he was feeling very groggy indeed.

His legs gave way but they caught him before he hit the ground. Someone supported him on either side up steps and into a building. He was propelled along, people pressing in from either side, a feeling of excitement, of urgency in the air. Then more steps, this time going down. He stumbled and had to be more or less carried the rest of the way.

Through a door, and his blindfold was ripped off. He blinked in light that was harsh after the darkness of the blindfold.

He was in the bank vaults! In retrospect, there did seem to have been something familiar about the steps he had been dragged up.

There were in all about twenty men in the vaults, variously armed with semi automatics, rifles and revolvers.

They stood before the pretty well impregnable bank strong room with its massive steel door.

Two men came from behind. One was obviously the leader, older than the others, probably in his forties, and with an air of authority.

The other was a surprise. It was a man David knew, Ali Abdullah Karim.

He focused his mind and dredged up from his memory everything he knew about this man. Ali Abdullah Karim was the manager of a small Pakistani bank. David knew him in the way of business. Indeed there had been many transactions between their respective banks in recent times. Quite a lot of these transactions had been the transfer of various sums of money. It had crossed David's mind at the time that the sums recently were unusually large, he had even fleetingly wondered if there was something suspicious about them. But he had let it go, the transactions had appeared to be perfectly correct and legal. But with hindsight it was apparent now that they hadn't been. He should have followed up his hunch. He should have investigated them more thoroughly. On the other hand, Ali Abdullah had an excellent reputation in the banking community and had been in charge of his bank for years and years. He was not someone anyone would have thought of as likely to be involved with an insurgency, though it was obvious now that he must have been all along. Indeed it was more than likely that it was Ali Abdullah who had run the various spying operations inside the Trucial Bank.

What David didn't know was that Ali Abdullah had joined the Islamic Jihad many years ago in Pakistan. He was a disciple of Sayyid Quatta who preached the purification of Islam and the removal of the corrupt influence of the West from Moslem lands. Sayyid Quatta was something of an intellectual and provided a lot of the philosophical underpinning to those movements which advocated that the end justifies the means. The end was to be a perfect Moslem society that would be brought about by a group of dedicated people who would lead the masses. To achieve this noble end, any means was acceptable and the means of the weak had by their nature to be more extreme than the means of the powerful.

In Khor Fahal, Ali Abdullah Karim had linked up with Ayatullah Abd Al Wahhab and the two men found that they had a lot in common. Ali Abdullah was in charge of all finance. He ran the whole funding operation for the planned uprising in all the Gulf states.

"We would like to get this phase of our operation over and done with as expeditiously as possible," Ali Abdullah said stiffly and formally now as if they were engaging in some regular bank business transaction.

"What do you want me to do?" David asked.

"Open the strong room."

There was silence. Everyone looked at David expectantly.

In his father's day, strong rooms were under dual control, with two sets of keys held by two people. This vault was also under dual control, not with keys but with memorised combinations. Apart from the record inside his head and that inside Mohammed's, the only other record by which access could be gained was lodged in the vault of another bank.

"I can't do that," David said.

The leader of the unit took over at this point leaving Ali Abdullah to stand back from this side of things. He nodded to a vicious looking youth who advanced on David and side swiped him with the stock of his machine pistol.

David felt a trickle of blood run down his face. He wondered if his jaw was broken, it felt like it could be. The youth sideswiped him again and he fell to the ground.

There was blood running out of his mouth. "I can't open the strong-room because I can't remember the numbers. I can't remember anything. I think you've damaged my brain. And anyway it's under dual control." Was he being silly attempting to be stupidly heroic? Of course he had his responsibilities and he took them seriously. But why should he get himself severely beaten up, maybe killed by resisting? What would that achieve?

"Why do you want to inflict this suffering on yourself?" Ali Abdullah asked. "What's the point? Open the strong room and we will let you go free."

David could feel the tenseness, see it in the eyes and attitude of the fighters who were straining on the leash to really have a go at him.

In the long run these people were going to get him to do what they wanted. One way or another. If that meant stringing him up, beating the soles of his feet, torturing him with electric shocks to the genitals or whatever, that was what they would do. He was already worried about his jaw; it didn't seem to be working quite right as if it was slightly unhinged. Another blow would do permanent damage.

"All right. All right." David said. "I'll try to remember."

So, for all the massive technological advances, for all the firewalls that were supposed to prevent all unauthorised access, for all the codes, all the checks and counter checks, for all the security, this is what it came down to in the end, kidnapping and brute force. Just as that was what it had come down to in the robbery of £26.000.000 by the IRA from the Ulster Bank, the largest bank robbery ever in Europe. It too had been carried out by kidnapping and threats.

Several of the unit dragged David to his feet and stood him in front of the strong-room door while their leader began to grind the mouth of his revolver into the back of David's skull.

David worked his combination.

As he was dragged back, he saw Mohammed being dragged forward. Of course. He should have guessed.

Mohammed looked dishevelled as if he too had had a working over. His usually immaculate white starched *thobe* was dirty and torn, his *kheffiya*, always neatly in place, was askew. He looked dazed and frightened, no doubt fearing for his life.

Mohammed didn't look at David or even in his direction as he began to operate his combination. Probably he felt guilty at what he was doing just as David did. He recalled all those long extended conversations with Mohammed during which he had sometimes wondered if Mohammed was a man to be trusted. Or if he was playing both sides at the same time. He felt a bit of a heel for having doubted him.

As Mohammed fumbled, he must have entered a wrong number, it struck David again how all the technological wizardry available in the building which had allowed him to contact and deal in financial markets around the world, to transfer large sums of money at the touch of a button, was totally ineffective and irrelevant in the present situation.

In the here and now the world had shrunk to this small crowded area in the vaults where physical violence, not technology, predominated.

There was a cheer as the huge strong room door, moving so smoothly despite its immense weight, swung open.

The armed fighters looked in awe at the stacks of ten tola gold bars and the high piles of currency, neatly sorted into one hundred dinar notes, fifties, twenties and tens.

The leader ordered his men to stand back while Ali Abdullah now took charge. As if David's continued presence would cause all that money to disappear, several men grabbed hold of him and began to hustle him back up the stairs. He was not going to be a witness to what followed. He wasn't needed any more.

A moment later he was back in the boot of the car for the return journey.

He had been tricked. Ali Abdullah's promise meant nothing. They had no intention of releasing him.

CHAPTER 51

Deborah got back home exhausted to find David's Land Rover missing. She looked all around the block and out in the street but there was no sign of it anywhere. It had obviously been stolen and there was little chance of her ever seeing it again. Now she had no means of transport, no means of moving around. She was cut off, isolated, on her own.

And the power was still out. After the fatigue of the long trek back on top of the emotional trauma of what had happened on the bridge and losing her own car it was all a bit too much. All she wanted to do was to throw herself on the bed and stay there.

That was the danger - that she would just give up, lose all resolve and do nothing. That was what she had to fight against at all costs.

She had also to forestall falling into a condition brought about by exposure to intense heat. She had seen people laid low by it. It came with physical symptoms, notably pains in the backs of your legs, but mainly it hit you like a paralysing drug that anaesthetised the mind. It drained your energy and made it virtually impossible to move.

To try to stop this happening to her, the first thing she did was to put a few spoons of salt in a glass of water and forced herself to drink it.

The next thing she did was take a shower. The water from the cold tap was really warm but nonetheless she stood under it for ages and that, combined with the effect the salt was beginning to have, made her feel better.

After her shower, she fed the dogs and dressed Poochie's wound. Poochie was still drowsy from the tranquilliser but the wound seem OK. Then she lay on the bed. She would have to have a couple of hours rest and recovery before going out in that debilitating heat again.

She fell into a sleep of exhaustion.

When she awoke, hours had passed. It felt like minutes but it was actually hours. The salt had done its work. Her strength had come back.

She began to prepare herself a salad. She sliced an onion, red peppers, chopped a few stalks of celery, spread the lot on wilted leaves of Chinese lettuce, opened a tin of mixed nuts and sprinkled them on top. Then she drank over a litre of orange juice, the juice was warm now but she knew that she had to take in as much liquid as she possibly could.

Then she considered what to do next.

Deborah began walking back towards the roundabout with the turn off to the Old City. She was burdened by her *abbaya* and headscarf that made her hot and uncomfortable but was a necessary disguise - she'd be mad to walk out as a female European in European attire. She made herself walk slowly to conserve energy. She paced herself, trying not to hurry, seeking out any small shade there was.

Reaching the roundabout, she turned off and headed towards the Old City. After a short distance, she managed to flag down a taxi. Previously a number of taxis had ignored her and driven by. A woman alone on this road was an unusual sight and might even be a dangerous fare: she might, for instance, be out without her husband's permission. She had begun to think that she would have to walk all the way to the taxi rank. So she felt lucky when a taxi pulled up.

The driver took one glance at the veiled form in his taxi but didn't speak beyond the obligatory greeting and didn't show any interest in her, perhaps he hadn't even noticed she was a European. The driver was giving all his attention to what was coming out over the car radio. She sank down in the back seat where the excited rhetoric coming over the taxi radio from the local station washed over her.

After paying off the taxi, Deborah first knocked lightly, then pounded on Eileen's door. The door was eventually opened and Eileen's little girl Fatima stood there. She was wearing the same brightly coloured dress as when she had last seen her and, despite all that was going on, was carefully groomed. But she didn't look like the same girl, she looked quite different. Perhaps that was because her appearance was altered by wearing her hair loose. Whatever it was, she looked older than she had seemed on their last brief meeting. She could be as old as eleven.

"Hello Fatima. Can I have a word with your mother?"

"She's not here," Fatima said in surprisingly good English with a strong

Dublin accent. She hadn't spoken a word of English all the time when she had led her through a maze of side alleys towards her car last time she was here. Obviously Eileen must have taught her English but the girl hadn't let on she knew any. Or perhaps Eileen had told her not to let on she spoke English.

Deborah was disappointed that Eileen wasn't here; it wasn't something she had anticipated or even considered when she'd set out. All her plans revolved around Eileen.

"I was hoping to see your mother," Deborah said. "It's very important. When will she be back?"

"I can't say. She went on that big march all the women went on."

"And your father?"

"He's away out too. He's always away. And nobody knows where he is. Not even my mother. He is a very important man, a Commander of a Unit," Fatima said proudly.

"Your mother and I are friends. We share the same nationality."

"Are you the lady she used bring her writings to?"

"That's right."

"But you didn't publish any of them."

"Not straight away. But I had it under consideration when I lost my job and was sacked by the Sheikha."

"I see," Fatima said. "If you like I can make you tea."

"Well, thank you Fatima. I'd like that. It's a thirsty day."

Deborah followed Fatima into the apartment and along to the kitchen. The house, which had been so full of the sound of voices and activity last time she had been here, was now hollowly empty.

"There's no one here," Fatima said. "I was left in charge. I'm here to take messages."

"Phone messages?"

"We don't have a phone. My mother says phones are not to be trusted. The government listens in. Phones are dangerous. We communicate by messages. Do you have a message?"

"I'm afraid not."

"Where did you leave your car today?"

"I didn't come by car. I don't have a car any more. I tried to cross the bridge earlier today and I, well, I left my car there."

"Did you see my mother on the bridge?"

"Not that I'm aware of." And even if I had, Deborah thought, I probably wouldn't have recognised her. One black-cloaked figure looked much like another.

"She was there. On the bridge. Helping make the revolution. Are you getting your car back?"

"I don't know. I shouldn't think so."

"Why were you on the bridge?"

"I was trying to get to the other side. You see my husband was kidnapped last night and taken away and I was trying to do something to find him."

"Why was he kidnapped?"

"I have no idea."

"He must have done something wrong."

"I suppose he must. But I was hoping your mother would be able to tell me where he was or at least what area of the city he was most likely to be held in."

Fatima considered this as she poured out a glass of tea.

"Well I can tell you that. I carry messages all the time. All prisoners are held in one of the places I go to. But if you want him you will have to pay a ransom. A big ransom."

"I see," Deborah said. "I wouldn't mind at all paying ransom money. To help the cause. My husband you see is not at all political. He works for an Arab bank."

"What bank?"

"The Trucial Bank."

"In that case he has lots of money. So he can pay a really big ransom. But how will we get the money? You must get it and bring it here."

"I'd certainly be prepared to do that."

"In that case I'll tell you where to look. More tea?"

"Thanks. This is really good tea."

"Yes," Fatima said, "my mother always drinks Earl Grey."

A little later, as Deborah was leaving, there was a great commotion in the apartment across the hall.

"What's happened? What's going on?" Deborah asked.

"Omar from next door has been killed by the police. I must go there now," Fatima said.

At that moment, there came through the open door of the apartment across the hall the sound of pandemonium and a huge explosion of emotion and grief in the room. The young man's relations began to scream and shriek and tear their hair out.

CHAPTER 52

Leaving Eileen's block, Deborah, in addition to her *abbaya* and veil, was wearing a mask with slits for the eyes. Fatima, who would herself soon be veiled, insisted this was necessary for her safety in the area she was going to. By the time she was fully attired, she was as formless and invisible as Arab women had learned over the centuries to make themselves.

Deborah felt awkward; indeed, she found it difficult to walk with the unaccustomed mask. It made her disorientated because it restricted what she could see. Basically, she could only see straight in front of her. She could only move along in a shuffle. So, after a short time, she took the mask off.

Deborah walked through the back streets of the Old City in the general area Fatima had pointed her towards.

There were plenty of people out and about, in fact there was a buzz, a sense of excitement in the air. She passed groups of armed men, some carrying rifles, and even some with rocket launchers. As one of these groups approached now, she turned aside into a vegetable shop, and, as they passed, bent over the vegetables. The last thing she wanted to be was conspicuous. She didn't want to draw attention to herself in any way.

Just after she had left the vegetable shop, there was a loud report, a bullet zinged past her and hit a trolley full of bottles of Coca Cola that a young boy was pushing along and calling out offering for sale. The bottles of coke exploded in slivers of flying glass. The boy grabbed his money bag and ran, abandoning his trolley, which careered into the street, an advertisement for Coca Cola, that most American of icons, stuck to its side in this most Arab quarter. What had that been all about? Was it that someone didn't like to see something as American as coke for sale in their own heartland?

Deborah looked at the crowd around her but she couldn't see, had no idea, where the bullet had come from or who had fired it. But it made her feel shaky. It brought home to her that this was no game she was playing and that it was highly dangerous to be wandering around on her own in this area.

But there was no way she would be here in this maze of side streets and alleyways if Fatima, who came here often with messages, hadn't been confident that this was the area where anyone taken prisoner would be held. Fatima had been quite sure about that. In fact, she claimed to have sighted some hostages. And, though she was young, she was clear-minded and observant and Deborah believed her.

Being directed by Fatima to the general area was one thing, but finding her way around it was something else. Every street, every laneway was extremely crowded in this extremely densely populated and very confusing quarter. There were hardly any street signs and those there were Deborah had great difficulty in reading. Not for the first time, she realised what a disadvantage it was not to have good Arabic.

She soon realised that tracking down someone held as a hostage in this area was like looking for a needle in a haystack. The streets were in chaos. Now that the police had been expelled there seemed to be no one in control. Everyone seemed to be out wandering the streets and she had no way of knowing whether they were criminals or terrorists or what they were and all of them seemed to be armed.

As an elementary precaution, she took care to avoid groups of people demonstrating. She didn't want to run the risk of being caught up in a demo again.

The more she penetrated into this area, the more she felt that she was getting in out of her depth. It had been ridiculous to imagine that on her own she would have any chance whatever of finding a cell of kidnappers holed up in this dense crowded ghetto where any room, any space down in any cellar, would be perfect for concealing people in an environment which was friendly to the kidnapper and would protect him while being extremely suspicious and hostile to all strangers. She hadn't a chance in hell.

It wasn't that Fatima had given her the wrong instructions, she had most likely given her the right instructions. But Fatima's instructions depended on her locating the central reference point. It was useless unless she could orientate herself.

The reference point Fatima had given her and she had to locate was the shop of a merchant called Malik al Samad in the street called Shakir Street. After a long time, when she was getting dizzy trying to read Arabic signs, she thought she had located the street and that gave her a lift. At last, she was getting somewhere. However, the street she thought was Shakir Street turned out to be a very long winding street packed with people. Moreover, although she walked its full length and back she couldn't find the shop of Malik al Samad which Fatima said was a hardware shop. In any event, the shop itself was not where the prisoners were held, it was only a guide, a reference point. If she found it, she had then to go down the laneway that ran at the side of the shop, turn right and right again and search for a *suq* guesthouse with a name that translated as The House of Rest for Weary travellers. That's where the prisoners were held.

Seeing on the other side of the road a hardware shop that she had the feeling was the right one, gave her a burst of hope even though the shop looked harmless with people browsing among its wares and an elderly owner in charge. She was nearly knocked down crossing the road only to find that it wasn't the right shop. There was no laneway to the side and no *suq* guesthouse.

It was hopeless. She was lost. She didn't really any longer know where she was. And it made no sense to give herself away by starting to ask questions. To open her mouth would give her away as a *Nazarani* and that would put her in danger right away. She certainly couldn't stop someone in the street and ask them anything at all. Not after she had witnessed that poor Coca Cola boy's barrow being shot up for no apparent reason, the bullet whizzing past her ear.

She began to feel increasingly discouraged and anxious. She was becoming confused and upset with the situation she was in. It was all hopeless.

There were dozens of little side streets, hundreds of shops and houses. She passed a few likely looking places where youths in black t-shirts were lounging around but then she soon passed another place exactly similar, there were possible hideouts all over this area. There was a myriad of places where David could be held, down any of these alleys, even at the backs of any of the shops, in any room or cellar.

And, anyway, what would she do if she did locate the right place. She might only find his headless body. They might have already executed him. And, even if they hadn't, if she asked questions they would more than likely kidnap her and hold her.

She was on a hopeless quest.

The best thing for her to do was to give up and get out of here before something happened to her. But she didn't know which direction to go in.

She didn't know which way to turn, and was wondering what to do, when she found herself suddenly surrounded by a group of black cloaked young women.

There was a babble of voices, young female voices made harsh by the Arabic they were speaking and somewhat muffled by the *yashmaks* they were wearing.

"Who are you, who are you?" was about all Deborah could make out, as far as her Arabic extended.

The group of black clad women clustered around her. At first, Deborah wasn't alarmed; these girls didn't seem aggressive. They were giggling, enjoying all the excitement of the revolution, enjoying being let out. They didn't get many diversions.

"Who are you? What are you doing here?"

"Why are you alone?"

"Where is your husband?

"What is your name?"

The girls pressed up against her excitedly, forcing her against the wall of a shop.

Pressing up closer against her, they tore her veil away. They exclaimed, "She is *Nazarani*. Her face is painted."

Deborah was wearing the lightest of make-up but that didn't seem to matter.

"Take off the paint," they shrieked excitedly, producing a piece of dirty cloth and, holding Deborah's face, rubbed it roughly.

"In our new state there will be no make-up," the girls said as they poked at her now and pinched her.

There was a commotion a few doors up, a fight broke out and the girls in black yashmaks ran away.

Deborah went in the opposite direction, her face sore and raw from being scrubbed. Her face smarting, she felt lost and frightened. She had to get out of here.

She kept walking and walking not knowing which direction she was walking in until she saw a taxi approaching. The taxi was already taken with a crowd of women in it but the driver stopped for her as she waved frantically.

She gave him a few dinars and squeezed into the back where she sat huddled up, one black bundle in a row of black bundles.

CHAPTER 53

---

eborah didn't get back home until the sun had set. The electricity was still off. She had just let herself into the apartment and was standing in the kitchen when she had the feeling that there was someone in the apartment. She felt that someone was watching her. She felt someone's eyes one her.

She looked around, swung her flashlight here and there but could see no one. It must just be her imagination. She was imagining things.

But the feeling of someone watching her persisted, she could hear someone or something breathing, a slightly wheezy sound. She swung the flashlight again and thought she saw a form quickly drawing back into the passageway that led to Abdul's quarters, into the shadows. Could it be someone from one of the other apartments? She didn't think that likely. It was more likely to be an intruder.

What should she do? This time she wasn't going to retreat to the roof. And, anyway, if there was somebody in the apartment, and she couldn't be absolutely sure, she would have to deal with them. She took a boning knife from the drawer and moved towards Abdul's quarters.

A man in a white, or once white, *thobe* and wearing a skullcap emerged from the shadows and stood looking at her with steady glaring eyes. He didn't appear to be armed. And he seemed to be on his own.

"Who are you? What are you doing here?"

The man who confronted her was thin, almost skinny. He looked ordinary enough. Except for his eyes. His eyes were red rimmed and staring.

"Abdul send me. I come instead of Abdul. He say I may have his quarters. I may have his job."

"What proof have you that Abdul sent you? Where is Abdul?"

"Abdul gone. Abdul finish."

"What do you mean finish?"

The youth drew his finger across his throat.

His eyes began to wander sideways.

"Abdul Sunni. All Sunnis finish. But I look after you. I can make tea, I can make goat stew, I can make Arab bread. I come look after you."

He smiled ingratiatingly or in an attempt, a mockery, of being ingratiating.

There was something definitely creepy about this character. She had an idea that he was a loner. He seemed to have come alone. He didn't seem to be part of a gang. Or indeed part of anything. Deborah knew that she was going to have to get rid of him or she couldn't go on staying here even for the night.

She approached him, carrying the knife. As she had seen on the streets, the revolution had brought all sorts of criminals and crazies out of the woodwork. Obviously this one thought he could move in where he liked, do what he liked. This one had a real mean dangerous look about him.

"I like that knife. It has good sharp narrow blade. Very good for cutting the throat of a goat and letting it bleed."

Deborah, pointing the knife at him, moved past him and let the dogs out of the room where they had been scratching at the door. As she opened the door, they rushed out barking.

Deborah returned to the kitchen.

"Get out," she said. "Now."

The man smiled as if bemused. He seemed to be weighing up the situation. He looked at the dogs. He didn't like dogs. Dogs are unclean. And they can be dangerous. Reluctantly he edged towards front door.

"You must get rid of those dogs if I'm going to work here. If you don't, I'll get rid of them for you."

Deborah said nothing. She was beginning to tremble.

"I am going now," the man said. "But only for the moment. I will be back. You have everything here. You are wealthy. But not any more. Everything is about to change. I can come stay here any time I wish."

With that he left.

But how far did he go? Deborah had the feeling that he hadn't gone far. She had the feeling that he was hanging around out there.

She locked all the windows and doors.

But when she looked out the window a little later, there was the creepy man squatting down in the compound staring up at the apartment. He obviously had no intention of going anywhere. He was going to stay put and wear her down. Even with the curtains pulled across, she could feel his eyes on her, see his form hunched up, see him down there waiting.

The dogs springing up suddenly startled her out of her light doze. There was someone at the door trying to get in. But, when she checked through the spy hole, there was no one there that she could see. Not that that meant anything. There could easily be someone just out of her line of sight. She thought she could hear creaks and the sound of someone moving about out there waiting. She was trapped in here like a rat in a cage.

Now and again she thought she heard people walking around in the apartment over her head and wondered if someone had come back. There was shouting followed by a loud thud. What was going on up there? Had marauders broken into Dr Rashid's apartment?

As she listened and waited, there was the sound of footsteps of several people coming down the stairs. They paused outside her door; they were arguing about something. Then steps continued down the stairs and out of the building. There was the sound of a pick-up truck starting up and, pulling the curtain slightly aside, she could see that it was loaded with what they had looted from Dr Rashid's apartment.

Then silence descended again. But the silence was more unnerving than the noise. Because, in the silence, she could hear small stealthy movements. The loner out there waiting his time.

Her imagination was too active for her to settle down. So she pulled a chair up to the window and sat looking out.

She could see the flashes and hear the sound of shooting coming from the area of the bridge and far beyond. This was followed by a huge explosion. Flames leaped up into the sky. Something big had gone up.

The revolution had unleashed all sorts of forces out there. The lid had been taken off and vile things had come crawling out. All around her was a descent into chaos.

But there was nothing she could do only sit in here trapped. And, even if she could have gone out, she wouldn't. She had to be here in case a miracle happened and David came back home.

It wasn't likely. The record was that when you were kidnapped in this part of the world you didn't get out. Unless a ransom was paid. In almost all cases it was either execution or a large sum of money handed over. Her only hope was that in some way the bank or CJ or someone had been contacted and could get cash to the kidnappers.

So Deborah, sitting on the chair at the window and holding on to this slim hope, waited and waited.

CHAPTER 54

T he new guards were rougher, kicking David as they threw him roughly back face down into his cell and slammed the door.

But, despite the rough treatment, they didn't either blindfold or handcuff him or chain him to the wall. Why? Was this omission intentional or due to a general lack of organisation? Or was it that they didn't care about him now that they had got what they wanted out of him? He had done what they wanted him to do and by doing so he had become disposable.

David hauled himself to his feet and looked about the cell which he had been in for so long but being blindfolded hadn't seen until now. The cell was an odd shape, long and narrow with nooks and crannies and crevices. There was one tiny iron barred window high up. The bare mud walls were damp and sweating. On the floor was some worn matting. The cell had a medieval look about it.

He stood waiting for the guards to come back. Surely they'd remember their omission and come back to handcuff and chain him. But they didn't come and he was left not knowing what his fate was to be. Whether it was to live or die.

The fact that he knew Arabic didn't mean that he could read the minds of his kidnappers. He knew that he could never fully understand the structure of their minds, their deeply fatalistic temperament, the philosophical outlook that allowed them so readily to accept suffering and, if necessary, annihilation. There was something at the core of such a mindset that was beyond his comprehension.

But he had at least learned a little. He had learned that these people's lives in every detail were dictated by Islam. These people had a basically different concept of how society should be ordered and this brought them into direct conflict with the western world. But how was trying to work out how his captors' minds ticked going to help him in his present predicament?

David jumped up and began pacing about his cell.

From what he had been able to work out during his removal from here to the bank and back again and from his previous deductions, he was reasonably sure that he was being held in the basement of one of the numerous cheap lodging houses in the *suq*. Hadn't someone said, if only mockingly, 'Very nice hotel. What time you like tea?'

The noises drifting in through the high barred window all confirmed this. In fact, he was pretty sure that the lodging house was carrying on at least some business. Wasn't this a little bizarre? Coffee in the courtyard and hostages, there were certainly other cells and presumably other hostages, in the basement.

The pleasure of having the freedom to walk about wore off after a time. He had briefly expected that they would release him as Ali Abdullah Karim had promised after he'd opened the strong room. That hope had been like a sliver of shining bright light but they had lied to him. They hadn't released him and hope that they might still do so was becoming ever dimmer, leaving him fearful of what his fate would be.

He tried to work out what the significance of bringing him back here and re-imprisoning him was most likely to be.

The only logical conclusion he could come to was that they didn't want any witnesses to their removal of the gold and currency from the Trucial Bank vaults; they didn't want anyone to spill the beans. That meant they were going to hold him captive for a very long time. Or perhaps behead him. Or otherwise dispose of him. Ali Abdullah Karim, who obviously held senior rank, would want any important outside witness like him to be kept out of the picture.

So what could he do to avoid his fate? What leverage was he left with? None that he could think of. His usefulness to them was gone the minute they got into the strong room.

David slumped down on the mud floor discouraged and depressed.

There flashed into his mind the image of Carolyn's tearful face as she held on to her gran's hand walking towards the plane. Would he ever see his daughter again? Or would she grow up fatherless?

Even more than Carolyn he worried about Deborah. What was she doing? Was she safe? Had she been molested? How would she cope if he didn't get out of here alive?

Hours crept by during every minute of which he expected the door to swing open and to be taken to another place.

But nobody came near him. After being left alone for a few hours, hope, irrepressible, illogical hope, began to creep into his mind, to lift his feeling of total dread of what was going to happen to him. The fact that no one had come so far must surely mean that at least he wasn't high on their list of priorities of people to be dealt with. Could they even have forgotten about him altogether?

He tried knocking on the door which was thick and spiked with iron spikes, though he wasn't sure if this was wise, if he might be better to just lie here quietly. But it didn't matter. No one seemed to hear him anyway.

He began to pace up and down again. He was incapable of sitting still. He had had no food or water since the chapatti and coffee for breakfast and by now he was extremely thirsty and ravenously hungry.

As the hours passed tediously by and dusk began to fall, he sank down on the floor exhausted.

Initially he had expected that someone would come, if not immediately, then quite soon. Although they hadn't come as yet, he still expected them at any moment. He waited in dread of their coming. He had flashes of that head in Death Wadi rolling towards him. Did his captors have an execution ground somewhere nearby, or was it just a room right here in this building?

Time went by and still no one came.

And, as the light began to fade, he began to wonder numbly if anyone would ever come near him at all. What about his guards? Had they abandoned him too, perhaps assigned to other duties? Was he going to be left here to die of hunger and thirst?

He sat there dazed by all that had happened to him and suddenly, by some shift in consciousness, he was no longer in the cell but gazing out on waving date palms which were being cut to pieces by gunfire while men screamed, blood stained the water of the river, bodies floated down stream.

David stirred, flicked a fly from his face.

As the hours moved on, David sitting there waiting and waiting, entered many dark places. Losing the discipline of consciousness, his mind collapsed inwards on itself, fragmenting, opening up vistas of horror he hadn't had any inkling were in there. He hadn't known that his mind extended that far, had never been out to its farther boundaries, content to keep within the necessary restraints of sanity.

From the cell next door a single long drawn out scream of the most incredible agony came to his ears. It was more a howl of pain and desperation than a scream. It was so distinct that it was as if he was right in there in the cell next door. The sound was of someone in mortal agony. It seemed to epitomise all the suffering and despair of the Middle East. And it seemed to go on and on forever.

Then it was abruptly cut off with a single shot.

The shot was followed shortly after by the sound of a body being dragged away. Followed by silence.

David was both horrified and terrified. The noises, the scream, the shot, heard without being able to see what was actually happening, was deeply disturbing. He couldn't help visualising what the tortured man had gone through before being shot.

There were no more sounds from the cell nearby.

After what he had heard from next door cell, he found it impossible to remain seated. Compulsively he paced up and down. He pummelled the door with his fists but only ended up hurting himself. Eventually exhausted he sank down again in a corner. He felt weak. His head and wrists throbbed. He put his head in his hands. He was in despair.

As he sat there, he had a tingling feeling on his leg. Something was crawling up along it. Slowly and carefully, he extended his right hand, caught the scorpion by its carapace and carried it to a far corner where he was about to place it down gently when he heard the scuttling noises of a nest of scorpions in a crevice. He had a horror of snakes, scorpions or any sort of creepy crawly. A disproportionate horror. He dropped the scorpion and backed away.

He retreated as far as he could and sat slumped on the ground with his legs hunched up defensively, waiting for the steps of the men who would tell him what his fate was to be.

He sat there in a daze, mulling over the bizarre turn of events that had ended with finding himself imprisoned in this airless basement with the expectation of meeting a fate similar to his father's.

He sank into the darkness for he knew not how long.

Then, gradually, through the mind fog, the miasma that had descended on him, he became aware of a noise outside his door.

He stiffened. There was a hard rock in his belly and darkness in his mind.

The moment had arrived. They had come to get him. His mouth went dry and he began to tremble.

The door opened and a guard carrying an oil lamp came in and set a jug of water on the floor, then left without speaking.

As he gulped the water down, he knew he should drink slowly but he gulped anyway, he noticed a faint line of light at the door.

The guard hadn't locked him in, not only that; he had left the door slightly ajar.

NOEL SCANLON

CHAPTER 55

For David the world had suddenly expanded after the confinement of his cell. A miracle had happened. Once out of the cell and hearing voices down below he had cautiously made his way up the stairs and on to the roof.

How did people survive locked up for month after month, year after year, often blindfolded and chained? How did they hold their mind together? He certainly wouldn't be able to.

Out now on the roof, he felt exposed as he picked his way past shrouded bundles on their string beds on this rooftop of baked mud and straw. Looking back, he saw a tatty sign declaring the house where he had been held to be The House of Rest for Weary Travellers.

He had escaped. But how had it happened? It could hardly have been forgetfulness on the part of the guard who had left the door open. He must have been bribed. But what about the other guards? How would they react when they discovered he had escaped? He had to assume they would come after him.

He stumbled and tripped over a sleeping bundle, picked his way between the string beds and over supine bodies. How could anyone sleep like that, completely enveloped head and all, how could they breathe, were they men or women, women probably but there was no way of knowing.

He came to a low mud wall and climbed over it on to the adjoining roof. Before him stretched a roofscape open to the sky where hundreds, probably thousands of people were sleeping.

Voices began muttering behind him, all around him. He was causing a disturbance, making himself conspicuous, the one thing he didn't want to be.

He had to get down off the roof. He couldn't go any farther because between this roof and the next there was a wide gap. Not that wide, but too wide for him to attempt to jump it. As he paused considering what to do next, a bullet whined over his head.

Behind him, black bundles had arisen from their string beds, shadowy figures were shouting and moving around. But who had fired the shot? Was it one of the guards alerted to his escape and in pursuit? Or was it just one of the aroused sleepers on the roof in this area where pretty well everyone carried arms?

Waiting for the bullet in his back which would precipitate him into another and more permanent state of darkness than being imprisoned even blindfolded and chained, David looked desperately about for a way down off the roof.

In a burst of light that seemed like fireworks being let off but was, he realised, tracer flares, he saw an outside cement fire escape and dived for it. The tracer flares petered out and, in darkness, he clambered down the cement stairs that had no railings of any description, grazing his arms and elbows trying to keep close in to the wall.

There was another tracer, followed by a burst of machine gun fire. There must be a police helicopter up there in the sky somewhere and the Shi'ite fighters were trying to take it out.

He stumbled into the courtyard of a rundown hotel or doss house just like the one he had been held in. The small dirty obscure building with a large hand painted Arabic sign was fronted by a walled courtyard with sand thrown on the hard ground, a building that in some other epoch had been white, with iron barred windows where, at any moment, a head or a barrel of a gun might appear. A few rickety tables were set out for customers and, on one of these, an oil lamp was guttering out. Beside this table, an unveiled flat nosed, black-faced woman slept among a horde of small children.

Someone shouted down from the roofs. In response, an old watchman arose from the ground clutching a blunderbuss. He tried to block David's way, but, in a frenzy not to be trapped, David knocked him aside and the old man collapsed with a groan on to the ground.

There were noises behind him and he thought he saw figures on the roof headed for the cement stairway. However, by then, he was out in the street.

Looking about for cover, he spotted the fruit and vegetable *suq* opening off and dived into it. There were fruit and vegetable stalls on either side of a narrow road. The stalls were empty now, only wooden frames. Rotting melons and other fruit and vegetables thrown on the ground were slippery underfoot and made him careful as he began to run.

From all his *suq* visits with Mohammed, this general area was familiar. What had become of Mohammed? What had they done with him? Had they let him go? Had they imprisoned him? Or had they done away with him?

There wasn't much light in this *suq*. The traders were closed up and sleeping or watching from behind closed doors. Here and there, lights were on indoors, filtering out from behind shuttered windows.

A veiled woman startled him as she scurried across in front of him and into a doorway. To avoid colliding with her, he tried to slow down but began to slip, sliding on the slippery litter underfoot.

Suddenly a bullet tore into the shuttered shop front he was passing and there was a crash of something breaking inside. Somebody was coming after him, he didn't know who. Whether it was one of the guards from the House of Rest for Weary Travellers or someone else, what did it matter? They knew where he was.

He spurted, but not for long. He was in a cul-de-sac. As he realised this, he ran into the end wall, slapping his hands up against it to save himself.

Above him, dimly apparent, was one of the many huge, blown up, enhanced and highly flattering posters of Sheikh Suleiman Bin Himyar al Yas that were posted up all over Khor Fahal. This one had been defaced and partly torn down. It looked like a ghostly remnant.

His way forward was blocked. He was trapped.

As he stood there, his back to the end wall, trapped and in, or shortly likely to be in, some gunman's sights, a figure appeared before him. A fighter in uniform complete with bandanna. This one had his face blackened.

A familiar voice said, "I rather think we'd better get you out of here."

Someone was pulling him to one side and into an opening between houses.

It was Sebastian!

NOEL SCANLON

CHAPTER 56

David was flabbergasted. "Jesus Christ. I thought you were dead."
"Well not exactly," Sebastian said, as he began to lead the way
between the houses.

"I can't believe it," David said following on. "You were dead and now
you are alive again. You disappear without trace. I find blood all over your
bedroom and the furniture in bits. I was really upset. I was certain you had
been abducted or dead or both. I thought the Ayatullah's men had rumbled
you and come to get you."

"They nearly did. That's why we had to stage that ruse so carefully. You
see they were beginning to have doubts about me. If I was to survive and
continue to be one of them, we had to find a way of boosting their belief in
me. We had to convince them once and for all that I was really with them.
And we did. We did it by, among other things, staging a police raid on my
apartment. A squad of police came roaring ostentatiously up to the block,
stormed into the building with guns drawn, broke down my door, beat me
up viciously and arrested me under the terrorism act. To make it realistic,
I had to be roughed up and they did rather overdo that a bit. Still, the ruse
worked. And, of course, you played your part in it as planned."

"Me? What part did I play?"

"You told Deborah what you had seen. Deborah told Eileen. Eileen
told her husband, Safwan Hisham, who checked up on its veracity. Luckily
for me, it stood up to scrutiny. It convinced him and the other leaders that
the police were my enemies and they were my friends."

"I never thought you could be so devious."

David's mind was racing putting it all together.

What Sebastian was telling him explained a lot. It explained why, when
he had gone to the police to report Sebastian's apparent abduction, they had
reacted the way they did. They had obviously contacted their superiors and

had been told from higher up to block his questions and get rid of him.

It all made sense. He already knew that Sebastian was with MI6. In addition, he knew he had infiltrated the Ayatullah's group under the guise of being an ex-IRA operative. It all fitted together.

"And to think that all this time I was sure you were dead."

"That's what you were supposed to think. It was essential for me to disappear in a hurry."

"And you never even dropped a hint."

"If I had, it would have spoiled the whole operation."

At that point, Sebastian held up his hand for silence indicating danger ahead and cutting the conversation off. He went on more carefully, leading the way through walkways so narrow that they bumped off the walls of the high houses on either side. All these *suqs* were interconnected.

What Sebastian had told David was true as far as it went. What he had not told him was that to retain the trust of the Ayatullah's organisation, he'd had to do more than arrange that police raid on his apartment. He had had to teach them some bomb making techniques. In the case of the bomb at CJ's, his call to his contact had been acted on immediately and given the police time to prevent that particular bomb from going off. In the case of Andy Wilson he had similarly called his contact but there had been some dreadful cock up, there had been some breakdown in communications and his message hadn't been passed on to the proper authorities in time. He greatly regretted it but there was a lot at stake here; if this uprising got out of hand, it could spread throughout the Gulf region. Moreover, his own life was at risk all the time. There were always people among the Ayatullah's men who remained unconvinced, who resented him and would put a bullet in his back at the first opportunity.

They were negotiating their way now through another alleyway, when the far end was darkened by the outline of a man's form. A volley of shots ricocheted off the mud walls of either side just above their heads. Turning and thrusting David to one side, Sebastian fired off a burst of automatic fire. The form disappeared.

David had instinctively lowered his head and covered it with his hands as dried mud flaked off the wall above him as he ducked into a doorway.

"Sorry about that," Sebastian said leading the way forward again. His skills evidentially extended a good deal beyond faking his own death.

As they made their way along, David said, "So it was you arranged for the door of the cell to be left open?"

"Of course."

"And how did you manage that?"

"Bribery, what else. Money passed hands. Bank money that your friend CJ was kind enough to make available."

David digested this piece of information. "Why did you go to so much trouble to get me out?"

"Because you're my friend. And because there's something you can help me with."

David couldn't imagine what. As it was, he was trying to hold down the tension that was jumping in his brain. It was impossible to imagine what use he'd be in present circumstances.

Suddenly and abruptly, they emerged into the market area where there were a great many people about all in a state of confusion and uproar. It was a state of total chaos.

"My car is just nearby," Sebastian said coolly, as if this was just an ordinary stroll in the markets.

They got into Sebastian's car which was parked behind a small grocery shop and Sebastian drove through groups of screaming men, past a shop that had been blown up just minutes before they reached it, the explosion rocking their car, throwing people and parts of bodies all over the place.

David was in shock. Nevertheless, despite that, he noticed the facia board of the showroom that was in flames. It read Jaffer Tasufin, a Sunni and a customer of the bank, the main Toyota dealer in the state. Jaffer Tasufin owned showrooms and blocks of apartments all over the place. He was a man of great respectability. Now his showroom was on fire and people were rushing about waving their arms and calling for help.

Sebastian drove on through it all without comment, appearing not to notice the shots and screams of the burned and injured. It was apparent that he had the type of sang froid of which David was totally incapable. David was beginning to realise that, despite their shared childhood experiences, Sebastian was a man he had greatly misjudged. He was beginning to think he didn't know anything about him at all.

Sebastian's demeanour since he had so suddenly and dramatically appeared in the cul de sac by the blown up poster where David had stood immobile waiting to be shot, had been one of nonchalant casualness. David's was the exact opposite. He was in a state of deep fear and uncertainty and trepidation in the situation in which he found himself.

Given his own extreme fear, David felt it almost impossible to understand how Sebastian could be so nonchalant. How was he able to ignore the terrible things happening around them, the danger they were in, and the risks they were taking by being here at all?

"Where are we headed?" David asked, noting that they were moving in the opposite direction from his home on the creek.

"We're driving to the fishermen's harbour," Sebastian said. "A dhow is lying out there with a large consignment of weapons. It's not an ordinary dhow, it's got high powered engines and a lot of work done on it. Anyway, my job tonight is to stop the arms it carries from coming ashore."

"And what's my part in all of this?" David asked.

"Don't worry," Sebastian said, swerving to avoid a truck. "You won't have to do anything nasty. We want you more in your capacity as a banker."

"It doesn't look much like a bank situation to me."

"Oh, but it is. You'll see in due course."

When they reached the fishermen's harbour, Sebastian dropped David off beside a warehouse and gave him some instructions. Then he said, "Now I have to be off. But I'll be back shortly. And, meantime, wait until I give you the signal to come out."

CHAPTER 57

As Sebastian disappeared quickly into the darkness, David took cover in a slit between two warehouses in the harbour area. Sebastian had told him to stay there out of harm's way until he gave him the signal to come out. His location wasn't far from the cafe where he and Sebastian had sipped tea, Sebastian in his *agal* and *kheffiah* looking like some latter day Lawrence of Arabia, whose sexual preferences he also shared. What a revelation Sebastian was.

He knew it was the same area though it looked very different now. When he had met Sebastian here, the cafe where they had drunk tea by the warm sticky water of the harbour had been a quiet spot, the fishing *sambuqs* of a design that went back to antiquity rolling at anchor. Now David could barely make out where the cafe was. What lights there were, were oil lamps and were on the pier and on the dhows in the harbour. And far from being a quiet backwater, the harbour area had become a scene of conflict.

This was what war and revolution achieved, a transformation from peace to mayhem, from tranquillity to suffering and death. Dark and unimaginable things were being perpetrated in the darkness out there where there were constant sporadic bursts of gunfire and from where came shouts and screams and wailing laden with unbearable suffering and pain and fear as scores were settled in blood.

Louder gunfire and explosions came all the time from the Old City. Revenge and looting were well under way as if the people required this emotional catharsis, this emotional outpouring, this lancing of the boil of their hatred and frustration.

In the middle of the mayhem they had driven through on the way here, David had seen people walking along the road with plasma screens, carrying and wheeling away fridges and freezers and cookers and furniture of all sorts ignoring or oblivious to the fighting all around them, determined to get their share of the loot. He had even seen two youths drive a Lexus straight out through a showroom window.

As they had driven through all this chaos, Sebastian had told him what was supposed to happen here tonight, though he had the feeling that he had only been told what he needed to know.

The guts of it was that a dhow was lying out in the harbour with a shipment of arms for the insurgents. They were about to land these arms but only after they received payment in gold, the gold they had stolen from the Trucial Bank vaults.

Sebastian's mission was to prevent this happening.

The dhow with the arms, a boat very much like the gold smuggling boats the bank's customers regularly dealt with, was riding at anchor in the harbour. Sebastian had pointed it out. There were a number of dhows out there bobbing about.

The plan was that the Ayatullah's people would hand over an agreed quantity of gold, and the armaments would then be brought ashore by a fleet of small boats, it being considered inadvisable to bring the dhow close in to the pier.

The consignment was to consist of rocket propelled grenades, mostly of the shoulder held variety, but others of a more advanced technology, together with a large consignment of machine guns, grenades, small arms, ammunition and all the odds and ends needed to pursue a revolution. Some had already been landed as an earnest of intent. The rest would follow after the hand-over of the gold.

Sebastian had been put in charge of the unit assigned to handing over the gold and receiving and checking the arms. Sebastian was the most suitable person they had to conduct this operation and particularly to check the arms. He was the one with the technical expertise learnt during his years with the IRA in Northern Ireland. He was the arms expert who would assure the quality and suitability of the arms and ensure that they were as ordered.

David heard the sound of a vehicle close-by and coming towards him fast. He looked out to see who it was, thinking it might be Sebastian.

Shooting wildly into the air, a load of crazed looking *Mujahadeen* drove right close-by as he poked his head out.

Their eyes seemed to glow unnaturally, silver bright, something, hatred perhaps, emanating from them. They loosed off some shots that hit

David's building and made him duck. These fighters looked so wild, their eyes so out of focus, that they must have taken something, either *qat* or some other stimulant, unless it was just plain religious fervour instilled in them by the power of the Ayatullah's words calling for *Jihad*. Whatever the drug was, chemical or religious, it was obvious that the men in that vehicle could be stopped only by death and martyrdom.

They represented the fervent upsurge of Moslem fundamentalism that was on the march, not only here in Khor Fahal, but throughout the Moslem world from Algeria to Pakistan, from Iran to Indonesia.

The men in the vehicle that had just roared past were par for the course. Fervent, dedicated, ready to die for the cause. But poorly trained. And lightly armed. In the heel of the hunt, they were, or in time would be, up against vastly superior armaments, vastly superior technology. And so far technology had won. It took a lot of conviction to die for a belief, but five hundred pound bombs, shells from tanks, missiles from aircraft, rockets from helicopters, could annihilate any number of believers, however fervent, however willing to die.

Technology reigned supreme. For the present. But long term? What would happen long term? People fuelled by ideas and religious beliefs have prevailed against the odds in the past. Could it happen again?

David kept watching shadows move, vehicles start up and stop. And he watched the dhows out to sea and lighters coming and going and he tried to work out which of them was ferrying in the arms.

Above and behind him, stars pierced a black sky. Somewhere behind him, light filtered from a window that had been opened slightly, pouring yellow splashes of light down on to his hiding place. Was someone looking down on him, taking an interest in him, would they pick him out? Or was it just someone anxious to find out what was going on?

Though David had experienced rioting before, this was his first experience of being in the middle of fighting of this sort. And what most struck him about it was how confused it all was. It was impossible to work out what was going on. At least impossible for him. Everything was confused. And chaotic. And arbitrary. Whether people lived or died seemed to be purely accidental, where you happened to be at a particular moment in time.

David stayed where he was and waited. And waited.

Hours seemed to have passed when, suddenly, in a lull in the fighting, from not far away, down by the pier, came the sound of a number of pistol shots fired into the air in quick succession. The signal he had been waiting for.

David broke cover and ran towards the spot where the pistol shots had come from, crouching as he heard shots being discharged and what sounded like a gun battle, short sharp and vicious, going on down there by the pier. There was incoming fire from the other end of the pier, and volleys of returning fire. Then, from really close by, the staccato sound of a machine pistol. Then silence.

David stopped in confusion, looking about him.

"Here. Here," a figure said as Sebastian appeared before him for the second time that night, this time his machine pistol that had obviously been fired recently, still at the ready. In the dim light, David could just make out bodies lying this way and that, lying dead where they had fallen, their black shirts and green bandannas wet with blood.

"They're all dead, I'm afraid," Sebastian said. "We ran into a most unfortunate ambush. All my squad killed I'm afraid."

"You're wounded," David said, noticing now the blood seeping through Sebastian's shirt.

"I'm afraid so. Painful but not serious."

"Can I do anything?"

"Not really. Though perhaps you could help me move one or two of these bodies.

As David helped place the bodies in the exact positions Sebastian wanted them in, he felt a mixture of nausea and revulsion at the cruelty, the viciousness, the insanity of it all. As he dragged the bodies into place, he noticed a tattoo on the exposed chest of one of the fighters.

"Is it true," he asked, "that every *Mujahadeen* has tattooed on his chest a *sura* from the Koran?"

"Possibly. But we haven't time for that now."

Peering closely, David could just make out a tattoo on the chest of the dead fighter he was carrying and from the couple of the words he read knew it to be a sura from the Koran. This insurgency was then, in truth, a Jihad, a religious war or was so regarded by these fallen fighters.

"There isn't much time," Sebastian said, when the bodies of the fallen fighters had been arranged to his satisfaction. David thought he saw movement among the dead bodies. But he didn't mention it and didn't investigate. "Come with me and I'll show you what I want you to do, what

I really brought you here for."

Sebastian leading the way, they had walked for no more than twenty or thirty yards when they came upon a large off-road Land Rover.

"A strong vehicle," Sebastian said. "Specially strengthened chassis and springing. Particularly suitable for desert driving. Will cross pretty well any terrain. It's your means of escape."

"You mean you're providing this vehicle just for me?"

"In a manner of speaking."

David walked around the vehicle and looked in the back. "What's in here?"

"The gold," he said. "The gold that all the kafuffle has been about. The gold you're going to take out of the state for us."

David was stunned.

Sebastian slapped the Land Rover on the side. "Here are the keys. It's yours. Take it away."

David felt, on the one hand, that he had been duped but, on the other hand, he'd been given a means of survival, of getting out of the state across the desert and a vehicle that was capable of doing it.

"And what about you?"

"I'm staying here," Sebastian said. "There's still a lot more I can do."

"Don't be ridiculous," David said. "You can't stay here. They are bound to rumble you. They're not stupid you know. Jump in and I'll drive you wherever you want."

"Not possible, I'm afraid. Get in and take it away."

David got in reluctantly.

Looking down from the front seat of the Land Rover, David saw Sebastian as a shadowy figure in a shadowy place in a shadowy war. What he was doing was his vocation. He had a talent for it. And a commitment. It is difficult to think of a stronger commitment than risking your own life. And if he stayed on taking the chances he did he would more than likely lose it. In the dark shadowy spaces around them shooting was still going on. This was a battlefield, a killing ground. It was a place where death, so eagerly embraced by the Arab fighters, was very close by and very readily available.

In one last plea David said, "You can't possibly stay here in this hell. If you do, you won't survive."

But Sebastian was already moving away into the darkness, his black fighters outfit stained red with blood. He was quickly swallowed up in the shadows of the harbour area.

"Good luck," David said after the retreating figure.

He settled himself in the Land Rover. It fired up smoothly.

He drove away, not turning the lights on until he was out on a main road and quickly entered the same mayhem Sebastian had driven them through on their way here.

Someone was screaming a warning over a loud hailer and then suddenly the voice was cut off by an explosion. Further screams and an outbreak of wailing told him there had been causalities.

As he reached the spot, people were making way for an ambulance with the markings of the Red Crescent, which was blaring its horn trying to get through from another street from where there came the sound of sporadic gunfire.

Stretchers appeared. Running beside them, firing off shots into the air, shouting and screaming, were lines of *Mujahadeen*. Women too ran along beside the stretchers, ululating, tearing at their clothes and hair. All the people in the area seemed to be shouting and screaming at the same time.

David blasted his horn, put his foot down and drove through them.

A little later, when he was in the clear, he looked back to the harbour area and saw a huge flash and flames leap into the air. An oil storage tank had gone up.

He kept going, headed for the creek road.

CHAPTER 58

Deborah opened her eyes on to darkness. She thought she had heard a vehicle pull up outside but whether that was a dream or reality she wasn't sure. A little later, she could hear someone coming up the stairs. Who? It was most likely the crazy who had never gone away and was back again now in the middle of the night when there was no one about.

Taking the kitchen knife from the side table beside her, she retreated to the passageway at the back. As the footsteps stopped outside her hall door, she stood watching with the lounge door slightly ajar to enable her to see whoever came in. The dogs who had refused to leave the lounge stood watching and listening intently, their ears pricked up.

The front door opened which meant the person opening it had a key. She crept forward to look. It could be Abdul though it was more likely the crazy. The dogs ran forward barking excitedly.

She played her flashlight on the entrance.

It wasn't the crazy. Or Abdul. It was David! A dishevelled looking David, his clothes sticking to him with sweat, blood on his shirt, a look in his eyes as if those eyes had just seen terrible things.

Deborah let out a shriek and ran towards him. They fell into one another's arms. "God I can't believe it." She was overcome by an immense relief, the feeling of being reprieved, rescued, pulled up from the black pit. Tears were running down her cheeks as the terrific build up of fear and tension began to drain away.

"Where have you been? What's happened to you? Where did all the blood on your shirt come from?"

"It's not mine. It's...someone else's. I'll tell you all about it later. But not now. All hell has been let loose out there. And it's getting worse by the minute. We have to leave straightaway."

She could feel the tension in his body, the thumping of his fast beating heart. "I never thought I'd see you again," Deborah said, holding him tightly. There had been part of her missing and now it was back, slotted into place. She was whole again. She couldn't stop herself from gushing. "I thought that they wouldn't ever let you out. I thought that they would do something unspeakable to you like they've done to so many people they kidnapped.

"I didn't know what to do when you were taken," Deborah went on. "I tried to cross the bridge to get help but they began to attack me and I lost the car. Eileen's daughter Fatima told me where you might be in the Ma'ala area and I went there looking for you but I got lost and in the end didn't know where I was. I was looking for a shop Fatima had told me to find but I couldn't find it and I couldn't ask or they would have seized me and I didn't have enough Arabic anyway and it was awful with armed men roaming around everywhere. I was terrified. In the end, I got a seat in a taxi and came back home but, when I got here, there was a crazy man in the apartment and he's been watching it since. I got so I was so terrified of everything..."

"I know how you must have felt," David said. "I can well imagine what you've been through. But, right now, we have to move fast. We have to get out of here straightaway before they come here to get me. We'll talk later. But just now you have to help me throw together a few necessities for a desert journey."

"Where are we going?"

"I'm a wanted man and our only way to escape is to go into the desert. We have no alternative. There's no way we could get across the bridge to the New City. So, the desert is the only way to go."

David was in no doubt that the Ayatullah's *Mujahadeen* would come after him. It was impossible to imagine that they would just accept the disappearance of their gold, the absence of which was even now holding up the landing of the armaments they desperately needed. Without doubt, Jeeps would have already been despatched to find the gold and bring it back. And him with it.

Deborah was running frantically about the apartment, stuffing things into bags with quick nervous movements. Since David's sudden appearance, she had gone from being totally exhausted to being all keyed up, excited and confused and fearful all at the same time.

She ran to the bathroom for all the medical supplies in the house, a first aid kit, bottles of disinfectant, plasters, and pitched them into a bag.

She was glad to be getting out of this close confinement, even if she had no idea where there were going.

She felt really hyped up and catching David's urgency she listened to every noise outside, the sound of each vehicle approaching in case it stopped at their block, in case it had come for them, in case they would be trapped.

So they both feverishly threw essential items for a desert journey into plastic bags and holdalls, moving at speed, taking what was left in the fridge that hadn't already gone off and emptying the kitchen cupboards.

"I'll fill as many containers as I can find with water, we have some big plastic ones," David said. "And you'd better take your jewellery and anything you particularly want, anything of sentimental value. And don't forget the money in the safe. This apartment is bound to be cleaned out. They'll track me to here sooner rather than later."

As they rushed about, the sound of a giant explosion from the direction of the Old City made them move even faster.

Lugging the sacks and holdalls they had packed down the stairway, David said, "Leave whatever else you want to bring at the door and I'll come back for it. I've got to fetch plastic containers from the garage for the spare diesel. The tank is pretty full but we'll need more. We have to get more diesel."

Deborah spotted the spanking new Land Rover parked in their compound.

"Where did that come from?" she asked.

"That's what's going to take us across the desert if things go right," David said as he threw the holdalls and black sacks into the back of the vehicle.

Finally, everything they were bringing with them was loaded, the dogs were sitting up alert in the back ready for their trip. David had muzzled them in order to prevent them from barking and giving them away. The apartment front door was closed and locked and they were ready to go.

Deborah, closing the gate behind her, looked back at the apartment block more empty and ghostly than ever now at night, with its verandas and the balustrade on the roof where she had so often looked out over the creek. If they came after David and found him gone they would most likely wreck the place, they might well torch it. But it was at peace now, sleeping. And yet the block had taken on a sinister appearance, full of shadows. She thought she saw the flicker of movement at a window, a tiny glow of light, unseen eyes watching them leave. It had an eerie effect on her. Were people hiding in the other apartments watching them leave? Or were they really empty? Or were they filled with ghosts?

Deborah, with her *abbaya* pulled over her jeans and t-shirt, felt nervous and jumpy.

As the gate clicked closed, she saw two eyes floating in the near darkness. Mr Tom miaowed questioningly. In recent days, it had been left to her to feed him. Thinking of the empty flats, Deborah said, "I hope someone will look after the cat. I hope he doesn't starve."

"Of course he won't starve. There are dozens of cats living along the creek. They don't starve."

Deborah didn't like the idea of Mr Tom becoming one of the wild creekside cats. But here was nothing she could do about it.

"Hurry up." David whispered urgently.

The tyres of the Land Rover crunched on the creekside road suddenly illuminated by David flicking on the headlights.

"Wouldn't it be better with the lights off?" Deborah suggested.

"Maybe," David said reducing the lights to sidelights. "Provided we can get to see where we're going."

Behind them came a flash of light followed by an explosion. Shouts and screams and the blasting of sirens reached out on to the creek road. The sirens were coming from the bridge area.

A Jeep coming at speed, braked at their apartment block and drove into the compound. It looked like they'd just got out in time.

David speeded up but, after a few hundred yards, had to brake abruptly.

"There's some obstruction on the road. It looks like a barrier of some sort," he said as he leaped out to investigate.

Deborah could see the barrier now. She strained her eyes to see if it was manned. She couldn't see anyone but that didn't mean there wasn't someone there.

David began to raise the barrier slowly or what seemed to be slowly but probably was not really. It was so quiet that she could hear the rasping sound of his breathing.

He ran back to the Land Rover and jumped in.

As he started the engine, a figure, shadowy and ill defined, appeared out of the darkness and began to lower the barrier. As he drove forward, the man moved out into the middle of the road shouting a warning, Kalashnikov in hand.

David aimed the vehicle at him, and the offside mudguard caught him a glancing blow as he jumped to one side. Then they were past and bumping wildly into the darkness as the man picked himself up and began firing after them.

Deborah imagined the feeling of the next shot entering her body and putting an end to it all. So much had happened in the last twenty-four hours, she'd had so many shocks one after the other that she felt numbed.

The man fired again in their general direction but missed. Then they were out of range bumping along with the headlights still off, as a result of which David nearly crashed a number of times. After a particularly narrow escape, he pulled abruptly off the road they were on, on to a rough back road, switched on the headlights and headed for the desert.

Soon the flickering lights of a shanty town lit only by oil lamps appeared to their right in the desert scrub. As they approached, there was the sound of activity, of shouting and screaming. Something clicked in David's mind and he knew that this was the shanty town from which the boy who used to help him on the boat came from.

This was a settlement the police claimed to be a hot bed of terrorists. They came here regularly, lifted scores of men, and bulldozed their shacks. Had the boy who used help him with the boat and who had been badly beaten up before disappearing completely, gone back to his shack, might even be there now? Was he about to be or had he already been arrested again and thrown into prison?

David had no idea, but he felt a sense of guilt that he hadn't done more for the boy when he had called on him for help. But what could he have done? He had suddenly taken off, disappeared and he had no way of finding him.

Maybe he was still out there somewhere having evaded the police, he was street smart after all and had lightening reactions, he could smell danger coming down the line. Or maybe after all that had happened to him, he had gone the other way, joined the Ayatullah's *Mujahadeen,* even volunteered to be a suicide bomber. He hoped not, he hoped that the boy's obvious love of life, his instinct for survival would prevent him from taking such a decision. But who could tell? Many other young people in similar circumstances had done just that. Not that he could even begin to understand the mental processes by which anyone could arrive at the decision to take their own life, to blow themselves up. It was incomprehensible to him.

David would have been horrified had he known that his boy was the suicide bomber who had blown himself up in the attempt to assassinate Sheikh Suleiman Bin Himyar Al Yas on the palace steps.

A little farther on, and for no apparent reason since there was no road and therefore no traffic, they came upon a large cement roundabout. It looked oddly incongruous, not to say ridiculous, out here in the wilderness, built a long time ago by an eccentric member of the Ruling Family who had seen roundabouts on a visit to Europe and copied them in this unlikely environment. Now the roundabouts were covered in sand and sinking into the ground.

Just beyond the roundabout, there was a filling station. The headlights shone briefly on a few ragged palm trees and thorn trees and a camel having a late night snack, curling its long lower lip trying to get at a hidden piece of greenery.

A sign in Arabic declared the filling station to be The Three Palm Filling Station and Desert Engineering Works. A battered sign bore the name of Shell. It was a decrepit place well off the main route even into the desert. Hardly anyone ever came here. On the rare occasion David had passed by, the proprietor Abdulla had been lying under some battered and broken down truck with Arabic lettering and decorated the way Arab drivers decorate their vehicles while an apprentice in dirty overalls idled the time away.

He pulled in now and cruised to a standstill.

It was dark and silent. He took a pocket flashlight from the glove compartment and approached the hut where he knew that Abdulla slept. It was a hut built of wood with a palm roof. He could hear snoring inside.

He edged the door open and shone the flashlight down on a sleeping sprawling figure. "Abdulla."

No reply. Was he drunk on the brew he made from tapping the date palms, a sort of poor man's *arak* and for the consumption of which he could receive a hundred lashes.

"Abdulla."

Still no reply.

He shook him but Abdulla only groaned. He seemed to be dead drunk.

David turned away and shone the flashlight around. There was practically nothing in the hut: a table with an oil lamp now extinguished, the leftovers of a meal, pieces of a chapattis. And a glass. He picked it up to smell it and, as he did so, he sensed a movement behind him as Abdulla emerged from his torpor and launched himself at him.

David shot his arms behind him in reflex and, hitting Abdulla's knees in a reverse tackle, brought him to the ground. Abdulla fell like a big sack of rice. If he had been sober or even half sober, he wouldn't have been able to handle him.

Abdulla was lying quietly on the ground but, just to be on the safe side, he tied him with a length of rope and gagged him with a piece torn off his shirt.

He shook him to bring him to. "Where's the key to the pump?"

Abdulla kept the pumps chained and locked with a big old lock.

After a couple of times of asking, Abdulla nodded towards a peg on the wall. David took the key and got out.

Abdulla had to be left tied; if not he might report what had happened. On the other hand, he might not. He was not a man who would be well in with the authorities. Still, better to be on the safe side. And he needn't worry about him being left here. The apprentice would find him in the morning.

David unlocked the pump, topped up the Land Rover and filled the plastic containers with diesel, using a hand pump, which seemed ridiculous in a state with one of the largest oil fields in the world, but there it was.

They drove on along a track that ran parallel to the coast with the sea always only a few hundred yards distant. As they drove, they passed small villages sunk in a sea of sand, with occasionally the ruins of an old fort. They were entering a scrub desert. The track they were on was only one of dozens of tracks meandering across this area. The problem was to work out where all these tracks led. Some of them were dead ends. Some of them curved back towards small coastal fishing villages. Some led only to *eigas* or inland lakes.

David made his choice and found himself on a track that had an under layer of hard subka and a washboard surface badly rutted and corrugated. These corrugations caused the Land Rover to vibrate and shudder, nearly tearing the steering wheel out of his hand as he tried to find the right speed for hitting the tops of the corrugations and thereby cut down on the jolting.

At he drove, he kept checking in the rear view mirror for signs of pursuit.

After a time, he began wondering if he had chosen the wrong track and if he should turn back and try another one. He was getting seriously worried that he had made the wrong choice when the subka track they were on came out into a wide-open gravel desert, which was quite flat and easy to drive over except for the danger of hitting rocks and boulders that rose up now and then in the darkness.

As they gradually began to move into the gravel desert, they were confronted by the most extraordinary spectacle.

On the horizon, the whole desert seemed to be on fire. He immediately realised what had happened.

"They've set fire to the oil pipeline!"

CHAPTER 59

In the distance, great flames were leaping high into the air, vividly illuminating the night sky. It was the most spectacular sight David had ever seen, that great pipeline that pumped millions and millions of gallons of oil a day cut in various places and torched but still pumping the gas that was keeping these huge fires going.

Deborah didn't respond. The immensity of the oil fires frightened her, made her think that the desert, which she thought was going to be a sanctuary, a place they could just disappear into, was turning out to be just the opposite. It was turning out to be a highly dangerous environment.

David drove for some time, awed by the great spectacle of the oil fires and the light they threw off and the great plumes of smoke rising into the sky. There was one at every point where the pipeline had been cut or blown up.

Watching them and dazzled by them, he hadn't noticed until now smaller pinpoints of light moving over the desert like little glow worms, that were, he suddenly realised, the side lights of vehicles. He could just make out that they were Jeeps racing over the gravel desert with heavy machine guns mounted in the rear and a complement of half a dozen armed men.

He immediately cut his engine, doused all lights and prayed that they hadn't been seen.

After a few tense moments, the patrol moved on and away.

They sat there listening and watching and eventually drove on slowly and tentatively.

They hadn't gone more than half a mile when they heard the sound of a vehicle very close to them apparently moving without any lights at all. David immediately braked, stopped, turned the engine off and sat taut and alert.

The vehicle slid past in the dark, apparently as anxious to be anonymous as they were. And David realised that what it was, was people like themselves escaping from the revolution. There were plenty of people wanting to escape from the state, he had seen them at the airport when Deborah's mother had left, people desperate to get on the plane, arguing and shouting at officials, on the edge of hysteria, knowing that their lives depended on getting out. Given that most of them had been turned away at the airport, many of them were bound to try the desert route. These people passing in the night were like themselves trying to get out into the desert without being cut off by the patrols.

They hadn't expected any of this activity in the desert, either the people trying to escape or the patrols.

They began to be hyper cautious. Every time they heard a noise of any sort, they pulled up, switched off the engine and waited.

What were all these Jeeps doing in this stretch of the gravel desert close to the city? The most likely thing was that they were on patrol out here looking for people fleeing from the city like themselves. David had an ominous feeling that these vehicles were after him in particular, had been assigned to intercept him and his cargo.

Gazing at the massive oil fires in the distance, leaping skyward, burning off thousands and hundred of thousand of gallons of the precious fuel the west so depended on, burning as if the whole earth was on fire, David said, "We can't just keep driving towards those pipelines. There's no way we could cross them, all the crossing points will have been destroyed."

The pipelines ran west from a group of oil wells and then turned at right angles down towards the coast and Khor Fahal harbour.

"We'll just have to change direction a bit to clear the pipelines and oil wells. It will be longer and mean more sand desert driving. But we've no option."

Just then there was a sudden flood of lights up ahead as a number of Jeeps that had been converging on one point suddenly turned on their headlights, pinpointing a single lone vehicle, which was evidently their prey.

There followed the staccato sound of machine gun fire. The occupants of the vehicle had been eliminated and their vehicle was set ablaze,

"God Almighty, they're burning them alive," Deborah cried out. She began to scream in shock.

David too was increasingly uneasy. He hadn't expected oil fires that would cause a change to their route. He hadn't expected to run into armed patrols intent on cutting off anyone fleeing the city. He hadn't expected any of these dangers and they left him shaken.

Maybe he had done the wrong thing in trying to escape through the desert. Perhaps they would have been safer to have just hunkered down somewhere. But where?

They waited until all the Jeeps had driven away before they drove on on an altered course, bumping wildly across the desert, trying to find another track.

As they went careering across this rough terrain, swerving to avoid boulders that suddenly loomed up in front of them, David didn't feel that he was fully in control, that he was in control at all. The dogs were in a terrible state in the back with their low penetrating whines and Deborah was trying to calm them down.

Eventually they entered a *wadi* where the going was easier. David reckoned that, if they headed up the *wadi*, it should eventually lead them into the Empty Quarter. They had been driving on sidelights all this time, afraid that full lights would give their position away. To continue like this would leave them in constant danger of crashing into a boulder or breaking a spring.

Nonetheless, they held off turning on their headlights until they were well into the *wadi*.

The headlights showed them that the *wadi* was wide, perhaps a mile wide, defined by escarpments on either side. The lights illuminated the brown slash of an ill-defined track.

As they sped up the *wadi*, the Land Rover cast a moving pool of light, a flicker in an intimidating desolation.

NOEL SCANLON

CHAPTER 60

They drove hard up the *wadi* for over an hour, all the time putting distance between themselves and the city. Another half hour and lightness began to seep into the horizon ahead of them and the emerging light began to swallow up the headlights and the darkness.

Gradually, as they drove on, redness began to suffuse the horizon and the desert sucked in its colour, changing from grey brown to orange tinted. Sunrise came with a rush, expanding their surroundings, plucking them out of the dark cocoon they had been hidden in since leaving the city.

Seeing there was no other vehicle in sight, Deborah was feeling a little better, a little less anxious. They had got this far but she wouldn't feel safe until they had crossed the border out of this state. She had expected the desert to be a refuge, empty and free and open, but it had turned out to be just as dangerous as the city they had left. She felt exhausted not only physically overtired but emotionally drained from all that had happened so that she drifted in and out of brief snatches of sleep from which she was always awakened by the jolting of the vehicle.

She came to with a start now as David pulled in behind a clump of camel thorn revealed by the quickly strengthening light of dawn. For the first time they were beginning to be able to see clearly what was around them.

With the engine turned off, a great silence closed in and enveloped them. In other circumstances, both of them would have found this silence peaceful and relaxing but, in present circumstances, neither of them could relax, not while they knew that the *Mujahadeen* could be anywhere in this desert and quite possibly pursuing them.

They climbed out of the Land Rover, both of them stiff and tired from the drive. David's arms and shoulders ached from driving over the rough terrain.

Deborah released the dogs from the back. But they didn't move far from the vehicle. Though there was lots of space all around, they didn't seem to want to explore it; they were as intimated by it as they themselves were.

David poured some water and, as they sipped it, he told Deborah about what had happened to him from the time of his kidnapping to the time of his release. She looked so shook up that he didn't know if she was taking any of it in.

But she was listening intently to how he got out, how the guards had been bribed with money put up by CJ. She had always heard that that was the only way to have people kidnapped in these parts released and certainly her own efforts, even if she had managed to locate the House of Rest for Weary Travellers, would have had no effect whatever. When he had finished she said, "So it was Sebastian got you out."

"Absolutely. Him and CJ."

Deborah had mixed feelings. David had told her earlier in the drive about the gold they were carrying. It made her feel that they were being used. On the other hand, without Sebastian, neither of them would be here. David would still be chained up and held hostage. That made Sebastian both the hero of the hour and a master manipulator.

"And did Sebastian have anything to say about what we were meant to do when we got into the desert?"

"He did. His plan is that we drive to the Omani border and cross out of the state at one of the less frequented crossing points far over to the west."

Deborah tried to conjure up the map of Arabia in her mind. "So that means we'll have to drive across the Rub al Khali."

"A bit of it. Not all of it"

"We can't do that," Deborah said. She had read about the Rub al Khali. She knew that until recent decades it had never been crossed except by wandering Bedouin. Even nowadays nobody went there unaccompanied if they could avoid it. Dismayed by the prospect, she repeated, "We can't do it. You have no experience of driving in the desert. We'd be bound to get lost. We don't know the way."

"Sebastian told me what to do in general terms," David said trying to be upbeat though he was as concerned at the prospect of what lay in front of them as she was. "It shouldn't be all that difficult. What it amounts to is that if we keep driving south we'll eventually reach the Omani border. It's a long border so we don't have to be too accurate. The main thing is to have a top class vehicle and we have one," David said trying to convince himself as much as to convince Deborah.

Deborah thought of all the obvious objections but she wasn't about to argue or even to think about what might lie ahead. If they had no alterative, what was the point of arguing? Anyway, she hadn't the energy. She was too drained, physically and mentally from what had happened to her in the last few days. Maybe if she had some rest, some time to recuperate, she would feel better.

So she didn't protest. She'd leave it to David to do what he thought best. What suggestions could she make anyway? She could hardly propose that they go back. All the same, she couldn't help feeling apprehensive about their chances in the desert. And, for all the front he put on, she could see that, like herself, David was having a reaction to what he had been through over the past twenty four hours. It must have been dreadful for him. It was hard to think of anything worse than being blindfolded and chained in a confined place with all the time the threat of being beheaded hanging over you. She could see that it had taken its toll. She could see it in his eyes. He looked jumpy and nervous. Which didn't auger well for the journey ahead.

Meantime David was walking about the Land Rover. He did indeed feel nervous and apprehensive. He'd been in sand deserts but it was a long time ago. He had really no experience of desert driving and that was probably why he was finding the Land Rover difficult to handle. At speed over rough ground the load was inclined to shift, he could feel it on the steering. He didn't always feel fully in control of the vehicle. Maybe he'd adapt as time went on.

To give himself confidence, he walked around the vehicle which was top of the range. Sebastian had told him that it was specially adapted for desert driving and reinforced to carry a heavy load. It was made for just this sort of terrain. It was certainly some vehicle from its 2.5 V6 engine to its Electronic Traction Control and its Hill Descent Control. At least he had a good vehicle even if he wasn't the best of desert drivers.

He tried to readjust the load which he felt was unevenly distributed and making it harder to steer. But he didn't have much success. The gold was packed in boxes of 10, 50, and 100 ten tola bars with a weight that he hadn't a hope in hell of restacking.

He checked the wheels and couldn't make up his mind though he thought one of the front tyres had somewhat lower pressure than it should.

He rummaged about for the foot pump and began pumping up the tyre which might also help to balance the load better.

While he was doing this, Deborah shouted, "Something's coming."

Looking back the way they had come, Deborah could see two small dust clouds in the distance that could only be moving vehicles. The sight of them made her feel the bottom fall out of her world. She had a feeling of certainty that they were going to be caught and killed. Those dust clouds reeled her in, pulled her back into the atmosphere of dread and panic that had pervaded the apartment by the creek during her days, cut off and alone there with the revolution going on down the road and the apartment an easy target for any marauder. At least here, if you had to die, it would be out in the open and not trapped like a rat in a hot closed apartment.

"Honey, Poochie," she called urgently. The dogs had moved a little distance away and were sniffing something. What was there to sniff in the desert? They came quickly and obediently to her call, picking up the urgency in her voice. She let them into the back seat and joined David behind the cluster of camel thorn bushes.

Crouching there as the dust clouds moved quickly across the desert about a mile away, they could see that one of the vehicles was a car and that it was being pursued by a Jeep of the sort they had seen in the gravel desert with a machine gun mounted behind.

Watching the pursued car, the perspiration running down her back to settle in a dark ring where her t-shirt met her jeans, Deborah felt a sense of complete helplessness. Who were the people in the car trying to escape having no doubt come into the desert only in desperation? Whoever they were, she empathised with them. It could just as easily have been her and David. They were lucky to have stopped by chance at this particular time. Being stationary, they weren't throwing up a dust cloud which was what gave vehicles away in the desert.

As they watched, the gap was quickly narrowing between the two vehicles. The car was a regular saloon model not at all suitable for this terrain. Suddenly it swerved out of control and, a moment later, there was the sound of an explosion and a burst of orange-coloured flame, which was swallowed up by the white light now pouring down from the sun so that the explosion didn't seem dramatic or significant in any way, muted here in the openness of the desert. Yet the lives of those people in the car had been extinguished, snuffed out.

The men in the Jeep were shouting and firing their guns into the air in triumph as if they had achieved a great victory by reducing living human beings to charred corpses. They rushed over to the car and began looking through it and it was clear that they were looking for something other than corpses.

Watching, a chill ran down David's back as he realised that they were looking for the gold. The gold he was carrying.

This incident only confirmed what he thought anyway. He had never assumed they had gotten clean away. That was highly unlikely. The Ayatullah's people needed the gold in the back of his vehicle to pay for arms shipments and weren't going to give up easily. So long as there was the slightest chance of getting the gold back, they would pursue him into and across the desert if need be. They might not know exactly what route he had taken and the desert was big and wide but they would definitely keep on trying to find him. They weren't going to give up.

They would send fighters after them into the desert and if necessary into the Empty Quarter itself.

NOEL SCANLON

CHAPTER 61

_____

After witnessing the grisly incident of the car being blown up and its occupants burnt, they weren't in any hurry to leave their shelter behind the clump of camel thorn. Even after the Jeep was long gone, leaving the charred corpses behind, and there was nothing else to be seen in the whole open desert, Deborah wasn't keen to venture out. Another unseen patrol could be lurking, waiting for them anywhere out there.

But they had no alternative other than to go on. They were committed. So finally, they left their refuge and drove on, Deborah looking behind her for any sign of a cloud dust that would betray a following vehicle.

And so they entered and began to crawl over an area of wind-scoured desolation where what little vegetation there was began to get rarer and rarer and the air got drier and the temperature soared, sucking up any moisture that was in the atmosphere.

All around them now the desert began to unfold in the emerging light that pushed the horizon back and back until it looked endless. The depth and vastness of it, so flat and stretching so far, was stunning. It was both awesome and intimidating.

Deborah had never been farther than the fringes of the desert where they sometimes went for a picnic. God, a picnic, the very concept of a picnic was something she could hardly conceive of. She had entered the desert and the desert had entered her. Its immensity, its emptiness, its atmosphere, had wiped her out.

By and large, most expats, even those who had spent years in the area, chose never to drive out here, and why should they, she wouldn't if she didn't have to. Margaret hadn't. Nor had Andy. Poor Andy. He had died quite by chance. The bomb could just as easily have been placed under someone else's car. Only it was placed under his.

Not even the journalists, by and large, came far into the desert if they came into it at all. By now the press corps would have based themselves on the Phoenix Bar; she could imagine them gossiping at the bar, picking one another's brains, sending their despatches to their papers or radio or TV stations.

After several more hours hard driving, they began to enter the fringes of the sand desert known as the Rub al Khali. There was no sign of the giant oil fires now. They had driven around them and past them. Distance and the sun had eaten them up.

The sun began to climb the sky, a glaring ball burning them up, incandescent, all those nuclear explosions going on inside it, this desert sun was not one anyone would want to expose themselves to. It was so hot and the air so dry that it began to cause an irritating dryness in Deborah's nose and throat. The air she drew into her lungs was hurtful.

Could it reach a temperature out here when the heat would actually burn you up? With the help of global warming perhaps, it could. Perhaps we had finally managed to release so much carbon dioxide into the atmosphere, carbon dioxide stored for millennia in fossil fuels and oil but being released now at such a rate into the atmosphere that we had finally managed to pollute it to the extent of upsetting the balance of nature. Perhaps the ozone layer they were always talking about had finally been stripped away over this piece of desert and they would be fried alive by the ultra violet rays.

How often Sally had told her as they chatted over the phone how much she hated the desert which she saw as a boring, trackless waste land infested with snakes and camel spiders and giant ticks that sucked your blood. The oil company had warned the staff never to go into it and Sally never had. Years ago a party of construction workers had got lost out here somewhere and walked in circles till they dropped and died from dehydration and Sally wasn't going to chance that. Even Eileen, for all her raving about Islam, had never been more than a few miles out of the Old City.

Abdul too had been strongly anti the desert, possibly because his ancestors had wandered around in it for so many centuries. "Desert no good place." So recently out of the desert himself, Abdul was all for the town, its comforts and amenities. Where was Abdul now?

As they drove on, Deborah began to fall into a dreamy state, the way you do on a long journey especially in extreme heat.

Once she saw a blob moving across the desert ahead of them, throwing up dust that lay snake-like behind it, and when she pointed it out to David, he immediately stopped and they stared tensely at the moving blob until it disappeared from sight.

As they started up again, she noticed that David looked totally exhausted and she wondered if he would be able to handle what lay ahead.

The size of the Land Rover had shrunk so that it was a tiny dot in a vast sea of emptiness, totally encompassed by sand. There was such a feeling of space all about that Deborah felt that they were tiny insects creeping across the surface of the earth. The sun glared down from a sky that it filled and dominated. It reflected upwards from the whitened-out desert.

In the time they had lived creek-side, going out in their boat or driving out of town for a picnic, she had known intellectually that there was a great desert out here. But knowing something exists is one thing. Experiencing the actuality is something else entirely.

Deborah felt as if she was slipping into another dimension. The desert all around her became like a dream rather then reality. She was in another dimension in which her thoughts began to wander about in a land of fantasy.

Meantime, David was concentrating on his driving, on staying awake. He had had very little sleep for days now and a combination of this, the tension and the extreme heat was getting to him as he drove with his eyes screwed half-closed against the glare of a sun that was spreading, enlarging, intensifying.

As they penetrated farther and farther into the desert, it swallowed them up and closed in over them. David felt that if anything should go wrong, if they had a puncture, for instance, he might get the spare on, but, if they got a second puncture what would they do then. They would be no match for this hostile desert, which was not, of course, actually hostile, any more than the sun was hostile, it was only, like all nature, indifferent.

David drove and drove, the live air dancing before him, blasting in hotly through the open windows and burning his skin.

And, as he drove, he thought of Khor Fahal and the revolution and CJ and Mohammed and wondered how the markets were moving, the FTSE, the Dow Jones and Nasdaq, and the currency markets. News of the revolution was bound to have hit the headlines by now and that would mean a further drop in the price of the dinar. He wondered about all that was going on back in the city. And he thought of Bank Street as he had last seen it being taken over by a mob and wondered what state it was in now.

As David drove and thought about all these things, there gradually appeared faintly outlined in the distance and seemingly moving about, changing position, a chain of high dunes that they would eventually have to cross.

He drove on and on in air that was shimmering in the heat until, suddenly, they hit a patch of soft sand they could not get through even with four-wheel drive and high gear ratio and gradually ground to a halt.

"We've dug in," David said.

He fetched the shovel and sand tracks from the back and began clearing the sand away from the tyres, digging out. This was a slow job because, as fast as he cleared the sand away, it slid back again. The sunrays punched down like blows on his head but he kept on shovelling, stopping only to drink some water, carefully, not too much, they had a strictly limited supply.

Before stopping, they had been protected, cut-off in the moving bubble of the car. Now they were exposed to their environment. Not a sound penetrated, not a movement stirred the air. Without the noise of the engine, it was silent with the silence of the deep desert. Deborah felt this intense silence disturbing. It was the silence before time began, the silence after the world ended.

When David had cleared as much sand as he could, he took the sand tracks down and placed one under each tyre. He got Deborah to sit behind the steering wheel and when he shouted to her, she eased the clutch out. But, instead of moving forward, the wheels began to spin, shooting out sand behind, digging them in deeper and deeper until Deborah felt a wave of panic and took her foot off the accelerator.

After several attempts, the tyres gripped and David was shoving at the back and shouting, "Grip, grip, grip," and they were inching forward but the wheels were still spinning, and the engine at full revs was whining in protest and then, when they were beginning to think they'd never get out, the vehicle shot forward with a lurch and they on more firm sand, though there was some slippage and then they were away, David running behind red-faced and sweating.

That was their first dig-in but it wasn't their last. There were numerous spots in the desert where the sand had a different consistency, not exactly quicksands but unstable sand which you could easily sink into and which it was almost impossible to identify until you were in one of them.

David was exhausted from digging out. And he was having difficulty with his concentration. Maybe it was one of the blows to the head he had suffered over the last few days, but, for whatever reason, he was having trouble in focusing which was difficult anyway in the vast monotonous desert with the sun in his eyes.

They seemed to be making no impression whatsoever on the distance between them and the distant dunes which they had to cross. As time went by, what with the monotony and heat, he got the feeling that his brain was disassociated from his body, that his consciousness was up there in the sky somewhere looking down on the tiny speck that was the Land Rover with himself and Deborah inside it.

They were getting nowhere fast, lost in the immensity of this desert, lost under a cruel sky, under light that penetrated his skull making his thoughts rattle about in his head like coins in an empty tin can.

In Arabia, there is either too much space so that you are crushed and annihilated by it. Or there is no space at all. Suqs seemed to have been built purposely narrow so that everyone is jammed closely together in narrow noise-filled spaces. The empty desert on the one hand, the crowded suqs on the other. Absolute loneliness and, in contrast, absolute conviviality. This conviviality, this crowding together, applied even in high-rise city offices where Arab businessmen managed to gather a crowd around them if at all possible, a throwback to the past when their Bedouin ancestors trudging over these lonely empty deserts huddled together at night over their camp fires, seeking noise and company to keep the great empty spaces, the profound silence of the desert at bay.

The West for a long time greatly romanticised the desert. Its love affair with this romantic concept of the desert reached its apogee with T E Lawrence, all flowing robes and camel riding and English endurance and indigenous tribes sharing their flyblown dates, romantic figures as they rode their camels across these deserts, performing incredible feats of endurance. It was a concept that embraced the freedom of the desert and the great open spaces and the poetry of emptiness, an emptiness that was awe inspiring and mysterious, the sweep of these great open spaces inducing a mystic spirituality.

But that was all in the past. Oil and prosperity put paid to all that.

Later on that day, in all that emptiness, David thought he heard the sound of a radio. Though he had tried frequently, he had not been able to get anything on his own radio only static so that when he first heard the sound he put it down to fatigue and a bit of mind wandering. He had several times already had the sensation that, as his body breathed and sweated, his mind had lifted itself clear of his body and drifted. But, when he heard the sound again, closer this time, he sat up and took note.

He locked on to the sound, drove up a sand hill and, there, in the hollow in front of them, he was startled to see a stalled car and the source of the sound he had been hearing. Booming from the car's radio came the sound of Arabic music. His first thought was that the Mercedes must have a better radio. He longed for news.

He drove over to the car. It was badly dug in. And there were people inside. But why didn't any of them move? Were they asleep?

Sand tracks and shovels were abandoned beside the vehicle as if they had given up trying to dig out. The bonnet was up, as if someone had been working on the engine.

He got stiffly down and yanked the Mercedes door open.

As he did so, the corpse of the driver fell into his arms and a strong stench assailed his nostrils. He looked at the dead man and recognised him. It was Faud bin Rasheed, a merchant who banked with the HSBC. David sensed a presence behind him. Turning, he saw watching him a Bedouin sitting on a camel, just like the camels he had become so familiar with in Mukulla in the Hadhramut all those years ago, a small man in dusty robes, a rifle slung on his riding saddle, one of the small and diminishing number of tribesmen who had once been the sole inhabitants of this desert, but were now reduced to a few small bands. Was this man alone? Probably not. More than likely he was a scout and outrider for a group of riders.

As David watched, the Bedouin abruptly turned his camel and rode away.

David eased Faud bin Rasheed's body back into the front seat. A sickening smell came from the rear of the Mercedes where he saw now three lightly veiled women and two children, their bodies limp, their heads lolling unnaturally sideways. Reaching in, he tried to locate a pulse, a heartbeat in any of them, but couldn't. From their condition, from the state of their clothes, it was clear that several of them had died outside and been dragged back in here by the last survivor. The bodies had been robbed of the gold rings and bangles and Faud bin Rasheed had been robbed of the gold Rolex he always wore. The Bedouin had looted the lot.

Closing the door carefully, he now noticed the body of a man on a little hillock above the car lying beside a spade. It seemed as if he had been trying to cover the car in sand by way of burial and had partially succeeded.

David moved around to the engine of the Mercedes, which had its bonnet up. It had been largely dismantled. The Bedouin had obviously taken what they wanted from both the car and the corpses.

As best he could reconstruct what had happened, the Mercedes must have dug in some time ago and they were unable to dig out. Whatever had prompted them to flee into the desert, it must have been something both unexpected and compelling. They must have been in mortal danger to have just taken off. There was little or no evidence of proper preparation. It looked like the Bedouin had found them dead rather than murdered them. Though he couldn't be sure. His best guess was that they had died without outside intervention. It didn't take long in this desert.

They had died trying to escape and he wondered how many other unfortunates had suffered the same fate. How many other vehicles had made it into the desert only to suffer a fate like this, the occupants dead or dying under this brutal sky?

CHAPTER 62

As David and Deborah drove away from the Mercedes, Deborah couldn't help dwelling on the appalling fate of the once comfortable, middle-class townspeople lying now in that desert hollow under a black cloud of flies, a wealthy family David had said they'd been, whose corpses would lie in their superheated car with the fierce sun beating down on them.

As they drove on, she felt dizzy with the heat and exhaustion. Diesel was becoming critical with more than half of the plastic containers they had filled at the Tree Palm Oasis garage now empty. Was there enough to get them through? Deborah started watching the gauge, willing it not to go down too quickly and, for a time, it didn't, but then she looked away for a moment and when she looked back it was definitely lower. She couldn't take her eyes off the gauge. It had a hypnotic fascination. Gradually, imperceptibly, it fell down into the red zone and they had to call a stop.

David, stiff and sore from driving for so long, fetched a container and poured diesel into the tank, careful not to waste a drop.

As he drove on, he half closed his eyes against the dazzle of the sun that seemed to be probing into his skull. It blazed down from a sky that it filled and dominated. It reflected upwards from the whitened-out sand.

How had he got himself into the position of having to attempt this drive? It didn't make any sense. All he had done was to accept a job in the Middle East, which CJ had been good enough to offer him and that seemed to be the answer to all their financial problems. At the time, there was no way he could have imagined that accepting a banking position in the Gulf could possibly lead to a chain of events that would end up with this wild drive across the desert.

For a long time they drove on like this, driving in a heat daze into the dead eye of the sun. Deborah kept watching the line of dunes, which sometimes seemed to have moved nearer and, then again, at other times, seemed actually to have moved away. They only seemed to be inching across the desert, making so little impression on it that she sometimes wondered if they were moving forward at all, or just driving in place, getting nowhere. She felt overpowered by the vastness, the loneliness, the desolation of that great desert. It made her feel very, very small.

But gradually, imperceptibly, they were getting closer to the Great Dunes. They entered an area of rolling terrain, an area of sand hillocks on the fringes of the dunes.

And now, suddenly, the weather began to change. The wind was getting up.

Deborah was becoming heat-drugged and relapsed into a state of torpor. She nodded off and, while she slept, the wind rose, whipping up the sand.

She was jolted awake by the sound of the wind that had increased to storm force strength. Funnelled between the dunes, it was lifting sand into the air by the ton, strictly limiting visibility. She glanced across at David. He looked wild, his face burnt, his eyes red orbs, his hair standing up, held in place by a mixture of sand and perspiration.

Just then, they both heard the drone of a vehicle, a faint sound that seemed to be that of an engine, though it was impossible to tell with the shrieking of the wind and impossible to see for any distance with so much sand dancing in the air. Though it might have been her imagination, Deborah thought she caught a glimpse of a Jeep with ghostly soundless waving figures, but the image disappeared so quickly it might well have been a mirage. She hoped to God it was.

But it wasn't a mirage. The sound came again, a sound like the drone of a vehicle. She hadn't imagined it and it was much closer this time.

She glanced at David. She didn't need to ask. She could tell by his taut, anxious look that he had heard it too.

While they were both looking about trying to locate the sound, there was a brief window when the visibility improved and, right behind them, was what was undoubtedly a Jeep. Then the window of visibility closed and the Jeep was swallowed up again in the sandstorm. But it was there all right. It was their pursuer.

Deborah's worst fear had been that they would in some way be tracked down by the Ayatullah's *Mujahadeen* before they could get across the border. And now her worse fear had been realised. They had been so long in the empty desert, driven so far without seeing anyone that she had allowed herself to think that they had got away. But they hadn't.

"The bastards have been after us all the time."

For the moment, the sandstorm gave them cover. But the occupants of the Jeep had spotted them, knew where they were. Through the howl of the wind, she could hear them shouting. A warning? It was impossible to tell; their voices were carried away in the wind. But it was obvious they were shouting something when a shot rang out and kicked up the sand in front of them.

David said, "Take the rifle."

With a feeling of unreality, Deborah reached back for the rifle Sebastian had given David for protection. It was heavier than she had expected, the metal warm to the touch. Holding it, she felt clumsy, awkward.

"I don't know how to use it," she said.

"It's easy." David's voice was hoarse. "Release the safety catch. Yes, that's it. All you have to do now is squeeze the trigger when I tell you. Press the stock hard against your shoulder or the recoil will hurt you."

Deborah looked down at the rifle. She didn't want to pick it up. She saw it as an instrument of death, uncaring and brutal. A few ounces of pressure, a few seconds in space and it would deliver death to whomever you aimed it at, tearing into some other human being's flesh and bone and brain, causing pain and destruction, oblivious to the complexities, to the wonder of human existence.

"Fire now," David said.

Deborah had been reluctant to handle the weapon at all. But it turned out that her sense of survival was stronger than her misgivings. Under David's urging, she leaned out of the window, aimed as well as she could in the general direction of their pursuers and pressed the trigger.

Nothing happened. She pressed harder. The kick of the recoil knocked her backwards against the seat so that she didn't see where her burst of shots had gone.

David floored the accelerator.

They were right up close now to the high, steeply banked Great Dunes. He swung the Land Rover parallel to the range, searching for a gap, a valley, however narrow, any possible way of getting through.

Scanning a dune face, David suddenly saw what looked like it might be a way through. As he headed for it, there was a spatter of shots behind them.

Immediately they entered this sand valley, there was some protection from the wind but, on both sides and seeming to hang over them as if about to engulf them, were precipices of sand. As they got farther into this narrow valley, they could hear the sound of whispering sliding sand as if the precipices of sand were about to collapse on to them.

They were caught now in a freak whirlwind, great spiralling cones that sometimes strike in this part of the Arabian desert, sucking up large quantities of sand which the whirlwind carries along with it and deposits elsewhere. It was an incredible sight. You wouldn't think wind alone could lift such weight.

David was finding it difficult to control the vehicle. It was obvious that they couldn't get much farther. And it was dangerous trying to make headway at all in such low visibility. The floor of the sand valley began to rise in front of them and, as it did, the engine began to labour, to slow. Finally, it stalled. With the weight of the load up back, it couldn't take the incline. The Land Rover came to a stop. They were dug in.

David slumped back in his seat. There was sand in his eyes, which the ferocity of the wind had somehow blown in. He tried to get the sand out of his eyes but only succeeded in scratching his eyeballs.

"Now we're properly stuck," he said. "Is there any sign of the Jeep?"

Deborah squinted into the sandstorm raging in the valley behind them. "I can't see anything."

"They can't be far away."

They sat still for a few minutes, their eyes straining for the sight of, and their ears for the sound of, their pursuers but there was only the shriek of the wind. They were in the middle of a full-blown sand storm. Whipped off the dunes by the wind, a miasma of sand danced and whirled madly all around. There was nothing they could do only huddle down to wait for the storm to pass, hoping it didn't bury them alive.

Settling down wasn't that easy, though. Honey and Poochie were crouched in the back terrified by the insistent rat-tat-tatting of hard grained sand blasting against the tightly closed windows.

Deborah listened to the roar of the wind as it tore unchecked across the wilderness. It was the loneliest sound in the world.

Time dragged slowly by. She had this fear that the sides of the sand valley were about to roll down on them like a huge wave at any moment. A huge wave, only solid. Whipped by the wind, the dunes stirred as if alive. Hadn't she heard or read that in sand storms whole dunes moved. It had sounded fanciful at the time. But not any more. When nature erupted you were overwhelmed by its force. You just sat it out helplessly and waited to see what would happen.

David had drifted into a sleep of exhaustion.

Deborah stared out at the sand dancing wildly outside. She didn't want to doze off, but staring at millions of flying grains of sand had a hypnotic effect and she felt drowsiness creeping over her. She tried to fight it off. The Land Rover was so stuffy that she had this fear that they might all die of asphyxiation in their sleep. She considered opening a window a tiny crack but was afraid to.

She fought the drowsiness but eventually exhaustion won and she fell into a troubled sleep.

In time, they all slept in the Land Rover, a dot in a swirling shifting sandscape, two humans immersed in their own fantasies coughing and choking and frequently changing position. And two dogs who twitched constantly as they too dreamt.

CHAPTER 63

Deborah began to awake. For a moment, she thought they were buried alive, that the sand had built up over them.

She opened her eyes. It was nighttime in the Great Dunes. She listened for the howling wind but it was completely still.

Through the window of the Land Rover, she could see a sky so full of stars that they seemed to be jostling for space. Starlight and moonlight made the desert appear a faint off-white. The dune they were on loomed over them like a great shrouded giant, silhouetted against millions of stars.

David was slumped over the steering wheel. He twitched and muttered as he slept. She put her hand out to touch the dogs but they weren't there.

She shook David. He muttered but didn't awake. He'd had such a hard drive that she didn't like to persist in wakening him. But she'd have to find out what had happened to the dogs.

She tried to open her door but couldn't. The sand blown by the sandstorm must have built up and trapped them in their vehicle. She felt an onrush of panic. She tried the door again. It was held firmly in place. Then she noticed that the back window had been broken, that's where the dogs must have gotten out. By scooping sand away with her hands she was able to squeeze through.

The air outside was wonderfully fresh. The sand under her feet was cool, cold almost. The air too was cool or seemed so after all the terrible heat of the day. She thought the dogs would be close-by and she'd find them in a minute, but there was no sign of them.

She stood leaning against the side of the vehicle that had sand half way up it. There was no sign of the dogs and they didn't come when she called. They weren't anywhere nearby and she didn't know in which direction to look.

Standing there wondering what to do, she heard a faint noise farther back in the valley and decided that's where they must be.

Climbing a huge hill of sand formed by the collapsing sides of the valley, she saw farther back, faint in the moonlight, the Jeep that had been following them dug in at an odd awkward angle. And from inside the Jeep was coming faintly but distinctly the voice of Ayatullah Abd Al Wahhab. The occupants of the Jeep must have carried with them tapes of the Ayatullah's speeches and had left one playing.

It was strange and eerie and disturbing to hear the passionate throbbing sound of the Ayatullah's voice, which she had only before heard in the crowded alleyways of the Old City, wafting through the night desert air, away out here amid the dunes. It gave her the creeps to think that he could reach not only into the houses and into the hearts and minds of his fervent followers in the city, but reach right out here into this desolate part of the desert.

She called out softly to the dogs and suddenly they came scampering up the sand dune towards her, panting and wagging their tails. They must have been down at the Jeep. They must have heard noises and gone to investigate.

She urged the dogs to stay quiet and hoped that the men in the Jeep hadn't heard them nosing around outside. It was unlikely they would with the sound of the tape playing, nonetheless, she was anxious to get back to their vehicle. She was aghast at how near their pursuers were.

Once the light of dawn came, their Land Rover would be spotted. She must do something. She must go back, waken David and somehow they must get out of here.

She had turned back and was hurrying away when she heard the whispering of the sand as one layer began to slide over another. The whispering noise sounded quite pleasant. It sounded like as if the dead desert had somehow come to life. The slope of sand she was standing on heaved and sighed. Dune whispered to dune and hollow to hollow until the whole area around was filled with whisperings.

Suddenly she realised that the whispering noise was the sand under her beginning to move and slide.

She raced away from the moving sliding sand about to engulf her. Despite her fatigue, she forced herself on, slipping and falling and picking herself up again, carried at times by the moving sand.

Looking behind her, she saw that the sand slide had grown into an avalanche now, falling on the Jeep back in the valley, sliding and sliding until it was well up the doors. One man emerged crawling out of a window and began firing his sub machine gun wildly in the air. But at that point the speed of the sand avalanche accelerated and, within seconds, the Jeep, with its occupants, was buried deep in a mountain of sand.

The voice of the Ayatullah ceased. There was silence in the Great Dunes.

Then an odd thing happened. She could feel an unseen presence towering over her. It seemed to cover a huge area, to reach down from the sky and touch her. She saw a patch of deep darkness flowing down the dune in a wave towards her. It could have been the darkness cast by a cloud. Only there weren't any clouds. It only lasted for a few seconds, but it gave her the eerie feeling that there was an unseen presence out there. At the same time she had to get moving as her feet began to sink into the sand and she had the wild feeling that the sand had become gelatinous, viscous beneath her feet, that it was trying to suck her down so that she had to struggle step by step to get away, to escape from its grasp, escape from something, some force that wanted to suck her down, to bury her alive, to hold her in its deadly embrace.

Running and panting, she followed the dogs until they were back at the Land Rover and, after the frightened animals had scampered back through the window into the vehicle, she crawled in after them.

She lay there staring open eyed into the darkness, seeing again the avalanche of sliding sand and feeling that strange eerie presence.

The dogs cosied up to her and they lay there close together in that great desolation waiting for the dawn.

CHAPTER 64

T he desert dawn had barely begun to dispel the night when Deborah and David pushed their way out of the Land Rover on to the side of a great dune.

Deborah still felt shaken and stunned by the sudden death of the men who had followed them for so long and who now lay in their Jeep buried beneath the sand avalanche that had engulfed them and covered them in a great depth of sand.

What a close call it had been. Nature doesn't pick favourites and they were well aware what a narrow escape they had had.

Now the sandstorm was over and it was as if it had never been. But so much sand had been moved that the terrain all around them had altered dramatically. Right behind them, where there had been a valley there was no longer a valley. God knows how many thousands and tens of thousands of tons of sand had been dumped into that valley where the Jeep lay buried.

Dunes began to be revealed all around them. With the rising sun, these dunes began to take shape. Rose-coloured in the dawn, dune backed dune in majestic ranks, casting great blue shadows on the sand. Each dune rose to its pinnacled crest, an ocean arrested in motion and flowed down in ridges so sleek that it was as if some massive hand had smoothed them.

The dunes looked incredibly beautiful. They were also incredibly dangerous. How quickly they extinguished life.

David, light-headed with fatigue but high on having survived so far, having driven across a desert he didn't think he had the capability to drive across, turned his mind to working out how best to approach and get through the dunes that lay ahead.

He tried to recall everything he had ever heard about desert driving. His father's driver had told him as a little boy when they had driven into the fringes of this same Empty Quarter in another time, in another state, that the golden rule was that you must keep your momentum up and, where possible, go for the hard sand between the dunes.

As they stood looking at the awesome scene around them, they ate quickly, anxious to get on with their journey, balancing the food on the bonnet that was still cool, food they had grabbed from the fridge and cupboards, salted cocktail biscuits, dates and overripe bananas. They drank all the water they could take. Their bodies had to have water if they were to get through the rest of the drive.

After eating, they both got down to the laborious task of clearing the sand off their partially buried vehicle. It was slow work because of the infuriating tendency of this fine dry sand to slide back just as soon as you had cleared it away.

But at last they had cleared most of it and then gone through the usual routine of wedging the sand tracks under the wheels. Now was the moment of truth.

David turned the key. The engine fired and he began to ease the clutch out. But, just as soon as he did, the wheels began the dreaded spinning and spewing out of sand, leaving them dug in worse than before.

"Fuck it," David said.

Deborah, watching, felt the fear that hadn't ever been far away beginning to creep back into her mind, the fear that they would never, not ever, get out of here, never stir from this spot where the sun would soon be fully up and they would suffer the same fate as the occupants of the Mercedes.

"Fuck it, it can't be done," David said getting down from the vehicle, already sweating heavily under the clear blue incandescent sky and covered in sand and perspiration. "It can't be done. It absolutely cannot. We'll never get out this way. We'll never shift this vehicle. It isn't possible. It's dug in too deep and it's too heavy. And, even if we did dig out, in no time at all we'd be dug in again. With the weight we have up, we haven't a chance in hell of going anywhere."

It was something that had been on his mind all along. From the very beginning, there had been this worry of getting through the dunes with such a heavy load up.

"What are we to do?" Deborah asked, feeling a sense of hopelessness come over her.

"There's only one thing we can do. We'll have to off-load the gold."

"You mean leave the gold here!"

"It's either that or stay here with it and die from exposure and dehydration. Even without all that weight up, we can't be sure we can dig out. But one thing's for certain, we can't get out with it on board."

"But it's bank gold."

"Fuck the bank. It's our lives are at stake. It's quite simply a question of dumping the gold or losing our lives. Which wouldn't do anyone any good anyway given that nobody would know where it was. It'd just lie here forever. Unclaimed."

They stood there considering, weighing the matter up, but they both knew perfectly well what they were going to do. And it wasn't to stay here and die a horrible death. Not if they could do anything about it.

So they began unloading the gold.

Even that didn't turn out to be all that easy. In the first place, it was far too heavy for them to either lift or carry, there was no question of that. But David managed to tilt the Land Rover in such a way that they were able to use the angle of the tilt to slide the boxes backwards and tumble them out into the sand.

As they unloaded the gold, David did a quick calculation. At the price of around $800 per troy ounce, one tola being 3.75 ounces, it came out at around $3000 per ten tola bar or $150000 per fifty. That would put the value of the yellow metal they were dumping at thirty million.

He couldn't help thinking of all the times he had sat in the bank, his fingers flicking over the computer keyboard executing customers' instructions for the purchase of gold which people in the state bought for smuggling to India and as a hedge in times of uncertainty. Gold has always been bought as a hedge in times of crisis. Currencies go up and currencies go down but gold goes on forever. Gold is real, gold is solid, gold is tangible.

Sweating to off-load box after box of gold on to the sand in this uninhabited place, it came home to him how far he was from where he should be in the normal course of events, back in the bank at the heart of the capitalist system flashing orders across the globe, not heaving and shoving and sweating to get these boxes out of the Land Rover and then try to get out of here alive.

As the last box tumbled out, they began shovelling sand. They had to cover the boxes well and they managed to do this in large part by sliding sand down the slope of the dune until the gold was well buried.

When they were satisfied that it was well concealed, they turned their attention to the Land Rover. This time, relieved of the weight of the gold, the tyres caught on the sand tracks and jolted clear.

They gathered up their things, anxious to get away, leaving the narrow sand valley they had spent the night in behind.

The last thing they did was to look back at where the Ayatullah's fighters lay buried. They could barely distinguish the spot so smooth did the sand lie without the slightest clue that underneath its smooth surface lay a Jeep and four men, clutching their now useless machine guns, their corpses still warm,

A little farther on, they found a valley that seemed to have a hard base between the dunes, and they were on their way, the Land Rover feeling incredibly light and more manageable without its load.

Suddenly there was a crackling from the radio, which David had left turned on all the time in the hope of hearing something from the outside world. By some freak chance of transmission the radio was all of a sudden picking up *Saut al Arabiya*, at first almost inaudibly, but gradually it became more audible.

Between bouts of crackling, David was able to pick up snatches of news from the outside world. He couldn't hear every word, it was all very frustrating, but there, in the heart of the dunes, the voice of the *Saut Al Arabiya* newsreader conveyed the startling information that the Phoenix Hotel had been heavily damaged by a car bomb that had been driven into it by a suicide bomber.

"The Phoenix!" Deborah exclaimed, remembering her last visit to the hotel bar and the few journalists scenting news who had already installed themselves there. "Was anyone killed?"

Translating from the Arabic, David said, "As far as I can make out, there were several journalists injured."

"My God," Deborah said. "That's terrible. I wonder if Lina Tabbara was one of those injured. How do they say the uprising is going?"

"According to this station, the government have counter attacked and re-taken most of the city."

The voice deteriorated into a crackling noise again. But, after a while, as they drove between the towering dunes, it came back on.

"What are they saying now?"

"They're saying now that several dhows in the harbour have been searched and a large quantity of arms intended for the insurrection seized."

At this point, the transmission went dead. David, punching in different stations, pressing the scan key, keen to hear more, faintly got a station calling itself *Saut al Hurriya*, evidently a rebel station. This station gave a totally different account of how things were going from that given by *Saut Al Arabiya*. This station claimed that the Shi'ites were winning, that the Shi'ites were on the march under the leadership of Ayatullah Abd Al Wahhab, that their enemies would be destroyed and glorious victory would be theirs.

Abruptly this transmission too went dead. They would like to have heard more news but no more news was forthcoming.

Without any sound coming from the radio, they drove on in the deep silence of the dunes.

The freshness of the desert morning, or the illusion of freshness, didn't last for long before being greedily sucked up by the sun. The colour of the sunrise had long since disappeared. The earth and the sky had whitened out. The super-heated air began to throb all around them, to pulsate in their brains.

No wonder the tribesmen who had crossed and re-crossed these deserts for thousands of years at the speed of a man walking or at best a camel trotting and without benefit of four wheel drive or Electronic Traction Control or even Hill Descent Control, no wonder they were so hungry for gossip around their camp fires making lots of chatter to keep out the crushing silence and loneliness of this vast desert bearing in on them all the time.

For David and Deborah, coming from a world with all modern conveniences and swamped with incessant noise and far more information than the human brain could process, the deep and utter silence all around them was, in a strange way, intimidating.

They were deep into the dunes now, driving in the valleys between them, looking for the hard firm sand, driving in the dazzling dance of sunbeams on the sand itself and reflected from the mica in the sand. On either side of them, the dunes were magnificent in their barrenness, in their aesthetic grandeur. Moving between these Great Dunes, they felt puny and defenceless, they were surrounded by a primaeval silence that reached back to before time began.

Driving here you felt that this was a place where you could imagine God walking abroad on the earth. In the desert, there were no material comforts, nothing superfluous. The wandering tribal Bedouin, largely subsumed now into the oil towns and cities, expressed themselves through their ability to endure hardship in order to survive in a hostile environment where survival itself depended on reaching the next well. By virtue of this lifestyle, the spirit and the body were detached from one another, became two separate entities.

But in the here and now there was the matter of survival. There was still the nagging fear that, although they had seen one Jeep loaded with *Mujahadeen* buried in a sandstorm, there could be others that had penetrated the dunes and were lurking waiting on the other side.

After a couple of hard hours driving, they were through the dunes.

All the time David had kept a close eye on the compass. Before starting out, he had marked the place where they had buried the gold as best he could. He had scribbled a map showing every surrounding feature and how the place of burial related to each feature. He had marked the spot itself with one of the spades, the handle like a flag post to which he had attached a silk scarf of Deborah's which would flutter there in that empty wilderness in the lightest of breezes.

Furthermore, he had set his compass direction east southeast and kept on a straight line. Also he had set the trip meter so that he would know the exact number of miles from the point of burial of the gold to the point of their arrival at the border, so that their drive out of the dunes could be done in reverse.

Suddenly the car radio, as if on a whim, began disgorging snippets of news again, this time from the Khor Fahal government station. A news bulletin announced that various western states had pledged support for the government and offered help in dealing with a terrorist attack on the state.

This attack had been repelled by the bravery of the people who had remained loyal to their Ruler. A number of people suspected of aiding and abetting the terrorists had been arrested and were presently being interrogated. They were being held as illegal combatants and were providing valuable information to the authorities.

A renegade Ayatullah hiding out in the Old City had narrowly evaded capture on several occasions but would soon be apprehended by the state security forces.

David wondered how much of this was propaganda and how much was true. He remembered his night in the harbour area with crazed looking fighters shooting wildly and apparently indiscriminately all around him. And there was Sebastian in the middle of it. There were many facets of Sebastian's character that David had had no idea existed. He had already had to revise his original perception of him on several occasions, but never more than on that night with the dhows loaded with arms lying off shore and the whole area a chaos of fighting and explosions.

It was that night in the harbour after he had heard the pistol shots and left his hiding place that he had fully come to realise what Sebastian was capable of doing and to what extremes he was prepared to go, extremes that both surprised and horrified him. He would never have thought Sebastian capable of doing what he did that night. He would never in a thousand years have expected it of his childhood friend. But the fact was that that night in the harbour Sebastian had murdered all the men in his unit, the ones David had helped carry and arrange in various poses. There had been no attacking force. Sebastian had killed them all himself.

How important Sebastian was in the general scheme of things David had no idea, though it was obvious that he couldn't have acted entirely alone.

Of course, it was no great surprise that this sort of undercover activity should be ongoing in the state. In fact, it would have been a surprise if it wasn't. There was too much at stake, too much oil that the West and the western oil companies wanted to keep under their control. There was altogether too much hanging on who ruled this area of the world that was so vital to the interests of the West for them to just let it go its own way without any interference.

The western clandestine activity came as no surprise. It was just a surprise, that a significant mover in it should have been his friend Sebastian.

The sun was well up now and they were slowly leaving the real barren desert behind them. They were entering an area where, instead of complete aridness, there were occasional plants. A lone cactus plant and the odd leafless shrub. Pieces of tribulous. It reminded Deborah that, although life out here in the desert was at a low ebb, hidden in the sand were the seeds of plants that would germinate miraculously when and if it rained. It was the miracle of the desert.

Ahead was an area of dull greenery and a few stunted palm trees. It wasn't much, but, after what they'd been through, after the heat and exhaustion, the cracked lips and the eyestrain, it was beginning to look positively lush.

They drove on and on until they entered a canyon that ran right up to the border and the crossing that Sebastian had selected. They had already hit David's estimated mileage figure. He had kept to a strict compass bearing and couldn't be far out.

He tensed knowing that this was the greatest point of danger. This was where vehicles would converge, and, if an intercept was going to be made, this was where it had to be.

CHAPTER 65

As they drove up the canyon, tracks became clearly discernible indicating people travelling this way. But who?

The tracks could be those of ordinary travellers. But they could just as easily have been made by the Ayatullah's *Mujahadeen*.

Thinking about this possibility David was hit by a feeling of uncertainty and a premonition that there were squads of *Mujahadeen* up ahead checking out the traffic on this side of the border, picking out particular vehicles that might be suspect and that would undoubtedly include him.

The feeling that he was driving into a trap was so strong that if at that moment he had enough spare diesel he would have turned around and headed for another crossing point. But he hadn't any spare diesel. They were already into their last container. He had to go on. He had no choice but to go on.

A helicopter buzzed overhead. Where was it coming from? It was probably Omani. Would the Omanis rescue them if they were about to be wiped out? The British had a lot of influence in the Oman. They were heavily involved in bringing the present Sultan to power by removing his father, the reclusive Sultan Said bin Taimur who lived in Salalah, where he vehemently resisted change of any sort. The old man was packed off to a nursing home in the south of England leaving his thousand odd slaves and numerous wives behind. He was replaced by his son Qaboos.

The British were involved too over an extended period of time, when British mercenaries, or contract officers, including SAS, fought with the Omanis against the rebel Peoples Front for the Liberation of the Occupied Arabian Gulf (PFLOAG) mainly in the province of Dhofar in an important but almost unknown and forgotten war among many other unknown and forgotten wars.

NOEL SCANLON

As they motored up the stony scrubby canyon, Deborah watched the thorn bushes and sparse dusty vegetation. The canyon was clearly defined now with irregular walls of sandstone springing up on either side. Flies began to appear, a sign of approaching habitation. And there were other signs of life not apparent in the barren desert. She spotted a lizard basking on a rock and then, a little farther on, a yellow butterfly whose delicate form seemed a wonder among all this harshness.

Suddenly a battered four-wheel-drive vehicle appeared from behind and passed them at speed, kicking up a cloud of dust. It too had just come out of the desert and was heading for the border. As they followed this vehicle up the canyon, Deborah heard the sound of another engine, and, looking behind, saw another dusty vehicle full of people on the last leg of their drive across the desert to the border.

The canyon narrowed further.

When the first shot rang out, Deborah couldn't see who was firing or where it was coming from though it seemed to be from a number of Jeeps in a protected position by an escarpment.

They were driving into a trap.

There was something ironic about driving towards the very Jeeps they had struggled so hard to avoid.

A machine gun started up and, as it did, David began to try to turn back but there wasn't time, it wasn't possible, it was too late, and, as he swerved sharply to the left trying to put some distance between himself and the firing, trying to get out of range, hitting bumps that sent them into the air to land with a shudder, he screamed at Deborah to get down just as little spurts of sand began to be kicked up all around them.

Deborah had a bewildering sense that she was living within two different realities. She could see what was happening but she couldn't fully believe that it was happening, not even the reality of the bullets that were whizzing all around.

At the same time, she felt the inevitability of it all, that, no matter what they had done, they were doomed from the outset, that they couldn't get through, that they wouldn't get through, that they would all die here and, as David floored the accelerator, shouting out something, driving towards their faceless executioners, and the Land Rover was being sprayed with automatic gun fire and the dogs were terrified and whimpering in the back, Deborah was dizzy with the imminent certainty of being shot, of twitching fingers firing compulsively, emotionally disconnected, killing as effortlessly and detachedly as in a video sequence that ignores pain and suffering and negates life.

The next blast of bullets struck the back of the Land Rover where the dogs were barking wildly and then a burst stitched along the side and struck David in his left arm so that the vehicle spun out of control. As he tried to steer with one hand, blood running down his arm and pumping between his fingers made his hands slippery with blood so that they kept slipping on the steering wheel making it difficult to steer.

Then came the explosion.

At first David was in shock not knowing what was happening. Then he realised that the *Mujahadeen* who had been firing on them had been hit by something substantial from across the border, probably an artillery shell and one Jeep burst into flames and then there were more direct hits and more flames and the fighters who had abandoned their Jeeps and were trying to escape were mown down.

As all this was happening, with the Land Rover bucketing wildly, Deborah screaming and the dogs howling, they crossed the border which was marked by a long stretch of razor wire and a barrier. On the other side was exactly similar terrain, a few stunted palms, a flag pole, and a number of border huts nearby which Omani soldiers were patrolling with personnel carriers and armoured cars.

They later learned that this force had arrived only a short time before having received a signal from Khor Fahal Intelligence which was working in close liaison with British Intelligence. The signal had directed them to come to this particular border crossing where they would find an insurgent interceptive unit.

While David spoke with Major Ahmed Kabani of the Omani armed police, groups of people who had recently crossed the border sat about in an assortment of vehicles, looking dazed.

They were the refugees who had made it through the desert. Apparently, many more had set out, no one knew how many. They might still arrive, or some of them might. That is what the people sitting in the hot sun were waiting for, relations and friends. But some would never arrive. Some were back there in the desert whiteness, silent corpses that would lie under the brightness of the desert sun.

David could see them stranded back there in the desert abandoning their vehicles and trying to make it on foot, bare headed and bare footed, scorched and dehydrated until there was nothing left but fleshless skeletons fleeing under the consuming glare of the sun in an empty world where nothing stirred in all the whiteness and there was neither sunset nor sunrise, nothing but the brightness of the sun shining on polished skeletons, into eyeless sockets. Skeletons that might as easily have been them.

Major Kabani took David to a Red Crescent post where he got basic medical attention for his wound. It wasn't life threatening but he had lost a lot of blood, and he did need hospitalisation.

Deborah was taken to one of the hot stuffy border huts where she was questioned by an Omani Intelligence officer who wanted to know about their escape and who else they had seen in the desert. The intelligence officer could see that she was in shock and went out of his way to be pleasant. He even managed to patch up a brief call home to reassure her mother and tell Carolyn she loved her and would be home soon.

Waiting for the Red Crescent to be finished with David, Deborah, thinking back over her time in Khor Fahal, realised that her initial hopes as to what she could do there had been completely unrealistic. There had never been any real possibility that *Al Jameela* would become the type of magazine she had envisaged. If it continued at all into the future, whoever won in the present upheaval, *Al Jameela* would be something entirely different from her concept. Where would all those women who had written in to her find an outlet for their views? They wouldn't, was probably the answer to that.

Whoever won in the present power struggle, it seemed inevitable that women would slide further into the darker hidden side of life, the life lived behind the veil, behind the *yashmak,* behind *purdah* screening in latticed rooms, confined to the house and domesticity.

Until the whole Moslem attitude to women changed, women in Khor Fahal would be repressed. There would always be rebels, always the odd girl showing a flash of brightly coloured dress or make-up or even high-heeled shoes beneath the *abbaya*, but would such girls ever have any effect, would their voice ever be heard as fundamentalism swept across large swathes of the world?

She thought of Eileen's daughter, Fatima, who had been helpful to her and told her where she thought David was imprisoned. What future was there for a bright girl like her? And she thought of Eileen who, however crazy her views seemed, had had the courage to act on them. What would happen to Eileen? What would happen to her and her husband? If the uprising failed, her husband would most likely be killed or imprisoned.

And what would Eileen do? Stay on in that crowded apartment in the Old City? Would she go on living under a strict patriarchal regime, one where the women were restricted in both movement and thought, an atmosphere surely completely foreign to an Irish girl. Perhaps she'd return to Ireland. If she survived.

And Deborah was acutely aware that the insurgency in the state of Khor Fahal in which they had become so deeply involved, even if it spread to some other states, was still only a small part of the complex power struggles, the clash of religions and cultures which beset the Middle East, the outcome and long term effect of which, God only knew.

Later that day, they were both flown by helicopter to the government hospital in Muscat and the dogs were allowed to go along with them. After some tests, Deborah was treated for shock, but later allowed to leave hospital and check into the Al Mansoor hotel, a hotel of unbelievable luxury after the hardships of the desert. Given the medieval city Muscat had been only a few decades before, the hotel seemed ridiculously luxurious though she wasn't going to object to being pampered over the next few days.

After having the bullets removed, David lay in bed listening, to the BBC Overseas Service business report reporting on a completely different world to the one he had been recently inhabiting. The Dow and the FTSE and the Nikki were all up. In the currency market the Euro was strengthening against the dollar. The Khor dinar was still falling.

And David remembered that today was settlement day for the first contract he had taken out. The rates being quoted over the radio by the BBC meant that the bank, less commissions, stood to make a little shy of thirty million on the order he had placed.

The parallel order he had placed on his own account would net him substantially over a million. Which wasn't bad when you came to think of it. It made the pain from his arm wound a good deal more tolerable.

NOEL SCANLON

CHAPTER 66

In his bed in the hospital, David took a call from CJ. After enquiring about how he was CJ said, "If you'd had any sense, you'd have laid low in your apartment and waited to be rescued."

"If I had, we'd have been dead meat long before anyone rescued us."

"Your problem is you don't put enough faith in the authorities. Chief of Police Qassim gave me his word that nothing would happen to you."

David remembered the Jeep driving up to their block minutes after they had got out.

"It'd have been nice to know that as we sat there waiting to be knocked off."

"You're lucky to have only been shot in the arm. You got off lightly if you ask me. You wouldn't have got yourself kidnapped in the first instance if you had stayed on the right side of the creek among the right people."

David changed the subject. "How's the revolution going?"

"How do you think? I always told you those fecking terrorists were totally incompetent. In the beginning, they made a lot of noise. They blew up the odd building here and there including the Phoenix with those poor people in it. And typically they did a lot of damage in the Old City where most of them come from."

"And the pipelines." David said. "We saw the pipelines on fire on our way out."

"That's all under control. The fires didn't last long when they stopped pumping oil into them. As I said, there was the odd bit of damage here and there but nothing significant."

"What about the bank building?"

"It's fine?"

"There was a huge mob around it when I left."

"There are always mobs in situations like that. But they didn't get to do the bank building any great damage. They were quickly dispersed when the armed police brought in their armoured cars and some serious firepower. And then the Khor Fahal air force began bombing the terrorist areas as soon as they could get airborne."

"You mean they bombed buildings with civilians in them?"

"That is sometimes necessary if the people won't persuade the terrorists to surrender. Anyway, none of that's our business. We don't take political decisions, the government do that as I'm for ever telling you. From what Chief of Police Qassim tells me, it's only a question of time now until those holding out in the Old City will be crushed. When they are, all suspected terrorists left alive will be rounded up and punished. And I'll leave it to your lively imagination to work out what that means."

David knew precisely what it meant. Summary executions. Torture. Imprisonment without trial. The whole gig.

"I heard on the radio that there were uprisings in Dubai and Doha."

"There's been some trouble. But it won't amount to anything. They'll be put down without any problem. Those troublemakers are on a hiding to nothing. The people in this area have got used to prosperity and they want to hang on to it. They don't want to give it up in favour of some crazy religious fanaticism."

David thought this to be an over optimistic view of the future of the Gulf but refrained from saying so.

There was a pause before CJ asked, "What happened to the gold?"

"What gold?"

"Don't take me to be stupid. Do I look stupid? Did I get where I am by being stupid? The bank gold of course, what else."

"The Ayatullah robbed it from the bank. Better ask him about it. I'm sure he'd like to talk to you."

"Don't fuck about with me. I haven't been here all these years without having my finger on the pulse. What happened to the gold you drove off with from the harbour?"

"Oh that," David said. "We had to dump it. It was so heavy that we kept sinking into the sand. We got dug in and there was no way we could ever have got out without off-loading it. It was our life or the gold."

"So you dumped it. Thirty million dollars worth of bank gold. In the sand."

"That's right."

"And where exactly did you dump it?"

"In the dunes."

"Where in the dunes?"

"Right in the middle of the Great Dunes. In a sandstorm."

"Could you identify which dunes?

"Have you ever been out there?

"No. And I have no intention of going. I don't like sand. It's wandering around in it for so long that has made the people in this part of the world so fucking crazy."

"Well the thing is that all these dunes look pretty much the same. And they keep changing all the time. Especially after sandstorms. And there are lots of sandstorms. Great whirlwinds that suck up thousands of tons of sand and dump it somewhere else. It was a whirlwind doing just that that saved us from the Ayatullah's men who were right behind us and closing."

CJ grunted. "Save me the drama."

"I'm only telling you what happened."

"What you're telling me is that the gold, the bank gold, is buried out there under some fecking sand dune or other and you have no idea where."

"That's exactly what I'm telling you."

CJ considered this.

"I don't believe you for a moment. The trouble with the Irish is that they're all fecking liars."

"It takes one to know one."

CJ let that go. He thought for a moment.

"The position is that I'm retiring next year. Mary won't stand for me staying on longer than that in this part of the world. Not after all the recent trouble. So I suggested to the board that you begin the process of taking over from me and they agreed."

"Thanks for that vote of confidence in me. But I can't give you an answer straight away."

"An answer to what?"

"Whether I'll come back to this part of the world or not."

"Don't fuck about. Of course you'll come back. You may be a bit off centre. But you're not crazy enough to turn down an offer like I'm making you. You'll be a multi-millionaire in no time for Christsake." He paused. "Now about this gold."

"What about it?"

"It occurs to me that since the insurance people have already been notified about the robbery, it might only confuse them to bother them with what was, after all, a course of action we were told to take by a government agency, and involving a highly secret joint intelligence operation. And it is our duty to protect that secrecy. Do you get my point?"

"I get it perfectly."

"Good. I'll arrange for you to have some leave to recover from that wound and so on. Then you'll be back in Khor Fahal. What we'll do then is arrange the recovery of the gold. I'll order up a vehicle with the most up to date technical paraphernalia, the latest in Global Satellite fixing and mapping and all that technical rubbish to make sure you don't lose your way. You'll pick the stuff up, bring it back, deposit it in the bank vaults and we'll sell it on to one of our gold smuggling customers. Proceeds to a numbered Swiss Bank account. Fifty fifty split."

"The only slight problem is I don't know where the gold is."

"Don't give me that. You marked where it is. You know fucking well where it is. But if you should have a lapse of memory, I'll withdraw my recommendation to the board. And, in addition, I'll have you up for stealing the gold."

"Which I didn't."

"What's that got to do with it?"

"Not much I suppose. Not in a local Khor Fahal court."

"Precisely. I'll give you a day or two to think about it. Then I'll want your answer."

CJ paused then went on, "By the way, that Irish friend of Deborah's, Eileen something or other. Her husband has been taken into custody as a terrorist. He's been interrogated. In my opinion when that Irish girl married an Arab terrorist she made her own bed and now she'll have to lie on it. I'll leave it up to yourself whether you tell Deborah or not." CJ put the phone down.

David lay back in the bed. CJ had been a sharp cold dose of reality. But right now he wasn't going to think about CJ or his proposition. Instead he thought about how lucky he was to be still alive. He'd had a narrow escape, or rather a number of narrow escapes. And he had very nearly replicated the fate of his father at the hands of his kidnappers.

He remembered the morning it all began, that early morning before he went out in his boat and found the mullah's body. He had paused for a moment at the garage door and stood standing looking out watching the rising sun splashing a line of red along the horizon. For a moment everything had been perfectly still, a moment of transcendent beauty with the waves whispering on to the sandbank across the creek. The sea was flat and the air was prescient with the mystery of a new day. If only all of life could be like that. But it wasn't. Shortly after on that same morning he had found the body of the mullah and after that everything began to fall apart.

Turning in the bed now he remembered looking down from the helicopter on to the desert on the way here and thinking what an inhospitable place the desert looked and how impossible to drive through.

But it wasn't impossible at all. All you needed was what CJ had promised: the best available off-road vehicle, proper supplies, proper organisation and backup, and it would be nice to have a satellite phone and all the other odds and ends.

One thing he was beginning to realise. Despite all the awful things that had happened to him, this whole area of Arabia had some sort of fatal attraction for him.

And if he did decide to come back he just might take a little trip into the desert, into the Great Dunes, and see if that flag he had planted was still blowing in the wind.